Just Whistle

Hannah Rae

KDP

Text design by Hannah Rae
Cover design by Hannah Rae
Cover art by Hannah Rae

Grateful acknowledgment is made for permission to include the following copyrighted material:

"Surprise is like a thrilling pungent" by Emily Dickinson.
Credit line: Reprinted by permission of the publishers and the Trustees of Amherst College from THE POEMS OF EMILY DICKINSON, edited by Thomas H. Johnson, Cambridge, Mass.: The Belknap Press of Harvard University Press, Copyright © 1951, 1955 by the President and Fellows of Harvard College. Copyright © renewed 1979, 1983 by the President and Fellows of Harvard College. Copyright © 1914, 1918, 1919, 1924, 1929, 1930, 1932, 1935, 1937, 1942, by Martha Dickinson Bianchi. Copyright © 1952, 1957, 1958, 1963, 1965, by Mary L. Hampson.

"On the Other Side of the Road" by Erick Macek.
Reprinted by permission of Erick Macek (www.erickmacek.com).

ISBN 1514735954

Visit the author online:
www.heyheyhannahrae.com
www.facebook.com/HeyHannahRae
www.twitter.com/heyheyhannahrae

For my mom,
because she dreamed about houses with too many rooms
and cried after reading the first chapter.

And for Baxter, whom I miss every day.
June 8, 2003—December 31, 2013

∞

"There's the past and there's the future
And the here-and-now between.
I want you close for all of it;
I want you here with me.
So even when we disagree,
When opinions just won't jibe,
Know that I'll be back again
To kick it one more time."

-Sebastian Porter, "Kick It One More Time"

1.
Charley

If reincarnation is real, and if my soul or my energy or whatever it is that makes me *me* can return for another shot at life, then I hope to return as a cardinal. Afternoons spent in the treetops, flitting from branch to branch, whistling chipper tunes with songbird friends… It's about as satisfying an existence as I can imagine. Worries such as health and heartbreak would be imponderable, and my most pressing concern would become the neighborhood cat's tendency to stalk furred and feathered things. I exhale an envious sigh, pull my gaze away from the crimson bird perched atop the traffic light, and press gently on the accelerator as red changes to green.

It's been a long time since my last visit to the tiny Pennsylvania town of Lake Caywood. The streets themselves look the same as they did a decade ago: there's the post office and the bank, and Doc Delaney's Tavern that seems always to be flooded with light and laughter, each in exactly the same location as it was ten years ago. But something feels different now. Unfamiliar. Like that piece of the town that once belonged to me no longer does, and I no longer belong to it. We were intimate for eighteen years, but time and distance have turned us into complete strangers.

Being in this place that no longer knows me… it causes me to question how well I truly know myself. Anymore, at least. And whether or not I actually do.

Remnants of Christmas linger on Main Street. Wreaths with red bows adorn every lamppost, twinkling icicles of lights hang from rooflines, and window displays consist of snowmen and scarves and wool stockings stuffed with thick peppermint sticks. They'll come down tomorrow, or maybe the next day, once the world has officially stepped into January. A shiver runs through me, but it isn't the anticipation of a new year that has me feeling jittery. It's the dread that sits like a dead weight in the pit of my stomach. Sensing this elevation of nerves, Rhett hangs his head over my shoulder and affectionately nuzzles my cheek. "Okay, okay," I mutter, reaching up to scratch the soft spot behind his ear. "I love you, too, but I'm driving right now. You've gotta sit down, pup. Rhett. Sit."

He does, but not until administering a final sniff that sprays the right side of my face with dampness. Dog snot. I wipe it away with my sleeve and drum my thumbs against the steering wheel. I should make two stops, but only intend to make one, so at the intersection of Copper and Main I turn left instead of right.

It's a tree-lined road, and for three seasons out of every year a canopy of leaves shades the pavement below, but for now the limbs are bare. Overhead, skeleton branches form webs of wood, barely moving in the still afternoon. The sky is that murky shade of grey that only makes an appearance in nature's palette during the coldest months. Sunlight filters down in the same manner that it would through clouded pond water and I instinctively gulp in air, suddenly fearful of drowning, making my lungs tight with oxygen.

I pull the Jeep onto the side of the road, gravel crunching beneath its tires, and grip the steering wheel with white knuckles, my foot pressed heavily on the brake. Rhett's nose finds its way to my ear and fills it with a loud sniff. "Okay," I say out loud, to him and to me and to no one. "Okay. So… okay. We're doing this." I glance down at the scrap of paper curled into my cup holder, triple-checking the address that's scrawled there, even though I know it by heart. I could probably navigate the rest of the trip with my eyes closed.

I know this road.

I know this land.

I ran barefoot through the orchards here, climbing squat apple trees to reach sun-kissed fruit that hung from the highest branches. I reached into lush bushes, braving brambles and thorns to fill buckets with plump berries that stained my fingers the color of calligraphy ink. I lay flat on my back, grass tickling my exposed skin, and stared up at those vines of hops that stretched into oblivion, imagining the giant I'd find if I climbed to the top. On August mornings I played house in the cornfield, and when it got too hot to bear the breezeless rooms, I sat on the banks of the pond, serenaded by chirping frogs, catching catfish and then tossing them back with a splash.

I know this land because I grew up here.

The road is deserted, but I use my left turn signal anyway.

"Five-nineteen Copper Drive," I say, sounding stronger than I feel. "We're really doing this."

At one point in time the roof shone like new pennies, sunlight glinting off of it; now its coloring is more of a sea-foam green. Dormant chimneys stand at opposite ends of the farmhouse, terracotta bricks contrasting with the blueness of the sky, and embraced between them is what I for so many years referred to as "home." My gaze slides from left to right, just as it would over the pages of a book, but it isn't a book that I'm reading. It's my past.

Once brilliantly white, the structure is now chipped and peeling. Ribbons of paint curl away from the siding, revealing wood that's been forced to weather the elements, and the porch railing looks as though it could have used a fresh coat at least four or five years ago. On the second floor, a shutter hangs slightly askew.

The sight hurts my stomach and my heart.

What have I been doing for all these years? I silently ask myself. Because at this moment in time, parked outside the old farmhouse with the Jeep's radio whispering to me, staring into windows that are too dark, all of those years spent in Michigan suddenly seem like a monumental waste of time. Where I should have been is right here.

But I'm here now, and showing up is half the battle. That's what *he'd* say anyway. I roll my eyes, suddenly irritated, because it's a phrase I've grown to hate. A person has to do more than just show up. A person has to try.

I shut off the engine and remove the key. As a result the heater stops blowing, the radio falls silent, and Rhett, sensing a furthering of adventure, rapidly wags his tail. "Okay," I tell him, and he leaps into the front seat, following half a step behind as I climb out of the vehicle. With all four feet on solid ground, he executes a full body shake, sniffs the soil, and promptly raises a leg to mark a fallen tree branch. He then sets out to claim additional territory—a fence post, a pinecone, a patch of already-dead grass, the trunk of a cherry tree growing not far from the porch—while I retrieve my bags from the trunk.

I haven't brought much, but it will have to be enough.

I have no idea how long I'll be staying.

My breath clouds in front of me as I walk to the porch, floating up and away in white wisps. The air is so crispy that I can just about crunch it. "Rhett!" I call before mounting the first step. "Come on, pup!"

He is across the yard, his nose in a hole and his butt in the air, but he raises his head upon hearing my voice. "Come on," I repeat, and allow him one more sniff before clapping my hands. "Now, Rhett. Let's go."

His muscular body bounds across the frozen ground, ears flapping, and he slams on the brakes just in time to avoid a collision with my legs. "Whoa!" I exclaim, laughing and running a hand through his wiry fur. "Careful."

Rhett pants happily and nuzzles my hand. Then he leads the way onto the porch, stands before the front door, and scratches once with his paw. "Hold on," I mutter. "Just be patient."

The key is in my coat pocket. I reach for it, grip the cold metal, insert it into the lock. For a moment I think that it doesn't quite fit, but then I jiggle it and something clicks and the heavy wooden door swings open. I half expect the air in the farmhouse to be musty, like it hasn't circulated for a while, but it just smells like Gramps: strong tobacco and lemon drops. To think that he was here three days ago, putzing around this very kitchen, makes me catch my breath. I blink once, twice, dismissing tears from my eyes, and step inside. I kick the door shut behind me and let my bags fall. Rhett scampers ahead, snout to the floor, exploring… but I just stand there.

Everything is exactly as I remember. Formica countertops, slightly dull after an uncountable number of swipes from sudsy dishcloths and years of housing pots of slippery potpie, screaming hot from the stove, set aside without the use of a trivet. There's the solid oak table, giant in stature, which required three uncles, two cousins, and a grandfather to finagle into the house. It's where it's always been: in the center of everything. We used to stand around it and talk around it and eat around it. When I was just little and Noni was still in good health, she'd tuck her white hair beneath an indigo bandana and roll piecrusts on this table while I nibbled discarded apple skins. Very seldom was it that we'd use the more practical table—the one meant for dining—when partaking of a meal. Everyone simply preferred this one.

The wallpaper is faded, the curtains are drab, and the wood beneath my feet is scuffed and splintered. And yet… this place still feels like home.

I leave my bags where they've landed and step farther into the house, flipping on lights as I go. Mahogany crown molding, once polished and gleaming, now hosts cobwebs and a thin layer of dust, and the rugs in the living room are no longer vibrant and bright. They're tattered from years of foot traffic. The area directly in front of Gramps's favorite chair, in fact, is practically worn through. Without him sitting there, pipe clenched between his teeth, the large leather armchair seems emptier than a chair without an occupant ought to seem.

Overhead, Rhett's toenails click-clack against hardwood floors as he explores the maze of rooms above me. I imagine him nuzzling doors open with his nose, poking his head under beds, experiencing scents that are completely new to him. He's never been here before, after all; this is his first trip to Pennsylvania.

I glance at the clock on the wall, which used to chime every hour, but stopped ticking well over three decades ago. Gramps kept it all these years because it had been a wedding gift, designed and built by a man named Oliver Clay. They'd been friends once upon a time.

The clock is useless, but the darkening sky outside suggests that five o'clock is within sight. For a lot of people, tonight's happy hour will include champagne. It suddenly occurs to me that my decision to disregard the stop I should have made was a bad one. Tomorrow might be Thursday, but businesses will no doubt be closed. I hurriedly retrace my steps and scoop my purse off the kitchen floor, rummaging in it until my fingers find my phone. Five missed calls and two texts, all from him, but he's not the person I need to be in touch with. I retrieve a scrap of paper from my back pocket, dial the number that's scrawled on it, and silently hope someone will pick up. It takes three rings.

"Turley's Funeral Home," a man's voice answers. "This is Leonard. How may I help you?"

"Hi Leonard," I say. "This is Charley Lane. Charlotte, I mean. Um… I'm calling about my grandfather's funeral. Jasper Lane?" I put a question mark at the end of his name, as if I'm not certain it's correct, but of course it is. Saying it out loud though, while speaking with a funeral director, just makes his death seem that much more real.

Papers shuffle in the background and Leonard Turley clears his throat. "Ah, Charlotte. Yes. I was actually expecting you to stop in at some point today. Did the trip take longer than expected?"

"It did," I lie. "I'm sorry I didn't call sooner."

"No, no, it's quite alright. I'm glad you called when you did. We're just getting ready to close up. But let me see…" He trails off and I can faintly hear the sound of fingers flying over a computer keyboard. "Okay. Here we go. The obituary appeared in the paper on Monday, as you probably know, and as far as Friday is concerned, everything is under control. The service is scheduled to begin at ten o'clock."

"And it's just for family, correct?"

"It is a private service," Leonard assures me.

Gramps hadn't even wanted that. "Just burn me up and sprinkle my ashes with the hops," he'd always said. But his brother Kirby, my great-uncle, has been insistent about providing a proper send-off. "People need to be given an opportunity to say goodbye," he'd told me on Monday when he called with the news. "And he needs to be buried beside his wife."

I'd agreed to a private service, but Gramps had been adamant about the location of his remains. "He'll be cremated," I'd stated flatly, leaving no room for argument, "and I'll scatter his ashes among the hops. It's what he requested, and it's what we're going to do." The conversation with Kirby hadn't lasted long after that, and the only communication I'd had with him since was a newspaper clipping—the obituary—that arrived in the mail earlier this week.

"Is there anything else I can help you with, Charlotte?" Leonard asks now.

I tell him there isn't, thank him for his help, and we hang up.

The house seems too quiet, too empty. Rhett still scampers about overhead, creating occasional clatters that remind me he's up to no good, but it's not that type of quiet I mean. It's a lack of laughter and voices and music. Gramps never spent New Year's Eve alone, and back in his heyday he used to pack the farmhouse with people from all walks of life: mail carriers, doctors, barbers, and waitresses. Dorothy Kirkland, wife of the local shoe salesman, always brought chocolate cupcakes piled high with her famous peanut butter frosting, and the staff from the Tavern came laden with more appetizers than could be consumed in a night. Gramps provided the beer, of course.

It was inevitable that someone would bring a guitar or a banjo, and once the strumming began, feet started moving. Floors shook and windows fogged and people mingled, clinking glasses at midnight. The dancing would last into the wee hours, and thinking back on it, I'm not sure how Gramps was able to squeeze everyone into the house at one time. But somehow he did.

He'd be disappointed in my current New Year's plans, since I have none at all. No music, no guests, and no bubbly. I intend to put on my pajamas, curl up on the couch, and if I'm still awake when the clock strikes twelve, I'll watch NBC's coverage of the ball dropping. Not much of a holiday, really.

Rhett's footsteps race clumsily down the stairs. He skids around the corner, charging into the kitchen, his tail wagging proudly. Held gently between his powerful jaws is a pipe. I reach down to take it from him, hoping his needle-like teeth have not marred the surface. "Drop it," I command, sternly. "That belongs to Gramps." Only after the words are out of my mouth do I realize I've used the wrong verb tense.

Rhett releases his grip and I cradle the pipe in my hands, inhaling the aroma of sweet tobacco. Two-toned, it has a marbled red bowl and a black stem. I examine it closely, searching for imperfections, but find nothing. "You know what?" I ask of Rhett, forcing the shakiness from my voice. "We might not have any champagne, but I bet we've got beer. The least we can do is toast Gramps."

Rhett sits on his haunches, cocking his head to one side and watching curiously as I walk to the refrigerator. It hums quietly, and when I yank on the door, light floods the shelves and pools at my feet, illuminating the appliance's contents. The sight causes me to laugh out loud. There's a Tupperware container filled with what looks like leftover spaghetti, and a bag of salad that's seen better days, but it's the top two shelves that make me smile. They are lined with row after row of beers: amber lagers, golden IPAs, chocolaty stouts, and coffee-colored porters. Gramps bottled each and every one of them.

I grab a pale ale, pry off the cap, and extend the chilled bottle before me. "This one's for you, Gramps."

2.
Juli

If it were two degrees colder, there'd be snow, but the precipitation that splatters against the windshield and hood of my truck is regular old rain. The wipers keep beat to something that's whispering through the radio, but I have the volume turned down low because I actually prefer the downpour's rhythm. It's steady and constant and fresh. I tap the tempo with my left foot since my right one's solid on the brake.

I've been stuck at the intersection of Howard and Copper for what seems like an eternity, waiting for the light to change so that I can make a left. I'm pretty much convinced it will never again cycle through that beautiful green-yellow-red pattern. Howard Avenue is apparently the one road in town that never experiences any traffic, or, if vehicles *do* travel on this pavement, the drivers must all have destinations that require a right-hand turn. I'm thinking that right is the way to go, even if it results in a roundabout route to the hardware store—and actually go so far as to redirect my turn signal—when I get distracted.

Turley's Funeral Home is located on the opposite side of the street, tucked snugly between a law office and a sandwich shop. This would normally be of little interest to me. Having grown up in Lake Caywood, I've attended a few memorial services held there: my grandmother, great-uncle Ralph, one of my mother's cousins whom I barely knew… It's not the establishment itself that filches my attention—it's what transpires on the sidewalk in front of Turley's Funeral Home. A woman who looks to be around the same age as me pushes through the front door and steps onto the rain-soaked sidewalk. She has no umbrella, but wears a black coat with a hood. It's cinched at the waist, which would normally emphasize an hourglass figure, but this girl is pretty much devoid of curves. She's built more like a rail than a timepiece, and while that can sometimes be not such a bad thing, judgment has to be withheld until I can clearly see her face… and the black hood she's wearing makes it impossible to do that. Her body language suggests intense frustration, though, and this is only reinforced when an elderly, heavyset guy storms after her a moment later. By this time, the woman is several paces down the block. The man—his fat cheeks and smooth forehead the same shade as a tomato—spots her, throws both hands into the air, and shouts something that causes the woman to not only turn, but to also take several steps toward him. The argument is obviously a heated one, so I doubt soggy attire is a main focus at this point in time, but as my truck's windshield wipers continue to swish methodically back and forth, I can't help but think both parties must be positively soaked.

And then the light turns green.

There's a part of me that's almost willing to sit at the intersection of Howard and Copper for a second eternity, just to observe this dispute between strangers for a few more minutes, but the urgency to purchase a new sanding belt wins out and I turn left instead.

It's true that Lake Caywood has an abundance of quirky shops lining Main Street, but my favorite place to spend money is probably Honey-Do Hardware. It's a mom-and-pop business, owned by Hank Duncan and his wife Eileen, who has to be the sweetest lady on the face of the earth. Eileen loves animals more than anyone I know; she works closely with the local shelter and always has at least one four-legged foster child with her in the shop. Last month she actually had *three* four-legged foster children: three-month-old orange tabbies who'd originally been found in a trash bag alongside a backcountry road. They were adopted almost immediately and now live in a big house on Lakefront Drive with a guy by the name of George Simmons. He hires me to pressure wash his house every spring.

Anyway, it's an admirable thing that Eileen does.

It's how I came to adopt my own dog, in fact.

I find parking on the street and feed money to the meter, turning my collar up against the steady downpour. Nevertheless, icy droplets still manage to splatter against my neck and slide down my back, making me shiver. My feet are completely soaked by the time I splash my way to the entrance of Honey-Do. The clank of a copper cowbell announces my presence as I slip inside, but I don't venture far from the front door, opting to allow a moment to drip on the oversized welcome mat instead. Aware of the fact that a customer has entered the store, Eileen wanders out of the plumbing aisle and fixes me with a bemused expression. "Juli Singer," she sighs. "When, oh when, are you going to give up those Chuck Taylors and invest in a proper pair of work boots? Your feet have got to be *freezing*."

"I'm fine," I assure her, even though she's right: my toes are probably the color of blueberries at this point in time. I wiggle them to make sure they're not frozen solid. "I came in to get some sanding belts."

"What size do you need?" Eileen has wispy blonde hair that she often tucks under a bandana. Today is no exception. Flyaway strands still manage to escape the red-fabric confine, though, framing her face in a way that reminds me a bit of a halo.

I tell her what I need and we walk through the store together, traveling past the lighting aisle, past the electrical aisle, and right down the middle of my favorite section: tools. There's just something about being among drills and power saws and nail guns... I can't fully put it into words, but I guess what I mostly feel is happy.

"Men and their tools," Eileen mutters, observing the slight sideways smile on my face. "I'll never understand it. Here are your belts. How many d'you need?"

"Two packs oughtta do it," I answer, and bend down to retrieve the sandpaper bands. As I do, something brushes against the back of my leg, nudging wet denim against skin. "You must be the new boarder," I say in acknowledgement of the droopy-faced Basset that's sniffing my ankle.

"This is Myra," Eileen informs me. "She moved in a few days ago."

I extend a hand, allow Myra to give it a good sniff, and then rub her long ears affectionately. "She's sort of quiet for a Basset, isn't she?" I ask, glancing up at Eileen. "I thought this breed was known for being pretty vocal. She didn't make a sound when I came in."

Eileen shrugs. "I know what you mean, but Myra doesn't seem to make a whole lot of noise. She's a timid little thing."

"How old is she?"

"Six or seven is what the shelter told me. Her previous owners abandoned her."

"How come?"

"Job relocation," Eileen says. "Couldn't take her with them."

I turn back to Myra and look into her sad brown eyes. "No wonder you're so quiet," I muse. "You're heartbroken. Poor ol' girl." I give her head a pat and hoist myself to my feet. Eileen gives me a knowing look. "What?" I ask.

"You're sure you don't want another one?"

"Oh, I'm positive. One dog is enough." I follow her to the front of the store and pull my wallet from my back pocket. Hank is standing behind the register. "You picked a hell of a day to be out and about," he greets me.

"Don't I know it," I say, placing the sanding belts and a twenty-dollar bill on the counter. "But duty calls."

Eileen squeezes behind her husband, places my purchase in a plastic bag, and hands it to me while Hank makes change. "Are you working on anything fun right now?" she asks.

"Sanding, staining, and sealing a flight of stairs for the Goodes. The steps are fine, but the banister's a pain, so… I want to make some progress on that. And then I'm heading back to my place because Asher texted a little while ago and said his kitchen sink is leaking."

"It never ends, does it?" Hank sighs. He places a few quarters and pennies into my hand. They jingle against one another, momentarily hiding the tiny *5* that's tattooed on my palm, and then I slide the change into my pocket, concurring, "It never does."

I say my goodbyes, give Myra a final scratch behind the ears, and attempt to dodge raindrops as I dash to my truck. The wet weather has me craving coffee, but once the heater's blowing on my feet, the desire for caffeine isn't strong enough to warrant another soggy sprint from vehicle to building. I drive past Bottomless Joe's coffeehouse without stopping and head away from downtown.

The Goodes live at the end of Newman Avenue. The road essentially becomes their driveway since theirs is the last house on the street. It's fairly massive and sits atop a large hill that overlooks the lake. The couple moved in about six months ago, shortly after their wedding. Had it been up to the town, the rundown house would have been bulldozed and a new marina constructed in its place, but when Old Lady Gallagher passed away last year, she didn't leave her home to the town: she left it to Petey and Jenny Goode. They're in the process of renovating it, and while they've already done quite a bit to make the home their own, it still needs a lot of work.

I steer my truck up their drive and park it beside the white picket fence that Jenny and I repainted in August. Since she's a teacher, she was home for the majority of that month, and when she told me she felt badly about watching me do all the work, I handed her a paintbrush. We got the job done in about half the time I'd anticipated it taking.

Because Lake Caywood students are currently in the midst of another holiday break—Christmas, this time—I expect Jenny will be the one to answer the door. I'm wrong, though. It's Petey who responds to my succession of quick knocks and ushers me inside. "You look like a drowned rat," he says in welcome. "You want a cup of coffee? First, take off your coat. Have you never heard of an umbrella?"

I slouch out of the sopping canvas and relinquish it to him, and he hands me a pair of dry socks. "Put those on," he instructs. So I kick off my sneakers, peel off my socks, and pull the warm woolen ones over my frigid toes. To ask how he knew to be prepared with this small kindness is pointless. I've known Petey Goode for a long time (we went to high school together, although he was a year ahead of me) and if there's one thing I've learned about him, it's this: he knows things in a way other people simply cannot. He'd make the ideal Boy Scout: he's always prepared.

With the circulation returning to my feet, I follow Petey through the living room and into the kitchen, where he hands me a steaming mug of freshly brewed coffee. I hold it beneath my nose, inhaling its scent and allowing the heat to warm my face. And then, noticing a sink stacked high with dirty dishes, I query, "Jenny's not here?"

Petey shakes his head. "Nope. Visiting her family in Washington. She flies back tomorrow." He follows my gaze and considers the crusty casserole, speckled silverware, and mound of smeared plates. "I should probably clean that up before her return."

"Yeah… You probably should." I give him a soft pat on the shoulder and head toward the foyer. "I'm gonna get to work on this staircase while you get to work on those dishes. Have fun, buddy."

The problem with sanding is that it makes a mess. I keep the Goodes' Shop-Vac handy, and use it regularly, but there's still a thin film of dust that clings to the wall and settles over the floor.

The other problem with sanding is that it's incredibly monotonous. I go over everything three times: first with coarse-grit paper, then with medium, and finally with the fine-grit belts that were purchased this morning. Around lunchtime, Petey informs me that there's a grilled cheese sandwich with my name on it waiting in the kitchen, but that's the only break I allow myself. By four o'clock, my eyes are itching despite a pair of protective goggles, my mouth is dryer than the Sahara, and I'm sneezing up a storm. I complete a last round of suction with the Shop-Vac and tell Petey I'm heading out. "I can stain it tomorrow morning if that's cool with you. It'll take two days 'cause I've gotta do it every other step. Do you get what I mean?"

"You're on a bit of an eighties kick today, aren't you?" is how he responds.

My cheeks burn a little, but I play it off with a nonchalant shrug. I'm more productive if I'm singing while I'm working; customers know this when they hire me. But Petey's right: I was definitely stuck on the Violent Femmes today.

"So, tomorrow morning," he says, chuckling. "Sounds good." He folds the newspaper he'd been reading, sets it aside, and introduces a completely new topic: "Jasper Lane's funeral was today. He was ninety-two. Did you know him at all?"

Jasper Lane had a full head of hair that was the color of snow, an unkempt mustache that flopped over his upper lip, and was never without his pipe. A bit of a Lake Caywood legend, he'll forever be remembered for the epic parties he used to throw in his youth. But I never really knew him.

"He hired me to clean out his gutters one spring, and we drank some *really* good beer together once the job was done, but that was my only interaction with him," I say in answer. "What about you?"

"Oh, I'd see him a few times a week," Petey responds, "on mornings that I was waiting tables at the Tavern. He'd come in, find a seat at the bar, and order his usual: black coffee, a spinach-and-cheese omelet, and toast with blackberry jam."

"Sounds pretty good."

Petey nods. "He was just a nice guy. Always happy."

"You didn't go to the funeral, though?" I confirm, suddenly remembering the sidewalk feud that was witnessed this morning.

"Nah. It was family only, which makes me wonder…" He trails off and runs a hand through his short hair. "Jasper talked about his granddaughter all the time, and might've mentioned a brother once or twice, but… I don't know. It's possible they're his only living relatives."

I don't share anything with Petey about the confrontation outside Turley's Funeral Home—I'm not much for gossip—but I don't forget about it either. Both the man and the woman were obviously upset about something.

Very upset.

I thank Petey for the use of his socks, promise to wash and return them in the near future, and jog back to my truck. The rain's let up a bit, but my windshield wipers keep a steady rhythm on the ride home. My place is located on the other side of the lake—just a short walk from town—in a little development where all the streets are named after trees. House number eleven on Sassafras Way is mine. I own the whole thing, but only live on the bottom floor; my good buddy Asher rents the upstairs.

And it's my good buddy Asher whose sink is leaking.

I throw the truck into park, turn off the engine, and sit for a moment in the driveway, contemplating how wonderful it would be to go inside, put on some dry clothes, and curl up on the couch with Scarlett. *Soon*, I promise myself. *This will happen soon.* I open the door with a sigh, grab my toolbox from the backseat, and head around the side of the house to the steps that'll lead me to the second-floor apartment.

Asher hears me coming and meets me at the door. "Hey, man. What's the matter with your eyes?" is how he chooses to welcome me.

"What d'you mean? Nothing's the matter with my eyes." I push past him and walk over to the sink, opening the cupboard doors below in order to inspect the pipes. There is definitely a leak. Asher's placed a pitcher right beneath the drip and little droplets of water continue to slide down the pipe and *plink* into the container, slowly filling it.

"They're all red," he says now, still commenting on my eyes, "like you were crying."

"I wasn't crying," I assure him. "I was sanding."

"Oh."

"Yeah. *Oh.*" I roll my red eyes at him, pass him the pitcher of sink water, and ease myself under the pipes for a better view. The cabinet ledge digs painfully into my back and I wiggle around, trying to get comfortable. "Do you have an old towel handy? And can you also hand me the adjustable wrench from my toolbox? I think it's your supply line."

Asher fulfills these obligations and then hoists himself onto the counter, bouncing his heels against a closed cupboard door. The sound is hollow and annoying. "What're you doing tonight?" he asks from above.

"Not sure. Why?"

"Annie's coming over. We're gonna order pizza and watch *The Godfather.* Wanna join us? You could bring Scarlett."

I was right about the supply line: now that it's tightened, the leak has vanished. I ease myself out from under the sink and sit on the kitchen floor, staring skeptically up at my best friend. "You're going to watch *The Godfather*?" I confirm. Annie's sort of a new presence in Asher's life, so I don't know her very well at all, but she does *not* strike me as someone who'd typically spend her Friday night watching a film about the mafia. If he'd said they were renting *The Notebook*, that would make sense to me… but not *The Godfather.* "Wow." I climb to my feet and shake my head in wonderment. "She must really be into you."

Asher gives me a confused look—"clueless" might be a better word to use—and I actually have to laugh. "You two have fun," I tell him. "I think I'll just order my own pizza and eat it on the couch. I'm pretty beat."

3.
Charley

The sounds that the farmhouse makes are still familiar, even after all this time. Some mornings I lie in bed—the same bed in which I slept nearly every night of my childhood—and listen to the faint creaks and squeaks and sighs the bones make as they settle. I used to do it as a kid, too… remain still as a statue, covers tucked tight under my chin with my eyes squeezed shut against the sun that spilled over the orchard and into my room, sniffing the air. And more often than not, some sort of fantastical aroma, courtesy of Noni's fine baking, would invade my nostrils: apple strudel dusted with cinnamon, decadent black raspberry pie with a sugared crust, syrupy peach cobbler. My favorite was always blackberry shortcake with a dollop of freshly whipped cream, slightly sweetened. Noni's the only person I ever knew who made it, and as far as I know, she kept her recipes inside her head.

It's been two weeks since the funeral and I've not one clue as to what I'm still doing in Lake Caywood, but I know for certain that I cannot return to Michigan. Some things were said there, and those things can't be undone, so the only place I have to travel is forward. Forward to where, I don't know… but reverse is not an option. Some words are simply too powerful for take-backs.

From where he's sprawled on the floor beside my bed, Rhett snorts. Then he raises his head, looks around, and wags his tail upon spotting me. "G'morning, pup." I have to smile; he looks so happy to see me.

Growing up, we always had a farm dog or two—and I loved every single one of them—but Rhett is, by far, the greatest canine companion I've ever encountered. He has gas that'll clear a room, and sometimes he's too stubborn for his own good, but he understands me in a way nobody ever has before. When I'm down, he'll act like a goof and attempt to cheer me up, and if that doesn't work, he'll sit beside me and place his head in my lap and just let me cry. If he were a man instead of a dog, I'd marry him. Farts and all.

I bought him from a pet shop, which is *so* something I never thought I'd do. But it was love at first sight: I saw him. I had to have him. So I bought him. The tag on his cage labeled him as a terrier mix, which is definitely not a breed recognized by the American Kennel Club, but I couldn't get over his scraggly beard, mottled grey and brown fur, and velvety ears that perked up when he saw me. His saddleback suggests Airedale, and there's a hint of German pointer as well, but whatever he is, he was worth every penny; I wouldn't trade him for the world.

Rhett stands, stretches, and nuzzles my arm with his nose. He's hungry, no doubt. It seems that each day we spend in Lake Caywood, our wakeup time creeps closer and closer toward noon. It's probably nearer to lunch than it is breakfast. I take a deep breath, brace myself for the cold air that's about to bombard my naked limbs, and throw off the covers. It takes no longer than two seconds before my arms are completely covered in goose pimples. I pull on a sweatshirt and socks while Rhett sits in the doorway, thumping his tail against the floor and anticipating a bowl full of fresh kibble. Having eaten nearly everything left in the house, I had little choice but to devote a portion of yesterday to a grocery run. I picked up the basics: eggs, bread, milk, cheese, a bag of Purina… Stuff like that. It'd been ten years, so even though Main Street Market is still situated in its old location, the establishment itself was different than what I remembered. The floors are Pergo instead of that old schoolroom, asbestos tiling; vertical banners sweep down from above, advertising pictures of vibrantly colored fruits and vegetables; thunder sounds before the produce is spritzed with water; and there's a Mediterranean bar. It used to be that green olives were available in a jar and black olives were available in a can and that was that. Now shoppers may not only choose from a variety of olives—kalamata, manzanilla, gaeta; garlic-stuffed, feta-stuffed, pit-still-intact—but those olives are also allowed to *intermingle* in a plastic tub. Plus, there are marinated mushrooms and artichokes that a person might add to the mix if so inclined.

I was so inclined.

Admittedly, my love for olives is fairly intense (I've been known to eat them for breakfast) but this morning is cold enough to warrant something hot. My culinary skills will never compare to those of Noni, but I do make a mean bowl of oatmeal. Nuts, raisins, a splash of heavy cream… lots of cinnamon and brown sugar. My stomach rumbles just thinking about it.

Rhett leads the way downstairs, his nails clicking softly against the hardwood, and I follow a few paces behind. Once in the kitchen, we veer in different directions: I stroll to the coffeemaker and my pup makes a beeline for his food dish. He stands beside it, tail erect, watching me with wide eyes. "Give me two minutes," I request, scooping hazelnut grounds into the machine. "Then I'm all yours."

I've neglected to turn on the lights and the kitchen is dimly lit, diluted sunshine filtering in through thick-glassed windows. Running water at the sink, I observe the outside world and wonder if it might finally snow; the sky is a cold shade of grey. Clouds blend together, forming a thick blanket of haze. If I squint hard enough, I think I might be able to discern minute flurries, but it may just be my imagination.

Rhett barks once from the other side of the room—a sociable yip that's meant to remind me of his famished state—and I turn my back on the gurgling coffeemaker, occupying my time with dog food instead. "Here you go," I say, depositing a scoop of kibble into his bowl. "Have at it."

He sits obediently and meets my gaze, awaiting confirmation. "Go ahead," I tell him. "Eat." And he does, first sniffing the dry morsels with his long snout and then chomping them between powerful jaws. I set to work on my oatmeal, heating a mixture of milk and water on the stove, and consider my surroundings while waiting for the liquid to reach a slow boil.

The floors should really be redone, and the countertop replaced, and the cabinetry refinished. And that's just what's needed in the *kitchen*. To renovate the entire house is a task too hefty for comprehension, but it's also a task that needs to be reflected upon. I can handle a drill just fine, and wield a paintbrush better than most people, but on the subject of home repair, I'm relatively uneducated. If I stay, though, I don't want the farmhouse to merely be my home; I want it to be a testament to Gramps's life.

If I stay.

There's only one way I can think to do that.

The thing is, Gramps left all of it to me: the orchards, the barn, the farmhouse, the hops, and everything in the bank. Kirby got the car—a Ford Model T that, with frequent tinkering, still runs—which is all he really cared about. We met with the lawyer last week to go over the will, and while I was completely blindsided by the inheritance, my great-uncle didn't seem the least bit surprised. He was happy with the car, but still angry about my refusal to bury Gramps beside Noni, so the meeting with the lawyer was just that: a meeting with a lawyer. There was no brunch date beforehand and no lunch date afterward, and Kirby and I haven't spoken since. Considering the magnitude of our post-funeral fight, I'm relatively certain we won't have much to say to one another for quite some time. I'll reunite my grandfather with his land when the moment feels right, and maybe his brother will want to be there when it happens, but for now Gramps is resting on the living room mantle.

I turn my attention back to the stove, reduce the heat, and dump dry oatmeal into the now-hot liquid. It bubbles up, threatening to spill over the rim of the pot, and I quickly lift it off the heat, stirring constantly. Rhett knows a second scoop of Purina won't find its way into his bowl until later this evening, so he settles himself beside the stove, resting his chin on my feet, hopeful that something edible might accidentally tumble to the ground. After a few moments in this position, as the top of my socked foot becomes unexplainably damp, I realize he's drooling. "Rhett," I sigh, taking a step back.

He stares up at me, obviously put out by the fact that I've taken his headrest.

I set to transferring my oatmeal to a bowl and adding all of the ingredients that will make it delicious. "Here's the game plan," I say to my pup, who watches me from where he remains sprawled on the floor. His reluctance to move requires me to step over and around him, depending upon my destination. "I'm going to eat, and then you and I are going to take a walk."

Rhett's ears—acute triangles that flop at the tips—stand taller than usual and he tilts his head to one side. "Walk" is his favorite word.

I carry my breakfast to the oak table in the center of the room and lift myself onto one of the tall stools. The scent of cinnamon wafts upwards, reminding me of the gooey sticky buns Noni used to make on winter weekday mornings that warranted two-hour school delays. I'd pull the warm dough apart with my fingers, unearthing pockets of finely chopped pecans slathered in syrupy sweetness. I miss those mornings. And I miss Noni and Gramps.

With no leash to confine him, Rhett bounds ahead, thoroughly sniffing at the bases of bare apple trees and snorting his way along withered raspberry bushes. He never runs so far ahead that I can't see him, and he makes it a point to double back every now and again. "Good boy," I praise him each time this is done, and give his wiry head a soft pat.

I've bundled up for the excursion, but it's chilly despite my wool coat and thick gloves. With every exhale, my breath floats up and away in wispy clouds of white. Frozen blades of grass crunch beneath my feet with each step.

We walk first around the pond, where cattails stand at attention on the sidelines with their bushy heads bobbing above a sheet of glistening ice, and then mosey among a grove of peach trees, their limbs gnarled and bare. Nestled among the inhabitants of this sparse orchard forest is a beautiful error: a lone plum tree, planted by mistake in the midst of warmer-hued fruit. As a young teenager, I spent many an afternoon here, hidden within a maze of branches, munching on deep purple plums as I dreamed about boys and a life outside of Lake Caywood. So consumed was I by these thoughts that I never noticed the juice sliding down my arms and dripping off my elbows; I'd go home sticky at the end of the day with no memory of how it had happened.

As it turns out, life on the other side of Lake Caywood isn't all that it's cracked up to be.

Neither are the boys.

Gramps kept all the P's to the property's south: peaches, pears, and plums. Apples, berries, and cherries grow toward the north end. I'm not sure if there was a purpose behind arranging it alphabetically or not; it might have just been a coincidence, or it may have been Noni's doing. She kept a vegetable garden behind the house—my bedroom overlooked it—and if I remember correctly, it too went from A to Z. Asparagus, broccoli, corn, cucumbers, eggplant… all the way to zucchini. Noni loved to pass her time within that maze of vegetation, pulling weeds and harvesting produce. We barely managed to put a dent in what she collected; so much of it was canned. To this day, I've never tasted a spaghetti sauce that compares to my grandmother's.

Gramps hired a crew to care for his orchards. Felipe, handsome and mustached, was a constant fixture in our lives, but the others would come in the spring and bid adieu in late October. Oh, Gramps would oversee everything and help out when necessary, but whereas Noni was the queen of her garden, Gramps was surprisingly hands-off.

Except for when it came to the hops, that is.

Located on the backside of the barn, this is the crop he valued most.

Rhett nudges my gloved hand with his nose and I give his ears a gentle tousle. "This way," I say, and motion to skirt the perimeter of the barn. The wooden giant, once painted a brilliant red that's now chipped and splintered, seems almost to be slumbering as we meander past it and enter the web of posts and wires beyond. Now, of course, the lines that cross above my head like low-hanging telephone cables are empty; the perennial green vines that clung to them in spring and summer months have since turned brown and released their grips and crumbled to the frozen earth below, but come March and April, fresh bines will begin to emerge from the soil. Gramps grew all types of hops, from Cascade to Willamette, and like his fruit trees, it suddenly occurs to me that they were organized alphabetically. How had I lived with him for nearly two decades and never realized this until now? I swallow my guilt and follow Rhett into the hop field, remembering September afternoons when I'd dart off the school bus, deposit my knapsack on the porch step, and race to help Gramps with the harvest.

I was drinking beer long before the law would have liked me to be. Gramps offered me a sip of effervescent ale on my fifth birthday and I accepted. Most kids probably would've scrunched up their noses and stuck out their tongues, trying to get rid of the taste… but I rather liked the sweet-bitterness of it. I learned from an early age what it meant to be responsible when it comes to alcohol, and by twelve or so, I was not only sampling the many ales, stouts, and porters that Gramps concocted: I was also helping him to name them.

He referred to the product as Old Orchard Brews, and although he did register the name to make it official, his creations were always gifted rather than sold. Nothing special to look at, the different beers were funneled into brown-glass bottles and labeled with masking tape and a Sharpie. The tightly scrawled names that appeared on the tags, however, would have certainly been worthy of complimentary artwork. Many of the titles related in some way back to the farm—like Berry Patch Summer (a wheat beer infused with juicy strawberries, plump blackberries, and tart blueberries) and Golden Delicious Lager (it had just a *hint* of apple)—but Gramps never felt restricted by the orchard; he didn't feel the need to relate every brew to a fruit. Instead, he liked to have fun with the names. Bellhoppin', for example, has always been one of my favorites. Citrusy in a way that instinctively puckers lips, and with an eleven-percent alcohol content, Gramps used to warn, "Don't drink more than one. If you do, you'll need a bellhop to carry both you *and* your bags."

He messed around with porters for a while, too, and came up with one that he referred to as Starched Collar. It was a deep, chocolaty brown in color and smelled pleasantly of roasted coffee beans. Perfect for a winter evening, my grandfather described the flavor as "rigid and mature," and every now and then he'd actually combine the IPA and the darker beer to create a black and tan.

Of course, he didn't *call* it a black and tan.

He termed it Top-Notch Service, because how could Bellhoppin', when paired with a Starched Collar Porter, result in anything else? I smile, remembering Gramps's creativity and the fun he'd experience each time a new batch of beer was ready to be named; I remember the way his face would light up and he'd clasp his rough hands together upon thinking of something especially clever. Like a roasted coffee stout labeled Chicory Dickory Dark, or a notably sweet and fizzy IPA given the title of Soda Hop.

The sudden rush of memories causes my vision to blur. I blink back my tears and consider my frostbitten surroundings. Three months from now, this field will be waking up from hibernation, and six months from now, fresh vines of hops will spiral upward in tendrils of green. I take a deep breath and fill my lungs with frozen air. Come June, the aroma emanating from this plot of land will be completely different.

Earthy.

Musty.

Dank.

I wonder if I will still be here in June.

I think that I probably will, if only because I owe this much to Gramps.

Rhett, like me, lifts his head and inhales sharply. Then he prances to one of the tall posts Gramps positioned years ago and sniffs the ground before marking his territory. "This is mine now," he tells the world. And I think that it really could be… for a while.

Or forever.

At this point, the two are pretty much interchangeable.

Something cold brushes against my cheek and as I reach up to wipe it away, I realize that flurries of snow have begun to fall from the sky, floating down like confetti, teaming together in an effort to paint the world white. I clap my gloved hands, the muted sound capturing Rhett's attention and directing his gaze to meet mine. "Let's go home," I say.

We trek back to the old farmhouse together.

4.

Addy

He sits on the porch steps, the wooden slats cold beneath him, watching as a platoon of snowflakes parachutes to earth. They fall slowly at first, enjoying the flight, but soon quicken the pace of their attack. Within moments, the lawn is tucked beneath a blanket of white.

Addy whistles to pass the time. The notes float upward to mingle with plummeting ice crystals, dodging and dosey-doeing and dancing across the yard. He watches their colorful paths—at first solid and bright, then diluted like watercolors—until the existence of each one is nothing but a memory.

With a cargo jacket the color of charcoal, a slouched beanie and fingerless gloves the same shade as ash, and a wardrobe consisting of all the hues found in a black and white film, it might be assumed that Addison Birch has a personal vendetta against color. That particular conjecture would be false, though. Addy sees color where others see none.

In fact, where Addy sees color, others frequently see *nothing.*

And so he sits, feet planted firmly on the bottom step, waiting and whistling and wondering.

Charley hears him before she sees him, and had his song not collided with her halfway between the barn and the farmhouse, she may not have recognized him at all. No longer is he that four-foot-tall boy with wide eyes and an all-the-time quizzical expression. He stands as she approaches and Charley is surprised to find that he is tall—taller than she is—with dark eyes that have narrowed with knowledge. He smiles in a way that keeps his teeth hidden and allows his hands to remain in his pockets. There will be no hug.

It's been ten years, but Addy would recognize her anywhere. When Charley moves, infinitesimal sparks follow in her wake, burning a brilliant shade of crimson before dissolving to extinction. She is the only one he's ever known to be that color.

There's a dog with her and he barks once upon noticing the boy's presence. It's a firm bark that serves as both a question and a warning. He turns to confer with his owner, pausing several feet from the stranger standing on the bottom porch step, and waits for a command. "It's okay," Charley says. "Good boy." The dog plunges ahead, obviously curious, and cautiously sniffs at the hems of this unfamiliar person's jeans. After a moment Charley warns, "That's enough, Rhett," and then tilts her head to the side as she looks up at Addy. She allows him to speak first.

Hands tucked deep in his pockets, he keeps his gaze lowered so that his dark eyes don't quite meet hers. "I heard you were back." His voice is so much lower than what she remembers. A decade ago, when they'd used to spend Friday evenings making English muffin pizzas together, that voice had been sweet and childlike… not deep and accusatory. But then, Addy had been a child at that point in time. He must have been no more than seven when she left.

Charley, not sure of how to respond, doesn't immediately speak. She instead reaches down to gently rumple Rhett's ears. The dog pants happily and thumps his back leg, satisfying an itch. The movement sends a spray of snow into the air.

Addy has never been one to overuse words, so although he does lift his dark eyes to find hers, he does not fill the void with additional talk. And eventually Charley contributes, "Gramps died."

"I heard about that," Addy says with a nod. "I'm sorry."

The young woman shrugs and miniature embers bounce from her shoulders. Crimson to fuchsia to gone. Her cheeks, already red from the cold, grow splotchy from the effort of holding back tears. "He was ninety-two."

To Addy, who will turn eighteen next month, this seems like a ridiculously long life.

"He left the house to me," she whispers.

Charley Lane has very green eyes and they peer up at Addy from beneath a dark hood, searching his face for *something*. An opinion? Affirmation? A hint of the anger he must feel toward her? But what he offers is a straightforward question: "Will you stay?"

She blinks once, but holds his gaze. "I think so."

"Good." There is no emotion in his tone. Addy reveals nothing; he simply steps off the porch and walks past her. Although his narrow form continues to move farther and farther away, the obscure little tune that he whistles remains audible. It lingers there in the snow-covered yard, much like his footprints.

He goes to the library. Not the very loud and very public library that sits across the street from the courthouse: the quiet one frequented by college students. Classes have been back in session for one week, so there's movement on the campus again, but last night was the first Friday since Christmas break and more than a few kegs were no doubt drained. As he strolls across the mostly empty university grounds, it seems the majority of the student body is still sleeping off its hangover.

The library is located about a block from the dining hall. Because of this, the air surrounding the building carries the sweet scent of maple syrup. Addy skipped breakfast this morning and the aroma causes extra saliva to pool in his mouth. He swallows, dismissing all thoughts of pancakes and waffles and flat discs of Canadian bacon, and takes the stairs two at a time. He passes the marble pillars, pushes through the tall double doors, and skirts the brightly lit lobby as quickly as possible. Where he likes to be is among the stacks, bumping his index finger along crisp spines and cracked spines and spines that have been nibbled by dogs.

Addy's love for literature is intense. He'll read anything and everything, no matter the genre, because it has the potential to transport him to a place far from Smalltown, Pennsylvania. He's lived his whole life in Lake Caywood, and although he occasionally dares to dream of a life after high school—a new start in a big city, an adventure on the Appalachian

Trail—he's never truly believed that this life could exist outside the town's boundaries. Graduation is less than five months away. College isn't an option, so where does that leave him?

Waiting tables at the diner on Railroad Street, where the sandwiches are mediocre at best and the drunks are plentiful at two A.M. Addy knows the tips he earns there aren't enough to cover even one year of higher education, let alone four. He's successfully dodged his guidance counselor for an entire semester; not a single college application has been submitted.

His long finger, its nail flat and narrow, glides over a very broad spine. *The Complete Works of Emily Dickinson.* It's been read, but not by many. The protective plastic book jacket that shields it from things like spilled coffee and rainy days is still crisp and glossy. Addy pulls the volume from the shelf, slides to the floor, and settles cross-legged with the book in his lap. He opens to a random page about a third of the way from the end.

Surprise is like a thrilling—pungent—
Upon a tasteless meat
Alone—too acrid—but combined
An edible Delight.

"Like Charley," he says aloud to no one, because she *is* the surprise, sparkling and red and unexpected, and his life is the tasteless meat. It hadn't always been this way, though. His childhood had been somewhat of an edible delight, but that was years ago... back when Charley Lane had acted as more of a mother to him than the woman who should have held that title. Oh, how he'd idolized her! Addy closes his eyes, rests his head against the bookcase behind him, and recalls a day in late August.

School hadn't yet begun, but its approach was close enough to make a person sentimental for summer. Tomatoes were abundant, along with zucchinis and cucumbers, and at the end of nearly every other driveway one would see a basket overflowing with produce and a handwritten sign that advertised Free. Not surprisingly, June Birch hadn't been around, so she'd requested that Charley watch over her six-year-old son. *Raise* her six-year-old son, really. Addy had overheard that particular set of early-morning instructions and can still remember them to this day: "I'm working a double," his mother had said, "and then I have a date, so I won't be home until midnight at the earliest. I can trust you to feed him, right? There's Chef Boyardee in the cupboard by the stove."

Charley, technically still a child herself, had known more about caring for kids than June Birch ever would. She didn't park Addy in front of the television or feed him canned ravioli that had been warmed in the microwave. What she did was buckle him into the backseat of her car and transport him to the farmhouse. Noni'd been in the process of making spaghetti sauce and the kitchen had been a sauna that smelled of fresh herbs. Addy imagines that his eyes must have grown to be the size of quarters—or maybe even half dollars—upon beholding all of the different tomatoes. Buckets and buckets of them! There'd been plump tomatoes with skins that had split; fleshy Roma tomatoes, perfect for sauce; round tomatoes striped with pink; tomatoes so dark they almost looked purple; and cherry-sized tomatoes the color of sunshine.

Noni put him to work at the high table in the middle of the kitchen, instructing him to pluck the leaves from long, reedy stems of oregano. Beside him, Charley chopped basil and parsley and rosemary, which her grandmother claimed to be a secret ingredient. "Sauce isn't sauce without rosemary," she'd said. "Rosemary and good red wine."

It had taken all day, but as the sun grew dim that evening, Addy had felt a sense of accomplishment as he marveled at the jars of sauce cooling on the counter. There were so many—enough to last through the winter—and he had helped.

There had been no Chef Boyardee for dinner that night. Noni served them garden-fresh salad, buttery garlic bread, and spaghetti saturated with sauce. Addy would be hard pressed to remember a better meal; he'd eaten until the button on his shorts threatened to pop.

He opens his eyes, happy to have the memory, but saddened by the knowledge that it cannot be repeated or relived, even with Charley back in the old farmhouse. The distance between them is vast, the likelihood of rekindling slim, and the realization of this truth is surprisingly heavy.

A high-pitched squeak and the soft shuffle of feet pull Addy from his thoughts. He glances to the left and there at the end of the row, pushing a cart laden with library books, is Miss Flora. She smiles when she sees him. "Why, Mr. Birch! I didn't see you come in. What are you reading today?"

Addy closes the book in his lap and holds up the cover for viewing.

"Dickinson," the old woman muses. "Rather a dismal read, I'd imagine."

"Rather," he has to agree.

"I expect that the pages are peppered with dashes."

This comment almost earns a smile from Addy. He's fond of Miss Flora, who exudes shimmers of yellow-green light and works as one of the college's part-time librarians, shelving books on Saturdays and Tuesday evenings. He's known her for years, although not well. Their relationship consists of book recommendations and research assistance, and the longest real conversation the two ever shared occurred when Addy borrowed *To Kill A Mockingbird* and Miss Flora confided, "That one's my daughter's favorite."

"You have a daughter?" he'd asked, and the old woman had smiled and said, "I did." Then, with frail fingers that shook, she reached behind her neck to unclasp a thin chain of silver. From it hung a simple locket, tarnished with age, in the shape of a circle. A delicate snowflake was etched on the front. "There," she'd directed, opening the locket and pointing to a small image captured inside. "She was four or five when that picture was taken. Wasn't she beautiful?"

Addy had nodded politely. Although the photograph was in black and white, it was evident that the little girl had bright eyes—most likely blue or green—that would have been quite striking against her dark hair. But just as he is now, he'd been a teenager, not especially interested in learning about a child he'd never met, and so he'd instead questioned Miss Flora about a trio of letters etched on the other half of the locket: F.H.C. "Were those her initials?"

"They're mine, actually."

Addy paused, thought, and then said, "But your last name is Higgins."

"It was, and then it wasn't, and now it is again," Miss Flora explained. "For a while I took the surname of Clay, but those days are gone. I've returned to my roots, Mr. Birch." She closed the locket then, snapping it gently shut so that it made a quiet *click*, and reached again with her quivering hands behind her neck, fumbling with the tiny clasp.

"What happened?" Addy had asked in that moment. "To your daughter, I mean?"

A sadness washed over Miss Flora's face; her wrinkles suddenly seemed deeper than ever. In a whisper she answered, "Oh, she died a long time ago." And then she placed Addy's book in his hands and said, "You enjoy that," thus ending the conversation.

Here in the present, the little librarian straightens a nearby shelf before reuniting Robert Frost with his fellow poets. She grins down at the young man, her eyes twinkling from behind bifocals. "Enjoy your time with Emily," she says.

Addy watches her shuffle away, guiding the cart over to join greats such as Shelley, Steinbeck, and Stowe. The high-pitched squeak grows faint with distance. Sighing, he turns back to the book in his lap and wonders what it would take to transform his life into something that the morose Dickinson *wouldn't* wish to write a poem about.

5.
Juli

If February only has twenty-eight days, then each of those days must be about thirty hours long. No way is it the shortest month… The calendar's gotta be lying.

It's only a little after three o'clock, but the sky is grey enough to warrant headlights. I flick mine on and steer the truck down Main Street, hoping to find an available spot in front of the Tavern. I wouldn't normally be meeting for drinks in the middle of the afternoon, but it's Asher's birthday and I told him I'd buy him a beer after school. He's thirty-five going on twenty-two; I swear his level of maturity decreases the older he gets.

Not surprisingly, the concept of Tuesday happy hour is less popular than, say, Thursday or Friday happy hour. I have little trouble securing a parking spot and shove a handful of dimes into the meter's mouth before ducking into the Tavern. The place is virtually empty. A table of three shares a late lunch (or maybe it's an early dinner—I'm not really sure) and an old man nurses a cup of coffee at the end of the bar, but those are the only customers. Except for Asher, I mean. He's occupying one of the barstools positioned closest to the taps, watching Petey Goode as he pours him a Guinness. I snag a seat of my own and shrug out of my coat. "Happy birthday, bud. Hey there, Petey. What's goin' on?"

"My students baked me a cake," Asher volunteers. "Chocolate with cream cheese icing."

"Homemade?"

He shakes his head. "I'm pretty sure the cake was from a box and the frosting was from a tub, but it was still delicious. There were sprinkles, too. Rainbow ones."

"Wow, rainbow? They must really love you."

Petey laughs and Asher elbows me sharply in the side. "You're just jealous," he says.

"Jealous that you have a beer and I don't, maybe." I turn to Petey, who's waiting for my order with a pint glass in his hand, and request a stout of my own. He wastes little time in fulfilling the request. Then I turn back to Asher and give him the birthday attention that he deserves. "So, which students hooked you up? Grace and Lily?"

"Grace and Savannah."

"Savannah..." I repeat. "I forgot about her."

Asher teaches math at the high school and each school year he manages to acquire a gaggle of girls who swoon over his surfer-dude looks: blonde hair, blue eyes, perpetual tan. He's largely oblivious to these crushes, never noticing the giggles and flushed cheeks that are often exhibited by female students, but he does seem to take note when there's food involved. I've been with him when we've bumped into kids from his class, though. The boys hit him up for high-fives and have a casual conversation about football or basketball or whatever sport is in season. But the girls are different. I've observed their shyness, their lack of eye contact, their inability to employ words that consist of more than one or two syllables... Simply stated, they're smitten, but Asher doesn't see it.

Although he may be ignorant when it comes to adolescent lust, Asher is surprisingly intuitive when it comes to the personalities and learning styles of his students. He understands them on a level that I wish every teacher could, and I get the impression that he's pretty good at what he does. I hear an awful lot of stories about school and students, and by the second semester, I've usually got about ten or fifteen names committed to memory. Grace and Lily and Savannah are just a few of 'em.

"They're in my first period class," Asher says now, "so I divvied it up and we ate it for breakfast."

"Did you turn it into a math problem?" Petey asks, placing my Guinness on the bar. It has a frothy head that bleeds into the coffee-colored beer below, creating a creaminess that reminds me of milk chocolate. I'm suddenly wishing I had a piece of that birthday cake.

Asher laughs in response to Petey's suggestion. "Probably should have. I could have proven that division *is* useful in the real world. I must not have been thinking clearly. It was early, and just the *scent* of that cake was giving me a sugar high."

"There's always next year," Petey states. He tells us to let him know if we need anything else and then wanders away to check on the Tavern's other customers. I take a sip of my beer. It's rich and heavy and pleasantly bitter. Perfect for February. "So," I begin, "what're your plans for the rest of today? Are you and Annie getting together?"

"Not tonight," Asher says, "but maybe this weekend. Kenny and Wes and some other guys from work are taking me out for trivia and wings later."

"Where're you going for that? Solomon's Pub?"

"Yep."

"Huh. Well, that should be fun." I say it, and I mostly mean it, but there's a part of me that's surprised by the fact Annie isn't included in his birthday plans. It could be she has to work, or already had something scheduled for tonight, but since it's really not my place to pry, I choose to let it go. We talk about sports and new tires for Asher's car and a disgusting clog that I dislodged from a bathtub drain this morning; then we order another round and discuss the odds of redheads becoming extinct and whether or not giant squids might really exist. Asher ate two Pop-Tarts *and* cake for breakfast, and partook of a delicious birthday lunch provided by his coworkers, so he's sober as a judge after draining two glasses of beer. I, however, skipped my midday meal and am feeling a bit of a buzz. If I were to say this out loud, Asher would no doubt offer me a ride, but then there'd be the hassle of retrieving my truck and I just don't feel like dealing with all that. Besides, I've got a short list of things to purchase from Honey-Do and that's well within walking distance. I pop a mint in my mouth, zip my coat, and head down the block. Asher honks as he pulls away.

The air is damp and cold and I lower my head against the wind, wishing I'd opted for a beanie rather than a baseball cap. Groundhog's Day has come and gone, and according to Punxsutawney Phil, we're in for six more weeks of winter weather. I shiver and quicken my pace.

The copper cowbell announces my arrival and Myra is there to greet me almost immediately. The past month has brought us closer together; when I squat down to give her a proper hello, she rolls onto her side and exposes her belly for a thorough scratching. I get her back leg going and she revs her engine for a good minute or two. Eileen stands behind the register and laughs. "Are you *sure* you don't want her?"

This question is posed each time I visit the shop, and each time I reiterate, "One is enough." Today is no exception. It's true that I've grown quite fond of the Basset, but if I took home every animal I fell in love with, I'd live in a zoo.

I give the hound a final pat, stand up, and go in search of drywall screws. Behind me, I hear Myra shake her floppy ears and droopy face (it sounds like a lot of muted clapping) and that noise is soon replaced with the quick click of her nails on linoleum. It takes a moment for her to catch up, but she does find—and then follow—me through the store. We debate cement screws together.

Not surprisingly, the winter months provide me with an abundance of indoor jobs. I've got a tiling gig lined up for tomorrow, some painting later this week, and at some point I need to install a new chandelier for my former chemistry teacher. That guy throws more dinner parties than anyone I've ever met; he's always working on *something* to make his dining room new and exciting, whether it's the wall color, light fixtures, or artwork. He's hired me for maybe four or five different projects and I don't think a single tablecloth has ever made a second appearance. He's a shopper; that much is clear.

From the front of the store, the cowbell clangs, and Myra, who's been using my leg for support as she reaches around to clean her back foot, clambers to all fours and hurries to investigate. I grab the screws that I need, hoist a fifty-pound bag of thinset into my arms, and take a moment to contemplate whether my trowel is in the truck or lost in the garage. It's a poorly timed thought—the thinset is heavy—so I grab an extra one and head to the register, determining that it's better to have two than none.

Eileen and the new arrival talk quietly at the counter. The customer is a woman with very short, very dark hair. I believe this is referred to as a pixie cut, but why I know this is beyond me. It's probably one of those things that my friends' girlfriends were rambling on about at some point and I just happened to be halfway paying attention to them. Anyway, her hair is almost as short as mine and her coat is black with a hood and it suddenly occurs to me that this could be the girl from outside the funeral parlor. I slow my pace a bit, wondering if a snippet of the conversation they're having might be audible, but Eileen foils my attempts when she glances over and catches me clutching my thinset several yards from the register. "Stop acting macho and put that down on the counter," she instructs with a roll of her eyes. "That stuff weighs a ton." To the pixie-haired customer she says, "This is the guy I was telling you about. Julian Singer."

"Juli," I correct. I unload my purchases with a thud and offer a now-free hand to the girl. She accepts it and offers, "I'm Charley." Her voice is sweet and her slightly upturned nose is adorable and her eyes are incredibly green. Emerald green. We shake, and then we release our grips, and then Eileen says, "Charley just moved back to the area and she's looking for a handyman. I suggested you."

"Yeah? Well, what kinds of projects do you have in mind?"

"Oh, jeez…" she sighs. "There's so much to be done. The hardwood floors need to be refinished, everything needs a fresh coat of paint, the front door needs a new lock… I'd sort of like to widen a doorway if that's even a possibility."

"It probably is. I mean, it's trickier if the wall's load-bearing, but it's likely still doable."

"How about a backsplash? Can you do that?"

"Sure."

She nods, seeming to take a mental note. "Have you ever installed swinging doors?"

"No, but that doesn't mean I couldn't."

"What about lights?"

I raise an eyebrow and tilt my head to the side. "What about 'em?"

A small grin brightens Charley's face. "Do you install them, too?"

"Depends. I do *some* electrical work, but not much, so if it's a job that I don't feel comfortable doing, I'll pass and give you the number of an electrician instead."

"Recessed lighting?" she asks.

"I'll get you that number," I say.

Charley laughs. "Fair enough. Do you have a card or something with your information?"

I fish one out of my wallet and hand it over. "I don't know what your schedule's like, or how soon you're looking to get started, but if you're interested I'm gonna have some free time tomorrow afternoon. I could maybe swing by and take a look?"

"Really? That'd be great!"

"Where's the property?"

"Way out Copper Drive, number five-nineteen."

"She's staying in Jasper Lane's old place," Eileen volunteers, and Charley nods, adding, "He was my grandfather. I, uh… I have some big plans for the house."

"Well, I look forward to learning what they are," I tell her. "Tomorrow, say, around two?"

"That's perfect, thank you." She says this to me, and then she repeats it to Eileen: "Thanks."

We watch her leave. As soon as the door swings shut behind her, Eileen gives me a mischievous grin and states, "She's cute." I say nothing, which doesn't necessarily mean I don't agree. Charley had been several steps above cute: she'd been beautiful. But if there's one thing I don't do well, it's relationships. The few that I've been in have failed, and my current schedule really doesn't allow for dinner dates and movie nights anyway. My career keeps me busy.

Disappointed by my silence, but sensing these lips will remain sealed, Eileen totals my purchases and swipes my credit card. "You know," she says, not quite ready to let the topic drop, "not all girls drink cosmos and spend forever on their hair and expect their boyfriends to talk on the phone for two hours every night. And just because you're busy doesn't mean you're *too* busy. Sometimes it's okay to put yourself first. You deserve to be happy."

"I'm happy," I assure her.

"Well, you deserve to be happy *with somebody*," she amends, and offers a slight smile.

I loop the plastic Honey-Do bag over my wrist and lift the weighty thinset from the counter, lugging it toward the door. Myra pads a few steps behind and Eileen's stare bores into my back; I can feel it. "You worry about me too much, you know that?" I call over my shoulder, and she laughs. "I worry about you just enough, Juli Singer!"

6.
Charley

I wake with a headache even before the sun has yawned its "good morning," pad to the kitchen with Rhett on my heels, and brew extra-strong coffee that I use to swallow three pills. It helps, but doesn't completely diminish the dull ache that has taken up residency behind my eyes. I rub my temples and squint at the clock: five-thirty. Too early to be up, but not worth it to return to bed since Juli will most likely be here by seven o'clock. He's been working split shifts at the farmhouse, putting in a few hours each morning and then coming back in the evening, and even working overtime on the weekends. It's been this way since that day in mid-February. He'd knocked on the door a little after two and I'd invited him in to see the premises. Upon stepping inside, his eyes had widened to about the size of plums. "Is it going to be that bad?" I'd asked, unable to read his expression, but he'd quietly responded, "It's going to be that *fun*!"

I'd taken him through the entire house and shown him every room. Juli noticed things that I hadn't and frequently hunkered down for a closer look at something, or knocked on a wall to determine the presence of a stud. I mostly observed, both his actions and his person. He's not your average handyman… he's got a walk and a soft-spoken sarcasm that suggest confidence, but he's not a know-it-all. And he certainly doesn't *look* like someone who mends broken house things for a living. Juli Singer wears Converse instead of Timberland, thermals instead of flannels, and sports creative tattoos all over his body. *Tiny* creative tattoos. I noticed it that day in the hardware shop. When we shook hands for the first time, there'd been a very small *5* on his palm. It might've simply been written there with a ballpoint pen, but when it was still visible the next day, when he'd visited the farmhouse for the first time, I'd gone ahead and asked about it.

"Footnote number five," he'd explained. "Nail gun accident. The details and date are recorded on the bottom of my right foot. It's how I keep track of my injuries."

It had taken several seconds for his words to register. "Wait," I'd had to confirm. "You have *footnotes* tattooed all over your body?"

"Just seven of them," he'd answered with a shrug.

"That's hilarious!"

Juli had smiled then, looking almost pleased. "Well, thanks."

Another not-your-typical-handyman trait that defines Juli Singer: he's got a lip ring. It's silver and he fiddles with it while pondering tricky solutions. That first day at the house he'd stood in the kitchen, scanning the counters and the cabinets and the walls, while all the time tugging at that silver hoop. And then he'd confirmed, "So you essentially want to turn this place into a restaurant?"

"A bar."

"No dinners?"

"Probably just appetizers."

"Huh. So this room will be off limits to the public?"

I'd nodded. "But a good portion of the house won't be. I know it sounds crazy…"

"I think it sounds cool." He'd offered me a lopsided grin, adjusted the brim of his baseball cap, and added, "But it's gonna be a lot of work."

"Yeah…" I'd fallen silent, wondering if the decision was a bad one, but Juli hadn't given the impression that such a monumental undertaking would end up being a mistake. He'd just fiddled with that lip ring and asked curiously, "D'you have a name for it yet?"

"I had the name before I had the vision. I'd like to call it the Brewhaha."

"B-R-E-W?"

"Gramps was all about drinking beer and having a good time," I'd explained.

And so that's what the past month has been: turning an old farmhouse into a bar. The project has been a messy one. I'd originally thought to widen the entryway from the kitchen to the living room in order to install swinging doors, but Juli, being far more skilled at construction than I, added quite a few doorways to the list. What he did *not* add to the list, however, is additional doors. I have this vision that there will always be live music on the first floor. Bluegrass, jazz, zydeco… Any and all of it is fine by me, but if that ends up being the case, Juli has suggested an open floor plan. This way all the rooms will open into one another so that people may move about freely, choosing to be close to the musicians or not. I agree with the logic, but the decision to connect everything has resulted in a lot of dust and noise.

Reciprocating saws create an awful lot of dust and noise.

With a mug of coffee warming my hands, I meander through the downstairs rooms, observing their current states of disarray and imagining how changed they will appear just a few months from now. The living room is virtually vacant at this point in time. Gramps's favorite leather armchair remains, hidden beneath an old sheet heavy with plaster powder, but the clock and the family portraits and the apple orchard watercolor, painted by my fifteen-year-old self, have all been temporarily relocated to an unused bedroom upstairs.

I've gotten rid of the rugs. As tattered and worn as they were, Juli helped me lug them to the end of the drive and place them beside the dented trashcan. I'll replace them in time, once the floors have been sanded and the walls painted and the doorways are again whole. There's really no rush. I have a finish date in mind, of course, but I am here and it is there and so many months exist between that I mostly just focus on today and maybe one or two tomorrows. It's a practice I've come to live by.

It used to be that a narrow hallway off the kitchen was the only way to access the study, master bedroom, and full bath found on the first floor, but Juli has remedied that situation. Now both spaces not only open into the living room, but also into each other. The bathroom, thankfully, still has only one door. I travel the circular path, stepping over extension cords and building materials that litter the floor, momentarily allowing myself to envision the future. In my mind, the hues will be warm: plenty of deep reds and burnt browns and polished wood. There will be at least one couch in both the living room and the bedroom—and perhaps even a chaise lounge for that latter space—but for the study I can't help but imagine an assortment of rather plush chairs, situated around a bold oriental rug, eager to welcome the animated debates of poets and politicians as they sip creamy stouts from chilled mugs. I sigh as I pick my way back to the kitchen, for the fun of design does seem ages away.

I find Rhett sprawled by his empty food dish, head resting dejectedly upon his paws, but he does raise a pair of wiry eyebrows and widen those chocolate-brown eyes when I eventually reappear. "Are you hungry?" I ask, and he thumps his tail in response. "Alright… here you go." I deposit a scoop of kibble in his bowl, top off my coffee, and am in the process of unwrapping a granola bar when the muffled *thwump* of a car door slamming sounds from outside. Rhett glances up from his breakfast, still chomping a mouthful of chow. I say to him, "Juli must be early," and peer out the window to confirm this theory.

He's traipsing across the lawn, a toolbox in one hand and a canvas grocery bag swinging from the other. His lips are moving, despite the fact that he's alone, but I've gotten to know him fairly well over the past several weeks and recognize he's more likely singing than talking to himself. That sign on the side of his truck doesn't lie: Juli Singer really does provide "Service with a Song."

I meet him at the door and he stops his tune in mid-verse, pausing to offer a sideways smile. "What're you singing?" I ask, and he shrugs. "Something by the Beatles. I brought breakfast"—he holds up the shopping bag—"and… I also brought Scarlett."

"Your dog?" I confirm.

He nods. "She's in the truck. I'll bring her in if it's okay with you, but I didn't want to assume that it would be. Rhett presents himself as the friendliest dog on the face of the earth, but there's always that chance…" he trails off.

"Rhett loves other dogs," I assure him, "and it's absolutely fine with me if she comes inside."

So Juli sets his tools on the floor, hands breakfast to me, and makes a quick return trip to his truck. I carry the canvas bag to the tall table in the center of the kitchen and Rhett dances along at my side, his nose detecting something edible.

His attention is immediately diverted when Juli returns with a hesitant pup trailing behind. She has glossy fur that's auburn in color and a shyness that's evident from the way her long, feathered tail remains hidden between her legs. "It's okay," Juli reassures her, tousling her floppy ears and removing the leash from her collar. "Rhett just wants to play."

Boy, does he! My wiry pup has his front paws on the ground and his butt in the air. His own tail stands completely erect; he's too excited even to wag it. Scarlett, cowering behind her owner, bravely pokes her head around Juli's knees and stares at Rhett, both timid and curious. Rhett offers a short, friendly yip and cocks his head good-humoredly to the side. He can be a clown and chooses to portray this side of himself now. The goofy behavior seems to put Scarlett at ease because she walks over to Rhett and delicately sniffs at his ear. Some sort of canine communication must exist between them in that moment because just like *that* they are off, dashing from room to room and exploring the torn-apart house together.

I laugh and Juli comes to stand beside me, unearthing a bakery box from the bag. "I stopped and picked up some cinnamon rolls from that new bakery on Lakefront."

"Piping Hot?" I verify, having noticed it the other day, and he nods. The establishment was cute with its aqua trim and yellow-striped awning, but I hadn't realized it was such a new addition to Lake Caywood. My ten-year absence has resulted in so many of the town's shops and restaurants seeming new.

Juli retrieves two paper towels from the dispenser by the sink, offers one to me, and then places a gooey breakfast spiral on top of it. "Did you go in?" he asks in reference to the bakery.

"Nope, just drove by. Rhett and I were out exploring. A lot's changed since I was last here."

"How old were you when you left?" He uncoils the cinnamon roll and tears off a piece of the flaky pastry, popping it into his mouth. Then he licks the sugary icing from his fingers, wipes them on his pants, and waits for my answer.

"Eighteen," I say, not elaborating, but the response isn't enough. Juli immediately follows it up with, "Why'd you go?"

It's a good question—Why *did* I go?—and my instinct is to answer it with a question of my own: Why would I *not* go? I'd been through with high school even before tossing my graduation cap into the air and felt that I'd seen everything this small town had to offer. Gramps had urged me to consider Lake Caywood University, but I refused to submit an application and took off for Ferris State as soon as the dorms would house me. I came home for visits a few times that first year, but then Noni passed away and the farmhouse seemed far too empty with just Gramps putzing around inside. So I stayed in Michigan and conveniently always had other plans when the holidays rolled around. "Sorry, Gramps," I remember apologizing over the phone to him one December, "but I'm heading to Colorado for Christmas this year. A friend invited me to spend break on the slopes." He must have been devastated, but all he'd said in response was, "That's fine, Charley. You have fun and be safe. Know that I love you."

Hindsight is twenty-twenty, of course, and I can see looking back that more time needed to be spent here with Gramps, helping with yard work and house repairs… and just letting him know that I loved him too. But I can't go back, I can only go forward, and I think that's why I answer Juli's question with, "I guess the real reason I left had mostly to do with Addy."

"Addy Birch?" Juli prompts right away, and his familiarity throws me for a loop. I lower the bite of cinnamon roll I'd been about to put in my mouth and meet his gaze instead. "You know him?" I ask.

"Sure. I mean, not very well, but everybody in town knows Addy Birch. Or at least who he is. Up until last year he was Lake Caywood High's star quarterback. Always on the front page of the sports section, usually above the fold, and then this past season he just… quit." Juli shrugs, wonders, "How do you know him?"

To say that I was his babysitter would be the understatement of the century. I helped to toilet train him, taught him his alphabet, and read him to sleep with *The Very Hungry Caterpillar* when his mom spent the night with her latest fling instead of her son; I introduced him to asparagus, showed him how to crack open a fresh coconut, and made sure he knew how to swim. Sometimes I picked him up from school and a few times I was still there the next morning to take him back, because his mom hadn't bothered coming home that night. He called me Char-Char at first—before he'd properly learned to talk, always pairing the two syllables with a little-boy smile—and then just Charley with time and practice. So how do I know Addy Birch? I raised him. And if I hadn't left when I did, with my whole life spread before me at the age of eighteen, then I don't think I ever would have.

"It's complicated," I say to Juli now, "but I used to watch him when his mom couldn't."

"I feel like I'm probably being pretty generous if I only refer to that woman as trashy," he states, swallowing the last of his cinnamon roll and crossing the kitchen to retrieve his tools. "She's always working a different dead-end job, but always spending her money in the same place."

"Duff's?" I guess, and Juli counters, "Where else?"

Duff's is one thing about Lake Caywood that hasn't changed and probably never will. Although the technical address is listed as Fourth Street, no one uses the front door. It's been painted one too many times and no longer opens with ease. Customers enter the establishment through the back, which requires a short stumble down Baker's Alley and some drunken coordination to navigate a narrow flight of stairs. The whole place smells like an ashtray and the haze of smoke, paired with a few low-wattage bulbs, means that it's never much brighter than a cloudless night with a full moon. Duff's is the kind of venue that serves beer for breakfast. I've been there exactly once and it wasn't because I had a hankerin' for cheap whiskey served in a cloudy tumbler.

Juli yanks me away from this cigarette-scented memory and plants me firmly in the here and now by announcing that today is one of those rare days that will bestow the old farmhouse with his full attention. He's apparently in it for the long haul, with no intention of disappearing for the middle part of the day.

"How'd you swing that?" I call after him as he disappears around the corner. His voice sounds hollow and is laced with echoes when he shouts from the living room, "Made my own schedule. I'd like to finish these doorways so we can start on the floors."

"We?" I confirm.

"Hey, you said you were good with a paintbrush. I'm counting on your expertise."

The comment brings a surprised smile to my face, despite the fact that there's no one around to witness it. I've maybe mentioned *once* that I like to paint; Juli seems to not only listen when I speak, but to also remember what I say, and from what I've experienced, that's a rather rare trait to find in a man. I agree to help him seal the wood when the time comes. Right now I set to work on brewing a fresh pot of coffee before decluttering the oak table in the center of the room. Breakfast is easy enough to clear away, as it involves tossing a bakery box and some crumpled paper towels into the trash, but a short stack of bills to be paid and some other odds and ends also litter the area. Thanks to Gramps's deep pockets (and the fact that he left what was in them to me), monthly payments and renovation costs haven't proven to be much of an issue; I just need to devote a chunk of time to writing checks. It's the other stuff occupying space on the table that I haven't felt much like dealing with: a handful of sympathy cards from long-ago acquaintances that I feel badly about throwing away; several scraps of paper jotted with notes that I don't understand, all scrawled in Juli's handwriting; a box of dog treats that Rhett isn't crazy about; that square, metal box dusted with rust…

Above me, the muted *click* of dog nails against hardwood filters through the ceiling. The sound disappears for a moment when I execute a long whistle—I imagine Rhett lifting his head and cocking it to one side, excited, while Scarlett glances around in alarm—and then those nails are suddenly thundering down the stairs, around the corner, and right into the kitchen. Rhett is running at full speed and just barely manages to slam on the brakes before colliding with my shins; Scarlett is a bit subdued, employing a pace more suitable for indoors. I command them to sit, which they do, and offer each a reward from the box of biscuits on the table. Scarlett is shy at first, reluctant to take the treat from my hand, but then she musters some courage and snatches it away, hungrily crunching it into several pieces that spill from her mouth and fall to the floor. She wastes little time in licking the hardwood clean.

Rhett, on the other hand, accepts the gift with a lack of enthusiasm. He sits before me, the beef-flavored bone held gently between his teeth, waiting to see if this is *really* the reason I so rudely pulled him away from his second-floor adventure. Realizing that it is, he stands and plods over to his food dish, where he slides to his belly and apathetically munches the unexciting snack. Scarlett trots over to his location and nuzzles his snout with hers, kindly offering to help.

"So that's one thing removed from the table," I say to myself, because it will be when the biscuits go home with Juli later today. I scoot them off to the side and slide the metal box toward me, running my fingers over its sharp edges and miniscule keyhole. Kirby stopped by last week to drop it off. It had been the first time we'd spoken since meeting with the lawyer and the first words out of his mouth as he climbed from the car were tinged with sarcasm: "So, did you scatter those ashes yet?"

"Not yet," I'd confided, "but you're welcome to join me when I do."

Kirby had shaken his head and stared over my shoulder instead of looking at me. His frustration was evident. "Ain't right," he'd grumbled. "Ain't right at all. When your grandmother passed away all those years ago, she did so with the understanding that her husband would be buried beside her, and now you're preventing that from happening."

"Because that's not what Gramps wanted," I'd reiterated.

But Kirby, who'd always had a soft spot for Noni, had continued to argue, "They should be together."

"They *are* together. They will *always* be together. It doesn't matter where they're buried."

"Or scattered," he'd muttered.

I'd wanted to say something then—something that I most likely would have come to regret—but I'd managed to hold my tongue and remain silent. Kirby'd harrumphed once and then he'd gruffly extended an arm, shoving the rusted box at me. "Here. Jasper left this for you. I found it in the Model T." There'd been a note with it, written in Gramps's shaky handwriting, that stated simply, *Please give to Charley. The key is in the game room. Corner pocket.*

It didn't make sense, of course; the farmhouse has no game room.

Kirby had only been able to deliver the package, not an explanation, and left shortly after the task was completed. I'd watched him go, standing there in the yard with the box in my hands, until the car's taillights were no longer visible and the evening air too cold to be tolerable without a jacket. That night and the next day and several days after that had been spent thoroughly exploring the house, wandering from room to room in search of something that might suggest cards had once been played there, or darts thrown. At least half a dozen times I'd gone looking, even venturing down to the dirt basement and out to the barn where Gramps kept his brewing equipment, but each time I'd come up empty-handed.

"And 'corner pocket' has *got* to refer to pool," I say now, out loud. My voice causes the resting dogs to glance up from where they've decided to nap. Looking directly at Rhett, I state, "There is no pool table in this house."

The coffeemaker gurgles and hisses and I notice its drip has slowed to almost a complete stop. I retrieve my mug from earlier and unearth another one from the cupboard. Juli takes his black, but I like a splash of cream in mine. A thin stream pours from the carton, hitting the steaming liquid and bleeding outward: white to caramel to rich chocolate brown. I grip a handle with each hand and call out to Juli, requesting his whereabouts. His answer is prompt, but vague—"Back here!"—so I listen for the whir of his mechanical screwdriver and travel in that direction. The noise seems to be coming from the study, but when I step through the jagged doorway, I find the room to be empty.

"Juli?"

"Right over here," he responds, and his voice is nearby. I traipse through the room, stepping around a few scraps of two-by-fours, and poke my head into the bedroom that opens into the office. I look left, and then right, but it too is vacant. "I give up," I announce to the unoccupied space. "Where are you?"

"In here."

As I turn toward the words, I realize they've been spoken from inside the closet. I walk over to the door, which is slightly ajar, and nudge it all the way open with my foot. "What're you doing in—" I begin to say, but quickly learn that what I had thought to be a closet is actually quite the opposite: the room is surprisingly spacious. Like everything else in the house, the wallpaper is outdated and the floor scuffed from years of foot traffic, but the lighting of the area is incredible. Tall, expansive windows occupy two of the four walls, allowing morning sunlight to spill in and affording an impressive overlook to the orchards below. A third wall presents glass pocket doors that open into the living room. But what really throws me for a loop—I actually blink several times to ensure that my brain's not playing some sort of cruel trick on me—is the baby grand piano in the center of the room. It's gleaming so brightly that one would assume it must have recently been polished. My jaw drops; I am completely speechless and utterly confused.

Juli stands on a stepstool in the middle of the room, carefully removing an outdated light fixture from the ceiling. With his arms raised above his head, his t-shirt rides up just a bit to reveal the elastic waist of his boxers. Grey with pink stripes. "Bulb's burnt out," he mumbles around a screw held between his lips. "Figured you'd end up replacing the whole thing anyway."

I say nothing and the clouded, glass dome detaches itself from the ceiling, falling into Juli's hands. He catches it softly and hops to the ground. "So what're your thoughts on this room? I didn't realize you had a piano… Pretty sweet. Are you gonna want to expand this doorway, or leave it intact?" He sets his screwdriver on the stool, places the light fixture in a cardboard box filled with metal scraps and other knickknacks, and walks over to accept a cup of coffee. I release one of the mugs but hold onto my words until Juli looks right at me, arches his dark brows, and asks pointedly, "What's wrong?"

"This room," I answer. "This room is not supposed to be here."

"What do you mean?"

"I mean that it is physically *impossible* for this room to exist in this space. Think about it. That door," I explain, motioning to the one propped open beside me, "is supposed to open into a closet, and the back of that closet is supposed to butt up against the porch, and this room is *not* supposed to be here. Come on; I'll show you." I grab his hand and lead him into the study, which is where my grandparents' heavy mahogany desk still resides. As I drag Juli along behind me, I remember the story that accompanies the piece of furniture, as told to me by my grandfather so many years ago.

A long time ago, soon after Gramps had returned from a stint in World War II, he got it into his head that a road trip might be in order. A person's only young once, he'd decided, and felt that a change of scenery would serve him well. So he'd packed some clothes and some cash and hitched his way west. The experience ended up changing his life. He hiked a portion of the Appalachian trail, stomped his feet to a few catchy beats in Nashville, stood awestruck at the Grand Canyon, and then, once he reached California, happened into a small bar called Babbo's, which was owned by a well-to-do fellow named Mr. Aldo Crocetti. Always interested in the stories of others, Aldo welcomed Gramps with a clap on the shoulder and a pint of home-brewed lager served in a very frosted glass.

It took no time at all for the two to become friends, and before the day was done, the brewmaster was schooling Gramps on everything he knew about beer. They talked a lot and drank even more, and as the stars were just starting to blink awake in the sky, Aldo extended an invitation for dinner—homemade pizza topped with tomato, mozzarella, and fresh basil—prepared by his beautiful daughter.

She had dark, wavy hair that would have reached almost to her waist had she let it hang loose, but instead she kept it secured in a sloppy bun, tucked beneath an indigo bandana. Her smile was sweet but shy, and when she spoke, Gramps compared her voice to the melody of a spring shower, fresh and true. Her name was Isabella, but of course I came to know her as Noni.

It was love at first sight; they married only a couple months later.

Aldo, despite his modest lifestyle, was actually a man of great wealth. Gramps ended up returning to Lake Caywood with three very unexpected things: the love of his life, more money than he ever thought possible, and an antique mahogany desk. "For you to sit and write letters to your babbo," Aldo had instructed his daughter.

The couple had bought the farmhouse and its surrounding orchards upon their return, and the desk found a permanent home in the study. As promised, Noni composed many a letter to her father from that spot, and Gramps, too, utilized the space when he corresponded with friends and managed his finances. It was, and still is, where the farmhouse's blueprints were kept.

The desk is currently hidden beneath an old sheet, protecting the polished wood from dusty elements, but I lift a corner of it and tug on a bottom drawer, exposing the paperwork hidden inside. I find what I'm looking for within a manila envelope, right under the deed to the house. "See?" I implore of Juli, spreading the prints on the floor. "That room doesn't exist. Or rather, it shouldn't exist… I honestly don't think that it *did* exist until today."

"That's impossible," Juli states, because it is. He kneels beside me and squints down at the white lines etched on blue paper, scrutinizing the farmhouse's floor plan. With an index finger, he walks his way from the living room to the office to the bedroom to the *closet.* A second walkthrough results in the same outcome and also earns a baffled sigh. "I don't know," he admits. "None of this makes sense. Are you sure those are the right blueprints?"

"I'm sure. And think about it—"

"It's physically impossible for that room to exist," he cuts in, acknowledging the exact observation that I made only moments ago. "But it *did* exist, right?"

"Unless we're both going crazy…"

"Do you think it's still there?" He shoots me a questioning look and clambers to his feet, accidentally sloshing some of his coffee onto the floor. We rush back to the room that may or may not be a mere figment of our imaginations.

The door stands open, just as we left it, and Juli's tools and stepstool are still there… but they reside in an unlit closet. Gone is the spacious room with its piano and beautiful orchard view. Gone as quickly as it appeared. Juli steps into the tiny space, knocks on the back wall, and then tugs on his lip ring. "What the hell?" he whispers, mostly to himself. "This makes no sense." But then he glances down, catches sight of the cardboard box filled with odds and ends, and cocks his head a bit to one side. There, resting among scraps of metal and shards of wood, is an outdated light fixture, its glass dome clouded from years of use.

7.

Addy

A high school cafeteria could easily and accurately be compared to a jungle. Monkeys may not swing from vines, and vibrant tree frogs don't chirp from high-above branches, but there are certainly students reminiscent of specific animals. Take Brooke Cooley and her group of friends, for example… always plucking and grooming themselves, and painting their faces with pink lipstick and brightly colored eye shadow. They're like parrots, or toucans, or cockatiels wearing too much blush.

Army ants make up the drama club. Most of the time they go unnoticed, but right before the fall play and spring musical they tend to join forces and monopolize the morning announcements, reminding the student body that tickets for *West Side Story* are only five dollars if purchased in advance. Nobody listens because nobody really cares, but the ants are diligent in their efforts.

The football team is primarily comprised of gorillas: big and burly and beefy. They carry themselves in a way that suggests power. Addy used to run with them, but now he prefers to portray himself as more of a chameleon, simply blending in with his surroundings. For the most part he goes unnoticed, but there are a few animals in the jungle with more wits than the others. Gabe Wynne, for instance, who's about as spry and quick as a tree-hopping squirrel monkey. "Gonna eat your pineapple?" he asks now, and swipes the plastic container before Addy even has a chance to respond. In fairness, Gabe doesn't merely assume that the answer will be "no"; he waits, the tongs of his fork angled toward the fruit and his hand holding steady, until Addy shakes his head. Only *then* does he indulge himself.

"So," Gabe wonders, his mouth full of pineapple, "how d'you think you made out on that pop quiz? I'm hoping I passed, but it's gonna be close."

Addy plays with the mound of mashed potatoes on his tray, smoothing them into a pancake and then building them back up again. The flavor is bland and the texture too thick; they'd benefit from some heavy cream, a little extra butter, maybe even a few cloves of roasted garlic, and definitely some salt and pepper. "I think I did alright," he admits. Although Gabe is a year younger, both boys have precalc with Mr. Coleman directly before lunch. Generally speaking, Gabe struggles and Addy earns A's without trying, and while their friendship officially started on the football field about two years ago, it's the after-school tutoring sessions that have brought them closer together.

Gabe takes another bite of pineapple and shakes his head, obviously frustrated. "It amazes me that you understand that crap. I swear Coleman's speaking Latin and writing in hieroglyphics. I mean, for real, when am I ever gonna *need* that stuff?"

Addy lifts his shoulders in a shrug. "It's probably beneficial for engineers."

"I wanna be a journalist," Gabe states, matter-of-fact.

"Then you're probably never gonna need that stuff."

Gabe throws his fork onto the table and his hands into the air. Little copper-colored fireworks explode all around him. "That's what I'm *saying*," he states. "Precalc is pointless. I hate it. Mr. Coleman can take his stupid 'section three-point-two exercise, numbers one through fifteen' assignment and shove it up his ass." This declaration is stated with intense finality and the expression Gabe wears is one of great seriousness, which of course brings the hint of a smile to Addy's face. And that, in turn, earns a slight grin from Gabe. He closes his eyes, takes a deep breath, and calmly returns his fork to his tray. And then he mutters one last time, just to make his opinion clear, "Stupid Mr. Coleman."

"Stupid Mr. Coleman," Addy agrees, because camaraderie seems to be what his friend needs in this moment, and Gabe nods his thanks with a very short, very adamant jerk of his head. The gesture coincides with the sound of the bell, and just like that the jungle creatures are on their feet and moving toward the exits. Gabe has art and Addy has study hall, so the boys drop off their trays and head in opposite directions.

If Addy intended to hang around for sixth period, he would've stayed in the cafeteria, put his head down on the lunch table, and treated himself to a forty-minute nap. He has absolutely no intention of doing that, though, because the study hall administrator never takes attendance and always has his nose buried in that day's newspaper. Completely oblivious to what it is he's meant to be monitoring, Addy has managed to skip class on thirty-seven different occasions without being marked absent even once. Lake Caywood High: Where Attendance Counts for Nada.

The place he usually chooses to spend sixth period is among books and today is no exception. Unfortunately, Mrs. Pennington has become wise to his mode of operating and is waiting in front of the library. "Addison Birch," she greets him, a wry smile curling the corners of her lips. "I thought I might find you here. Has your homeroom teacher neglected to give you every single one of the passes I've written? You know: the ones that excuse you from sixth period in order to visit me, your favorite counselor, in the guidance office?"

Addy hangs his head. It's a rhetorical question; he currently has one of those very passes in his back pocket.

"Come along," Mrs. Pennington says, linking her arm companionably through his and guiding him down the hall. "I'm not nearly as terrifying as you seem to believe me to be…"

Terrifying is, in fact, *not* how Addy perceives his guidance counselor. Small in stature and not much wider than a pencil, she has shoulder-length hair that's worn in a ponytail and purple reading glasses that are frequently perched at the end of her nose. She smiles a lot, laughs even more than she smiles, and has raised her voice at a student approximately never. In addition to this, little flecks of green follow her like glitter, and green is by far the gentlest color. Addy hasn't been avoiding her because he's afraid of her… he just doesn't want to discuss life after high school.

Mrs. Pennington steers him right into her office and instructs him to take a seat, which he does. She must have his schedule or his transcript or something like that already loaded on her laptop because she wastes zero time on small talk and jumps right into the real reason he's currently being held hostage. "Straight A's, with the exception of physics, in which you're holding strong with a B-plus, and no extra-curriculars to speak of since you said so long to football, unless you count detention for occasionally *skipping* physics, which I don't, but even without participation in a sport or a club, your college applications would be good… except for the fact that you haven't submitted any." She rattles it off in one long, run-on sentence, employing a definite touch of sarcasm, and then peers at him over the top of those purple glasses. "So," she says, "how about you tell me what's going on?"

"Not much," Addy answers. He stares at his sneakers, black with white laces, and racks his brain for a more meaningful response. "I've been working a lot," is what he settles on.

"At the diner?"

He nods.

"What are your hours like?" Mrs. Pennington wonders.

"Weekends. And after school a few days a week." What he doesn't contribute is that his shifts last into the wee hours of morning and that he has, on occasion, actually traveled directly from work to school. When he's desperate for sleep, he feigns a migraine and catches a nap in the nurse's office, but mostly study hall is sufficient. It's easier for Addy to close his eyes at school than at home. There are nights when his mother doesn't come home at all, but when she does, she typically has a friend with her. These friends are rarely the same from one night to the next, but they all seem to have two things in common: they are men, and they are looking for a good time. Addy imagines it would take every finger of every student in the building to count how many times he's woken to the sound of drunken laughter, the rough clatter of furniture being bumped, the stale scent of cigarette smoke slipping under his bedroom door… On nights that he doesn't have to go home, he doesn't go home, and because school has become his only respite, the idea of preparing for a life after graduation is too heavy to imagine. So he just doesn't think about it at all.

One might assume that with the hours he works Addy would have a substantial stash of spare change lying around, but that's sadly not the case.

For as many jobs as June Birch has held over the course of the past year, she probably should have been able to cover a full month's rent on her own once or twice. However, if she did that she wouldn't be able to afford her vodka tonics, Lucky Strikes, and biweekly manicures. Addy doesn't really have the option of saying no, either; if he did, he and his mother would be receiving an eviction notice expeditiously.

If Mrs. Pennington knows anything about Addy's life outside of Lake Caywood High, she doesn't make mention of it now. She also doesn't pose the age-old question: What do you want to do with your life? Instead, she closes her laptop, crosses her legs, and stares at Addy until he raises his gaze to meet hers. Then she asks very simply, "What do you like?"

This is met with a blank expression.

"What do you like?" she repeats. "What do you enjoy doing? It obviously wasn't football, because you quit that, and your B-plus in physics implies that maybe matter and energy aren't your main interests… so tell me, Addison: what do you truly *like*?"

"I like cooking," he says, and the answer surprises even him.

"Cooking?" Mrs. Pennington confirms. She seems pleased with his answer.

"Yeah," Addy repeats. "Cooking. I like to cook."

"Well, please feel free to cook for me anytime," his guidance counselor tells him, and then she asks for the story behind the interest; wonders how he came to realize that the kitchen was a fun place to spend time.

So he tells her.

It happened when he was five, on a Saturday morning in the middle of January, on a day that intermittently spit snowflakes that repeatedly coated the ground and then melted. At that point in time, his mother had been employed at a department store located in a neighboring town and was scheduled to start work at nine. Charley showed up around eight-thirty. She had with her a brown-paper grocery bag. "What's in it?" Addy had asked, and then watched as she'd removed each item and lined up everything on the counter: eggs, a thick loaf of bread, vanilla extract, milk, a bag of chocolate chips, some bananas, a brick of cream cheese, confectioner's sugar, and a small carton of whipping cream. All fresh ingredients, and nothing like the boxed mac 'n' cheese and frozen fish sticks that June spent her money on.

"We're making French toast," Charley had informed him, "and we're stuffing it with chocolate and bananas."

She'd allowed him to crack the eggs, and then helped to pick bits of shell from the bowl when the procedure didn't go quite as planned. She'd taught him how to read a recipe, how to use a hand-held mixer, and how to mash bananas with a fork. Charley had sliced the bread and Addy had dredged it through the egg mixture, and while the thick slabs toasted in the oven, they had created whipped cream that didn't come out of a can. Until that day, Addy hadn't realized such a thing even existed, and when the timer went off, they'd eaten breakfast at the kitchen table instead of in front of the television.

All of this is disclosed to the guidance counselor, although Addy does not volunteer Charley's last name or the fact that she is back in town. These details are not important to the story. Mrs. Pennington brings her hands together; fingertips touch but palms do not, forming a sort of steeple. "Have you thought about culinary school?" she queries.

Addy shakes his head.

"It's worth considering. At the end of two years, you'd have your Associate's degree." She watches Addy, who watches his feet, and then says, "At least let me give you some information. I'll be right back." She hops up, her ponytail bouncing, and slips from the office. While she's gone, Addy studies the artwork that decorates the walls. There's a poster for Lake Caywood University, another that promotes an end to bullying, and a third that advertises the importance of individuality. Some pictures of family members—a husband and three dark-haired daughters—and colorful student sketches cling to the side of a metal filing cabinet, held up with magnets. One of the drawings is a cartoon version of a stegosaurus and written in each of his plates is a virtue: ambition, confidence, kindness, love, modesty, respect, responsibility… There are actually more than seven traits listed, but the words narrowly scrawled inside the spikes on the dinosaur's tail are too difficult to read from Addy's angle. He thinks that maybe one of them is "trust," but can't be sure.

Mrs. Pennington returns a moment later with three pamphlets. Two contain information regarding nearby culinary schools and the third provides details about acquiring financial aid. Addy accepts them, and even pays attention while his counselor breezes through the brochures with him, but he knows that nothing will amount from this lesson on higher education. He will earn his high school diploma, graduating toward the top of his class, and continue to work at the diner, serving scrambled eggs to drunks at three o'clock in the morning. Part of each paycheck will go to his mother, who in turn will pay each month's rent with perfectly manicured nails. This has always been the cycle; Addy doubts it will ever change. He does thank Mrs. Pennington for her advice, despite the fact that he won't be listening to it, and trudges back upstairs for seventh period.

English with Mr. Kent is Addy's favorite class and the only reason he doesn't duck out of school before lunch. It's a place where literature comes to life and characters stumble through lives more dismal than his own. Heathcliff, Oliver Twist, Frankenstein… but Mr. Kent has saved the best—or rather, worst—for last: Macbeth. The poor guy was taunted by witches, manipulated by his wife, and eventually beheaded. The majority of the class isn't yet aware of the King of Scotland's demise, though. Mr. Kent has them reading aloud, speaking with accents for extra credit, and the process, while amusing, is slow. They're only just now delving into the first scene of act four.

"Double, double toil and trouble; Fire burn and cauldron bubble," Eleanor Ames recites. She makes her voice quiet and crackly; her impersonation of a Scotswoman, however, could use some work. Addy smiles a little but keeps his head down, eager to maintain his sans role status. Having already read ahead to the play's conclusion, he's presently exploring a new storyline—one that may or may not have been inspired by Shakespeare's work. *Something Wicked This Way Comes* is tucked inside his giant textbook, hidden from view, and while Mr. Kent probably suspects that Addy Birch isn't following along, line by line, he's also not going to make an issue of it. He knows when he stops the class in a moment to revisit the apparitions, determining their shapes and significances, Addy will be the one to rattle them off without even glancing back at the text: "an armored head, a bloody baby, a kid wearing a crown and holding a tree." He's one of those rare students who's able to split his attention and focus it fully on two completely different topics.

Mr. Kent is in awe of the ability. He understands that modern technology has had an effect on the human brain, and that the teenagers who pass through his classroom each day are better at multitasking than he'll ever be, but to have a gift like Addison Birch… The kid doesn't miss a beat.

"'Great Birnam wood to high Dunsinane hill,'" Mr. Kent quotes now, directing his students' attention to words spoken by the third apparition. "What's meant by that? Confer with the text. Posthaste!" He claps his hands, trying his best to instill a sense of urgency.

Eleanor Ames studies the passage, rereads the line, struggles to decipher its importance. She is one of few, though; most students cast their eyes downward, *pretending* to analyze the language of Shakespeare, while several others fix their teacher with bored, blank stares. But Addy—his nose in a book that's not even part of the twelfth-grade curriculum—slowly raises his hand.

Mr. Kent stifles a grin. "Addy?"

"Unless Birnam wood moves to Dunsinane hill, then Macbeth is safe." He pulls his gaze away from Bradbury and looks up. "It'd be like moving Lake Caywood to Gettysburg."

"So it's impossible," Eleanor deduces, but Mr. Kent shakes his head ever so slightly. Flickers of blue spring from his skin, taking flight, and then vanish almost as quickly as they appeared. "Don't be so sure," he warns. "Nothing is impossible."

As much as Addy respects his English teacher, he has to disagree with his statement.

Some things are definitely impossible.

8.
Juli

Because my ma is someone who worries that I don't eat enough vegetables, she makes it a point to always serve salad when I swing by her house for lunch. It's not my favorite meal, but it's also not the worst, and she typically makes it bearable by pairing the garden fare with something more substantial: grilled cheese, potato soup, poached salmon… whatever she happens to have on hand. Today it's a chicken salad sandwich on multigrain bread, complete with lettuce, tomato, and provolone. "This is good," I mumble through a mouthful of food. Scarlett, my little Irish setter, sits beside me and rests her head on my lap, imploring me with those hazel eyes of hers.

"Come over here, Scarlett," Ma says, and claps her hand against her thigh. She'd been working her way through a basket of warm laundry at the kitchen counter, uncrumpling inside-out shirts and folding them into smooth packages, but this task is temporarily abandoned upon witnessing Scarlett's intense desire for a bread crust. "Do you need a snack, sweet girl?" she asks, and walks to the pantry. Scarlett straightens her posture and redirects her gaze; she knows that the pantry houses delectable cheese- and poultry-flavored treats. I expect Ma to satisfy her with a simple biscuit, but what she produces is actually a decent-sized rawhide. "Look what I have for you," she coos, and Scarlett quickly abandons her stance beside me in order to perch expectantly before my mother. Ma extends the bone, Scarlett clamps down on it, and then she is quickly prancing into the living room, eager to gnaw away at the rawhide in private. I raise my eyebrows at Ma and she shrugs, asking, "Is it really so wrong for me to spoil my granddogger every now and then?"

I roll my eyes and shake my head, slightly amused.

Ma returns to the laundry. She's quiet for a while, content to watch me eat my sandwich and pick at my salad, but eventually she wonders about the goings-on in my life. Specifically, the old farmhouse. "How's it coming along?"

Truthfully, the farmhouse has proven to be a lot of work… but I've enjoyed most of it. The renovation itself has been fun (I like the challenge of merging a bar and a house) but there's a part of me that also acknowledges the fondness I've developed for Charley. She's quirky—definitely quirkier than anyone else I've ever known—and her thoughts are so very different than mine. It could just be that spring is in the air, but there's for sure something about her that appeals to me.

Spring, as much as I love it, is probably my busiest time of year. When the flowers start to bloom, my phone starts to ring. People want their houses pressure washed, their decks stained, their conceptualized patios made tangible. I did the best I could to split my time between work and the farmhouse, but it admittedly did take all of April to finish the doorways and sand and seal the floors. Charley helped as much as she could, and is currently in the process of painting each room, but the fact remains that it's already the middle of May and neither the kitchen nor the home's exterior have been touched. The first-floor bathroom is a work in progress. In addition to a toilet and a pedestal sink, the space also houses an old claw-foot tub. "We could tear this out and build some cabinetry," I'd suggested last week. "It'd give you a place to store cleaning supplies and extra toilet paper." But Charley had shaken her head and said, "Nah. That stuff can go in the towel closet. I'd like to use the tub as a garden." She intends to fill it with potting soil and houseplants. I share this with my mother and she laughs. "Charley Lane sounds like a real character."

"Oh, she is," I assure her. "She's one of a kind."

Ma fixes me with one of those eyebrows-in-the-air looks. The kind that asks without asking, "Do you like her?" And since she doesn't officially ask it, I opt not to answer it. I wouldn't know *how* to answer it. Do I like

Charley? Absolutely. I like that her emerald eyes glisten when she talks about Rhett, and that there's a crease that appears to the right of her mouth when she smiles, and that she always seems to have holes in the heels of her socks. But I confide none of this to my mother, just as I've confided none of it to Eileen… despite the fact that the Honey-Do owner has conspiratorially asked on numerous occasions, "So? How're things with Charley?"

"Charley's good," I answer every time. "Things at the farmhouse are good."

Eileen never pushes the issue, but my mother is not Eileen. When her unspoken question fails to receive a response, she takes it upon herself to offer a few words of wisdom: "Sometimes it's difficult for a girl to determine what a boy is feeling."

I fill my mouth with a forkful of lettuce and wait for her to continue. She doesn't. "Sometimes it's difficult for a son to determine what a mother is implying," I eventually counter.

The expression she wears is one of bemusement as she tosses a pair of rolled socks at my head. I duck just in time. "What I mean," she clarifies, "is that Charley may not know how you feel about her because she is essentially *paying* you for the time that you spend together. Maybe you need to initiate an opportunity to spend time together *outside* of the farmhouse."

"Like a date."

It's not a question, but Ma answers anyway. "Like a date."

"Charley and I *have* gone to the hardware store together," I point out, "to purchase new doorknobs." The comment results in another overhand pitch and a pair of my father's argyle socks hits me squarely in the left ear. "Hey!"

"Shopping for doorknobs is not a date. Take her out for dinner."

I have to laugh. I know as well as anyone that a trip to the Honey-Do is very different than a trip to the Tavern, but dates have never been my strong suit. I'm not great at talking while sitting still. I'd rather have a conversation during the installation of a ceiling fan or the grouting of a backsplash; there's a lot less eye contact involved. Nonetheless, I promise to take my mother's suggestion under advisement and load up the dishwasher with my lunchtime accoutrements. "Come on, Scarlett!" I call from the side door, jangling my keys to let her know that I'm serious. She's beside me a moment later, firmly clenching a half-chewed rawhide in her jaw, her tail wagging pleasantly. I open the door and she hurries ahead to the truck. Ma gives me a tight squeeze and adjusts the brim of my baseball cap. "Love you, Juli."

"Love you too." I give her a halfway grin and pull the door shut behind me.

Time to get back to work.

The first thing I notice is that Myra doesn't greet me at the door. "Where is she?" I ask, directing the question to Hank. He's stocking shelves in the plumbing aisle.

"Myra got herself an invite to join the Finleys," I'm informed. The family's son, Sam, stopped in last week to purchase materials for a school project and Myra apparently fell head over heels for him. Hank claims she even followed him out the front door and onto the sidewalk. Fortunately, Sam felt the same palpitations in his heart that the Basset was feeling in hers. He dragged his parents into the shop to meet her yesterday and she was adopted right then and there, happily ever after. "So it's just me," Hank concludes. "Eileen's at the shelter as we speak."

It's excellent news. The Finleys have hired me for more than a few odd jobs and I really like the entire family, so I don't doubt that Myra has found herself the perfect forever home, but I will certainly miss seeing her at Honey-Do. I'd gotten used to having her around.

Hank leaves his cardboard box of flanges, drains, and strainers on the floor, wipes his hands on his pants, and comes over to meet me. "What's the game plan for today?" he wonders, and I know that he has accurately assumed my afternoon will be spent with Charley.

"Removing wallpaper," I groan, anticipating that the task will be a tedious one.

Hank sympathizes by volunteering a groan of his own. "Got a scoring tool?" he asks. When I nod, he leads the way to an assortment of liquids and gels stored in large, plastic jugs. He grabs a blue container by its handle and pulls it from the shelf, passing it to me. Then he follows that up with a pack of synthetic paint roller covers and says, "That right there's your best bet. Spray it on real good and heavy. Let the paper get a good soak before trying to peel it off."

I end up buying a couple of new paintbrushes, too. Charley accidentally ruined my favorite two-inch brush the other day when she forgot to clean it. I sometimes think that her brain takes random vacations. I mean, how does a person spend almost eight hours painting and then forget to clean her tools? That's Charley, though. We ended up losing the tail end of a gallon of paint, too, since she left the container wide open overnight… It wasn't a big deal by any means, but she felt horrible about it and must've apologized at least a hundred times.

Once the items are paid for, I lug them to the truck and load them into the back. Scarlett waits excitedly in the front, whimpering with anticipation when I finally climb behind the wheel. It's a bit of a challenge, since she likes to occupy that seat when I'm not in it, but I eventually coax her into riding shotgun instead of driving.

We make it to the farmhouse right around two o'clock. Rhett must sense our arrival because his deep bark is audible as soon as we pull up; it escapes the open windows and invades the front yard, causing Scarlett to chime in with her own high-pitched whine. I suddenly find myself surrounded by a rather ear-splitting serenade. "Make it stop!" I shout to Charley when she appears behind the screen door that I installed two weeks ago. "Hurry!"

The wish is granted immediately and Rhett darts outside. He dashes initially to me, feeling obliged to sniff my pants and snort at my shoes, but his attention is quickly diverted to the truck's interior. He tilts his head to one side, swinging his tail back and forth like a pendulum. Scarlett stares down at him from her driver's-side perch, eyes bright and playful. It is only when Rhett offers a youthful yip that she decides to leap. Her red body sails over him, landing lithely on the soft ground, and they are bounding across the yard in no time, racing toward the berry patch. Charley steps onto the porch and claps her hands, warning the dogs to remain within view, and I can't help but look at her for a few extra seconds. She's wearing paint-splattered jeans and a grey t-shirt and her short hair is doing its own thing by sort of standing up in the back. Like Dennis the Menace.

Either my extra-long gaze makes her self-conscious or she reads my mind because she reaches up to smooth the flyaway wisps before walking over to join me beside my truck. "What'd you bring this time?" she asks. My back is to her, but I can feel her behind me, peering over my shoulder to see what I've brought. I pass her the bag of brushes and rollers so that she can peek inside. "Painting?" she confirms.

"Not painting," I correct, and reveal the jug of wallpaper remover. "Not yet, anyway."

Charley narrows her eyes and nibbles at her bottom lip. "I think I'd rather paint."

"I *know* I'd rather paint." There are actually quite a few things I'd rather do than pry brittle segments of yellowed paper from the walls in the bathroom, but this is the next task to be crossed off the list. I follow Charley into the house, through the kitchen, and straight down the hall to the torn-apart room. The tub, sink, and toilet were relocated during the sanding process. The latter two items, both stained from years of use, were put out with the trash, but the claw-foot tub is currently residing in the study across the hall. I found Rhett sprawled inside of it the other day, gnawing away at a loafer that must have at one point belonged to Jasper Lane. Charley had been upstairs at the time, sorting through closets in an effort to determine which items should be saved, which should be donated, and which should simply be thrown away with the trash. The loafer had originally been going to the rescue mission, but Rhett altered its destiny and the shoe was retired instead. Contrary to what might be expected, though, its partner was not. "What if a man with only one foot happens to be shoe shopping?" Charley had rationalized. "This loafer might be perfect for him."

"Well, if your hypothetical shopper only has his left foot and happens to also wear a size ten," I'd reluctantly agreed, "then I suppose that loafer might indeed be perfect. But I'd just toss it."

"I'm not doing that." She'd been adamant about the decision. I watched her add the lone loafer to a box of rescue mission-bound donations, rolling my eyes at the gesture… but smiling nevertheless.

Without fixtures, the bathroom is really just a closet-sized space that boasts a gleaming wooden floor, hideously papered walls, and pipes that poke through in random spots. It does have a window, so the lighting is fairly good, but there's a lot to be done in such a small area. Charley stands beside me, observing our surroundings, and while she's probably thinking about what color she'll eventually choose for the walls, I'm contemplating whether or not a day at Lake Caywood's berry festival could constitute as a date. Before I have an opportunity to ask Charley if it's even something she'd be interested in checking out, she opens her mouth and says, "I'll be more than happy to paint this room when the time comes, but I think I'll pass on the wallpaper removal. Have fun. I'm going in search of the dogs."

I swallow my courage and watch her go. A moment later, her voice carries through the open window, sing-songing Rhett and Scarlett's names, and the metallic jangle of dog licenses bouncing against rabies tags sounds in response. I hear the screen door squeak open, slam shut, and dog nails click-clacking against hard wood. Both pups make it a point to stop by for a visit, but Charley must find something else to occupy her time because she doesn't come back. I spend the next hour scoring ugly wallpaper, rolling gel-like remover over it, prying it up at the edges, and singing a crazy number of Sublime songs. I'm in the midst of belting out "What I Got" when the doorbell rings. Rhett barks, of course, just in case his owner has somehow missed the surprisingly loud *ding-dong* that resonates through the house, but Charley has heard it and is hustling to the door. I hear her bare feet slapping against the wood floor, but this time there is no squeak of the door swinging open. If I really strain my ears, I can detect the muffled sound of voices—one male and one female—but whoever has come for a visit must still be standing on the porch, speaking to Charley through the screen. I decide that it's probably someone from the electric company, here to read an outdoor meter; or a farmhand, seeking an orchard-related answer of some sort; or it could even be one of those random churchgoers who likes to stop by and encourage complete strangers to join their congregation for Sunday morning prayer. I always pretend I'm not home when those visitors come to the door, but maybe Charley is a better person than I am. I go back to singing and tearing strips of paper from the wall, certain the person on the porch is no one of interest, but then the door *does* squeak open.

"She is not going to read the Bible with a complete stranger," I mutter to myself in disbelief.

There's no talking at first, just the shuffle of uncertain footsteps. They travel across the kitchen and stop, I imagine, right in front of the oak table because Charley suddenly says, "Just set 'em there. What's on top?"

The response is muffled, but I definitely catch the name "Rosemary."

"Mmm... That sounds delicious!"

Unless Charley Lane is a cannibal, the aforementioned rosemary must be an herb rather than a person's name, because whoever is with her in the kitchen has brought something edible. The masculine voice speaks again, so quiet that it's almost impossible to make out, and whatever is being shared must be a real mouthful because Charley is quiet for a long time. When she finally does speak again, she is obviously moved. "Of course!" I hear her exclaim. "I'm so flattered that you asked! I just can't believe—"

The man apparently cuts in with another comment, one too soft even to detect, and I suddenly find myself hoping it isn't sweet nothings into her ear that he's whispering. Am I jealous? Maybe a little... I narrow my eyes and focus really hard, straining to pick up the rest of the conversation.

Whatever mysterious remark the guy *did* quietly make, Charley counters it by stating, "I wouldn't miss it for the world." Her tone is about as serious as I've ever heard it.

I listen for further discussion, but there is none. Feet travel back across the kitchen, the door opens and closes, and then Charley is hurrying down the hall. "Hey," she says, poking her head around the doorjamb. "Are you hungry? Addy Birch just stopped by with fancy English muffin pizzas. We used to make 'em all the time when he was a kid. Want one?"

"What's on top that makes them fancy?"

"Tomatoes, rosemary, mozzarella, lemon zest, parsley, pepper, salt," she rattles off.

I shrug. "Sure. I'll try one."

I climb to my feet, remove a few bits of wallpaper from my jeans, and prepare to follow her to the kitchen. Charley doesn't budge right away, though. Instead she scratches her right earlobe, chews her bottom lip, and sticks her hands in her pockets. With her gaze directed slightly downward, she volunteers, "The real reason he came over was to invite me to his graduation." She pauses, and I wonder if I should say something, but the way her lips remain slightly apart makes me think that she's not quite done with what she's trying to say. So I wait. "He has four tickets," she continues. "His mom will go, you know, and I'm sure she'll take whichever guy she's planning to sleep with that night… but he gave the other two tickets to me." She looks up, fixing me with those green eyes. There's a hint of vulnerability in her voice when she asks, "Do you think you'd want to go with me?"

"Absolutely." I don't need to think about it; I provide the answer immediately.

"Yeah?"

"Yeah," I assure her. "When is it?"

"June fifth."

"Yep, that'll work. The only thing I have going on that day is renovating an old farmhouse, but I think I can probably skip out a bit early and be cleaned up by six or so. Does that sound about right?"

Charley grins. "That sounds exactly right. It's a date."

She turns away at that point and I'm sort of glad that she does. "Just give me a minute to clean up here," I call after her because my cheeks are unusually warm and my temperature unusually high. I wish the sink were working so I could splash some cold water on my face. I am not someone who blushes easily, but Charley Lane has managed to make me do just that.

9.
Charley

I replaced my Michigan phone number with a set of Pennsylvania digits approximately two weeks after the decision was made to stay in the farmhouse. Because of this, there are very few people who know how to contact me: Juli, his electrician, Kirby, the doctor's office, the vet's office, the owners of Honey-Do Hardware… and other people of that nature. I am, for the most part, off the grid.

Or, I was… until just a moment ago.

It's become customary for Rhett and me to take a jaunt to the mailbox each morning. Sometimes I raise the red, metal flag and deposit a payment for pickup; other times I simply collect a pile of bills or a bank statement or a catalog. Today I do both of these things, swapping a check made out to the electric company for a grocery sales flier, a glossy handout advertising L.L.Bean's latest merchandise, and a short stack of envelopes. I flip through them, the spring morning seeming like any other until I take notice of that familiar handwriting. The R is what gives it away, since it's always capitalized, even when appearing in the middle of a word. Like my name.

The sight of that R takes my breath away and I temporarily lose track of time. Behind me, Rhett gives the mailbox a final sniff—I hear him snort into the weeds at the post's base—and lifts his leg to reaffirm that this territory is, in fact, his. Satisfied that the other neighborhood dogs will understand and respect this, he prances after me, the gravel of the drive crunching beneath his feet. He falls into stride beside me, keeping my pace for half a minute until a squirrel diverts his attention. Rhett shoots across the yard like a bullet, chases the bushy-tailed creature up a tree, and then stands with his tail erect, eyes wide, watching for movement in the branches above. I am equally aware of all of this and none of this, because even though I whistle for my pup to return to me, my thoughts are not entirely focused in the present. A good portion of what's in my head is actually lingering in the past.

It takes just about all of my willpower *not* to tear the envelope open before I've reached the house. But I manage. I wait until I'm in the kitchen, standing by the tall oak table, before slipping an index finger beneath that sealed flap. As I rip through the paper, I can't help but think that *he* secured whatever is hidden inside. *He* was the one to moisten the adhesive and press it shut. *He* took the steps to track me down. And as my fingers fumble with the folded sheet of stationery, those words that he always used to say pop into my head: Showing up is half the battle.

"Please don't let him show up," I say out loud, because it suddenly occurs to me that this is now a possibility. He has my address. Therefore, he knows where to find me.

What he's sent is a letter and a picture of us standing in the rain, a red umbrella doing its best to protect us from the elements. My hair was long then, spilling over my shoulders and framing my face; his was short, but not so short that those golden bangs didn't fan across his forehead, barely brushing the tips of his long lashes… Oh, how I'd loved and envied those lashes. Not even with mascara could mine compete with his.

The snapshot was taken before the truth was spoken, so we both wear genuine smiles that expose our teeth and reach our eyes and indicate to all the world that we are happy. And we were, at that point in time. We *were* happy.

The letter is brief. For as much as he loved to talk, he was never much for writing, so what I find scrawled in his capital-R handwriting are eight measly sentences:

> *Remember when this pictuRe was taken? Two days into histoRy's soggiest thRee-day festival, Right befoRe youR favorRte band stoRmed the stage. You weRe so excited. Anyway, I found it tucked inside that copy of The ThoRn BiRds that you loaned me thRee yeaRs ago. I'm Reading it now (finally fulfilling that*

pRomise to you!) but I'll find my own bookmaRk; I thought you might like this one back.

I hope you'Re well, ChaRley. Please take caRe of youRself. And happy biRthday.

I read it three times, analyzing each word and searching between the lines for even a hint of animosity. But there is none. Concern is evident, as are hurt and confusion, but he has apparently accepted the decision that's been made rather than hold it against me. Maybe he's come to terms with the fact that acceptance will result in less pain. Or maybe he's doing what he's always done, which is put me before himself. I blink away the tears that have pooled in my eyes, not wanting to think about Michigan or rainy concerts or the way his skin seemed always to smell of soap and sunshine. Instead, I return the letter to its envelope and carry it into the study where it can be hidden among deeds and blueprints and other fine-print paperwork. But the photograph isn't buried in that bottom drawer. I keep that with me, caressing its smooth edges as I meander from room to room, finally allowing myself to *really* imagine what the farmhouse will look like once the renovation has been completed.

With the exception of the kitchen, the first floor looks quite a bit different than it did five months ago. Wider doorways make the rooms appear more welcoming, the newly polished floors are slick enough to slide across in socked feet, and all of the walls boast a fresh coat of paint. I've stuck with a rather natural pallet, incorporating various shades of red and brown and gold, because while these colors are reminiscent of Golden Delicious, Braeburn, and Bosc, they are also the chroma of milky stouts, amber ales, and honey-hued lagers.

It's been a long time since I've played a part in beer production, but a good chunk of my time has lately been spent in the barn with the brew kettles. There are currently a few things in the works: a coffee-chocolate stout, a grapefruit-infused IPA, and a noble attempt at a red lager, although, after visiting the walk-in refrigerator and observing the sealed kegs and hundreds of brown bottles that are housed there, it's hard to imagine we'll run out of beer anytime soon. Nevertheless, the one thing the Brewhaha must never run out of is the beverage it's named after, so I've been diligently brewing away.

As much as I know about beer, there's twice as much that I *don't* know, so I took a suggestion from my handyman and recruited the assistance of a local bartender who has proven to be highly educated on matters pertaining to alcohol and absolutely everything else. Petey Goode is probably the most intelligent person I've ever met. He graduated one year ahead of Juli, finished out four years at Yale, and currently holds about five different jobs… none of which requires a college diploma. Petey seems happy enough with his multifaceted employment, though, and I've gotten the impression that he really enjoys the science that goes along with brewing. He has a definite knack for combining flavors—the grapefruit infusion was his idea—and has formed a working relationship with Oscar, Felipe's nephew, who has essentially grown up on this land and is now in charge of the other migrant workers who come and go with the seasons. An incredibly hard worker, Oscar can be seen patrolling the fields each morning at the crack of dawn, pruning limbs and eliminating pests. He does enjoy a cold beer now and again, which is evident on days when the recycling gets carried to the end of the driveway. Saturday seems to be his preferred night of indulgence; I actually witnessed him and Petey sharing a six-pack last weekend.

Considering all that's been occurring inside the farmhouse, I'm more than content to relinquish control of the beer; as long as I get to periodically contribute my two cents and always sample the final products, I'm a happy camper. There's just so much stuff to consider in addition to hop combinations… like furniture, for example.

Furniture is at the top of today's to-do list; artwork holds the slot right beneath it.

Juli has said that he'd like to start working on the kitchen and has arranged for a crew of helpers to show up around nine o'clock. I could certainly stick around, assisting with the removal of the Formica countertops that Noni used to swipe with her damp dishrag, eliminating dried drops of gravy and thin films of flour that accumulated during the preparation of Sunday dinner, but although I understand that granite is better than laminate, it's hard to say goodbye to these things I've always taken for granted. Much of my childhood was spent in the kitchen. It was there that I learned the secret ingredient of piecrusts (vodka, chilled in the freezer), the best way to slice a peach (not along that little ridge where the cheeks come together, surprisingly), and how to chop onions without crying (just whistle). To watch the kitchen I've known for such a long time disappear piece by piece is simply too difficult a thing to endure, so I've opted to drive into West Orensdale instead. I have a list of items that need to be purchased and my goal is to find at least one piece of furniture for each room by the end of today.

Like most men, Rhett isn't a huge fan of shopping, so I plant a kiss on his wiry head, offer him a rubber bone that's been stuffed with peanut butter, and quickly slip out the door in an effort to escape before he has time to realize that he's been left. Juli will be here soon enough, anyway; I trust him to care for Rhett while I'm gone.

West Orensdale is about a thirty-minute drive from Lake Caywood, but it takes longer than half an hour for me to get there. I swing by the pharmacy to fill a prescription and end up occupying the next fifteen minutes or so by browsing the bath aisle. Loofahs in all different colors, shower gels in all different scents, bars of glycerin hand soap that glisten like birthstones. I splurge on some lotion that smells of lavender before returning to my Jeep, and then to the road.

The route is a fairly scenic one, winding through intermittent farmland and towns that are tiny enough to function without traffic lights. I keep the windows down, allowing the cool morning air to gush in and tousle my hair. It's been an unusually mild spring, and although it's been a decade since last spending an April or May in Pennsylvania, everything seems to be blooming a full week later than what I'd anticipated. One of my most vivid childhood memories is that of my tenth birthday, when Noni taught me the proper way to make strawberry shortcake. I'd been to a friend's house the week before and had received an invitation to stay for dinner. Grilled flank steak, baked potatoes, and a giant salad were served, and all of it had been delicious, but the dessert was exceptional: vanilla pound cake layered with strawberries and whipped cream, served with a scoop of ice cream on the side. "Marissa's mom called it strawberry shortcake," I remember saying to Noni, who had scoffed and responded almost snootily with her slight accent, "A pound cake is not a shortcake. I will teach you. First, the Italian way. Then, the Pennsylvania Dutch."

And so it happened that on my happy-birthday eve I experienced puff pastries filled with juicy strawberries, dusted with confectioner's sugar, and topped with a dollop of freshly whipped cream. Not surprisingly, it was far better than what Marissa's mother had served. Gramps and Noni had lit colorful candles and filled the house with song, and then I had wished for a new bicycle before extinguishing all ten little flames. I went to bed with my belly bulging and woke up the next morning to yet another birthday lesson: how to make strawberry shortcake that's suitable for breakfast. "See?" Noni had asked as she'd used her fingers to cut the butter into the dry ingredients. "Very crumbly. We add milk now."

The consistency had ended up being like that of cookie dough, and she'd smoothed the entire hunk of it into the bottom of a deep-dish pie pan. While it baked, we washed and sliced and sprinkled sugar over two quarts of strawberries that had been plucked from the garden earlier that morning. And then, when the timer finally sounded, Noni crumbled a thick slab of shortcake into a bowl, ladled berries on top, and drowned the whole thing with milk. "Eat," she'd told me, and I had. Once my bowl was empty, Noni eyed me with suspicion and wondered, "Which you like better?"

A part of me had thought to lie and say that I'd preferred the Italian version—because it had indeed been scrumptious—but at age ten I was exceedingly honest. "With milk," I'd admitted, and the confession brought a huge and very unexpected grin to Noni's face. "Ah… I thought so!" she'd exclaimed. "I like it that-a way too!"

It was eighteen years ago to the day that I ate strawberry shortcake for breakfast and completed a scavenger hunt that led me to the plum tree in the peach orchard, against which was propped a new bike. It was yellow with a horn and a basket; rainbow tassels hung from the handles. I loved it more than I have ever loved any bicycle before or since, and I've no idea what ever became of it. My grandparents used to have a picture of me riding that bike, its little wicker bin brimming with sun-kissed peaches and a bouquet of flowers, as I pedaled home from a lazy day spent in the orchard. For the longest time that photograph had been in a frame that occupied space on their mahogany desk. I haven't seen it since my return from Michigan, though. Perhaps Gramps tired of the image and relocated it to a box in the basement or something… If I could find it, I'd consider hanging it in one of the downstairs rooms, but I'm just not quite certain of the artistic approach that I'd like to take regarding pieces for the Brewhaha. Nostalgia seems a logical route, but the farmhouse is surprisingly lacking in selections; for as many bureaus that I've emptied and closets that I've cleaned, old photographs have yet to make an appearance. My hope lies in today being a day of discoveries.

I steer the Jeep into the parking lot of Brass and Brickman's Junque and Antiques and shut off the engine. West Orensdale is larger than Lake Caywood, though not excessively so, and because of this it offers a wider range of shops. My intent is to purchase seating and rugs for the downstairs rooms, and I figure that the consideration of time-period pieces might be a good place to start.

I half expect the store to smell old, like cobwebs and woodchips, but what it actually smells like is lemon-scented furniture polish. I pause just inside the door, considering my surroundings. There's a round table, stained a deep red, situated directly beneath the most amazing chandelier I've ever seen. It's makeshift in nature, consisting of a medley of what looks to be recycled streetlamps. Long cords, none of which are the same length, stagger the lights so that they form a rather chaotic cluster in midair. Their luminosity bounces off other odds and ends that have claimed spots on the ceiling: copper pots and pans, a rain shower of tarnished stopwatches, giant ladles that shine like newly minted pennies. I cannot recall ever before stepping into a place quite as eclectic as this.

The owners of the fancy junk shop must have an affinity for rocking chairs because there are several of them situated about the cluttered space. Some are solid, others slatted, and a few have bentwood frames with caned seats and backs. They stand alone in corners and companionably beside ornate sofa tables; they congregate around heavy wooden chests that serve as tables laden with ceramic pitchers and thickly walled glasses. The displays make me flashback to summer evenings spent on the farmhouse's porch, when Gramps and Noni and sometimes Uncle Kirby and I would each claim a chair and rock until the stars blinked awake in the sky. This was long before Gramps succumbed to the modern convenience of air conditioning, back when humidity still claimed permanent residency in the kitchen and the day's heat snuggled into bed on the second floor, making sleep difficult at best. We'd gather outside, sticky and content after having indulged in one too many helpings of Noni's crispy fried green tomatoes or crunch-battered drumsticks or dense cornbread that contained the perfect hint of sweetness. The adults would sip pale ale from sweating glasses and I would drink pulpy lemonade and the night sounds would include laughter and crickets and the melodic clink of ice cubes bouncing against one another. It's a memory with a message: I will need to buy rocking chairs, for both inside and out, and I make a note of this on the spiral-bound pad that I carry in my purse.

When I woke this morning and decided to purchase some furniture for the Brewhaha, West Orensdale was obviously on my radar. One-stop shopping, however, was not. I'd certainly noticed Brass and Brickman's before—had driven past it when I'd needed to visit the neighboring town for things like orthodontist appointments and elementary school birthday parties held at the only roller-skating rink around—but I'd never thought to stop and explore the treasure trove inside. Now, looking around, I realize that it offers just about everything on my list, and while many of the items are indeed from years past, there is definitely furniture that only *looks* as though its been around for decades. In actuality, quite a few of the pieces are brand new. There are wing chairs and cozy reading chairs and simple dining chairs made of various types of wood. Some are carved from rich mahogany and others are lighter, made of maple and oak. I find myself drawn to patterns of red and gold. I walk among the furniture, running my fingers over the different fabrics and testing their cushions for comfort. I have just plopped down on a very long and deeply buttoned leather sofa when a stooped salesman approaches. He has thin white hair and spectacles that seem to magnify his watery blue eyes. I like him immediately for the simple reason that he wears suspenders, which is something Gramps used to do. "What do you think of it?" he asks, his voice crackling a bit as he does. He perches across from me, choosing to occupy a high-backed chair upholstered in cream-colored velvet. As he sits down, his nametag glints: Joseph.

"I really like this one," I confide. "I've actually found quite a few things that I really like. I'm in the process of refurbishing an old farmhouse and it has a lot of rooms." I don't tell him that it might have more rooms than it should; I don't tell him that I think I once walked through the backside of a closet and found myself in a beautifully lit space that contained a baby grand piano and offered an impressive orchard view. I don't tell him that there's a part of me that worries I'm losing my mind, and that even though Juli *insists* he saw the room too, I still can't be certain that the reality I experience on an everyday basis hasn't somehow been altered. I just tell him that I'm going to need to buy a lot of furniture.

Joseph is happy to help and so together we walk through the store, tagging items of interest. I opt for two leather couches—one with a dimpled back, the other much wider and plusher—and splurge on both a chaise lounge *and* a loveseat for the master bedroom. An assortment of wing chairs, each with its own distinct style, is selected for the study. I also choose a hodgepodge of dining chairs to be scattered about the living room and a mishmash of end tables to be used throughout the house. "People will need a place to rest their drinks," I rationalize, and decide to add an overly large chest to my list of purchases as well, determining that it will make a creative coffee table.

My bill is exorbitantly high, as I knew it would be, but I can't help but feel a sense of satisfaction as I return to my Jeep empty-handed and thousands of dollars poorer. The goods will be delivered to five-nineteen Copper Drive later this week; before that happens, I aim to procure a few rugs. Having already made Joseph's day with my five-figure payment, I head over to George Floor Man to scope out the selection.

Unlike Brass and Brickman's, I've actually been inside this establishment once before, soon after I received my driver's permit. Uncle Kirby had volunteered to take me out for some practice, but there'd been a stipulation: I'd been responsible for helping him find the perfect birthday gift for Noni. "How about jewelry?" I remember suggesting. That's what Gramps would give her each year, and the excitement that accompanied the annual box of black velvet seemed always to be so genuine. But Kirby had shaken his head and said that a rug was what he wished to give her.

I'd raised my eyebrows and given him a quick sideways look. "A rug?"

"To go in front of the kitchen sink," he'd elaborated, "with a good, thick pad underneath so her feet don't ache so much. That's what I want to give her. Your grandmother spends a lot of time at that sink, you know, and there ain't no reason in the world for a person to hurt doing what she loves doing the most."

The words had been both surprising and touching. It was common knowledge that my uncle had a soft spot for Noni—he'd often stop and have a cup of coffee with her in the morning, and he was incredibly reliable when it came to fixing those things that Gramps tended to neglect... like when the icemaker would jam and make a terrible grinding noise instead of simply dropping cubes into a waiting glass. But until he made mention of the unfairness of sore feet, I'd had no idea that he was quite so thoughtful.

So that is how I came to learn about George Floor Man so many years ago, and as luck would have it, the shop is still in business.

Contrary to what one might expect, George Floor Man is actually owned by a woman named Georgette and Georgette is, in fact, what she prefers to be called—not George. She has unruly curls, rather wide hips, and likes to pair long skirts with work boots. Her voice is scratchy, but not as a result of cigarettes: rather, she has a benign polyp on her vocal cords and speaks in a low, raspy register because of it. These are things that I learned as a sixteen-year-old shopping for a runner with my uncle, and for whatever reason, this trivial information is still available to me now, twelve years later. I can't help but marvel at the memories that stay with a person, and I'm smiling a bit as I push through the shop's front door.

George Floor Man is much different than Brass and Brickman's. It's somehow crisper, if that makes any sense, like the air is able to circulate more easily because there's less chaos occupying the space. Rugs hang from above, sure, but they are not *directly* overhead, and the high ceilings provide an aura of spaciousness. Beneath my feet, all different types of flooring are represented: light-colored wood in herringbone patterns, wide boards of birch that appear almost rustic, and reedy lengths of bamboo; bricks laid to represent the weave of a basket, subtle patterns depicted in sheets of vinyl, and checkerboards created from ceramic tiles. The possibilities are overwhelming and endless, but fortunately I am not here to decide on a new floor. I turn my attention to the selection of rugs hanging against the far wall and start toward them. As I do, Georgette appears from the back with a rolled carpet over her shoulder and greets me with a gruff hello. "Lookin' for an area rug, are you?" she says after I've told her about my mission. "Then this'll make you happy: we're in the midst of spring cleaning, so all of my rugs are marked down by at least thirty percent."

"I picked a good day to come in," I say.

"Sure did," she agrees. "Let me know if you need any help."

The rugs are attached to sturdy metal rods and customers are able to flip through them just as they would a display of posters at one of those craft and hobby stores. The scale is much larger, but the principle is the same. I go through them quickly, only pausing every now and then if something really catches my eye because I feel that I will know it when I see it.

Know *them*, rather. The goal is to buy more than one rug, after all.

I find something for the living room first. It's excessively large and supremely plush and has a circular design at its center that reminds me a bit of a sun. The colors, too, are perfect: a medley of rich reds with touches of cream and gold. Unlike most of the other rugs, it doesn't have an ornate border, and as soon as my gaze lands on it, I feel confident that it is the one. I run my hand over the design, dig my fingertips deep into the thick wool, try to imagine it among leather sofas and fun-patterned throw pillows. It is exactly right; I can *feel* that it is exactly right.

It takes a bit longer to stumble upon something that will work in the bedroom. The palette is the same throughout the house and incorporates the many shades of autumn, but what I eventually settle on is a rug that introduces a bit of dark blue to the soft browns and muddied yellows. Something about pulling navy into the mix causes me to envision an inky night sky lit by twinkling stars and I have to wonder if the reason for this stems from Maurice Sendak. The colors of the rug are the colors found within the pages of *In The Night Kitchen*, and that particular picture book is one of the few memories of my mother that I've managed to hold onto.

Gramps and Noni never stopped talking about her, of course, and I know quite a bit of her life… Like, for example, she had a dusting of freckles across her nose and cheeks that became more noticeable with exposure to the sun. Her favorite food was homemade applesauce, her favorite book was *To Kill A Mockingbird,* and she was allergic to bees. When she was seven, she fell while running up the porch steps and sliced her shin so deeply that she required stitches. I *know* all of these things but I don't *remember* them; what I remember is *In The Night Kitchen.*

Mickey and his near-escape from the batter of a morning cake had been—and honestly still is—my favorite bedtime story. It was the one book that my mother would read aloud to me each and every night. Oh, she'd always pair it with something else too, like *Strega Nona* or *Owl Moon* or *Make Way for Ducklings*, but Mickey and those triplet bakers were whom I really wanted to hear about before closing my eyes on the day. Our routine was always the same: I'd take my bath, pull a nightshirt over my head, and snuggle into bed beside my mother. She always wrapped an arm around me, holding me close, and I would inhale her sweet scent of tea rose, which, in a word, simply smelled pink. And we would read about Mickey being mistaken for milk, and molding an airplane from dough, and securing that oh-so-necessary ingredient for the bakers just so that we could all have cake in the morning. She would then kiss me very lightly on the forehead and say in her singsong, motherly voice, "Goodnight, sweet Charley. I love you so much and I will see you in the morning."

Until one day when she *didn't* see me in the morning.

I push the sad bits out of my head and focus instead on the task at hand, which is determining which floor covering would be best for the study. Whatever it is will have to go nicely with a mahogany desk and an assortment of mismatched chairs, because that is the room where I imagine most of the world's problems will be solved. I can almost see the big-thinking men who will gather there, sipping their brews and voicing their loud opinions and playing the role of devil's advocate whenever the opportunity presents itself. It occurs to me that this will probably be the room I frequent least of all, but still I want its atmosphere to be just right.

Georgette, sensing a lull in my shopping success, appears at my side and asks in her sandpaper voice, "Can't find what you're looking for?"

"Not quite. I think I need something that's round, not rectangular."

The big woman nods and motions to a short stack of rugs located in a far corner. "Over here," she instructs me, leading the way. "The round ones are hard to hang, so I've just got 'em in a pile. You'll have to dig a bit, but there're some nice ones."

I think that she will leave then, but what she does instead is peel the top rug from the heap and fold it back on itself, revealing half of the carpet underneath. It's dark brown with a burgundy border and highlights of cream and gold. "I'll take that one," I say without thinking, and Georgette's eyebrows shoot skyward. "You sure?" she wants to know. "I've got a whole stack. This here's number two out of, oh, about thirty-five different patterns."

"No," I assure her, because I am confident in my decision. "That one is perfect."

She shrugs, happy to have the sale either way, and rolls the rug into a very tight and very long bundle. "This one and the other two, right? Just give me a few minutes to tie 'em up and then I'll figure out what you owe."

It ends up not being as expensive as I expect and Georgette helps me load the purchases into my Jeep. The one for the living room takes up almost the entire length of the automobile and is only a few inches shy of touching both the front and back windshields at the same time, but we make it work. I head back to the farmhouse with nearly everything crossed off my list.

Artwork will have to wait for another day; I'm worn out.

By the time I make it back to five-nineteen Copper Drive, it's almost five o'clock. Juli's truck, another truck, and an unfamiliar van are parked outside the house. Little regard has been paid to the driveway; all three vehicles have been backed across the yard and positioned near the front porch. I notice that the bed of Juli's truck is piled high with debris from the kitchen. The sight of it causes a rush of emotion to wash over me: excitement, because the renovation is a new adventure, but also sadness, since snippets of my childhood can be found among the wreckage.

Rhett must alert Juli to my arrival because both men appear on the other side of the screen door before I've even made it to the steps. One whines and paws at the doorframe; the other grins a sideways smile and says, "I'm glad you're back. I think I've got an idea."

I can't help but laugh. "You only think so? You don't know so?"

Juli shrugs. "I mean, yeah, I definitely have an idea. I'm just not sure what *you'll* think of it."

"What is it?"

"Come in here," he instructs, and opens the door for me. Rhett steps onto the porch and greets me by sniffing first my feet, then my knees, and finally my hands. Satisfied with the aromas on my person, he wags his tail and snorts into my open palm. "Thank you," I say, and promptly wipe the wetness onto my jeans.

Juli escorts me into the kitchen, pointing out obstacles and guiding me around them. There are tools and stepstools and broken pieces of countertop. There are also men I've never seen before, three of them, whom my handyman friend introduces along the way: "That's Sid. He's in charge of all the electrical stuff. And over there under the sink is Theo—" (a hand waves in my general direction) "—and this here is Ernie."

"Hi Ernie," I say to the man crawling across the floor. He has a slim frame, red hair, and holds a measuring tape in his left hand. "What're you doing down there?"

Ernie grins, but keeps right on moving, and his words when he does respond are directed to Juli rather than me: "Did you tell her?"

"Not yet."

"Tell me what?" I demand, and Juli nods his head in the direction of the extra-wide doorway that leads to the living room. "I know the plan is to hang a set of swinging doors right there, and to turn that side entrance into the main entrance, but the *real* main entrance opens into the kitchen."

"I know this," I say. "I'm aware of the floor plan."

"Well," Juli begins, making the single-syllable word last much longer than it's actually meant to. "What if we were to keep the main entrance where it is?"

"Then customers would have to walk through the kitchen," I point out. "Not a good thing."

"Unless the kitchen is meant to be walked through," Ernie pipes up, and Juli adds, "Just think about it for a minute: what if the food prep section of the kitchen was separated from the section of the kitchen that's meant to be used for dining? Like, what if the thing that separated the two was an actual bar? We wouldn't need to create a new entrance and we wouldn't need to install swinging doors. We'd just need to build a bar… and a bar is the only thing that your *bar* is currently missing."

He has a point. It seems like a ridiculous thing to have overlooked.

"You said yourself that the focus is beer, not food," Juli continues, "so if appetizers are the only things being prepared, then wouldn't an open kitchen like this be okay? There's plenty of room for both a bartender and a cook."

"And you could squeeze at least two, maybe three, little tables into a dining section," Ernie points out. He's still on the floor, but at least now he's upright, balancing on the balls of his feet. I realize that what he'd been doing was outlining where a bar might best be situated.

Juli watches me, trying to read my expression, but I guess that it must be indecipherable. "It's something to think about," he concludes with a slump of his shoulders, and it takes me a moment to understand that he's expecting me to reject the idea. A look of surprise lights his face when I say, "I think we should do it."

"You do?"

"We can't have a bar without a bar, Juli. That'd just be dumb."

I'm going to have to make a second trip to Brass and Brickman's.

10.

Addy

It's been a balmy spring. There's been just enough rain to coax the flowers from the ground and just enough sun to make them bloom. The temperature has sneaked up into the seventies once or twice, but mostly it confines itself to the upper sixties, and this evening is no exception. A person really couldn't request nicer weather for a high school graduation.

The festivities will take place in the stadium, situated across the same one hundred yards that Addy used to run on Friday nights. As much as he liked football, he'd never loved it, so stepping onto the freshly cut grass at this moment in time doesn't initiate a pang of sadness like it might for some of his classmates. He has fond memories of storming the field to the opening riffs of "Welcome to the Jungle," of the scent of buttered popcorn hanging heavy in the air, of the sound of the crowd stomping its feet against metal bleachers while the marching band played "The Hey Song," of cheerleaders shaking their gold pompoms beneath the fluorescent lights... and maybe he'll miss the experiences every now and again, but Addy Birch tries not to dwell in the past. He considers it much more important to focus on the here and now.

This particular here and now has him maintaining a challengingly slow pace beside Eleanor Ames, who happens to meet all the criteria needed to qualify as a graduation walking partner. First of all, she is a girl. Secondly, she's nearly the same height as Addy. And last but not least, she too has a GPA that places her among the top ten percent of her class. Both students wear the gold stoles that set them apart from the majority, and both will occupy chairs in the first two rows of seating. They have spent the past week practicing for this night, congregating in the school lobby at eight-thirty each morning and running rehearsals in the stadium *and* auditorium (in the event of inclement weather). Mr. Kent and Mrs. Ellsworth ran the operation—have run it for years, in fact—and the one thing that students are *not* supposed to do while walking to their seats on graduation night is have a conversation of any type. "This is an incredibly formal affair," Mrs. Ellsworth must have reminded them no fewer than seventy-five times. "There's to be no chitchat while walking to your seats. Do I make myself clear?" She'd been as serious as a heart attack, too; the expression she wore almost *challenged* a student to disregard her warnings. And despite this, Eleanor, looking straight ahead, mutters from the corner of her mouth, "Did you notice Dr. Raubenstein? He looks like a studious owl in that getup."

Addy stifles a laugh and glances at the superintendent. He does, in fact, resemble an owl that spends too much time in the library. Tufts of grey hair curl out from his mortarboard and the very round spectacles perched on the bridge of his beak-like nose only add to the effect. The entire faculty dons graduation garb for the big night, but Dr. Raubenstein is rocking the ensemble better than anyone else. Addy's grin lingers, but his gaze wanders to the bleachers.

Hundreds of people fill the seats. Each student receives four tickets for family and friends, but those tickets are only really necessary in the event of rain. If the weather cooperates, then there's no reason to utilize the auditorium since the stadium offers room to spare. He knows his mother is somewhere among the crowd, outfitted in her favorite dress with its hem that's too short and its neckline that's too deep, and probably snuggling inappropriately with her current catch. Addy's met him once. The introduction impressed him *almost* enough to commit the fellow's name to memory; it begins with an M, but the following letters are unknowns. The boyfriend'd had a thin, sallow face and glassy eyes like that of a goldfish. They'd met last week in Addy's living room, when the teenager had passed through at around one in the morning on his way to bed. It had been a long shift at the diner and all he'd wanted to do was crawl beneath the covers and close his eyes on the world, but there had been his mother, cuddling with Mr. M on the couch and giggling like a schoolgirl. The tinkle of her laugh had been sickening; Addy fell asleep with a pillow wrapped around the back of his head to block out the sound.

June Birch is not the person Addy most hopes to spot amidst the bleachers' swimming faces, though. It's Charley he's searching for. He scans the crowd, his eyes moving from top to bottom, left to right. He can't imagine that she'd miss his graduation—she'd seemed so flattered upon being asked to attend—but nowhere does he see her. Sighing, he pulls his gaze away from the audience and redirects it to the chairs lined up neatly on the field. He and Eleanor file into the first row and stand, waiting for their classmates to fill the seats behind them, while the high school band performs "Pomp and Circumstance" on repeat. It takes a while, but eventually the march comes to an end and the students are given the signal to sit.

Mr. Richards, the principal, is the only one to remain standing. He's a great bear of a man, both stocky and tall, with peppered grey hair and a beard that's not quite as trim as one would expect to find on an administrator. He approaches the podium, adjusting the tassel of his graduation cap before unearthing his words, apparently jotted down on a single index card, from one of his robe's many folds. He clears his throat, taps the microphone, and officially opens the ceremony by welcoming everyone to the graduation of Lake Caywood High School's senior class. "Today we deviate from our normal routines," he continues, "because today is the day that a child, a sibling, a cousin, a dear friend, a niece or a nephew, closes one door and steps through another, concludes one chapter and begins to write the next. Today is a day of goodbyes—to familiar faces that have passed us in the hallways for the past four years, to jammed lockers and oversized bathroom passes, to taco bar Tuesdays in the cafeteria, and to Mr. Kent's ten-page analysis of *Macbeth*—" (this gets a laugh) "—but today is also a day of hellos. Each of the two hundred twenty-six graduates seated before you will be greeting a new challenge in the days to come; whether it be college, a new job, trade school, or the military, they will say hello to new opportunities and obstacles, and while these opportunities and obstacles may be intimidating, they will also be exciting, because these students seated before you today are *prepared.* They are *ready* for what lies ahead. They have the skills to hit any curveball that life throws their way."

The principal is a good speaker, but Addy has trouble concentrating on Mr. Richards' words, and as much as he attempts to focus his thoughts on the present, they eventually force their way into the past, to a commencement of a different type.

Charley had been adamant that he learn how to swim, and thinking back on it now, he wonders if the money for his lessons had been supplied by his mother or by his babysitter. Never once had June sat poolside with her feet dangling in the water, cheering each time Addy emerged from underwater and offering encouragement in the form of smiles and kind words. That had been Charley's job. She'd sat there with the other mothers, probably listening to them as they swapped recipes and shared stories about their husbands and children, contributing very little to the conversation because she was really only a child herself.

Swimming lessons must have lasted for about six weeks—it's hard for Addy to remember for certain—but at the completion of the course, there'd been a graduation of sorts. The students had shown their skills by motoring from one side of the shallow end to the other, floating on their backs, and holding their breath underwater. At the end of the performance they'd tossed their brightly colored swim caps (purchased especially for that day) into the air, accepted an official document that certified each student had completed a course of guppy-leveled lessons, and toasted glasses of lemonade. Afterward, Charley had taken Addy out to lunch and then to a little art shop in town, Whirligigs and Whatnots, where they'd bought a frame for his diploma. They hung it above the desk in his room, so that he could look at it while coloring or completing homework or whatever, and it had continued to hang there until the day Charley disappeared. Then, hurt and angry, Addy had torn it from the wall and carried it outside to the dumpster, where the trash collectors had disposed of it a few hours later.

So lost is Addy in the past that by the time he returns to the here and now both the salutatorian and valedictorian have spoken, Mr. Richards has presented the class to the superintendent, and Dr. Raubenstein has nearly finished delivering a speech of his own. In a matter of moments, the dean will walk to the podium and the names of students will be read aloud, their syllables echoing throughout the stadium while family and friends clap politely from the bleachers. The graduates will return to their seats, Mr. Richards will provide a few final words, hats will be tossed joyfully into the air, and then the whole thing will be over.

"Over," Addy hears himself whisper very quietly, and Eleanor, to his left, wears a giant grin when she turns to face him. "I know!" she agrees. "Isn't it exciting?"

Addy nods, but his nod is a lie. He's experienced the real world already—has been fully submerged in it since about the age of seven, which is when Charley took off and left him to fend for himself—so to realize that now he has *only* the real world, and not the safety of school, is a terrifying revelation. Despite the mild night, Addy shivers.

The dean is at the microphone now and the front row is standing. As each name is called, the students shuffle their positions just a bit. They've practiced for this moment, have run through it multiple times for the past several days, but right now is the first and final performance.

Mr. Richards stands a few yards from the podium, making it a point to say *something* to each and every student. Eleanor Ames is with him now. Her posture is perfect, proud and tall, and she is smiling from ear to ear. Addy sees her laugh at something that the principal whispers to her, and then her name is being spoken and she is accepting her diploma and Addy is stepping forward… trying to catch his breath… almost walking right past his principal—but Mr. Richards places a firm hand on his shoulder and holds him back, saying, "Whoa, Addy!" with a laugh in his voice. "A little eager to be done with high school, are we?" he jokes, and Addison Birch, with his lungs struggling to hold enough air, doesn't know how to tell him that leaving this high school is the very last thing he wants to be doing. That he'd stay here forever if he could. But instead of speaking up, he swallows his words, and then his name is called and his feet are carrying him across the field to the podium and he is shaking the dean's hand and receiving his diploma and somebody somewhere is clapping.

In fact, more than one somebody appears to be clapping.

Addy scans the bleachers, searching for his mother and her date, but the person standing on the top row, silhouetted against the dipping sun with shimmers of red sparking off her skin, is none other than Charley Lane. And she's not alone: she's brought with her a small cheering section. From this distance, Addy recognizes none of the people surrounding her, but for the first time all evening he feels the slightest hint of happiness.

"I'm so proud of you!" Charley gushes, charging Addy on the football field and wrapping him in a tight hug. It's an embrace that he hasn't felt for a long time, but it's an embrace that still feels just right, and he realizes if there's anyone he can confide in regarding his trepidation about saying goodbye to Lake Caywood High, it's this woman who now, despite being absent for an entire decade of his life, is still more of a mother to him than June Birch ever has been. He opens his mouth to speak the words, and is about to allow them to spill forth, but then he catches sight of the people following in Charley's wake. Perhaps this is not the right time for a confession; perhaps the appropriate setting is not a football field illuminated on graduation night, with Green Day's "Good Riddance" blaring over the loudspeaker.

Charley loosens her grip on Addy and takes a step back, standing with her hands on his shoulders. "So proud of you," she reiterates. "What an accomplishment! I had no idea you were among the top students in your class!" She musses his hair, much like she used to do when he was only five or six, as if no time at all has passed.

"Thanks," Addy says bashfully, and averts his gaze from the trio who's congregated behind Charley. "And thanks for coming."

"Of course!" she exclaims. "I wouldn't have missed it!" And then, glancing around, something suddenly occurs to her. There's fury hidden in her expression, but her tone reveals nothing. It's the hue of the red sparks bouncing from her skin, suddenly brighter and more intense, which indicates her level of anger. "Is June here?"

Addy doesn't need to answer: the look on his face says it all. If his mother is here, she hasn't made it known, and if he had to wager a guess, he'd guess that she's currently occupying a barstool at Duff's.

Charley's cheeks grow splotchy and she purses her lips, but she doesn't waste any additional breath on the whereabouts of June Birch. Instead, she motions toward her posse of cheerers and says, "You may or may not recognize these faces: Juli Singer, handyman extraordinaire; Petey Goode, a guy who knows an awful lot about all sorts of stuff; and Jenny Goode, seventh-grade English teacher. Everyone, this is Addy Birch. He's kind of a big deal."

As hard as he tries not to, Addy blushes, and he doesn't quite make eye contact with anyone as he shakes their hands. All three members of Charley's cohort look familiar—Mrs. Goode especially, since she was a new and very talked-about teacher when he was in the eighth grade—but none of them are actually *known* by Addy. Nevertheless, he smiles and thanks them for coming and answers their questions about the graduation ceremony, fibbing about life after high school. "Maybe culinary school," he hears himself say to Petey, referencing past conversations with Mrs. Pennington. "I'm going to work for a year and then decide."

"I get that," Petey responds. "Why waste money on an education if you're not sure what you want to do with your life? You've got plenty of time to figure it out."

What with Addy being the center of attention, it's not surprising that he carries the conversation. Mr. Coleman, his precalc teacher, comes over at one point and claps him on the back, praising Addy on the four years of intense studying that earned him a seat among the top of his class. Promptly following this congratulatory display, Mr. Coleman receives a fair amount of playful criticism from Juli regarding his graduation garb. It turns out the two are best friends. Addy rather enjoys listening to their friendly back-and-forth banter because it allows him the opportunity to observe an unknown side of his math teacher. The person who would most benefit from this experience, of course, is Gabe Wynne, but Gabe isn't here tonight on account of needing to attend his cousin's graduation from West Orensdale. "It's a conflict," he'd stated last week, slumped there in the cafeteria, his elbow propped against the lunch table so his hand could support his head. He'd been eating a Honeycrisp and the surrounding air smelled like apples. "I can't be in two places at once. That's impossible."

Still, Addy makes a mental note to eventually inform Gabe of Mr. Coleman's humanness.

Despite the fact that summer has officially begun, the evening is chilly. A cool breeze makes all of them shiver and Charley, standing beside Addy, rubs her palms up and down her bare arms in an effort to keep warm. Little goose bumps dot her skin. She's wearing a simple sleeveless black dress with black sandals, but the sweater she'd meant to bring is draped across the banister back at the farmhouse.

Juli isn't oblivious to her chattering teeth. He shrugs out of his own jacket and wraps it around Charley's quivering shoulders without so much as a word. Addy observes the gesture, wondering if maybe Juli Singer is slightly more than just a handyman. There's a part of him that hopes this to be the case. The embers that dance around Juli are blue—almost the same shade as those that leap from his English teacher, Mr. Kent—and this is comforting, because more often than not, those who spark blue are gentle. Calm. Consistently reliable.

Charley accepts the jacket, melting into its warmth, but thanks Juli with only a word and not a gesture of her own. The group stands for a while longer, talking and laughing and taking in the magic of the moment, but when "Somewhere Over the Rainbow" starts to play and it becomes apparent that the night is winding to a close, Charley speaks up. "How about joining us for a late dinner?" she suggests. "Burgers and sweet potato fries from the Tavern?"

Addy wants to say "yes"—the word is right there on the tip of his tongue—but he knows that if he places himself in that situation, surrounded by people both curious and concerned about his future, the meal will be anything but enjoyable. As much as he loves to read and write, acting has never been something at which Addy excels. He doesn't want to spend the next few hours *pretending* to be thrilled about the fact that his high school career has come to a close. *Pretending* that he has a plan for his life. *Pretending* that he's excited for the future. And so that is why he bites his bottom lip, waiting for the word "yes" to evaporate into thin air, before saying instead, "Thank you, but… I think I'm going to head over to a friend's house. He's having a party, so…"

"Are you sure?" Charley confirms, knitting her brows.

"Yeah, I'm sure," he insists, and so she gives him a hug, and the others shake his hand, and everyone says "Congratulations" for the umpteenth time, and then Addy watches them walk toward the parking lot, their buoyant laughter floating upward to mingle with the stars.

There's no party. There could be if that's where Addy really wanted to be, because he had been invited to a few different gatherings, but solitude is what he prefers at this moment in time. Oddly enough, he ends up at Main Street Market, wandering the aisles and considering the many food items he's never even thought to purchase. Like throuba olives. Although significantly larger and darker than raisins—almost black, in fact—they have just as many wrinkles. Addy's never tried this particular type, but imagines it tastes just as salty and briny as all the others. As a kid, when he got hungry, Charley would often prepare a snack of exotic cheese and crispy bread and different varieties of olives. She had a special spoon for fishing the pimiento-stuffed fruits from their jars, and even though Addy never loved them as much as his babysitter did, he made it a point to sample each kind because it made her so happy.

It had been the cheeses that Addy'd looked forward to trying. Most kids his age were munching on American and cheddar and Monterey Jack, but Charley introduced him to smoked Gouda and Asiago and Manchego. That last one had been one of his favorites. Thinking of it, he abandons the Mediterranean bar with its olives and marinated mushrooms and stuffed grape leaves, and saunters instead to the cheese counter, where items are organized by consistency.

The display is situated within a round, refrigerated table; a wooden sign hanging from above advertises it as the Cheese Wheel. Addy circles the perimeter, scanning the labels of Boursin, Brie, and Gorgonzola, buffalo mozzarella, Muenster, and Balsamic BellaVitano, until finally his eyes land on a thick wedge of Manchego. He picks it up, examines the price tag: twelve dollars and ninety-five cents. It's practically as much as what a burger and fries would have cost him at the Tavern. "Do I really want to spend that much on cheese?" he mutters to himself, barely audible, so when somebody responds to the query, Addy actually jumps.

"The question you should really be asking yourself, Mr. Birch, is whether or not the enjoyment you'll experience upon consumption of that cheese will total the amount that it's worth." Miss Flora punctuates this nugget of wisdom with a firm nod and then squints through her bifocals to give him a once-over. "You're a bit overdressed to be grocery shopping," she observes, noting his black pants, white shirt, and charcoal-hued tie.

Addy forces a smile, but hangs his head all the same. "Tonight was my high school graduation," he says. "That's why."

"Well, now that's *something*, Mr. Birch!" Miss Flora exclaims. "I imagine that congratulations are in order. But tell me… why on earth are you spending your evening at the supermarket? Surely there's someplace you'd rather be?"

The teenager sighs and his shoulders slump. "Not really," he considers saying, because the only other place he has to go is home, but then he hears himself lying yet again: "I'm on my way to a party. Just something small that my mom's throwing together—a few of my friends will be there—but she forgot to pick up the cheese. You know," he continues, the quickness of the untruths alarmingly natural, "to go with the crackers. I said I'd take care of it." He holds up the Manchego, employing it as evidence, and fixes Miss Flora with the biggest grin he can muster.

Miss Flora studies him a tad longer than necessary, really scrutinizing his expression before speaking. It's as if she's not quite certain whether the words he's said are fact or fiction, but with no way of knowing for sure, she eventually presses her lips together, narrows her eyes, and says, "Well, then… that sounds just fine. Congratulations again, Mr. Birch. A high school graduation is something to be proud of, for sure." She pats his hand, ever so gently, before turning and walking away. Her small cart, containing little more than a cylinder of oatmeal, a bag of apples, and a box of raisins squeaks along in front of her, leading the way to the dairy aisle. Addy watches until she disappears, glancing quickly to his left and then his right before discreetly sliding the wedge of Manchego into his trouser pocket. The weight of it is heavy against his leg as he navigates his way to the exit.

Straight to the exit, because Addy does not stop to pay, and nobody follows him, save for the notes that he whistles ever so softly. They traipse over his shoulder, float up to the rafters, and break into a million pieces too small to warrant an echo.

11.
Juli

Different seasons offer different mornings and a summer morning can end up being pretty busy in downtown Lake Caywood. The heat of the day hasn't yet made itself known at seven o'clock and there are runners who take advantage of its absence. They wear neon sneakers and mesh shorts and t-shirts that advertise past athletic endeavors: autumn's Around Town Marathon, an end-of-season Santa Sprint, West Orensdale's Barefoot Bolt, and Biglerville High School's annual 5caKe. Their rubber soles pound the sidewalks, dodging lampposts and elm trees, dashing from one corner to the next, where they jog in place while waiting for red to change to green. To me, it seems like a miserable pastime, but I guess it must be more fun than it looks. I mean, there sure are bunches of people who appear to enjoy it, but I'd rather get my workout by building a deck or a patio. Not only is it more rewarding, but it earns me a paycheck, so when I drive the streets of Lake Caywood before the sun has fully risen, I relate more to those businessmen booking it to Bottomless Joe's, their only mission to secure a tall coffee before arriving at the office.

I occasionally find myself waiting in line behind these suit-clad men with their shiny shoes and fancy ties, but despite the early hour, caffeine is not my game plan. Today isn't a typical workday anyway; it's Saturday, and the only reason so many people are awake and wandering the streets beneath the still grey-painted sky is because of the Lake Caywood Jamboree. Held on the college's campus, the Jamboree was originally a festival to celebrate summer's first harvest: the berries. Over the years, though, it's become a festival for all fruits. Even if strawberries and raspberries and blueberries are the only things officially in season, their orchard cousins are represented in the form of preserves. There's always a rainbow of options available: strawberry-rhubarb, sour cherry, cranberry-apple, sweet apricot, peach-chipotle, plum, apple, green tomato, blackberry… the list goes on and potential customers are invited to sample all of it. When I was just little and my parents accompanied me to the Jamboree, Ma would make it a point to purchase at least a dozen of the squat jars with their handwritten labels. "Smucker's is good," she'd admit to us, "but homemade is better."

The best part of the festival, in my opinion, has nothing to do with jellies or jams or other things found in jars. I like the sugary stuff. In the past, bakeries from several of the surrounding towns have set up shop right there in the college's courtyard, selling blueberry cobblers and strawberry shortcakes and raspberry-custard pies; mixed berry Danishes and chocolate-dipped strawberries and warm crepes stuffed with raspberries and cream. Just thinking about the sugar-dusted concoctions causes my salivary glands to work overtime and a sense of urgency (disguised as a deep rumble in my gut) propels me to challenge the speed limit ever so slightly as I speed down Copper Drive.

Rhett is patrolling the yard, his nose close to the ground; Charley supervises from the front porch, a steaming mug wrapped in her hands. "Hey!" she calls out as soon as the truck's door swings open. "D'you want a cup of coffee before we head out? I made extra."

"Sure," I say, because coffee with Charley has become a part of my morning routine, "but then we have to get going. I'm hungry."

"Yes, sir," Charley responds. She sets her mug on the banister and gives me a playful salute before heading inside to retrieve the promised beverage. There's a smile on her face, but I nevertheless feel the need to provide further explanation: "I've literally been *dreaming* about raspberry popovers and lemon-blueberry scones!"

"*Dreaming* about them?" she confirms, her voice laced with laughter, sing-songing through the kitchen's open windows. I imagine her rolling her eyes as she pours the coffee.

"Dreaming about them!" I insist, and walk beneath the flowering limbs of the cherry tree to take a seat on the porch steps. Rhett prances over and gives me a sniff before plopping down at my side. He rests one of his big wiry feet on my lap and stares at me with those deep chocolate eyes of his, an expression of utter longing on his face. "I don't know what you expect me to give you," I say to him, holding up my empty hands. "I don't have the scones *or* the popovers yet. If I did, I'd offer you a bite."

"Really?" Charley wonders, skeptical. She pushes through the screen door, letting it clap shut behind her, and passes a mug of coffee over my shoulder. "If I did," I correct, meeting the yearning gaze of the pup, "I'd let you lick my fingers."

Charley snickers. "That sounds more like it." Having reclaimed her own breakfast brew, she joins us on the steps, running a hand along Rhett's back and then scratching his haunches. When she hits him at just the right spot, he starts thumping one of his back legs, as if revving his engine, and when I reach behind his ear to give it a good massage, a look of euphoria washes over his face. We're quiet for a couple of minutes, the only sound that of Rhett's foot keeping beat against the wooden step, but then Charley removes her hand and wipes it against her pants and says, "You know what I could go for? A really good muffin."

"Like a blueberry muffin?"

She shakes her head and takes a sip of her coffee. "Nah. Like one of those blackberry-cream muffins that Noni used to make when I was a kid. They were crispy on top, moist in the middle, and positively exploding with juice. *That's* what I want. Well... that and a strawberry milkshake. Or maybe just strawberry ice cream."

"I'll probably gain at least five pounds today," I tell her. "Maybe more."

"It's good to have a goal," Charley says, deadpan, but then I give her a sideways look and the corners of her mouth angle upwards. When she can't fight the smile anymore, she allows it to break through, and the happiness on her face somehow makes her bright green eyes brighter. She must catch me looking because a rosiness invades her cheeks. "Drink your coffee," she orders, "so we can get a move on."

"Oh, I see how it is... Yes, ma'am!"

She blushes an even deeper shade of red, insisting, "Well, now you've got me thinking about food, Juli Singer! Just... hurry up." The inky brew is hot, but I drink it as quickly as possible; the roof of my mouth is only slightly scorched when we climb into my truck a little while later. I turn the key in the ignition and both the engine and the radio come to life. "I love this song," Charley says immediately, approximately two notes into the tune, but it takes a moment before I recognize it.

"*There's the past and there's the future, and the here-and-now between,*" the artist lilts, his voice somehow lively and serene at the same time. Like he's happy, but calm about his happiness. "*I want you close for all of it; I want you here with me.*"

It's the certainty in the musician's tone more so than the lyrics themselves that allow me to identify the singer. "Sebastian Porter," I state, naming the lead voice of Lake Caywood's very own rock band. "We went to high school together."

"That's so cool," Charley sighs. "Did you know him?"

"Not so much back then—I was a freshman when he was a senior—but I've gotten to know him and his girlfriend over the years. They still live here, you know. Well, I mean, Bas lives here when he's not touring. Those guys spend an awful lot of time on the road."

"I bet." Charley lowers the window and rests her bare arm on the ledge. Summer's warm breath enters the truck in the form of a breeze. It tousles loose hair, rustles a folder of invoices on my backseat, and threatens to claim a recent gas receipt as its own. Charley catches hold of this last item, tucks it securely into the glove box, and says, "Flannel Lobster is my absolute favorite band. I've seen them in concert on eighteen separate occasions, but not once have I seen them perform in the state of Pennsylvania. Crazy, right?"

"That is pretty crazy," I have to agree since I've been to about eighteen of their shows and every single one of them has been not only in Pennsylvania, but in their hometown of Lake Caywood. They used to play at the local coffeehouse all the time. "Do you have a favorite song?"

"This one," she says, nodding in the direction of the radio controls. "I know it's a generic answer—everyone loves 'Kick It One More Time'; it's the song that made 'em famous—but those last couple of lines…" She trails off and I realize that it's because Bas Porter is in the process of *singing* those last couple of lines: "*Know that I'll be back again to kick it one more time.*" The chorus is repeated a few times before the guitars fade out and the drums quiet down. I expect Charley to follow it with an explanation of some sort, but all she says is, "I just really like the idea of coming back to kick it one more time."

"Coming back from where?" is what I think to ask, but I don't because we are at the college and my focus is on finding a parking spot. The streets running through the campus are lined with vehicles and there are volunteers clad in matching outfits at the entrance to each lot. They wear red t-shirts and hold walkie-talkies and direct traffic with never-faltering smiles. I secure a spot behind the library, throw the truck into park, and turn to face Charley. "First stop, breakfast?"

"Scones, popovers, and muffins," she responds. "Let's do this."

I tuck my keys in my pocket, Charley loops her purse over her shoulder, and we are on our way. The admission fee is ten dollars and I offer up a twenty to the money-collector before Charley even has a chance to open her wallet. "Hey!" she exclaims, but I simply pass her the brochure I've been handed and tell her that it's my treat. She scrunches her face into a look of defiant indecision, contemplating what's just occurred, but eventually decides that the generosity is acceptable as long as I'll permit her to pay for my scone.

"Deal," I agree. "That's it, though. One scone, and then we're even."

"And a popover," she attempts to bargain, but I shut her down: "No. Not 'and a popover.' I'll let you buy me a scone, but I refuse to accept additional offerings. I might purchase additional offerings for *you*, but that's allowable because I asked *you* to accompany *me* to the Jamboree."

"Juli…" she sighs.

"Charley…" I sigh back.

She tilts her head to one side, brings her brows together to form a bushy caterpillar, narrows those emerald eyes of hers and just stares for a good, long while. I look at her lips (which are slightly chapped), and I look at her nose (which is dusted with the faintest of freckles), and I look back to her eyes (which are green enough to make me think about lawnmowers), and then, just when I think that I can't take it anymore, her chapped lips form a small grin and she asks, "Is this, like, a date?"

As much as I'd wanted Addy's graduation to act as our first date, it really was more of a get-together with friends. Petey and Jenny Goode had ended up tagging along, since Jenny is a middle school teacher and recognized some of the students receiving diplomas, and then we'd all headed to the Tavern for dinner and drinks. Even Addy had been invited. He'd declined on account of having a party to attend, but maybe he shouldn't have. Dinner ended up being on the house, courtesy of Doc Delaney, owner of the establishment, and we all walked away with full bellies *and* full wallets.

Now, standing beside Charley, I look at her and she looks at me.

"It can be *like* a date, or it can be a date," I eventually answer. "Which do you prefer?"

My words come out sounding fairly nonchalant, but there's a part of me that worries my heart will beat right out through my chest. It's not a question I'd anticipated asking today—let alone ever—and now that it's out in the open, I'm terrified that Charley will choose the simile rather than the literal language. A long time ago, I did in fact read ("skim" might be a better choice of word) *The Merchant of Venice*, but not until this moment have I ever fully understood what it means to wait "with bated breath." It's as if my lungs are suddenly statues; they'll neither expand nor deflate.

"I think," Charley finally begins, and then pauses for effect. "I *think* that we should maybe just go with a straight-up date. But, if that's the case, then I'm not buying your scone."

The comment catches me off guard, but I find it to be hilarious. "That's fine," I assure her. "I'm happy to pay for my own scone. I'll even get one for you, if you like."

"No, thank you. A muffin is all I need."

"Suit yourself." I give her a lopsided smile and she gives me a bashful grin and without thinking, I reach out and take her left hand in my right one. "I'm starving. Let's find some breakfast so that I can pay for it, okay?"

We walk across the courtyard, right past several booths with jarred fruit for sale. If she were here, Ma would have to stop and sample the pear preserves, orange marmalade, and fig butter, but we ignore all of it and make a beeline to Piping Hot. The aromas wafting out from under their tent can best be described as delectable. I lick my lips and point to a poster board menu. Food items are listed in blue magic marker; prices are written in red. Someone with a bit of artistic talent has also added a bounty of berries at the bottom of the page, sketching mounds of strawberries and blackberries and blueberries.

Lemon-blueberry scones are at the top of the menu; raspberry popovers are about halfway down. I scan the options three times, but sadly, blackberry-cream muffins are not on the list. I buy a scone and two popovers, hand one to Charley, and motion to a booth on the other side of the quad. Even from here we can read the silver-on-purple lettering: Nothin' but Muffin. "If they don't have what you're looking for, then nobody will," I deduce.

Nothin' but Muffin is a little shop in Fillington, located approximately two and a half hours from Lake Caywood, that specializes in—you guessed it—muffins. Most of our town's people know about these ridiculously good breakfast cakes because of the Jamboree, but I've got an aunt who lives in Fillington and she's known to throw a doozy of a family reunion. The morning after, when the kids are hungry and the parents are too hung over to even think about scrambling eggs, Aunt Jean hands a wad of cash to one of the cousins and instructs him to purchase breakfast for everyone. Before I turned twenty-one, I was the cousin who made the muffin run, but now I stay at the house, sipping coffee and downing ibuprofen while someone else secures the grub. So admittedly, it's been a long time since I've actually set foot inside the tiny café known as Nothin' but Muffin, but I do remember the shop's selection and it is vast. Charley's eyes widen when she sees the size of the menu. "Wow," she whispers, a note of awe evident in the single syllable. "There are so many options!"

The list is alphabetical, starting with apple streusel and concluding with zucchini-spice, but there are far more than twenty-six possibilities. Fortunately, blackberry-cream is wedged right there between banana-nut and blueberry. "That's it," she says. "That's what I want."

In addition to the muffin, I request two cups of coffee: one with cream and one without. "Want to eat under that elm tree over there?" I ask, motioning to it with my chin since my hands are full, but Charley isn't paying any attention to me. In fact, as I'm talking to her, she's wandering away from me, her attention captivated by a crimson tent with the words Red Feather Art printed in white across the front. "Charley?" I call after her, and when she still doesn't respond, I'm forced to quicken my stride in order to catch up.

The tent houses a long table cluttered with all sorts of knickknacks: glass bottles of various shapes, sizes, and colors; little ceramic creatures with painted pale blue eyes; pinch pots glazed in earthy tones; old books with hollowed out pages; silver hoop earrings and gold chain necklaces. Here, in front of the jewelry, is where Charley stops. "Hey," I say, coming up beside her. "What're you looking at?"

She snaps out of it then, shaking her head to clear away the fog. "Sorry, I just… I don't know. I saw those words, 'Red Feather Art,' and decided to investigate. I've been having trouble finding art for the Brewhaha, you know, and thought that maybe…" She trails off, and though she motions to the table with its random odds and ends, her gaze doesn't leave the little box of rings directly in front of her. "There's obviously nothing here that will work for the farmhouse," she admits, "but…" And now she reaches into the box, plucks a copper band from the assortment of silver and gold, and holds it up for closer examination. Soldered to the small loop is a solitary black typewriter key: the number eight. "I need to buy this," she says with absolute confidence.

I don't ask why; I assume she will share her reasoning when she's ready.

The explanation comes sooner than expected.

We carry all of our purchases—food, beverages, and jewelry—to the base of an elm tree situated outside Landon Hall. Charley sits with her back against the trunk and I do the same, so we're sort of facing away from one another. My stomach is singing a woeful song of neglect, so I unearth my raspberry popover and dig in, but my companion's appetite must be temporarily subdued because rather than tear into her blackberry-cream muffin, she opens the bag from Red Feather Art and slides the copper ring onto her finger. "I like the number eight," she volunteers, "because it can be more than just an eight. It can go on forever if it needs to."

"Like an infinity sign, you mean."

Charley holds her hand out in front of her, considering her purchase and how it looks. "Like an infinity sign," she agrees. And then, as she unearths her muffin and pulls a chunk of the crispy, sugared crust from its top, she asks something that catches me a little off-guard: "Do you believe in reincarnation?"

My mouth is full of crumbly scone, which buys me a bit of time, but even factoring in some extra chews and a long swig of coffee doesn't allow me a lengthy enough moment to formulate my thoughts. Charley waits, almost imploringly, that chunk of muffin suspended halfway to her mouth. "I'm not sure," I hear myself admitting. "It's not something I spend a lot of time thinking about."

Now the bite of muffin moves, is consumed, and Charley redirects her gaze to the happenings on the lawn. A little girl with blonde curls and a yellow sundress toddles after her mother, holding some sort of sugar-dusted pastry that's almost as big as she is; three boys, around the age of fourteen or so, lick giant ice cream cones piled high with pink and purple scoops, all the while jostling and jabbing at one another; an old man with a cane plops down at a picnic table, opens a newly purchased jar of midnight-hued jam, procures a plastic spoon from his back pocket, and takes a big bite of the gooey goodness—no toast necessary. It makes me gag, but Charley just laughs, and then she queries, "So what do you think happens to people when they die?"

It's a deep question, and not something I ever fathomed we'd be discussing at Lake Caywood's light-hearted Jamboree. Nevertheless, I have no qualms about the topic and am more than willing to share my beliefs on the matter. "I like to think that people mostly go where they imagine they'll go. Take Asher, for example. He goes to church almost every Sunday and buys into the idea of Heaven, so I think that when Asher dies, he'll end up in Heaven. I'm not sure that *I* believe in Heaven, though. I mean, it's a nice idea—"

"But I'd rather come back," Charley cuts in. "I'd rather come back to be with my friends and kick it one more time." She gives me a grin, pleased with her use of the Flannel Lobster reference, and then adds, "My mom's dead, you know. She died when I was five."

"I'm sorry."

Charley shrugs. "My memory of it is foggy. She was killed in a car accident on New Year's Eve. It wasn't her fault, either. She hadn't even been drinking. She wouldn't have been out at all—she was off that night, home with me—but her friend needed a ride to work." I listen without interrupting, learning of the fight that had occurred between the friend and her scumbag husband, who had gotten angry and thrown his wife's car keys out the window. It had been snowing that night, so the keys were instantly buried beneath an icy blanket of white, and since the woman couldn't afford to lose her job waiting tables at the all-night diner, she called the only person she could think of for help: Charley's mother.

"She asked a neighbor to watch me for an hour, picked up her friend and dropped her off at the restaurant," Charley continues, "but then on her way home, she slid on the ice and the driver of the oncoming car didn't react at all. Because *he* was drunk. Both of them were killed instantly."

"So that's how you came to be raised by your grandparents?"

"Yep. Noni and Gramps were there when I woke up the next morning. They told me what had happened, helped me pack a suitcase of books and clothes, and trundled me back to the farmhouse. It was a really hard time, but…" She bites down on her lower lip and turns to face me. "I'm gonna tell you this, but you might think I'm crazy," she warns.

"Okay."

"Well, my mom loved the snow. *Loved* it. I don't have very many solid memories of my time with her, because I was pretty young when she died, but I do remember making snow angels with her and catching snowflakes on our tongues. It's kind of ironic, if you think about it, since maybe if there hadn't been snow on the road that night, she wouldn't have slipped, and then she might still be alive. But we'll never know that for sure, right? So… anyway. She loved the snow, and because of that, whenever it snows I can't help but feel there's a little piece of my mom with me. Like that's her way of sticking around."

I don't say anything, and when I don't immediately fill the space with words, Charley keeps going. "On the day I decided to stay at the farmhouse, right after I made that decision, it started to snow. And ever since then… well, I've just felt that it was the *right* decision. Is that crazy? Do you think I'm absolutely nuts now, Juli? Be honest."

"I think you're fascinating," I tell her. "Not crazy or nuts. Just fascinating."

She knits her brows and narrows her eyes, trying to determine whether or not I've spoken the truth. Deciding that I have, she says, "Thanks."

"You're welcome. What about your father? Was he ever a part of your life?"

"Never," Charley informs me. "I don't even know his name, and I think that's because my mom was never really certain of who my father was." She pauses here, smirks a little, adds, "My mom was a *badass*. Until she got pregnant, that is. Then she changed."

I'm not sure of how to follow this statement, so I eat my raspberry popover instead. It's mostly sweet and slightly tangy and as soon as it's gone, I'm regretful, but Charley reads my mind and offers me half of hers. "If you get a chance to come back as something else," she begins, "like snow or whatever, what would you want it to be?"

"Maybe a dog," I answer, surprising myself with the speed of the response. "But it'd have to be a dog that's well cared for. I'd hate to live outside, chained to a post, starved of affection for years on end. That'd be miserable." I look at her and raise my eyebrows. "What about you?"

She answers immediately: "A cardinal. One of the really red ones."

"You'd be returning as a boy," I point out, but Charley merely shrugs. "I guess so, yeah. But a soul is a soul, and I don't think that souls themselves have genders."

It's something to consider—something I wouldn't *mind* considering—except that I'm distracted by the blueberry that collides with my right temple. It bounces off my shoulder on its way to the ground, where it comes to rest among the soft blades of summertime grass. "You have to admit," Asher laughs, raising his hands to show that his status has changed from armed to defenseless, "that was a good shot."

I roll my eyes and climb to my feet. Charley does the same. Although I do agree that Asher's aim is impressive, I can't help but feel that by the end of any given school year, he acts more like his students than he does his coworkers. That must be what happens when a person spends most of his time with teenagers, though…

Asher has Annie with him and she's looking pretty cute in her denim skirt and old-school Jamboree tee, the words "Spread the Fun" smeared across the chest, as if they've been painted on with jelly. I used to have the same shirt, as did a good chunk of the town's population, but mine's been missing for years. That's what happens to my clothing, though: I wear it until it's so covered in paint and plaster that the best place for it becomes the trashcan, not my dresser drawer.

"Do you guys want to get some ice cream? That's where we're headed," Asher explains.

With one and a half popovers and a giant scone inside of it, my stomach is feeling a bit convex. "We just ate breakfast," I say, to which Asher responds, "There's homemade blackberry ice cream, dude. *Homemade.*"

I look to Charley, who raises her shoulders and points out, "You *did* set that goal…"

We end up accompanying them to the ice cream truck, where Asher, Annie, and I each indulge in a single scoop of the creamiest blackberry imaginable, and where Charley eventually decides on and acquires her strawberry milkshake. "Mmm…" she manages around a mouthful of the frozen treat. "This is insanely good."

"So good," Annie agrees. "After this, we should get lunch and head over to the stage. Jazzberry Jam is playing this afternoon."

I have to scoff at the mention of lunch, but I'm all for listening to some music. There will be several local acts performing throughout the day, but Jazzberry Jam is sort of a special thing. They play exactly one gig each year and the Jamboree is it. The members of Jazzberry Jam come and go, and one can never be sure of which instruments may be in attendance because the band's setup is essentially this: any musically-inclined teacher from the Lake Caywood School District—elementary, middle, or high—is encouraged to show up on the day of the berry festival, armed with an instrument, to open the afternoon concert series. Asher could join them if he wanted to, except for the fact that he doesn't play an instrument and he's completely tone deaf. But he's still turning out to see it. Just about the entire town will be.

Jazzberry Jam is scheduled to perform at noon, but we start to meander in that direction well before then. Already I can see groups of students congregating in front of the stage, eager to witness their teachers making utter fools of themselves, so there's not a doubt in my mind that the crowd will be fairly impressive. Annie's thought to bring a picnic blanket, which was smart; Asher carries it under his arm. Our goal is to claim a small portion of the hill that slopes away from the stage and set up camp. That way, we'll be able to see and hear everything without having to jockey for positions with the teenagers. We have plenty of time to kill, though, so when Charley reaches out, grips my wrist with her hand, and asks, "Is it okay if we stop and look at those paintings?" I'm happy to stick by her side while Asher and Annie go on ahead.

The tent that we duck under is white, like most of the others, but that's about where the similarities end. The only furniture is a wooden stool, upon which sits a little old lady with wispy white hair, and an easel. A metal cashbox sits in the grass by her feet and at least a dozen cardboard boxes—sturdy ones, like they might have been used to ship books—litter the ground. In the boxes are canvases, probably hundreds of them, and each one contains its own masterpiece. Everything is done with acrylics; nothing is framed.

The artist, focused on her easel and the work-in-progress that is propped there, doesn't even look up as we enter, so Charley squats before one of the cardboard galleries and I do the same. There seems to be no rhyme or reason as to how the paintings are organized; the one in the front is the portrait of a scruffy goat and the one behind it is a meadow of sunflowers. Because the system is so very catch-as-catch-can, it is somewhat surprising when Charley pulls the very last painting from the box and holds it up for closer inspection. "Juli," she gasps, nudging me in the side with her elbow. "Look!"

The canvas contains a brilliantly red barn with vines of ivy growing behind it, an orchard in the background. "Ivy doesn't grow like that," I point out, which makes Charley groan. "Because that's not ivy," she informs me, "they're hops. And that's Gramps's barn, back when the paint was fresh, and those are his peach and pear orchards behind it. I'd recognize it anywhere!" She bounces to her feet, clutching the painting to her chest, and walks over to the woman wielding a paintbrush.

"I'd like to buy this one," Charley announces, and when the old lady finally looks at her, the expression that darts fleetingly across her face is one of startled recognition. I expect her to say something—like "My goodness, look who it is! I haven't seen you in ages!"—but she simply blinks, twice, her bifocals magnifying kind eyes, and smiles brightly. She points at the stickered tag on the back and squints. "What's the price, dear?"

"Oh!" Charley exclaims, extending the canvas for the woman to see. "Eighty-five, I think. Did you paint it? Are you the initials in the bottom corner, F.H.?"

"I did," the old woman responds, now wearing a bemused smile. "And I am. Flora Higgins."

"I'm wondering if you knew my grandfather," Charley continues. There's a definite hint of excitement in her tone. "This is his barn, and those are his hops. His name was Jasper Lane."

This time I'm certain of it: startled recognition washes right over Flora Higgins' face, and this time she doesn't try to mask it. "If Jasper was your grandfather," she reasons, pausing long enough to put her thoughts in order, "then that makes you Charlotte."

Charley nods and grins a wide grin. "That's right! So you did know him?"

"Oh, no more than anyone else did. He was a personable man, your grandfather. He knew just about everyone to an extent."

"I suppose that's true," Charley muses. "I just thought that he might've been a friend since, you know—" and she cuts herself off, substituting the painting of the barn for the second half of her sentence. "I thought you might've known him well."

Flora Higgins must observe the disappointment on Charley's face because as she relinquishes her change, she confides, "There was a brief moment—many, *many* years ago—in which your grandfather played an integral role… but that was a different time. Practically a different lifetime. I was sorry to see he'd passed away, Charlotte. He was a truly wonderful man."

I can tell that Charley has a million questions she'd like to ask, but the artist turns back to her work, thus making it quite clear that she has nothing more to share, and we walk away in silence. It's not until we spy the blanket on the hill, with Asher lounging beside Annie, that Charley finally speaks. "That was a little bit weird back there, wasn't it?"

I reach out and give her hand that's not holding the canvas a squeeze. "Definitely a little bit weird," I have to agree, "but at least you finally found a piece of artwork, right? We may need to celebrate with mixed-berry smoothies."

"So much for five pounds," Charley mutters. "My money's on ten."

12.

Charley

I've never been a big fan of kissing. Quick pecks are okay, like for saying hello or goodbye, or even for just letting the guy know that he's done something too adorable for words, but as for full-fledge make out sessions on the couch… unless it's a preamble to sex, I don't see the point.

At least, I didn't until last night.

Juli kissed me. It happened in the hop field, beneath a canopy of vines dotted with musty-scented cones of green. I wasn't expecting it, although I *had* been expecting it the week before, when he dropped me off after a day of overeating at the Jamboree. But I guess that Juli was feeling pretty pregnant with a food baby at that point in time and wasn't much inclined for romance, so he merely walked me to the porch, offered an awkward hug, and we said goodnight.

As usual, he's spent a portion of each of this week's workday at the farmhouse, and so on Monday I thought he might do it over coffee, and on Tuesday I wondered if he'd attempt it after an end-of-day beer, and on Wednesday I escorted him to his truck as the sun was going down and figured he'd lean in for a kiss at that point in time.

He didn't.

By Friday I'd begun to think that our "date" had been nothing more than a fluke. I was, in fact, starting to find Juli's abnormally aloof behavior to be positively maddening, but then he joined me when I went out to check the growth of the Willamette hops and did what he should have done almost a week ago: kiss me.

Juli Singer at his smoothest, it was not. He'd been softly singing some sort of tune from the sixties—"Runaround Sue" or "The Wanderer" or something like that—which was nothing out of the ordinary, and then he'd stopped and reached down for my hand and said, "I think that I probably messed up a little bit when I didn't kiss you after the Jamboree. Is it okay if I do it now?"

I'd given him a look of disbelief—it was meant to be a look of disbelief—but Juli must have mistaken the incredulity for mild disgust or disappointment because his face had fallen and his shoulders had slumped. "I'm sorry," he'd muttered, tugging at that silver lip ring of his and looking endearingly sheepish. "I'm not good at this. I've never been good at this. I don't—"

"You need to be assertive," I'd interrupted. "Confident."

Juli had lifted his gaze then, almost bashfully, and I'd seen the blossom of color on his cheeks: splotches of pink on white, dusted with the slightest hint of afternoon stubble. My chest ached when I noticed the timidity in his eyes. "You *should* have kissed me on Saturday," I agreed with him. "I *wanted* you to kiss me on Saturday. And then when you didn't, I hoped you would do it on Monday, and I wished it again on Tuesday, and by mid—"

And that's where he cut me off.

He placed a hand on either side of my face and pressed his lips against mine and a little jolt of electricity coursed right down my spine and tingled my toes and for a very brief and wonderful moment, my breath was literally taken away.

My breathing was shallow when he eventually stepped back; I didn't immediately speak because I'd been so incredibly focused on filling my lungs with air. But finally, with oxygen once again flowing to my flustered brain and the butterflies settling in my chest, I'd gathered my thoughts and fixed Juli with a wide-eyed stare and finished, "And by midweek I figured that maybe it just wasn't meant to be… but I guess I was wrong."

He'd grinned one of those lopsided grins and the pigment that colored his cheeks at that point in time hadn't been a mark of embarrassment. Rather, Juli had simply looked happy. Happy… and maybe also a little bit proud.

Thinking of that kiss now, while tucked snugly beneath the covers of my bed with the morning sun streaming across the blanket, I shiver. It's a full-body shiver—one that goes all the way from the top of my head to the bottom of my feet—and its unexpectedness makes me giggle. "Juli Singer kissed me," I whisper, just to say the words out loud, but the sound of my voice rouses Rhett. I hear his tail first, thumping pleasantly against the hardwood floor, and then the metallic jangle of his collar as he lifts his head to make sure that I am, indeed, awake. I reach down to assure him that this is the case and his damp nose nuzzles my palm affectionately, relocating my hand so that it lands atop his head. A nice wake-up scratch behind the ears is what he's jonesing for, and so I appease him for a few minutes, massaging that velvety flap while Rhett grunts funny, deep-throated sounds of satisfaction. When his back leg starts motoring, I know that he's in the zone, and I allow him to stay there for a very brief time before proposing one of his favorite things: "Breakfast?" I ask, making my tone more animated than one might expect it to be when talking about dry kibble. "Are you hungry for breakfast?"

Rhett lifts his gaze; his eyes are bright. He sprawls there, as frozen as an actor in a movie still, waiting for confirmation, and when I provide it, he clambers clumsily to his feet and paws the bed. "Calm down," I instruct, but he fails to listen, choosing to occupy his time by prancing back and forth from the bed to the door. I throw back the covers, slip my feet into a pair of cheap rubber thongs, and pad along behind. The flip-flops create a soft shuffle of *thwap-whack* as I follow my pup through the hall, down the steps, and into the kitchen.

Organized disarray is the best way I can think to describe this particular room. While the majority of the first-floor living area has come together quite nicely, the kitchen remains very much torn apart. Insulation of one wall is still exposed; remnants of broken drywall unite in the corner, forming a small and jagged mountain; a ladder stands at attention in the middle of the room; and beside it, a Shop-Vac that appears to have taken up temporary residence. I do my best to wear blinders when I enter this room because it makes me a little bit sick to think that the Formica countertops upon which Noni used to cool sour cream-peach pies have been broken to pieces and discarded with the trash; my chest hurts when I remember the deep metal sink, which was just last week swapped at the scrap yard for cash, where I used to wash tomatoes and peaches for sauce. "Always a peach," Noni would say, "instead of the sugar. It's better that way."

The past month's construction has prevented me from storing much food in the house, and a rather ridiculous amount of money has been spent on eating out. Breakfast generally consists of a granola bar and lunch is typically a salad, kept fresh in the barn's refrigerator, but dinner is most often provided by a restaurant that's willing to deliver. The kitchen is, for the most part, off limits, so Rhett, having grown accustomed to the new accommodations, loops right through it and into the bathroom, where his food and water dishes have been stationed beside the tub.

With honey-hued walls, white fixtures, and wooden floors the color of coffee beans, I feel that the bathroom's makeover has turned out a great success. Although Juli thinks I'm a fool for filling the tub with potting soil and plants, I find the ferns and philodendrons to be quite charming. I intend to embellish the wall behind the tub with a few photographs taken while in the hop field: one of the spindly vines, a close-up of the yellow-green cones, another of the worn path that runs between the thick growth of Cascade and Centennial… There are five in all, taken once upon a time by Gramps himself, back when he dabbled in art. The images are currently in the possession of Whirligigs and Whatnots, where they're being matted with white and framed in black and should be ready for pickup sometime next week. The piece that I acquired at last weekend's Jamboree is there as well.

Gramps had experimented with various artistic endeavors—photography, paintings, poorly shaded charcoal sketches—but had stuck with none of them. And yet, I can remember the masterpieces being displayed around the house, propped on the mantle in the living room or tacked to the bulletin board in the rarely used upstairs office. Everything has since been secreted away, though; I only happened to stumble across the photographs because Juli handed me a kitchen drawer still cluttered with odds and ends. Noni's squirt gun had been right there toward the front (she was a firm believer that every kitchen should have one), but there'd also been a yo-yo with a broken string, a nearly empty book of matches, and a stack of random owner's manuals. "Junk drawer,"

Juli had noted before promptly passing the wooden container to me. "You might want to sort through it before it gets pitched." So I had, and what I found was largely worth tossing, but there, tucked between pages eight and nine of a booklet about the refrigerator, were five fairly decent snapshots of the hop field. The discovery made me think that there must be other artwork hidden within the house.

My plan for today is to find it.

Rhett whines, reminding me that his stomach is empty, and I bend down to plant a kiss on his wiry head. "I'm so sorry," I say, scooping Purina into his bowl. "Here you go, pup. Happy eats."

He pays little attention to my words, but acknowledges my offering right away. I stand by his side for a moment, watching him chomp away at his breakfast, enjoying the soft crunch that the food makes as it crumbles between back molars. Rhett is a methodical eater—he always has been—and even though it might seem silly, there's something satisfying about the way he so calmly and meticulously empties his food dish. My observation is brief, for today does come with a mission, and so I disappear back upstairs before Rhett has finished his breakfast.

Juli hasn't had a chance to do much to the second floor of the farmhouse. He did refinish the stairs and banister leading up to it, but that's where the renovation stops. The hardwood in the hallway and all of the rooms that branch off of it still need to be sanded, and until that happens, it's pointless to paint, so I've left the walls as they are.

The upstairs consists of three bedrooms (one of which has an attached bath), an additional bathroom with fixtures the color of avocado, and a very small space that Gramps and Noni referred to as an office, despite the fact that all of their finances were managed at the mahogany desk in the study. It is the office that I intend to investigate, though, so I walk to the end of the hall and open the door. It sticks initially, but when I give it a nudge with my hip, it swings open with a slight creak.

There's only one window in this room. It looks out on the apple orchard, affording a nice enough view, but providing little light. I touch the wall, flip the switch, wait for the overhead dome to awaken...

Nothing happens.

The bulb has apparently entered a permanent state of slumber. "Great," I mutter, and walk over to the desk. There is a green glass-shaded lamp that squats there and when I tug on its chain, it blinks immediately to life. The glow is not especially illuminating, but it casts enough light to make examining the desk's contents a possibility. I perch on the swivel chair, its cracked vinyl upholstery stabbing the back of my thigh, and tug on the middle drawer. It slides open easily, revealing an assortment of pens and a small calculator that no longer works. I toss it into the trash before continuing with the investigation, but it doesn't take long to realize that nothing of value is hidden here. I rock back, cross my arms, raise one hand to my mouth in order to nibble a thumbnail with my front teeth. Only two other pieces of furniture are housed in this room: a narrow bookcase filled with Nancy Drew mysteries, and a small recliner upholstered with scratchy fabric. I make a mental note to get rid of that chair—I've never liked it—and consider the storage space on the other side of the room.

Too small to be considered an actual closet, the storage space is a funny little alcove that's about three feet wide and four feet deep, with a short half-door that swings outward. Noni used to store sweaters inside during the summer months, because some were too bulky to fit comfortably in bottom drawers, and in the spring the Easter bunny always made it a point to conceal one egg in the shadowy confines. The first year that nook was employed as a hiding spot, the egg that was hidden there stayed missing for more than just Easter Sunday; we'd found it almost a month later, when a rank smell made itself present on the second floor, wafting down the hallway to greet us at the top of the steps each night as we traipsed tiredly to bed. Upon discovery, the shell had been dotted with tufts of blue fuzz, and in the years following that foul-scented event, I'd made it a point to always tote my basket first to the office, where I'd examine the alcove's contents before exploring the rest of the house.

Months ago, while sorting clothes to take to the rescue mission, I'd not thought to check this particular nook. I'd actually not even thought to enter this room, seeing as it was so very infrequently visited by both my grandparents and me. But now that I'm here… I lift myself from the chair, walk to the undersized door with its wrought iron latch, open it toward me and drop to my knees. It's dark inside; the bulb of the desk lamp uses wattage too low to project light this far. I squint, willing my eyes to adjust to the shadow-infested space. There's a flashlight downstairs, but I don't feel like racing to get it, so I crawl forward and feel around with my hands, touching a fleece blanket and a forgotten teddy bear and then the wall behind it. As my fingers creep up and along the flat surface, though, I'm surprised to find that the height of the wall isn't what I'd expected. It should be about three feet high, but there seems to be a ledge approximately seven inches off the floor. "Like a step," I think out loud.

Had Juli not already discovered a mysterious room with a baby grand piano in its midst, I'd probably think nothing of this apparent abnormality, but I grew up in this house and I know for a fact that there's never before been a staircase off the back of this alcove. I'm about to venture in farther, but the sound of Rhett's heavy feet on the stairs, rumbling like thunder, gives me pause. His nails click down the hall, into the room, and then he is beside me, pressing his wet nose against my ear. "Hi," I greet him, turning my head when I speak in an effort to avoid a mouthful of fur.

Rhett squeezes right past me, hitting me in the face with his wagging tail, and proceeds to clamber up the mysterious set of stairs. He spends not even a full second considering where it may lead, for he is a fearless and sometimes foolish fellow. "Rhett!" I call after him, a hint of panic in my voice. "Rhett, come!"

Of course he doesn't listen; he is part terrier, which makes him stubborn, and when partaking of something exceptionally exciting, he only ever exhibits selective hearing anyway. I take a breath, try to calm my fast-pulsing heart, and start up after him.

The stairway seems to spiral and widen the higher I climb. My feet follow the steps, slowly and steadily, while my right hand grips the rail with white knuckles. I wish that Juli were here. I wish that he were leading the way, feigning confidence to appease my own fear, reaching back with his left hand to grip mine in his. Rhett must read my thoughts because there he is at the top of the stairs, stalwart and stoic, waiting to share a proper tour of the place with his favorite human. I join him, showing my thanks with a gentle tousle of his ears, and take in our surroundings.

We appear to be in a studio. One that's both flooded with light (the excess spills down the spiral staircase like a waterfall) and high above the orchards. The ceiling is incredibly high and the windows are insanely vast and the few sections of wall that aren't occupied by glass are surprisingly narrow. I spin around, taking it all in, and suddenly come to the realization that we are somehow *on top of* the farmhouse. "We've found a tower, Rhett." I speak the words out loud because I have to. Otherwise, the truth wouldn't seem real.

Outside, the view encompasses all of Gramps's land: the grove of apricot trees, heavy with fruit not quite ripe enough to be picked; the cattail-lined pond, where Rhett enjoys chasing frogs into the shallows and snapping at the splashes created by their narrow escapes; Noni's garden, in need of some serious weeding; and the hop field, where Gramps now dozes among his favorite crop. I fulfilled that request a few weeks ago, in early spring, right when the fresh-green vines were beginning to tendril toward heaven. I'd invited Kirby to join me, but he'd curtly declined, and so Rhett had been the only one to accompany me as I carried the urn across the yard and around to the backside of the barn. I'd quoted a song that I'd heard once, written by an indie musician from some small town in Pennsylvania or somewhere, whose name I don't remember… if I'd even known it to begin with. But I can recall the opening lyrics pretty clearly—"There are times in our lives where you can't run on the gun / There are times in this world where you just gotta let go"—and this is how I bid farewell to Gramps.

This is how I'd chosen to let go.

I had done what he'd asked: scattered his ashes among the hops, mixing them into the soil so that he'd forever be able to have some input in the brewing process. I'd buried the urn beneath the Nugget vines because they had been Gramps's favorite; he'd loved the bitter taste and the aromatic smell. Sometimes I'd catch him rubbing the cones between his hands and then raising perfumed palms to his nose, inhaling deeply. The memory of it makes me smile.

The studio looks out on all of this and when I focus my attention on the inside, I realize that this magnificent landscape has been represented in multiple mediums. There's an easel with a canvas still perched there, its image depicting a canopy of color stretched above an asphalt road. I recognize it as Copper Drive in the fall, before the trees that line the street have dropped their leaves and crusted the ground beneath with a topping as crackly as pecan pie. Before paper-thin sheets of burnt umber and saffron and burgundy have tumbled through the air, floating downward, eventually landing with a soft *swish* among the many shades of autumn.

But the orchards are portrayed too, as are the pond and the barn and the house itself. Images of all sorts—acrylic and watercolor, charcoal and pastels—line the room's perimeter, propped against the low windowsills. A solitary wooden table, tall and rectangular with built-in shelving, hosts an assortment of supplies, but other than this, the easel, and a lone stool, the room is virtually void of furniture.

Rhett, constantly curious about new scents, puts his nose to the floor and darts in zigzags across the room, detecting smells that I can only imagine. Every now and then he'll execute an especially solid snort, and once he sneezes, but he manages not to damage anything until he rounds the worktable and disappears behind it. That's when the crash occurs, and that's when Rhett scampers back into my line of vision, and that's when I finally venture forth from my stance at the top of the staircase.

"What'd you do?" I demand, because my wiry scoundrel of a dog is wearing a look of pure guilt. Judging from his downcast gaze and the tail tucked between his legs, I'm expecting a small catastrophe, but all that I find on the other side of the table is a very large leather portfolio that has fallen onto its side. I reach for Rhett before I reach for the giant folder. "It's okay, pupper. Come here. You're fine. You're a good boy."

He approaches with his head down, still not certain that he's deserving of this particular title, but his tail does come out from hiding. Rhett inserts his snout into that hollow beneath my chin. I give him a hug, kissing his velvet ears and scratching his rump, and wait for him to tire of the affection. It doesn't take long, and when eventually he pulls away, I sit down in front of the portfolio and open the leather flap. Inside, separated by sheets of blank newsprint, are dozens and dozens of paintings. Watercolors. I pull them out one by one, examining each, while Rhett settles in beside me and rests his chin on my lap.

"Gramps painted these," I whisper, recognizing a soft-edged peach that had hung on the refrigerator when I was a child. "He must have painted all of these." And as I continue to go through the stack, there is his name at the bottom of each piece, printed with shaky handwriting: Jasper Lane. Sometimes there is a date, though not always, and from what I can tell it seems that the majority of the artwork was created long before I was a thought… probably long before even my *mother* was a thought. But of course that makes sense: Gramps would have had more time then. Raising a child tends to consume a sizeable chunk of each day; I learned that firsthand with Addy.

The landscapes and still lifes appear to be in chronological order, with the most recent creations residing at the top of the pile. The technique is certainly better—Gramps's early works tended to be overly blotchy thanks to the use of too much water—but despite this, I will certainly be able to display several of these pictures throughout the farmhouse. I appreciate all of them, because they were designed by Gramps himself, but there are a few that really speak to me. For example, his Ford Model T is captured in one. It's true that the edges are blurred in some spots, and the headlights look to be lopsided, but overall, the effect that it generates is quite nostalgic. I spent many a day watching Gramps tinker with that car, never fully comprehending the mechanics that went into it, but always content to listen to the stories he'd share while he worked.

And there's another painting that I like too, although I'm not sure why. It's the profile of a dark-haired woman, poised before an easel, a paintbrush in her hand. Her features are somewhat obscured by the long locks that frame her face, and at first I think it's Noni… but Noni, for as artistic as she was in the kitchen, knew very little about media outside the realm of food. The woman's identity may need to remain a mystery, but the artwork does not; I intend to hang it in one of the downstairs rooms so that anyone frequenting the Brewhaha might see it.

There are only a few pieces left in the portfolio. I expect the quality to be rather rough, since they're examples of Gramps's first attempts at art, and my assumption is mostly accurate, but the painting on the very bottom of the stack takes me by surprise. Causes me to lose my breath, in fact.

It's an acrylic, not a watercolor, and the creator of it was *definitely* not my grandfather. But that's not what makes me exhale all of the oxygen in my lungs and forget to take in more. That's not what makes my heart skip a beat. The thing that's so very startling about the piece is that the subject is *me*. Charley Lane. And it's an image that I recognize well.

I'm perched on the seat of a yellow bicycle, coasting down the dirt driveway, dark hair—longer back then—bouncing around my shoulders. Tassels, all the colors of the rainbow, flail from the handlebars, catching the wind, and there's a basket of peaches and flowers mounted to the front. The flowers are purple and gold and are probably little more than weeds plucked from the orchard's outskirts; the peaches are orangey-red, as if the sun has bent down and given each one a kiss. It's the exact picture that used to reside on my grandparents' mahogany desk… except for the fact that this isn't a photograph. It's a painting, with initials instead of a name: F.C.

"F.C.?" I ask of no one in particular. "Who in the world is F.C.?"

Rhett peers up at me, wondering if my words are of importance to him. Determining that they are not, he settles back into his half-sleep state and returns to a dream of meaty bones or quick-footed squirrels or whatever it is that dogs see when they close their eyes.

Unlike those of my canine companion, my eyes remain very much open. They scan the painting for additional hints, but find none, and so I flip the canvas board over to examine the back. There's a note there, its corners taped so that it lies flat, and the handwriting is neat and small. *Jasper,* it reads, *Thank you for the photograph. She's a beautiful girl, and looks so very much like her mother. It must be comforting to always have a piece of Fiona nearby. Stay well, and love to you always and forever.* But there is no signature.

Why Gramps would have sent that picture to someone—a woman, I assume—is beyond me. And why a woman other than Noni would conclude a brief note with "love to you always and forever" is a concern. That's the type of language that exists between paramours, which certainly isn't a label that would be used to describe Gramps. His middle name was technically Thomas, but it might as well have been Faithful because he never would have cheated on Noni; he loved her wholeheartedly.

Sighing, I return all of the paintings to the portfolio and hoist myself to my feet. Rhett does the same, eager to embark upon a new adventure, and trots over to the spiral staircase. It occurs to me that he hasn't yet been outside. "I'll bet you have to pee," I say, and he wags his tail enthusiastically before darting down ahead of me. Armed with an abundance of new artwork, I bring up the rear, stooping and then eventually crawling because the ceiling is only a few feet high once I reach the bottom steps. The hardwood presses unforgivingly against my knees, causing me to quicken my pace. I enter the office headfirst, and despite the overwhelming desire to stand up and stretch, what I do first is pivot back around and reach into the alcove, feeling for that back wall.

It's there, too, just as it should be. The stairs that had led up to the tower are gone. Another room, gone. But then… was it ever really there to begin with?

And are there others?

The key is in the game room. Corner pocket.

A memory of those words, written in Gramps's shaky handwriting, suddenly comes to mind, and I can't help but wonder… But, no. To bank on the appearance of a nonexistent space is beyond silly; rooms don't simply come and go.

Or do they?

I shake my head, puzzled. If I weren't still clutching the portfolio of art, I'd diagnose myself as crazy right here and now… but I *do* have the art. It's the only thing that allows me to believe my brain hasn't ceased functioning properly.

Downstairs, Rhett paws at the front door and barks once, alerting me to the fact that he'd like to go outside, so I dutifully climb to my feet and set out to oblige. I know that the classic phrase is "Dogs have owners. Cats have staff," but there's a part of me that realizes Rhett also has staff. He's the kind of pup who will continue to stand at the door, barking at one-minute intervals, until someone shows up to offer assistance. When I invite him to go in the Jeep with me, he's willing to plant his front feet on the seat, but he considers it too much of a bother to exert the effort needed to jump inside. Rather, he tends to glance first at his backend and then up at me, as if to say, "Are you going to get that?" And the answer is always, "Yes. I am going to get that," because I always do.

I find him just as I expected I would: in the kitchen, standing at the door, staring unblinkingly at the knob. "Here you go," I say, opening it for him. "Be careful."

He bounds off the porch, landing lithely in the grass, and is in the process of relieving himself on a bush when Juli drives up. There's a bicycle in the bed of the truck and a passenger in the front seat. I step onto the porch and walk to the stairs, but stop there. Rather than meander out to the men, I lean against one of the porch's vertical posts and watch from a distance. As suspected, it's Petey Goode riding shotgun, and as he hops out, he gives me a big grin and a friendly wave. My guess is that he'd been pedaling out this way on his bike, probably to check the status of some pumpkin ale he's been brewing, when Juli had pulled up beside him in his truck.

"Your handyman gave me a ride," Petey explains as he walks toward me. "I wanted to get out here and check on that batch of pumpkin before my shift at the Tavern. What're you up to?" He eyes my baggy linen pajama bottoms and casual foot attire. "Enjoying a wake-up-slow kind of Saturday morning? Jenny was doing the exact same thing when I left this morning. I swear she had on an identical outfit, too…"

I laugh. "She's a smart girl with an obvious appreciation for comfort."

"Tell me about it," Petey agrees. "During the school year, the first thing she does when she gets home from work is pull on a pair of sweatpants."

"When quittin' time rolls around," Juli contributes, sauntering over to participate in the conversation, "that's very often the same routine that I follow." He greets me with a crooked smile, and when he does, I can't help but notice that his gaze floats directly to my lips. "Hey, Charley."

"Hey," I say back.

Petey must pick up on some sort of not-quite-normal spark between us because his eyes do a little dance back and forth—first to Juli, then to me—and a hint of realization lights his face. He does stick around for a few minutes more to brief me on a potential chocolate stout, but then he excuses himself to the barn. We watch him go (wait for him to go, really), and once he's no longer in sight, Juli joins me on the porch, lightly touches my cheek with his hand, and then leans to brush my lips with his. He smells like woodchips and Listerine. "I found another room," I blurt out as soon as he pulls away. The comment isn't romantic in the least, but my eagerness to share the news causes the words to explode from my mouth without permission. "An art studio. In a tower off the back of the alcove. I had to climb a spiral staircase to get there. Rhett saw it too."

"Whoa," Juli says. "Back up. You lost me right around the point when you mentioned a tower… You did say 'tower,' right?" He glances up, even though an overhang prevents him from viewing the full exterior of the old farmhouse, but I understand the point he's trying to make: there is no tower.

"Let's have coffee," I decide, "and I'll explain the whole story from start to finish."

Which I do, beginning with the burnt-out light bulb and concluding with Rhett's full bladder. I even share the background information about the moldy Easter egg. And when I'm done, Juli furrows his brows and tugs on his lip ring and says, "I want to see it."

I shake my head, dismissing the notion. "You can't. It's gone already."

"Still, I'd like to check for myself." So we go upstairs together, hurry down the hallway, and enter the office, where I direct him to the funny half-door so that he can reach inside and have his own hand make contact with a wall rather than a flight of stairs. "Told you," I say, smugly, but pair it with a playful grin.

Juli sighs, obviously disappointed. "Damn. Do you think I could look through the portfolio?"

"Sure."

We end up taking the artwork to the living room and leaning it against the chest that I'd purchased to serve as a coffee table. "Have at it," I say. "Let's see if we have the same taste in art."

Juli begins at the back, which means that he ends up viewing the acrylic piece first. I expect him to comment on the bike, or the basket of peaches, or the rather cryptic note taped to the back. What I do not expect him to say is, "Your hair used to be long."

I nod, reaching up to feel the short layers that taper down to my bare neck.

"What made you want to cut it?"

The truth is, I hadn't *wanted* to cut it. And the other truth is that I hate revealing that side of myself. So I shrug and say simply, "It's a pretty lengthy story. Would you like it better if it was long?"

"No," Juli answers, and I can tell right away that he is being truthful. "Not at all."

"My ex-boyfriend liked it better long," I volunteer, surprising myself, and the expression on Juli's face lets me know that I've managed to surprise him too. "He was an artist—a photographer—and he used to tell me that I was his number one model. Which, I mean, I think was true. But I know for a fact that part of the reason he liked to photograph me so much was because of my hair." I glance up, meet Juli's gaze, hold it for a considerable stretch of time. "I had great hair, Juli. *Really* great hair. It was long and wavy and beautiful, and then when I chopped it all off… well, I guess it wasn't quite as much fun to photograph me." I punctuate the story's conclusion with a slump of my shoulders and slouch into my chair.

But Juli, still holding the painting of a ten-year-old me on a yellow bicycle, tilts his head to the side and asks, "Was it really that great? Your hair?"

"Would you like to see a picture?"

"If you have one."

"I do."

I go to the study, stand before one of the floor-to-ceiling bookcases, slide *The Thorn Birds* from where it's nesting between *Gone With the Wind* and *To Kill A Mockingbird.* It seemed only fitting to store the snapshot there, since that's where he'd been keeping it.

I carry the novel back to the living room and sit down on the couch beside Juli. "That's my ma's favorite book," he says right away. "Forbidden love and all that… Poor Ralph and Meggie."

"You've read it?" I confirm, not bothering to hide my disbelief.

"A long time ago." He shrugs. "I had to. It's my ma's favorite book."

"It's *my* favorite book," I tell him. "I can't believe you've read it!"

"Well, you know, what can I say? I guess I'm a sucker for a good love triangle."

I laugh and open the novel, flipping through its pages until I stumble upon the photograph. "Here," I whisper, passing it to Juli. "See? It was great hair."

I watch him study the image, taking all of it in: the red umbrella, the dark locks cascading over my shoulders, the golden-haired boy with his arm looped around me. "We were attending a three-day festival in Michigan," I contribute, "and it rained the whole time. That picture was taken approximately ten minutes before Flannel Lobster took the stage."

"And that guy beside you was your boyfriend?"

"He was."

"What's his name?"

"Does it matter?" I counter. "You wouldn't believe me if I told you."

Juli lowers his hand, resting the photograph on his knee but not releasing his grip. "Try me."

I look at the boy in the picture, take in his crazy-long lashes and the slight dimple that would form to the left of his mouth anytime he smiled. "Charlie," I admit. "His name is Charlie, but with an i-e instead of an e-y."

"Charley and Charlie?"

"Yep."

"Well, that's sort of funny."

"Yep," I repeat. "All of our friends thought so too."

Juli grins, lifts the photograph from his lap, and holds it up for a second round of examination. I watch him scrutinizing it, and wonder if he's looking at me or at Charlie, but then he says, "It *was* really great hair, but you know what?"

"What?"

He reaches over with his right hand, resting his tattooed palm on my cheek, and uses his thumb to softly caress the bangs that touch my forehead, brushing them aside. "I think I like it better short."

13.

Addy

July is different this year. In the past it had been the only month not touched by school; not a single one of its thirty-one days had ever been occupied by homework or vocabulary quizzes or football practice. Once upon a time Addy had loved the month of July because it had contained so many of life's small pleasures: Coppertone-scented afternoons by the lake, where he'd snacked on cheddar Goldfish crackers and fruit-flavored ice pops and attempted to catch silver minnows in a plastic pail; lightning bugs flickering on and off and high above in the night sky while he'd stood barefoot in dew-soaked grass and watched; evenings laden with the aroma of charcoal and blackened hotdogs split down the middle, a line of ketchup coursing along the v-shaped crack. July had been the month in which Noni prepared apricot crumble, crusted with sweetened coconut and topped with homemade almond ice cream. It had been the month that Gramps took him to the classic car show in West Orensdale, where they'd not only gotten to sit in a few vintage vehicles, but had also eaten the best pulled pork sandwich Addy ever recalls consuming. July had been wonderful because July had signified long days spent with Charley.

But then Charley had left, and when she did July became just another breezeless month with too much humidity and no end in sight. June Birch had decided that the chain-smoking neighbor lady in the upstairs apartment, Mrs. Grady, would make a sufficient sitter and so Addy had spent the next several summers with her, choosing to pass most days outside on the lawn with a book rather than behind hazy windows, filling his lungs with ashtray-scented air. It was around that point in time, aged eight or nine, that

Addy had realized his school was more of a home than his own house. His school had provided him with food and shelter and adults who looked after him, which was more than June Birch ever offered, but now that graduation day has come and gone, there is no more school. There's no light at the end of the tunnel, and every day seems like just another day in July.

Addy sighs, finishes tying his left sneaker, hoists himself off the bed and to his feet. His shift at the diner starts in thirty minutes, and since he doesn't have a car, he needs to get moving. Railroad Street may not be that far from the apartment, but he'll have to maintain a pace that's more brisk than it is leisurely, so he zips up a charcoal backpack, loops it over his shoulder, and pulls his bedroom door shut behind him on the way out.

The home that Addy shares with his mother isn't anything special: two bedrooms, one bath, a small living area, and an even smaller kitchen. Unless there's some sort of emergency, the landlord really isn't interested in being informed of any problems, so the windows are drafty, the plumbing leaks, the heater is shoddy, and the air conditioning is nonexistent. Addy does make it a point to keep the place clean—he takes it upon himself to mop and vacuum and dust every week—and so this is the reason why the kitchen's chipped linoleum floor, peeling up at the edges, isn't smeared with dirt and debris. And this is why the cream-colored laminate countertops, yellowed with age, gleam rather than sport a film of crumbs and grease. This is also why the sink is void of dirty dishes and the table's glass top is free of fingerprints and the faintest whiff of lemon can be detected beneath the always-present odor of stale Lucky Strikes.

Addy coughs as he enters the kitchen and June, sitting at the table with a freshly lit cigarette dangling from her lips, looks up from the want ads over which she is pouring. Her shoulder-length hair, over-dyed and brittle because of it, is pulled into a sloppy ponytail and her caked-on makeup could use some work. Too much mascara, eyeliner that's thicker than necessary, lipstick the color of Pepto-Bismol… Addy wishes that she could view herself as the rest of the world probably does: more clown than mother.

June's denim miniskirt, skimpy tank top, and to-go cup of gas station coffee suggest that last night was most likely spent in a bed other than her own. "Hey baby," she drawls when Addy enters the room. "You going to work?"

Like everyone else, little embers spark from June's skin, leaping off her bare shoulders and fizzling to nothingness once they hit the air. They're the color of wet cement, grey and cold, and they don't fly far at all. Sort of like June Birch is already a little bit dead inside. Like she doesn't have much to live for.

"Yeah," Addy answers.

"Today's your pay day, ain't it?"

He nods and walks to the front door, already tired of the conversation.

"I was thinking," his mother continues, "that since you're working more, maybe you oughta consider puttin' a bigger chunk of that paycheck toward our rent. Think you could do that, baby? To help make ends meet?"

"Sure," Addy says with a shrug. His fingers find the knob, grip it hard, turn it to the right.

"You know I love you, right?"

The words ignite a fire in his stomach that spreads to his chest. The heat of it burns his throat. "Right," he mutters without turning around. "I've gotta go." And he pushes outside, down the stairs, taking in great gulps of the morning's humid air in an effort to eliminate the taste of bile mixed with ashes that lingers in his mouth.

Addy's feet guide him across the yard, onto the sidewalk, down the street. As they pound the pavement, some of the anger he feels toward his mother begins to dissipate. Not all of it, of course; it will never completely vanish because the well that holds it is too deep. He will never forget the night of his high school graduation, when he returned home with a wedge of stolen Manchego to find his mother passed out on the couch, an unfamiliar man sprawled beside her and a half-empty bottle of tequila on the coffee table. She'd stirred groggily as Addy had passed through, lifting lids heavy with mascara and blinking several times to bring him into focus. "How was it, baby?" she had asked. And then, not really caring to hear the answer, had continued, "I'm sorry I couldn't make it. The big boss offered me some extra hours and we need the money, so…" She'd hiccupped, offered up a drunken smile, tilted her head to the side. "You look so handsome," June Birch had cooed. "My handsome baby boy, all growed up."

The memory of it results in a wave of fresh rage. It spills over him, clouding his vision and tingeing everything with red. Addy quickens his pace until he's actually jogging, running away from that moment that continues to live in both the past and the present. Fury fuels his step. It makes his chest heave and his heart race and his head pound, and when he finally turns onto Railroad Street, he's literally gasping for air. Gasping for hope.

Addy stops, bends at the waist, rests his hands on his knees, panting. There's a sob stuck in his throat, threatening to escape. He swallows hard, forcing it downward, and keeps doing this until some of the anger melts away. It drips off of him like rain, puddling at his feet, draining back into that well of outrage and animosity to be stored until the next flood of emotion. And then when he feels that he can face his life for at least a little while longer, Addy stands, wipes his forehead with the back of his hand, and takes a step forward.

The diner is located on a tree-lined road just off the main drag. Although one might consider the atmosphere halfway decent during the day, it turns into a real cesspool at night. The drunkards roll in around two, shortly after the bars have declared last call for alcohol and deadbolted their doors. They tumble into booths, noisily perusing laminated menus and ordering things like scrambled eggs doused in hot sauce, or French fries smothered in melted cheddar cheese. At that hour, with an abundance of booze in their bellies and a night of blurred memories in their heads, even the food that the diner has to offer ends up tasting pretty decent. Sometimes the tips are good because the customer's too bleary-eyed to know whether he's leaving a handful of ones or a handful of tens, but most often employees make out better serving lunch to the sober folks who wander in. That's the shift Addy's scheduled to work today. He's approaching the diner, which is constructed from a retired train car, when Gabe Wynne barrels down the steps. "Hey!" he exclaims, noticing Addy right away. "I was just in there looking for you!"

"Oh, yeah?"

Gabe nods once in that matter-of-fact manner of his. "Yeah. What are you doing two weeks from today? In the evening? That's, like, the second Friday in August, I think."

"Probably working," Addy answers. "Why?"

"The Franklins are hosting an almost-end-of-summer bonfire. Want to come? There'll be s'mores."

"Maybe. It'll depend on my hours."

Flecks of copper explode from Gabe's skin as he stands there, not saying anything for a long minute as he fixes his friend with a look of concern. He has serious eyes and it's hard to imagine what he might be thinking, but after a while he asks, pointblank, "Are you okay?"

"I'm fine," Addy responds too quickly. "Just tired. I've been working a lot lately."

Gabe wears an expression of skepticism, but says nothing, so Addy continues, "I'll let you know about the party. I promise." And because accepting this answer is really the only option, that's exactly what Gabe ends up doing.

If July was hot, then August is a sauna. The air seems thicker than it ought to be and lightning dances in the sky almost every night, summoning low rumbles of thunder and occasionally fast-moving sheets of rain. Lawns turn brown, the diner adds peach pie to its dessert menu (which admittedly isn't very good), and local shops advertise back-to-school sales in their front windows. Each time Addy passes by Whirligigs and Whatnots' display of notepads and number-two pencils, or the shoe store's exhibit of new sneakers, he feels a little pang of sadness. There will be no return to Lake Caywood High in the weeks to come; the only thing Addy has to look forward to is long shifts at the diner.

Even now, at eight o'clock in the evening with just the *hint* of a full moon taking shape in the sky, the air is sticky and damp. The humidity has taken up residence in the town, quiet and motionless, like a stubborn fog that refuses to clear out.

Addy scuffs down the sidewalk, moving as fast as he dares through the saturated atmosphere, hands tucked deep into a pair of black slacks. In his pocket he can feel a handful of coins and a bundle of bills, mostly with George Washington's face on them: thirty-two dollars and seventy-three cents. A slow day at the diner makes for a long day at the diner, especially when there's nothing to show for it when quitting time rolls around.

By this time, Lydia Franklin's party is in full swing. Gabe dropped by earlier today to provide a reminder—"It starts at six, but show up whenever"—and Addy promised to *try* to make an appearance, but that was really just a polite way of declining the invitation. Everyone in attendance will either be moving into a senior year of high school or a freshman year of college, not stuck in neutral, working shitty hours and earning lousy tips at a dead-end job. The disconnect that Addy feels from the kids with whom he's spent the last twelve years of his life is surreal; as much as he'd love to swap Mr. Coleman stories while toasting marshmallows around a bonfire, he knows that's not his life anymore. It never was, if he's being honest with himself, and so he heads to Main Street Market instead, opting to spend his evening among exotic spices and fancy extracts rather than former classmates. He whistles as he makes his way downtown.

Even as a kid, Addy loved the grocery store. Not when his mother would take him, dragging him down the aisles with all the prepackaged foods, like Hamburger Helper and Chef Boyardee and chicken noodle soup in a can. Those visits weren't especially fun because all forms of creativity were frowned upon. But when Charley took him? Well, that was fun. They'd plan a menu ahead of time, choosing tastes *and* colors that would compliment one another on a plate, and then they'd make a list. Charley showed him how to map it out like the store, so that produce appeared at the top and frozen foods, like ice cream, didn't appear until the end. "If you follow the store's layout," she'd explained, "then there's no need to be constantly backtracking. Make sense?"

It had, and in addition to teaching Addy how to construct a logical list, Charley had also taught him that overripe bananas are best for baking, purple beans turn green once they're cooked, and plain Greek yogurt adds a tang that sour cream doesn't. She'd educated him on the differences between condensed milk and evaporated milk, introduced him to gnocchi, and taught him to appreciate the fishy flavor of salmon. Had Charley not come into his life, Addy might not have known the power of pesto—or that pine nuts *do* make all the difference, even if walnuts are a cheap alternative.

He'd made pesto the other week, in fact, with a pouch of pine nuts that he'd swiped from the baking aisle. At ten dollars per pack, he had no intention of actually buying them, but they'd fit neatly into his pocket and so he'd taken them.

One packet.

It had been just enough to make him feel something other than anger.

Addy pretends to consider store-brand cinnamon versus McCormick cinnamon, but what he's really thinking about is the price of saffron: almost twenty dollars for a few grams. He studies the orange-red powder from the corner of his eye, wondering if the container will slide easily into his pocket or if it might fit more comfortably in his knapsack. The bag is how he'd secured two pounds of frozen shrimp just last week, and no one had noticed when he executed that particular stunt, so it seems unlikely that a tiny jar of saffron will arouse suspicion. He needs it for a paella recipe he's been eager to try…

Addy looks left, then right. There's an elderly gentleman at the other end of the aisle, thoroughly studying the coffee selection, but other than that he's alone. He reaches for the cinnamon, hesitates, and then before he can change his mind, swiftly snatches the saffron instead and slips it into his pocket. A quick glance over his shoulder offers assurance that the old man saw nothing, and with an almost-cocky confidence in his step, Addy makes his way to the front of the store. He whistles an upbeat tune, so softly that no one other than Addy can hear it.

He's still whistling as he steps into the warm night, but stops rather abruptly when he notices the police officer leaning against a black and white patrol car. "Going somewhere?" the officer asks. "Let me give you a ride."

14.
Juli

The cowbell clanks, copper against glass, and Eileen looks up from her stance at the register. "Must be hot out there," she says, eyeing my bare legs. "I probably don't need more than five fingers to count the number of times I've seen you in shorts."

"I wear shorts," I counter, "just not usually when I'm working."

"So you're not working today?"

"No, I am," I admit, "but it's already, like, a hundred degrees in the shade and it's not even noon yet. Denim on a day like today would likely cause heat stroke." I give her a smug smile, tuck my hands into the deep pockets of my cargo shorts, and jangle my keys as I walk down the hardware aisle. It's lined with various bins of hooks and fasteners and hinges, all of them shiny and metallic.

Brackets are why I'm here. Lucy Campbell called me last Thursday to ask if I might have time to install some floating shelves in her pottery shop on Main Street. I'd told her sure, and promised to complete the task in the very near future, but time had somehow slipped away from me. Now here it is more than a week after the fact and I haven't even purchased the hardware. I sigh, settle on some brushed-nickel brackets that'll support shelves up to a foot deep, and slide ten of them from the metal arm on which they're looped. Then I head back to the front counter to purchase the goods.

Eileen is not alone at the register. I don't notice her four-legged companion right away because he's curled behind a bag of charcoal briquettes, but his emission of a singsong-like mew does make me glance sideways. He blinks his yellow-green eyes, lazily licks a front paw, and squints up at me. "Hi," I say, extending a hand for examination. "Who are you?"

The black cat considers my offering before giving it a good sniff. He must deem me an uninteresting non-threat because following the inspection, he tucks his head back into his chest, covers his nose with a furry arm, and returns to his nap.

"That's Robert," Eileen informs me, running a hand down the cat's curled form. "He moved in a few days ago. A real sweetheart, but I think he's depressed. His owner died—I don't know the details—but that's why he was at the shelter. He's interested in sleeping… and that's about it. Not even food gets him excited."

"But he *is* eating?" I confirm.

Eileen nods. "He likes that flaked fish and shrimp stuff that Fancy Feast makes, but turns his nose up at everything else." She shrugs, concluding, "It'll get better. He's grieving, and grieving takes time. Is this all you need today? Just some brackets?"

"Yep, that's it." I reach behind the bag of charcoal to give Robert's head a quick pet. He flicks an ear, but that's about his only response. He does not purr. "Poor guy," I mutter. "He does seem sad."

"He'll be okay," Eileen assures me, passing a bag of brackets and twenty-three cents worth of change over the counter. "I fully intend to spoil him rotten. My husband carries him around every chance he gets, if you can believe it… cradling Robert like a baby. The man claims to be a dog person, but I'm not so sure anymore."

The image of Hank with the cat in his arms, uttering soft cooing sounds while rocking him to sleep like an infant, suddenly pops into my head. I stifle a laugh and head to the door. "Thanks, Eileen," I say over my shoulder.

"Stay cool, Juli!" she calls after me.

This proves to be a challenge. Despite cracking the windows, sitting in the truck is equivalent to taking a steam bath, and the air conditioner struggles to produce even a mildly cool breeze. Hot air pours out of the vents; it might be moving, but it's not refreshing. Everything feels damp, as if it's been misted by the spray of a hose. The back of my neck is sticky, the cotton fabric of my shirt clings to my skin, and I can feel droplets of sweat forming behind my knees and sliding down my calves. A cold shower would feel great right now. So would a dip in the lake. Heck, at this point I'd settle for the chilled air from an open refrigerator spilling over me, but instead I sit in my sweltering vehicle and drive it straight down Main Street to the opposite end of town, where the sidewalk literally ends.

Lake Caywood's very first post office existed on the outskirts of town, not among the general hubbub that occurred on or around the square as one might assume. I'm not sure why this was—I've never thought to research it or anything—but I do know that a new post office was eventually erected in a more central location. The original structure has since been bought and sold many times, housing everything from ice cream parlors to bike shops, but nothing seemed to stick until Lucy Campbell purchased the property and turned it into a pottery studio. She calls it Simply Clay, because that's her medium of choice, and she seems to do alright selling her creations to the locals. Of course, she will periodically host an event like Wine at the Wheel. It may sound like a bad idea, but the "wheel" in reference isn't a steering wheel: it's a pottery wheel. Lucy teaches people how to throw pots while providing them with a glass or two of wine. I attended a class one time; my mom ended up with a pretty decent salad bowl afterward.

Although a giant magnolia tree does tower over Simply Clay, the small building is mostly surrounded by redbuds. They explode with color in the early spring. A flagstone pathway leads from the sidewalk to the porch, which is dotted with various containers (all handmade by Lucy) and potted with shade-loving plants. Hardy hostas sprout from the front beds, their large variegated leaves dimpled and leathery, their long-stemmed flowers slanting away from the porch rail.

There's a kiln around back, which is most often used for firing clay, but has on occasion been utilized as a pizza oven. I know this for a fact, since I'm lucky enough to be among the intimate group of people who receive invitations to the small and impromptu gatherings that Lucy and her boyfriend, Bas, sometimes host. The events are rare, but always fun, and often end up occurring in the backyard of Simply Clay rather than at the couple's home. It's quieter here, I suppose. More secluded. Many an evening has been passed on that private patio… Dining on brick-oven pizza, nursing really good beer, and singing along to whatever song ends up being strummed next. This particular summer has been void of those backyard jam sessions, but that's to be expected. The band's been on tour. And besides, I've had other things to occupy my time.

I park my truck beside the last bit of sidewalk, swing the door open, and hop out. The air here is still hot, but it's somehow not *as* hot. I chalk it up to the trees and the shade and head up the walk to the studio, swinging my toolbox beside me.

Once natural wood, the shop's vertical siding has since been painted a pale shade of grey and the front door a brilliant aqua. The trim is dark teal—Lucy's favorite color—and so is the front porch. I've always thought that Simply Clay would look just as at home at the beach as it does in the woods of Lake Caywood.

I step inside, thrilled to find that the air is approximately twenty degrees cooler than it is outside, and smile at Lucy. "Hey," I greet her. "Sorry it's taken me forever to get out here. Tell me where you want these shelves."

"Your timing is incredible," she laughs, and gives me a big smile. "I've literally spent the last fifteen minutes walking around the shop, trying to determine how to incorporate these new pieces into already-existing displays. It can't look cluttered, you know?" She's holding a mug in one hand and a platter in the other, and she uses them to motion to a long wall of floor-to-ceiling bookcases. The shelves are already lined with bowls and pitchers and teapots; I can understand why she's having trouble finding room for new additions.

"I get it," I say. "So are you thinking that the shelves will go here?" I move across the room to a canvas of empty wall space. A narrow wooden table has been pushed snug against it and topped with a medley of different pots: some are tall and thin, others are short and fat. The colors range from speckled blue, like a robin's egg, to the warm reddish-brown of steeped tea, to that yellow-green hue that only appears in nature as the grass and the flowers resurface after a long winter. The pots vary in patterns, too. Many of them are two-toned, one glaze dripping over another, while others are solid and etched with viny patterns that curl around curved surfaces.

More pottery can be found under the table. I'm especially drawn to a tall planter painted with a vibrant red glaze that bleeds to teal. It's approximately three feet high and would look pretty neat if some of those giant-leafed coleus that my ma likes to grow were sprouting inside it.

Just as much as the giant pot, though, I appreciate the life-sized jack-o-lantern to its left. It sports a jagged grin and skinny triangles for its eyes and nose. Lucy's placed a candle inside and it flickers, illuminating the shifty expression, and rather than a stem, the pumpkin wears a top hat upon its head. "That's fun," I acknowledge, pointing to the Halloween artwork. "I like that."

"Yeah?" Lucy seems pleased. "I'm trying something new this year. We'll see if they sell." She relocates the platter and mug that she's been holding, setting them beside the register so that she can pull her loose blonde hair into a sloppy ponytail. It's short enough that only about seventy-five percent of it stays in place; the rest executes an immediate escape. "I'm actually thinking of displaying plates on this wall," she informs me, "and if you have time, I might ask you to help with that task, too?"

"Sure."

"I'd like to put the shelves behind the counter."

I follow her gaze, considering the back wall. Five floating shelves, staggered, would actually look pretty good there. Especially when Lucy shares that the model she's chosen has hooks attached to the bottom. "For mugs," she explains. "Let me run to the back and grab them."

"Do you need any help?" I call after her, but she simply waves a hand to indicate that she doesn't. I walk to the register, setting my bag of brackets on the counter and my toolbox on the floor. I can hear Lucy rummaging around in the storage room, shifting boxes in order to unearth the shelves she purchased several weeks ago. There's not much for me to do until she returns, so I pick up today's newspaper and skim over the front page. There are plans for the local swimming pool to be resurfaced this fall; Lake Caywood High School has hired a new cross country coach, so a get-to-know-you piece is featured; and the Marina will be hosting a Labor

Day celebration—complete with fireworks—that the entire town is invited to attend. I fold back the front page and peruse the inside information, briefing myself on local goings-on and upcoming events, not especially interested in any of it until I skim a succinct report found beneath the heading of "Police and Fire." It reads:

> At 9:03 p.m. on Friday, police arrested Addison Birch, 18, 97 Blackstone Dr., Apt. 1, Lake Caywood, and charged him with shoplifting by asportation. Police made the arrest at Main Street Market.

Today is Wednesday; Addy was arrested on Friday. Since Charley doesn't get the *Lake Caywood Times*, I can't imagine that she's aware of any of this, and I hate that I will most likely be the one to break the news to her.

"Anything exciting?" Lucy asks, emerging from the back. She's carrying a stack of five slim boards, each painted a different shade of grey, which I quickly move to assist her with. She continues, "I figured that if the top story is the resurfacing of the pool, then there can't really be *that* much to report, but I haven't read past the front page. What do you think of the shelves?"

I'd been expecting them to be packaged in cardboard, purchased from someplace like Lowe's or the Home Depot, but the ledges appear to be handcrafted. "They look great," I say. "Did you make them?"

"Nol's boyfriend did," Lucy explains.

Nol—short for Magnolia—is Lucy's boyfriend's almost-sister. She would have been his stepsister if the marriage between Nol's mother and Sebastian's father hadn't fallen apart at the last minute, but I suppose that's just how life goes sometimes. Despite the botched relationship between their parents, Bas and Nol have remained close. "How is Nol?" I wonder, positioning one of the shelves and looking to Lucy for approval.

"Oh, she's fine. Move it to the left a little."

I obey, asking while I do, "And what's Bas up to?"

"That's good. Mount that one there." She hands me a pencil so I can mark the location. Then she continues, "Bas is touring. He and the band are in Germany right now. They started in Asia, bounced around there for a while, and now they're traveling through Europe. I feel like I haven't seen him in *ages*."

"Because you probably haven't. When will he get back?"

"September second, and then he's home for at least a month." She smiles when she says this, obviously excited about the upcoming reunion. I can't imagine what it must be like to be in a serious relationship that only enables you to see your significant other in spurts, but it's a lifestyle that Lucy and Sebastian have managed to perfect; they've been together for as long as I can remember. "What about you?" she asks now. "Are the rumors true?"

I raise my eyebrows. "What rumors?"

"You and Charley Lane?"

"Where'd you hear that?"

Lucy laughs. "From your mom. And from your roommate."

"He's more of a tenant," I say around a screw that I'm holding between my lips. "I could never actually *live* with Asher. He'd drive me nuts. He *does* drive me nuts."

"And yet, isn't he your best friend?"

I'm quiet while I drill one of the brackets into place, considering the question. There was a time when I would have answered with an exuberant "Yeah!"—back when Asher and I shared the weekly routine of splitting a pitcher or two at the Tavern every Friday night, and got together on Wednesday evenings to make fancy grilled cheese sandwiches in his upstairs apartment, and just generally spent more time together… But the truth is, we've drifted apart.

"I don't know," I confide to Lucy, shrugging. "I guess."

She narrows her eyes at me. I can feel them boring into the back of my head. Eventually she says, "I like Asher—I really do—but he's a bit of a numskull," which makes me laugh. "He is!" she insists. "How old is he? Thirty-five?"

"Thirty-six."

"Well, he acts like he's in his early- to mid-twenties. Everyone around him is settling into their lives, moving forward and maturing and growing as individuals, and he's somehow managed to come to a complete standstill. He needs to wake up to the fact that he's not a kid anymore. He needs to grow up."

"I don't disagree," I say, because Lucy has pretty much hit the nail on the head. "You're right: Asher is, indeed, a numskull."

"I'm sorry," she apologizes. "I know the two of you are close."

I hang the first shelf, double-checking to make sure it's level, before I speak. Then I offer, "But that's just it… We're really not that close anymore. Not like we used to be. And, I mean, if I had to label someone as my best friend these days, it'd probably be Charley."

"So the rumors *are* true," Lucy muses.

"We're not dating," I tell her. "Not officially."

Lucy picks up the platter that she'd set on the counter a while ago, carrying it to the other side of the room. Over her shoulder she contributes, "But you should be. If she's your best friend, then you really should be."

"What are you saying about me and Charley?"

"Charley and me," my mother corrects. "And not much, seeing as I've never met her. Why?"

"Nothing. Never mind."

We are at the Tavern, sitting across from one another at a tall booth, but now Ma lowers her menu and fixes me with an expression of intrigue. "What is it that you *think* I'm saying about you and Charley?"

"That we're together?"

"Well, you *are* together a lot of the time," my mother smartly acknowledges.

"Together-together," I elaborate. "Like, dating." It seems unnecessary to mention Lucy's name since I'm not the least bit angry. Just curious.

Ma goes back to the menu. "I think I'll just get a salad. It's almost too hot to eat."

I cannot imagine ever ordering a salad as an entrée when out to eat at a restaurant. If my meal comes with a side salad, I'll pick at it, but that's about it. Give me a burger and fries any day. "So you're not spreading rumors?"

"About you and Charley?" Ma verifies. "I don't think so. I did mention to Lucy Campbell that you've been seeing a lot of her lately since you're renovating that old farmhouse, and that she seems to make you very happy, but I can assure you that the word 'dating' was never used." I roll my eyes, but my mother doesn't notice. Instead, she wonders, "When will I get to meet her?"

"I don't know. How's the second Saturday in October?"

She knits her brows. "What's happening the second Saturday in October?"

Before I have a chance to respond, Petey is standing at the end of the booth, smiling wide, clutching a pen and a notepad and ready to take our orders. "Have you two decided?" he asks. "I can come back if you need more time."

"No, I think we're ready," Ma says. "I'll have a cup of gazpacho and the chicken Caesar salad."

"And I'll have the mushroom-and-Swiss burger with sweet potato fries."

"Good choice," Petey praises, jotting it down. "Hey, what're you doing this Friday? Jenny and I are playing at Bottomless Joe's if you want to check it out. Show starts at seven. We'll just be doing covers and stuff."

"Sounds fun. I'll see what Charley's up to. Maybe we'll make an appearance."

"Great! Have you talked to her yet today?"

I can feel Ma's gaze on me, but I ignore it. "Nah, not yet. I'm going out there after lunch, though. Why? What's up?"

"She and I bottled some *really* good beer last night. You've gotta try it."

"The pumpkin ale?"

"Nope. That's not quite ready yet, but it will be for opening weekend. The one we bottled last night is an IPA with a hint of nectarine. Super tasty."

"Really?" I don't verbalize it, but that particular combination of flavors does not sound very appetizing. Petey is furiously bobbing his head up and down, though, so I agree to sample it later and text him my honest opinion of the concoction. Satisfied with this promise, he disappears to place our orders and I turn my attention back to my mother. "Opening weekend?" she says before I have a chance to comment on it. "Is *that* what's happening the second Saturday in October?" There's excitement in her tone.

"Yep," I inform her. "Mark it on your calendar."

I don't tell Charley the news about Addy right away. She's in such a good mood when I arrive, having just returned from Whirligigs and Whatnots with a huge stack of newly framed artwork, and she enthusiastically leads me by the hand around the entire first floor, debating where to hang what and rationalizing why. Every now and again I'll provide my two cents, but mostly I just let her gush.

"So do you think that I *should* hang the bicycle artwork?" she asks upon the conclusion of the tour. "Or not?"

"Hang it," I say. "It's a cool piece. Who cares if you don't know the artist? It's got you as the subject, and I can't think of a more pertinent subject to grace the walls of this farmhouse. So go for it."

Charley stands on her tiptoes and gives me a quick peck on the cheek. "Okay. That's what I'll do. Want to help me hang all of these?" She waves a hand at the many paintings that line the perimeter of the living room, propped up against the walls, early-afternoon sunshine glinting off their new glass fronts.

"I was going to start on the exterior stuff," I inform her, thinking of the crooked shutters hanging on the front of the house. Now that a date has been set for the grand opening, the stress of completing the renovation has me feeling more than a little on-edge. Charley widens her eyes and gawks at my words, though. "You can't work outside," she insists. "It's close to a hundred degrees! Stay in here where it's air-conditioned."

"All of the inside stuff is done, though," I point out. "On this floor, anyway, and I'm not really too concerned with the upstairs at this point in time. I am, however, eager to get the siding painted and the shutters painted and re-hung. So… that's what I'm going to do."

"But it's close to a hundred degrees!" she reiterates.

I give her a sideways smile, but shake my head to let her know that my mind is already made up. "I'll drink plenty of water," I promise, "and then when I'm done, you and I can try some of that nectarine IPA that Petey brewed."

"The Fuzzless Hopper!" Charley exclaims. "I've already tried it, and it's delicious!"

"The Fuzzless Hopper?" I confirm. "Were you guys drunk when you came up with that?"

"Maybe a little…"

I roll my eyes and leave the living room, choosing to visit the kitchen's newest addition: a stainless-steel, commercial-grade refrigerator that currently contains several varieties of nonalcoholic beverages, an assortment of homebrewed beer, and a few basic necessities for everyday cooking. "What're you going to do once the Brewhaha opens?" I ask, retrieving a bottle of water from the top shelf. "Always eat dinner at the bar?"

Charley shrugs. "I don't know. I haven't really thought about it."

Her answer surprises me. I'm not one for spending a lot of time in the kitchen, but I don't think that I'd much care to cohabitate with my staff and customers day in and day out. A small area upstairs—even if it weren't to contain much more than a sink, microwave, and mini fridge—would help somewhat. If it were me, though, I'd rent my own place off the premises. I doubt that I'd want to always be at work; having Asher as a tenant is quite enough. "You seriously haven't thought about it?"

She shakes her head. "Not really, no. I've been much too busy thinking about other things."

"Like…?"

"Hiring a staff."

"Oh. I guess you will be needing one of those."

"Yep, I sure will." Charley bites her bottom lip, suddenly looking worried, and so I walk over to her and place my hands on her shoulders. "Hey," I assure her, "this is all gonna work out the way it's supposed to. We can strategize the best way to find employees later, over chilled glasses of Fuzzless Hopper, but right now you're going to hang pictures and I'm going to hang shutters and progress is going to be made. Understood?"

"Understood," Charley whispers. "Just… drink a lot of water while you're out there. It's, like, almost a hundred degrees, you know?"

I obey Charley's order, guzzling water every chance I get, and although I probably down eight or nine bottles of the stuff, I don't stop to pee even once. I figure that I lose all the liquid I consume and then some in sweat alone; I'm dripping even in the shade cast by that old cherry tree out front. Generally speaking, when I'm on the clock, no matter how hot it is, my shirt stays on. Today is the exception. I tolerate the damp cotton glued to my back for almost an hour, but by two o'clock I'm down to my shorts and sneakers. Flecks of the structure's once-brilliant white paint flake off and stick to my chest and forearms, speckling my skin. It takes forever; I scale the house again and again, removing shutters, unscrewing rusty hardware, repositioning the ladder, climbing back up. When I feel too lightheaded to focus, I sit on the porch steps and rest my head against my knees, but my goal is to have every one of the house's shutters in the barn, a first coat of paint sprayed and drying on them, before calling it quits for the day.

It takes until a quarter to six, which is coincidentally when Charley finds me in the barn and announces that she's ordered a pizza. "Mushroom and extra cheese. It'll be here in half an hour. Want me to hose you down, or would you rather take a shower?"

"Both options sound great right about now," I confide, "but I could definitely benefit from some soap."

"I agree," she says, wrinkling her nose as she approaches. "You smell awful." Her unbelievably green eyes meet mine, but they don't stay there for very long. I watch her gaze drift downward, scanning my bare chest, lingering on my bellybutton, and then finally traveling all the way to my feet. On the way back up, she stares hard at my left knee and observes, "Is that a seven?"

"Yep."

"What happened?"

"Sliced it with a circular saw."

"Ouch," she winces, and then wonders, "Do they all coincide with power tool injuries?"

"Nah, not all of 'em. Like this one on my back? Number three?" I turn so that she can see the faint burn that mars the skin near my waist. "Camping accident. One of my buddies was pissed that I drank the last beer, so he threw an on-fire marshmallow at me. I wasn't wearing a shirt, so it left a mark."

"Is he still your buddy?" Charley wants to know, and I shake my head. "Not so much, no. We sort of lost touch after college."

This answer seems to please her. She turns her attention from the tiny tattooed *3* to the shutters drying on the ground and squats to examine my hard work. The airy dress that she's wearing falls a couple of inches above her knees, billowing around her as she bends down. "These turned out nicely. I like the color. Do you?"

At first, I hadn't. Charley ended up choosing a deep red, the color of pomegranate seeds, and I'd originally thought it would look funny with the farmhouse's copper roof, which oxidized a long time ago. It's now reminiscent of the Statue of Liberty, not of shiny one-cent coins. With the building's white siding, I'd had some concerns that the place might appear entirely too Christmassy, but now that the shutters have been sprayed and I can view the paint's hue on a larger scale, I'm beginning to understand why Charley chose it. "I do," I respond in answer to her question. "I didn't think I was going to, but I do."

She smiles, exposing a row of perfect teeth, and I suddenly want more than anything to kiss her. "Hold your breath," I instruct. "Just for a minute."

"Why?"

"Because I smell like an old gym sock, but I really want to give you a kiss."

Charley crinkles her nose, feigning disgust, but then she puckers her lips and says, "Make it fast."

I laugh, lean in, press my lips firmly against hers, and even though she's crazy to do it, I feel her reach up with both hands and grip the sides of my face, running her fingers through my sopping hair. Then she pulls away, shakes my sweat from her fingers, and says, "I need to wash my hands, and you *really* need a shower. Come on."

Living in Lake Caywood, I've gotten into the habit of always keeping a pair of swim trunks and a change of fresh clothes in my car. I grab some shorts and a shirt on the way to the house, and then head upstairs (since the first-floor tub has been planted with ferns...) for a much-needed scrub down. "Give me ten minutes," I tell Charley, "and have that beer ready to go when I get back."

"I will!" she assures me. "I promise!"

The mushroom-and-extra-cheese pizza is from Luigi's, which is where I order my pies most of the time, but for some reason tonight's meal tastes better than ever before. We eat it in the kitchen, perched on high stools at the giant oak table, because despite the fact that the sun is in the process of settling in for the night, the air is still holding moisture like a sponge.

Charley feels strongly about bars having signature glasses. I warned her that this will likely result in thievery among customers, but she insisted and placed an order with an online company. The shipment arrived last week; we're breaking in the glasses tonight. Admittedly, the design is clever: a tree of life, with roots that run deep and all sorts of fruit—apples, pears, peaches, plums, cherries—hanging from the branches. The word Brewhaha appears beneath the tree, arching with the roots to form a subtle smile. "You like it?" Charley asks, watching me study the glass.

"It's a cool design."

"Do you like the *beer*, Juli?"

"Oh! Sorry. Yes, I do like the beer, very much. Fuzzless Hopper. It's better than expected."

Charley takes a sip and a hint of froth lingers on her lip like a thin mustache. "It's delicious," she states. "Just admit it."

"Fine," I agree. "It's delicious." I lift another slice of pizza from the box, threads of cheese stretching like rubber bands across the lip of my plate, and ponder how to introduce the next topic of discussion. It's not something I want to talk about, but Charley needs to hear the news about Addy from someone and it might as well be me. She reads the change in my mood immediately, lowers her glass to observe, "You're abruptly distant. Why are you abruptly distant? What are you thinking about?"

"Addy," I admit. It seems pointless to beat around the bush.

"Addy Birch?"

"Yeah."

She stares at me with those deep emerald eyes, her pizza and beer momentarily forgotten. "What about him? Is he okay?"

I glance at the table, back up to her, off to the side. "Not really," I say. "He's gotten himself into some trouble." And then I tell her about what was printed in the newspaper, and share the very few details to which I'm privy, and squeeze her tight while tears of frustration stream down her cheeks. "What is he *doing*?" she asks over and over again. "What is he doing with his *life*?" But it's not a question that I can answer. I can only hold her while she works through the anger and disappointment that she's feeling.

15.

Charley

The brain is a funny thing. How it can process and rationalize and make sense of situations just so that it can live in harmony with what the heart wants…

A year ago, I probably would have taken some time to consider Addy's arrest, and why it happened, and whether or not getting involved is the right decision. But time is fleeting. It doesn't grow on trees and it doesn't stop when the hands of a clock come to a standstill. Once time passes, it's gone for good, so I allow a solid twenty-four hours and not a minute more between hearing the news and taking action.

Considering how often June Birch jumps from one job to the next, and the frequency at which she invites new men to share her bed, it's pretty surprising that she and Addy haven't moved away from Blackstone Drive. I conferred with the newspaper, though: they're still living in the same shabby first-floor apartment that they were in ten years ago, with the screen door that sticks and the drafty windows that have never quite closed and the thorny, overgrown bushes out front. The paint is dingier than I remember, the shutters more crooked, and while this place, like the farmhouse, has experienced years of neglect, the damage extends beyond loose shingles and squeaky hinges and clogged drains. This damage stems from an absence of love, and that's something in which the farmhouse never lacked. That's something that *no home* should ever lack… but Addy grew up without it.

I stand on the sidewalk for a minute, catching my breath and thinking about what I might say. I haven't written a script or run through a multitude of different scenarios in my mind; I haven't mapped out my words past "hello." I've only thought far enough ahead to get me to this point in time:

alone, outside Addy's apartment, the sky an odd blend of orange and purple as the sun disappears on yet another day. I inhale deeply, lift one foot off the ground, step firmly onto the front lawn. My flip-flopped feet carry me across the grass, overly shaggy, tickling my bare toes. At the door I knock once, loudly, and take a step back, waiting. My heart taps the beat to a fast tempo, the rhythm pounding in my head, and it occurs to me that I'm surviving on the same breath that was taken on the sidewalk. I replenish my lungs with fresh oxygen, wipe my sweaty palms against my jeans, and then cross my arms for something to do while I wait.

It's possible that he's not home; he could be working a shift at the diner or out with friends. But as I'm in the midst of wondering these things, the door swings open and Addy appears on the other side of the screen. His hair is rumpled, his cheeks shadowed by several days of scruff. He wears a wrinkled undershirt and dark, baggy jeans and when he sees me, his eyes narrow to dark slits, meeting my gaze for a moment before sliding downward to linger at my feet. "Hey," he mutters, propping the door open with his foot and directing his words at the ground rather than at me. "I'm guessing you heard."

"I did."

"And?"

"And I'm wondering why? Why'd you do it?"

He shrugs, still staring at the ground. A story behind the story isn't volunteered. His lips stay sealed; his gaze remains averted.

"So that's it?" I prompt. "That's all I get? No explanation; just a slump of your shoulders? You can't even look at me?" Anger quickens my heartbeat until it's thumping like a jackhammer. Fire courses through my veins, singeing the tips of my fingers and burning my cheeks. When I speak, my words are louder than I expect them to be: "What is going on with you? You're *better than that,* Addy. You are so much *better than that!*"

And now he looks up. Now his eyes find mine and hold the position, his glare filled with rage. "I'm better than that?" he whispers, but he might as well be shouting. "How the fuck would you know? You *left,* Charley. You *left.* That day I broke my arm. Remember? Because *I* sure do. It was June sixteenth, and it was hotter than hell, and I fell out of that tree, and you—"

"You don't know the whole story," I interrupt, but Addy cuts me off.

"YOU LEFT ME AT THE HOSPITAL!" He screams it, his fury punctuated by little specks of spittle that collect in the corners of his mouth. "You left me at the hospital, and then you left for good, and you never once thought to say goodbye! And do you know what I was stuck with?"

"Addy!"

"*No!*" he insists, shaking his head once, very quickly. "I need to say this. Do you *know* what I was stuck with? Do you remember?"

I swallow, forcing the truth into my stomach so that it may lie dormant for a while longer. Addy's eyes, cold and grey, brim with tears. Frustration, fury, pain. He's feeling all of it. "No," I admit to him. "I don't."

"Your name on my cast," he grimaces. "I was left with your goddamn name on my *cast*."

"I'm sorry," I offer, but Addy ignores the apology, choosing to pretend that I haven't spoken. Or perhaps he's so lost in his memory that my words have truly fallen on deaf ears. A tear slides down his cheek, leaving a saltwater trail that he quickly wipes away. "C-H-A-R-L-E-Y," he whispers, tracing an invisible tattoo on his forearm. "I wore it there for six weeks, wondering when you would call, or write, or just show up. I used to sit in the yard and wait, you know. For you or the mailman... whoever showed up first." He laughs, the sound bitter and flat, and then closes his eyes. "The mailman always won, but all he ever brought was bills."

"Addy..." I try again, but he's not ready to hear what I have to say.

"You could have written."

It's more accusation than statement, and it pummels me in the stomach with the force of a closed fist. I gulp air, fight back a sob, force myself to say, "And I should have."

"But you didn't." Addy looks at me, through me, seeing things that other people can't. "I've hated you for ten years, Charley Lane... but I've loved you for eighteen. And I don't know what to do with that. So... you want to know why I did it? Why I stole a twenty-dollar container of saffron and probably ruined my life in the process?"

I nod, cautiously, and he says, "I did it because I wanted to *feel* something. That's why. I'm tired of feeling angry all of the time, and I wanted to feel something different—something *better*—so I swiped a jar of saffron and I got caught." He blinks, almost smiles. "I was going to make paella."

The silence hangs heavy between us, providing us both with an opportunity to think. And as I stand there, twirling the infinity ring on the fourth finger of my right hand, I realize that what Addy needs is not the truth of the past, but rather the hope of a future. So this is what I offer: "You can make paella for me."

Addy rolls his eyes.

"For the Brewhaha, I mean. You can make whatever you want. I'll hire you as my lead chef."

"Really?" he scoffs, his tone saturated with skepticism. "Why would you do that?"

"Because I need a lead chef, and because you seem to know your way around the kitchen... and because it's probably the least I can do to make up for the fact that I abandoned you all those years ago. But it's mostly because I want to."

His eyes dart quickly away, and then back, tentatively holding my gaze. "You do?" he confirms, softening a bit. "And you'd be able to... to trust me? Even after...?"

I nod. "I have a few stipulations, though."

Addy scuffs his shoe against the door's threshold. "Like what?"

"Like you'll have to find a place of your own," I say, because I don't want June Birch taking more from him than she already has. "And you'll have to do some research on culinary programs, because I'll be expecting you to enroll in one for second semester. I'll help with the initial payments, for the apartment and for school, but then you've gotta start helping yourself. And if I find out that a chunk of your paycheck is going to your mom..." I look right at him, needing him to understand this. "I'll fire you, Addy."

I expect him to put up a fight, or to simply state that no child should be punished for supporting his own mother, but he surprises me by saying none of this. What he does do is stand up a little straighter, lift his head a bit higher, and ask, "When will you need me to start?"

∞

The beginning of a headache is curled at the base of my skull, throbbing dully but not yet making it impossible to function. I rummage in the Jeep's glove box for a prescription bottle that's kept there, finding it hidden behind an out-of-date roadmap. Green plastic with a childproof cap. The label has been peeled off—only sticky scabs of paper remain—but the pills inside are fresh. My doctor would instruct me to take two, but the accompanying side effect is severe drowsiness and I need to be alert for this next order of business. I study the container, considering my level of discomfort, and decide to wait. I opt for a quarter instead of the pills. That'll allot me enough time on the meter; I don't expect my visit to Duff's to last long.

It's not quite nine o'clock as I make my way down Baker's Alley to the back entrance. Despite the fact that Thirsty Thursday has no doubt already secured a substantial turnout at the Tavern, I don't expect more than a handful of deadbeats to be patronizing this shady establishment. There will be a few toothless drunkards, of course, slumped at the bar since early this afternoon, sipping Jim Beam and chain smoking Pall Malls and voicing opinions that aren't worth voicing. The men who frequent Duff's are the men who speak crudely of the opposite gender and ignorantly of local politics and negatively of anyone who may have favored a woman or an African American in a national election. These are men who will still be intoxicated twelve hours from now, stumbling home to sleep it off at a time when most people are groggily heading into the office, armed with leather briefcases and travel mugs of strong coffee. These are not men with whom I generally associate; they are, in fact, men I try to avoid. But I know that they will be at Duff's, and I expect that June Birch will be with them, and so I prepare myself for the atmosphere that exists on the other side of the warped, wooden door.

I have been to Duff's exactly once before: ten years ago, on a day every bit as hot as this one. I was eighteen, and Addy was seven-going-on-eight, and we'd gone to the orchard to gather ingredients for an upcoming birthday celebration. He'd requested blueberry pie and lemon ice cream, which at the time had seemed like a strange combination, but Noni'd insisted that the flavors would blend beautifully and had sent us out to pick berries while she ran into town for a few other necessities.

We filled a large basket with the plump, inky fruits; by the end of the day our fingertips were stained and Addy's teeth were purple rather than white. We stopped to cool our feet in the pond, talking and splashing and calling hellos to the bullfrogs hiding in the reeds, and then we'd cut through the peach grove on our way back to the house. I remember commenting on the plum tree, pointing to it and sharing that it's one of a kind, and Addy had stood a few feet from the gnarled trunk and turned his face skyward, squinting into leafy branches. "Are there plums up there now?"

"Green ones," I'd told him. "They're not ripe yet."

But he'd raised a hand to shield his eyes, not fully believing my words. "Are you sure?"

"Pretty sure. You can climb up and double check if you want to, though. Just be careful."

I'd relinquished the basket of berries and given him a boost, watching as he scampered lithely into the tree, navigating the treetop as only a child can. My job had been to spot from below, monitoring his movements and verbalizing caution when it seemed necessary, and after a short romp among the branches, Addy determined that I had been right: not a single plum was ready for harvest. So he'd started his descent. And everything would have been fine if I'd managed to catch him… but as he'd scrambled down the trunk, preparing to land in the soft grass at the tree's base, I realized that the likelihood of his feet colliding with the berries was high and so I bent to relocate the basket.

And that is when he fell.

It wasn't a tremendous tumble by any means—there were no initial tears—but when Addy clambered to his feet and found that his left arm insisted upon hanging limply at his side, panic ensued. I scooped him into my arms, abandoning the blueberries altogether, and buckled him into the backseat of my car.

Contrary to what I know now, my knowledge of hospitals was limited back then. I'd never broken a bone or undergone brain surgery or had my appendix removed; I'd never had my wisdom teeth taken out or sat with a friend while she'd received chemotherapy. But I did know enough to take Addy to the emergency room.

I knew *also* that June Birch should really be there to offer support.

When I called her place of employment, though, the manager explained that her shift had ended hours ago. And when the phone at ninety-seven Blackstone Drive continued to ring incessantly, the never-ending *brrrrriiinnngg!!* sounding shrilly in my ear, I realized that Addy's mother wasn't at home either. So after the doctor had molded a cast around Addy's arm, and after I'd procured a blue Sharpie and written my name on the dried plaster, I'd asked Carrie, the friendly nurse with the polka dot scrub top, what to do. And she had said that because I was not a family member, June Birch's presence was needed, and had promised to keep tabs on Addy while I did my best to find her.

Not until then did I leave, and I only left because I had to find Addy's mother. I'd never intended to stay away, though. That decision hadn't been mine to make; June Birch had made it for me.

I'd found her at Duff's, perched on a barstool and sipping a weak beer. The air was hazy with stale cigarette smoke and an old Loretta Lynn song played on the jukebox. June had draped her arm across the shoulders of a man sitting beside her. He looked like a stereotypical mechanic: dark blue Dickies smudged with grease, pale blue button-down shirt smeared with oil, big hands with black-rimmed nails... He might've been cute if he'd bothered to take a shower and clean himself up, but I can remember cringing as I approached from behind. If you didn't count the bartender, June and the mechanic had made up more than fifty-percent of the bar's population (it *was* only about two o'clock in the afternoon); the only other customer was an elderly gentleman with white hair and leathery skin and clothes from the seventies. He sat three seats away, gripping a tumbler of whiskey with both hands, his head ducked in a way that made me wonder if he was asleep.

I'd been scared, out of my element, and had kept my eyes trained on the back of June's head. She still hadn't noticed me, even when I stood directly behind her, and I had to clear my throat in order to capture her attention. "Excuse me, Ms. Birch?"

She'd turned then—just her head—and tried her best to bring me into focus. She blinked several times, her lashes caked with thick mascara and her lids smeared with pink shimmers, racking her brain for a name until one finally popped into her head: "Scharley," she'd slurred. "What're you doin' here? Where'sh my boy?"

"Addy's okay," I'd begun, "but he's at the hospital. He fell out of a tree and broke his—"

"He's *where*?" June had interrupted. "What're you sayin'? Addison's in the *hoshpital*? Why? What'd y'do to 'im?" And then she'd slapped the mechanic on the arm, causing some of his beer to slosh over the brim of the glass and onto the bar. "Are youse hearin' this?" she'd demanded. "My goddamn *babysitter* put my goddamn *kid* in the *hoshpital*! What the… what the fuck is wrong with you, Scharley?! What the *fuck*? I *trusted* you! I *trusted* you with my *baby*!"

"It's only a broken arm," I'd tried to explain. "Addy's fine. You just need to—"

"I'm *sorry*?" she'd cut me off. "Are you telling me what to do?"

I'd felt about two inches tall answering, "Well, the hospital needs you to—"

"Oh, no," June had said, waving her finger in my face. "You need to listen here, bitch, because you need to undershtand that *you* don't tell *me* what to *do*. And wanna know what else you don't do? You don't babysit my kid. That's what. So just… just get outta here. Get outta our lives. I never wanna see you again, Scharley Lane. Good riddance. And, and I'm warnin' you now: if you so much as *try* to contact him—if you even *try* to get a hold of *my* son—you'll regret it. I promish you that. I can *promish* you that."

I'd tried to reason with her, but June had been scary that night. Livid. She'd slid off the barstool, landing on her high-heeled feet, and tucked her clutch under her arm. "Never again," she'd repeated, and jabbed my chest with one of her manicured fingernails. "This right now is goodbye. Forever."

She'd left, presumably to visit the hospital, and I had left because it seemed like the only option. I was eighteen, and the mother of the person I cared most about had not only threatened me, but had told me pointblank to stay away from her child, and so I'd done the only thing that seemed to make any sense at all: I bid adieu to Lake Caywood and welcomed Ferris State with open arms and stepped into a new chapter of my life. And if someone had told me I'd be making a return trip to Duff's ten years later, in search of the woman who altered the course of my life with her words, I wouldn't have believed it. But here I am, standing in the doorway of the shadiest bar in town, staring at June Birch's profile as she raises a whiskey sour to her lips.

There isn't a mechanic beside her this time, but there is a man. He's built like a beanpole, tall and thin, but does have a soft pouch of a stomach. I attribute this to the pint glass in his hand and the half-empty pitcher of beer on the bar. Addy's mother rests one of her hands on his thigh and throws back her head, laughing at something he's said. The sound of it is tinny and hollow, as if she's forgotten the melody of real joy, and I actually wince when I hear it.

June Birch has aged. Her fingernails have been well taken care of, but the rest of her has not, and although she still wears clothes that are seductively short and makeup that is overly vibrant, the painstaking effort she must exert is really quite worthless because she merely looks like an old woman who's gone shopping in her teenager's closet. Her hair is thinning, there are bags under her eyes, and the lines around her mouth look to have been etched there with an artist's tools. I lock my gaze on her and head in her direction, taking it one step at a time, not exactly nervous… but not entirely eager to say what I've come here to say. I don't aim to be impolite, but there will be no "Excuse me, Ms. Birch" this time around.

I walk slowly across the bar, my eyes fixing themselves on her left ear, and when I am almost directly beside her, June swivels her head and acknowledges my presence. There's a glimmer of recognition that washes over her face, but I too have aged over the past decade. She seems unable to place me; my short hair, combined with her semi-inebriated state, causes her to tilt her head and ask, "Do I know you?"

"You did," I answer. "A long time ago. I used to take care of Addy."

Realization dawns on her. Her eyebrows go up, she considers me from head to foot, and then she purses her lips in a way that makes her look *mean.* "I thought I told you—"

"You did," I acknowledge, cutting *her* off this time around. "You did, and I listened, but now it's my turn to speak." The dull ache in my head has intensified, and the bar's smoky atmosphere isn't helping. I blink once, twice, trying to subdue the pain so that I can concentrate on what needs to be said. "I've hired Addy," I inform her. "He's coming to work for *me*, at *my* bar, and you are not to set foot on the premises. Do you understand? You are *not* welcome there."

June's eyes form angry slits. She glances to the guy with the half-empty pitcher, but he's currently offering his undivided attention to his pint glass, so she turns back to me and asks, "And what if I do?"

I shrug, feigning a nonchalance that I do not feel at this moment. "If you so much as *try* to visit the Brewhaha," I say, referencing her own warning from all those years back, "you'll regret it. It's as simple as that."

I don't give her an opportunity to issue a threat of her own, or poke me with a painted fingernail and blame me for things out of my control. I simply turn away from her and walk back across the barroom, eager to be gone from this dismal space. Once in the alley, I press my fingers to my temples, massaging them, and gulp down breath after breath of fresh air. My vision is splotchy and the taste of bile lingers at the back of my throat. I swallow, attempt to think of something other than the blinding pain in my head.

I should have taken the pills—that much is obvious now—but never before has a full-blown migraine surfaced this quickly. I maneuver the narrow stretch of asphalt one step at a time, allowing my right hand to trail along the exterior bricks of Duff's in order to maintain my balance and sense of direction. It takes approximately three minutes to make it back to the Jeep, but those three minutes feel like an eternity. I fumble with the key, insert it in the lock, swing the door open, climb inside. More than anything, I wish to close my eyes… want to close my eyes, but "No," I say aloud. "No." My fingers find the latch for the glove box and it falls open with a soft clatter. The medicine is there, snug in the green-plastic vial, and I manage to pop the cap, shaking two of the pills into my open palm. The pounding in my brain has become so intense that I actually crush the tablets between my back molars, grinding the chalky substance into a sour paste and gagging as I force it down. I fold my arms across the steering wheel and rest my forehead against them, hoping and praying for some form of relief, whether it be sleep or death.

Because at this point, I don't care where the darkness comes from: just so long as it comes.

16.

Addy

The college students are back. They arrived in droves just over two weeks ago, with the freshmen leading the pack. Minivans, SUVs, and rugged Outbacks lined the streets and filled the dormitory parking lots last Saturday as recent high-school grads and their parents unloaded boxes and suitcases, carting them up several flights of stairs to deliver them to shoebox-sized rooms with two beds and two built-in desks. "This will be your home away from home for the next nine months!" mothers cooed to their children. "Hang your posters with putty, not tacks," fathers sensibly added. And the freshmen had rolled their eyes, attempting to seem grown up, while in fact they were feeling much younger than they'd felt in a long time.

Addy had observed the goings-on from a distance, imagining what it would be like to experience Lake Caywood for the first time as an eighteen-year-old and to not have the memory of a childhood spent in this town. He'd marveled, too, about how it would be to live on his own, sharing a room or an apartment with somebody who'd expect him to do his own laundry and clean up after himself, but not to sacrifice a portion of his paycheck every other week to cover costs that weren't Addy's to begin with. That wonderment is what gave him the idea, and that's why he's currently dashing up the steps of the library, taking them two at a time like he always does.

There's a bulletin board that hangs in the lobby of the library. Addy has noticed it on several occasions—has even stopped to skim announcements for college movie nights and guest speakers—but he has never had a reason to tear a paper tab from the bottom of a "Roommate Wanted" flier and call the number that is printed there. The stipulations provided by Charley have changed that, though; now he stands before the bulletin board, actively searching for an apartment in need of another inhabitant.

There are several from which to choose, but the one that catches Addy's eye is very different than the rest. To start, it doesn't have a bold title stretching across the top of the page. Instead, a sketch of a suitcase occupies that space, and beneath it, a quote that discusses how difficult it is to live with someone who appreciates a higher standard of luggage.

Addy would recognize the voice of Holden Caulfield anywhere. He's read J.D. Salinger's masterpiece no fewer than ten times and can't imagine that a roommate who also appreciates *The Catcher in the Rye* wouldn't make for a decent fit. He quickly scans the rest of the flier. Typed right below the Salinger quote is a blurb about the apartment's location (Main Street, above Whirligigs and Whatnots) and its current occupant, who's written: "People call me Mac. I'm nineteen, very sarcastic, and looking for a roommate who won't be bothered by the fact that I frequently keep my art supplies on the kitchen counter. I like to read. I rarely clean the bathroom. I don't like coffee, but I do drink tea. I utilized one duffel bag and a bunch of cardboard boxes on move-in day. If you've got similar suitcases, give me a call. If you shop at Samsonite, don't bother."

Addy is smiling as he tears the contact information from the bottom of the page and tucks it into the pocket of his jeans. He understands that he shouldn't procrastinate on making the phone call, but he also realizes that it is Tuesday, and that on Tuesdays Miss Flora can generally be found shelving books. Addy hasn't seen her since the night of graduation, when he spoke with her at the market's cheese counter. Since then, and for reasons he's not quite sure of, Addy has been avoiding the library. He did pick up as many extra shifts as possible at the diner on Railroad Street, so the summer really hasn't afforded him much reading time, but now that he's concluded his last late-night shift of waiting tables, a good book seems like a smart idea. He leaves the bright lobby and heads for the stacks, passing by a few college students who have already begun research for the ten-page papers their professors assigned on that first day of class. Or maybe they're studying for their first college exam, memorizing dates and names and battles that changed the outcome of wars. Addy knows not what the notebooks and textbooks lying open on the tables in front of them contain; he knows only that for the first time in a long time, he's interested in reading something light. Airy. Refreshing.

"Like a beach read?" Miss Flora queries when he shares this desire with her.

"Sort of," Addy says, resting his elbows on the circulation desk. "I want something funny."

"Like a Nursery Crime?"

The tall boy cocks his head and knits his brows. "I don't know what you mean."

"Nursery Crimes," Miss Flora repeats. "It's a series by Jasper Fforde, about Inspector Jack Spratt and Detective Mary Mary. They solve mysteries, like…" And here she pauses to unearth a book from behind the counter, displaying its cover so that the young patron may see it. "…who killed Humpty Dumpty?"

Addy grins. "Have you read it?"

"I have, several years ago, and I do recall chuckling quite a bit." Miss Flora hands *The Big Over Easy* to Addy and waits patiently while he skims the book jacket's inside flap. The corners of his mouth curl slightly upward while reading the summary, and when he finishes he says, "I'll give it a try."

Miss Flora brings her hands together in a noiseless clap, celebrating the decision. As she accepts his card and signs the book out in his name, she comments on the fact that Addy seems happier than he has for quite some time. "Like a weight's been lifted from your shoulders," she observes. "Is it my imagination, or are things on the up and up?"

"It's not your imagination," Addy admits. "Things are changing." He briefs her on completing his stint as a waiter, confiding that when he delivered his two-weeks notice, it was one of the greatest feelings he'd ever experienced, and he tells her that his visit to the library has more to do with apartment hunting than it does with literature, since he's finally taking the steps to improve his living situation. And when Miss Flora asks where he'll be working now, he proudly states, "The Brewhaha. Charley asked me to cook for her. She wants me to be her lead chef."

There's a glimmer of recognition that washes over the old woman's face, and with a frail hand, she reaches up to touch the silver locket around her neck. Her thumb caresses the snowflake that's etched there, a faraway look in her eyes. "Charley Lane," she says, but it is not a question.

"Charley Lane," Addy confirms. "Do you know her?"

"Not well," Miss Flora answers, "but I know who she is. Tell me about the Brewhaha."

So the subject is altered, veering away from the person and focusing instead on the farmhouse. "I barely recognized the kitchen," Addy shares. "All of the appliances are new, and the countertops are granite, and there's a bar with five taps. The grand opening is next month. You should come."

"We'll see," Miss Flora says very softly. "We'll see."

The phone rings three times before a friendly voice answers, "Hello?"

"Hi. Is this Mac?"

"Sure is. Who's asking?"

Addy leans against one of the library's marble pillars and stares across the college courtyard. "My name's Addy Birch. I'm calling about the apartment. The only piece of luggage I own is a backpack, so I think you and Holden both have me beat."

"So you got the reference?"

"Yeah. I got the reference."

"I'm impressed. What're you doing later today? Wanna swing by for a tour? We can scrutinize one another, jump to a conclusion about compatibility, and maybe talk about rent. Any time after five works for me."

"Great."

"Use the back entrance," Mac adds, "off the deck. I'll see you later." And then he hangs up, rather abruptly, not especially interested in a formal goodbye.

Addy slides his phone back into his pocket. The quad is littered with students today. Some leisurely toss a Frisbee back and forth, the red disc gliding almost effortlessly through the air, while others sprawl on blankets and talk to old friends about summer vacations. Addy watches them, whistling an obscure little tune as he does, the notes drifting up and away as they dance across the college campus and eventually disappear. He loses himself in the melody, not noticing when the Jeep pulls up to the sidewalk, bumping the curb, and comes to a temporary standstill. Charley has to honk in order to capture his attention.

"Hey!" she laughs as Addy slides into the passenger's seat. "That must've been quite the daydream. What were you thinking about?" The red sparks sizzling on her skin are dull today—considerably duller than they'd been that day at his house—but then, she'd been angry with him. Colors intensify with different emotions.

"Just stuff," he responds. "Apartments and appetizers and opening night. Simple food. That's what you want, right?"

Charley puts on her turn signal and eases back into traffic. "Right. Do you have some ideas?"

"Pumpkin-Brie quesadillas, autumn chowder served by the cup, and maybe some apple fries dusted with confectioner's sugar. Is that enough, or should the menu be bigger?"

"Keep it simple," Charley tells him. "The kitchen isn't that big and I've never envisioned the Brewhaha as a full-fledge restaurant. Snacky stuff is perfect. I thought we could roast pumpkin seeds, too, and put them on the bar. Like peanuts, but different. I'll have a lot of pumpkin seeds to roast because I intend to carve a lot of jack-o-lanterns for the front porch. You can help if you want."

Addy drums his fingers against his knee, keeping beat with the song playing softly on the radio, and asks, "Do you remember when we made that pumpkin totem pole? It was, like, five jack-o-lanterns high."

Charley laughs. "Yeah, I remember that. We made the bottom pumpkin look like he was wincing. His eyes were squinty and his mouth was open in a wail and there was even a tear on his cheek, wasn't there?"

"It was supposed to be a tear," Addy says, "but it looked more like a crater. I messed up."

"You were five."

"That was the year I dressed up as the Trix Rabbit and collected candy in an empty cereal box." Addy remembers it well. Charley had decked him out in a white sweatsuit, safety-pinned a tail to his backside, painted his face with a pink nose and whiskers, and rigged up a pair of floppy bunny ears. June Birch had been working, of course, so Addy and Charley had walked around the neighborhood, gathering peanut butter cups and chocolate bars and miniature packets of Twizzlers that they then sorted into piles on the living floor. All of his early Halloween memories include Charley; had she not been around, Addy probably wouldn't have experienced trick-or-treating until a classmate invited him to tag along with his family in the fifth grade. He's not in the mood to relive the past right now, though, and so he pushes the long-ago thoughts from his head and returns to the present. "What are we shopping for today? Plates?"

"And bowls," Charley answers. "And silverware… and pots and pans… and anything else you think you might want. This shopping spree is basically for *you*, so if you notice something you think you'll need, speak up and we'll add it to the cart. We're going to that restaurant supply store in West Orensdale. I've heard they have everything."

Addy knows what she's referencing; he's driven by Friedrich and Company on several occasions, but has never had a reason to stop. It doesn't look like much from the outside—just a giant concrete box with four sets of double doors and an orange sign stretched above them, advertising the business's name—but the inside winds up being to a cook what a candy store is to a child. Floor-to-ceiling shelves offer everything from cooking utensils to red and yellow condiment containers. Addy's eyes grow to the size of small kiwis as he basks in his surroundings, taking it all in. "I think," he eventually stammers after a full minute of gawking, "that we'll probably need more than one cart."

There's a lot to consider when purchasing items for a bar, and the more Addy and Charley put into their carts, the more they realize they still need to buy. They grab metal mixing bowls, spoons, and spatulas; enormous pots for big batches of soup and sturdy trays for serving meals; terrycloth bar mops, a commercial grade coffeemaker, and a few solid bottle openers. "Do we need corkscrews?" Addy wonders, but Charley shrugs. "Maybe just one. We won't serve wine," she tells him. "Or mixed drinks either. Gramps was all about the beer, so that means *we're* all about the beer."

"Fair enough. What about the dinnerware? The stuff not behind the scenes?"

"Well… nothing's really behind the scenes, you know. The kitchen's wide open. If someone orders a pumpkin-Brie quesadilla, then the odds are that person is also watching you fill the order. You can't pick your nose and then add a pinch of salt to the soup," she warns with a smile, her green eyes glimmering. "We'll lose business if you do that."

Addy gives her a sideways look. "I'm pretty sure that if I *ever* did that," he says, "then I was, like, three."

"Four," Charley corrects. "You were four when you added boogers and salt to the soup. It was chicken noodle and it smelled really good, but I didn't eat any. You did, though. You were eating your boogers pretty consistently back then, so I didn't think chicken noodle soup boogers would hurt. At least they were cooked."

"That is disgusting," Addy declares, rolling his eyes and trying to hide a smile. "Totally disgusting. And I *promise* that I will not add boogers to any dishes served at the Brewhaha. I will, however, need dishes for the Brewhaha… which leads me back to my original question: what are we doing about dinnerware?"

Charley smiles, impressed by the segue, and answers matter-of-factly, "We're going to buy some. I did order pint glasses already, but we still need everything else: plates, pitchers, water glasses, bowls, mugs, forks, spoons, knives… All of it. And I guess you ought to be the one to choose the colors, since you'll be the one plating the food."

Addy doesn't disagree with her; she makes a valid point. But he's never been one for an excess of color. "Let's look at what they have," he says, because that seems the logical thing to do. But he does have an idea in mind.

There's an entire aisle's worth of plates. They come in all shapes and colors and patterns. "I want it to be round," he mutters, "and probably white," and when he sees the simple pattern on a middle shelf, he knows for sure. "This one." It's rimmed with red—the same shade that he associates with Charley—and so it only makes sense for this to be incorporated into the Brewhaha. "Definitely this one."

They find bowls and mugs to match, stock up on standard flatware, pack yet another cart with plastic pitchers and water glasses and crimson paper napkins. "I think we have to stop," Charley says when a gigantic package of straws tumbles from the mound of supplies and lands on the ground with a soft *thud.* "If we buy anything else, it's not gonna fit in the car."

It's a struggle to maneuver the overflowing carts through the store, but somehow the duo accomplishes it. They unload everything onto the conveyor-belt counter before piling it right back into the carts. Addy's jaw drops when the saleswoman somberly provides the total, but Charley takes it all in stride. She seems unperturbed by the astronomical amount, merely sliding a credit card from her wallet and passing it to the cashier. "Courtesy of Gramps," she explains to Addy on the walk to the Jeep. "He had more money than he knew what to do with. And do you know what he did with it?"

"What?"

"Absolutely nothing. So now I have twice as much money as I know what to do with." She grins and shakes her head. "Don't get me wrong—I'm not complaining—but it makes me wonder why he didn't at least hire someone to help him with the farmhouse's upkeep. I mean, he had Felipe and then Oscar to care for the orchards… but the house was completely neglected. It's as if he stopped caring about it."

Addy secures the coffeemaker on a backseat, taking the time to buckle it in, and asks, "Why would he do that, though?"

"No idea," Charley says with a shrug, "but there's a part of me that wonders if he wasn't depressed. I really should have come back sooner, Addy. I'm sorry. I am *so* sorry that I stayed gone for such a long time. If I could take it back, I would in a heartbeat."

The tall boy turns around and meets her gaze, holding it for a moment before speaking, and when he does find his voice, he says, "I know you would. And I know you are. Sorry, I mean. And I forgive you. Completely. I think your Gramps probably does, too."

Charley turns away, wiping her eyes so that Addy won't see the tears brimming there. "I hope you're right," she whispers, almost too softly for him to hear. "I really hope you're right."

The Jeep has been sufficiently stuffed with restaurant paraphernalia, to the point that the rearview mirror is of little use. "Are you sure that you don't want me to go back to the farmhouse with you and help to unload it?" Addy asks, standing on the sidewalk in front of Whirligigs and Whatnots, talking to Charley through the vehicle's open window. "I don't mind."

"No," she insists. "It's okay. Juli and his friends Ernie and Theo are over there now, painting the house's exterior, so I'll have plenty of assistance. Are you coming by tomorrow? I want to hear all about this potential roommate who houses art supplies in the kitchen. What's his name? Max?"

"Mac," Addy corrects. "And yes: I'll swing by tomorrow, probably in the afternoon." He takes a step back from the Jeep, waving goodbye as Charley pulls away, and then turns to face the art shop behind him.

Whirligigs and Whatnots is located directly beside the Tavern, which is owned and operated by Philip Hiram Delaney (Doc, for short) and is probably Lake Caywood's longest-standing restaurant. The establishment is known for its sweet potato fries, but Addy's favorite thing on the menu has always been the chocolate shake. It has the *faintest* hint of cinnamon, and that hint of cinnamon is what makes all the difference. He certainly wouldn't mind living this close to his dessert of choice.

There's a narrow alley that runs between the two businesses and Addy heads down it, following it around to the back of Whirligigs and Whatnots. Mac had mentioned a deck and there is definitely one suspended above him, a rickety stairway leading up to it. Addy plants a foot on the first step, testing its stability, and then carefully heads up to the second floor. A canvas folding chair and a plastic patio table are the only pieces of furniture on the deck; each item, along with the unfinished wood surrounding them, has been splattered with various shades of paint. Addy walks to the sliding glass door and raps his knuckle against it. The sound that it makes is hollow.

Inside, someone emerges from a back room. He's barefoot, sporting baggy jeans and a button-down shirt that hangs open in the front. Dark hair fans across his forehead—sort of greasy, but not completely unkempt—and both his clothes and his skin appear to be speckled with teal paint. He grips a paintbrush between his teeth and holds a rag in his right hand, using his left hand to flip back the deadbolt with a *click*. Then he slides the door open, removes the paintbrush from his mouth, and says, "Hey. You're Addy? I'm Mac. C'mon in." He steps back, ushering Addy into the kitchen, which does indeed appear to be a large closet for all things art. Tubes of paint adorn the countertops, juice glasses filled with milky water and half-clean brushes reside in the sink, and canvases, propped up against cabinets and sugar canisters, take their time drying. "So this is where I toast my Pop-Tarts each morning," Mac says. "I like the brown sugar ones, no frosting. That stuff'll rot your teeth. Follow me and I'll show you the living room."

Addy can't imagine that much living occurs in the living room. It's big enough for a couch and a recliner and an eighteen-inch television—and Mac's managed to cram all of that in here—but every seat is already occupied by a massive painting. Some look like Jackson Pollack was involved; others are weirdly beautiful abstracts of local landmarks. Addy takes it all in, pondering whether or not this setup could actually work, and continues to follow his tour guide down the hallway to a bathroom (Mac wasn't kidding when he said it rarely gets cleaned), an already occupied bedroom (the walls are literally *cluttered* with canvases), and then a completely empty room with a big window that overlooks Main Street. Addy imagines his bed here, and a desk, and maybe a bookcase containing his favorite titles, and a closet full of clothes that don't smell like the inside of an ashtray. The idea of it is almost too much to fathom. He glances to Mac, considering his unusually casual attire and lifestyle to match. "You don't smoke, do you?"

"Not cigarettes," Mac responds with a smile.

Addy bites his bottom lip, thinking. "Then this might work."

Mac laughs and leans against the door jamb, crossing his arms over his stomach. "Hold up, young'un. I have some questions for you, too, you know."

"Like what?"

"Like… Okay. What's your favorite book?"

"*The Adventures of Huckleberry Finn*," Addy responds, not needing to think about it.

"Do you take more than one shower per day?"

"Not usually, no."

"What do you get on your pizza?"

Addy shrugs. "It depends on my mood. I'll typically eat whatever. What about you?"

"I'm not a huge fan of pepperoni. Otherwise, anything works. You might be right."

"About?" Addy asks, raising his eyebrows.

"About this," Mac informs him. "That this might work. Rent's three hundred each month, utilities not included. Interested?"

"Yes."

"Then let's shake on it and choose a move-in date," he says, extending a paint-splattered hand, "so that you can go home and start packing. I'm expecting a knapsack and several cardboard boxes. If you show up with some sort of wheeled contraption that has an extendable handle, though, the deal is off. You got that?"

"Got it," Addy assures him.

When he leaves, his palm is smeared with remnants of teal paint.

17.
Juli

"Hey!" Asher calls from an upstairs window, his face shadowy behind the screen. "Do you have a minute? The kitchen sink is leaking again!"

I sigh. It's been a long day. The opening of the Brewhaha is less than forty-eight hours away and while the outside of the farmhouse is looking pretty sharp, the second floor is nowhere near completion. There's some wallpaper that needs to be scraped, fresh coats of paint applied, and a bathroom floor in need of tiling. I *have* managed to sand and seal the hardwood that runs down the hallway and into the rooms, so at least the air won't be thick with dust for opening day. When Charley declared the second weekend in October as "go time," I realized immediately that the renovation would still be in progress, but I had hoped to at least have the upstairs painted by now…

My muscles ache, my knees throb from spending a good portion of the day kneeling on them, and my skin feels as though it's covered in grit. What I want is a hot shower, but I don't share that with Asher. I simply lower the brim of my baseball cap, take a deep breath, and say, "Give me five minutes. Then I'll be up."

Scarlett is waiting at the door. She has an old tennis ball in her mouth and her tail is wagging furiously. I give her soft ears a tousle and bend down to kiss her forehead. "I bet you have to go out," I observe. "Come on. You can tag along."

She slips past me, races into the yard, chases a squirrel up a tree and then rolls around in the grass, releasing some pent-up energy and having fun in the process. I return to my truck and grab my toolbox from the backseat. Odds are it's the supply line again, and probably all that's really needed is an adjustable wrench, but if that's the only thing I take with me, I know that the situation will be jinxed. I whistle for Scarlett and head for the side steps; she gallops over to join me. Fallen leaves, red and gold, cling to her glossy fur, rustling with each step. I attempt to brush them off while we wait for Asher to answer the door.

He's still dressed in his work clothes—khakis and a button-down shirt—when he finally responds to my knocking. There's a loose tie looped around an upturned collar. "Sorry," he greets me. "You could've just let yourself in. I was on the phone… trying to sort something out with Annie."

"Everything okay?" I ask, because his tone is tinged with frustration.

"Oh, who knows," Asher mutters. "Do you want a beer?" He walks to the refrigerator, grabs a bottle from the door, and waits for my response. I'm in the process of unloading the assortment of sopping wet products from under the sink: a bottle of grapefruit-scented dish soap, a damp container of Comet, a package of sponges that has never been opened, a roll of paper towels still wrapped in plastic… I open these and use them to mop up the puddle that's formed beneath the drip. "Nah," I answer. "I'm okay."

"Have a beer with me," Asher insists. "I could really use a beer."

"Fine. I'll have a beer."

"All I have is Budweiser," he informs me. "Are you cool with that?"

"I guess I'll have to be," I point out, easing myself under the sink and wincing as the lip of the cupboard digs into my spine. Scarlett senses my discomfort and does her best to offer support, but her nose in my face provides little help. "Ash," I manage, my voice hollow-sounding. I turn my head to avoid being exfoliated by my pup's tongue and ask, "Are you able to offer some assistance here?"

I hear him laugh, twist the caps off the bottles, set them on the counter with a dull *clink*. "Scarlett," he singsongs, "come over here, girl. Come on…"

She gives me a final sniff, licks my cheek, and ducks out of the cabinet. Her nails click on the linoleum as she pads over to Asher and plops down at his feet, anticipating a treat. "Sorry," he says, and I imagine him extending his hands as proof that both palms are empty. "I've got nothing for you." Then to me he confides, "Annie's best friend from college is getting married next weekend."

"Is my adjustable wrench out there?" I wonder, craning my neck to see if I can spot it. As suspected, the problem is once again the supply line; my toolbox could have remained in the truck. "And can you hand it to me?"

Asher passes the wrench to me. "Are you listening to what I'm saying?"

"Annie's best friend from college is getting married next weekend," I say in response.

"Yeah. And she wants me to go to the wedding with her."

Despite the fact that I wiped up the puddle, the back of my shirt has grown damp. It sticks uncomfortably to my skin and I wiggle around, trying to loosen it. No luck. Above me, Asher continues, "The thing is, Annie's *in* the wedding, which means there'll be a rehearsal dinner the night before, and she wants me to go to that, too. Plus, the whole thing's taking place down in Virginia, so we're staying in a hotel." He shares all of this in the same tone that one might use if lamenting the misfortune of needing to have eight cavities filled at the same time.

I give the supply line a final once-over before sliding out from under the sink and sitting on the floor, my arms wrapped around my knees. Scarlett prances over and tucks her head into my armpit; I run a hand down her silky back and rest my own head against her shoulder. "Is that such a bad thing?" I ask of Asher. "I thought you liked weddings."

"I *do* most of the time," he grumbles, "but this one's different. I'm not gonna know anyone, and Annie'll be busy all day on Saturday. Hair, makeup, pictures… other wedding stuff that girls do…"

I will my eyes not to roll, but they do it anyway. "Really, Ash? You don't think you can find a sports bar and entertain yourself for an afternoon? It's not the end of the world by a long shot."

"No, I know, but…"

He trails off. I give him a minute to resume the dialogue, occupying the time with beer retrieval and a long swig, but when he remains silent, I go ahead and prompt, "But what?"

"But nothing," he sighs. "I just wish she didn't mind going alone."

"Please tell me you didn't suggest that," I say, "because if Annie asked you to go, then she wants you to go." I stare at my friend, who merely shrugs, and realize that this poor suggestion *was* made. "I don't get it, Ash. Do you not *want* to be dating Annie?"

He narrows his eyes so that his brows knit together, almost angry. "Of course I do."

"Oh."

"You don't believe me?"

The bottle of Budweiser in my hand is sweating, fat drops of condensation rolling down its glass neck, and I pick at the label, peeling it off in one piece. I reach up to set my beer beside the sink and use both hands to fold the sticky rectangle in half, then in half again, until it's nothing more than a small square. I consider telling Asher the truth—that Annie's gotta be ridiculously confused by the weird, mixed signals he's sending—but it's really none of my business. Asher is always somewhat enigmatic when it comes to women, which is probably why his relationships rarely last longer than a few months, and the only reason I'm more aware than usual of his impossible-to-read behavior is because Charley appears to have been cast from the same mold. I can sympathize with Annie because I can understand the puzzlement that she must be experiencing on a daily basis.

I've spent many a sleepless night staring at the ceiling, my mind running laps at a dizzying speed, trying to make sense of Charley Lane. She'll meet me in the driveway with a kiss and a steaming mug of coffee one day, and then the next day she'll dodge every single one of my advances. It's as if she's afraid to get close—to open herself up—and for every step forward that she takes, she follows it up with at least two back. I can't get a read on her. It's been close to five months and our relationship hasn't progressed past *kissing*. I'm well aware of the fact that some girls like to take things slow, but we've settled into a pace that wouldn't even register on a speedometer. I mean, if a sloth challenged us to a race, the sloth would win.

All of these thoughts zip through my mind, and I briefly consider sharing them with Asher, but the words that eventually fall out of my mouth are simply, "It doesn't really matter what I believe, does it?"

But Asher surprises me by saying, "It might." He hoists himself onto the kitchen counter and passes my beer down to me. "I like Annie, man. I like her a lot. But, I don't know… you think I'm handling it all wrong?"

I sigh and the sound causes Scarlett to turn her head, scanning my face for signs of distress. Finding none, she plods a few feet from where I'm sitting and lies down, resting her chin on her paws and blinking sleepily. I tug on the brim of my baseball cap, lowering it so that it shields my line of vision, and admit, "From where I sit, Annie looks to be giving you about one hundred ten percent while you're offering up *maybe* eighty-five, and that kills me because…"

"Because if Charley would give that much, then I'd be the happiest guy on the planet," is what I almost say, but don't. I cut myself off, take a swallow of beer, and finish, "If you like her, Ash—if you really and truly like her—then jump in with both feet. You're thirty-six years old. It's time to grow up." It comes out sounding harsher than I intend it to, and Asher retaliates with an "Ouch! Okay, Dad… Thanks for the lecture."

"Hey, I'm sorry—"

"Don't be," he interrupts. "What you said? Well, you're right. I do need to grow up. But…"

I stare at the last inch of beer in my bottle, debating whether or not I want it. "But?"

"But you should probably take some of your own advice, Juli."

"I think I do a pretty decent job of acting my age," I muse.

Asher tosses an abandoned beer cap at my head. It bounces off my hat, bumps against my knee on the way down, and hits the linoleum with a metallic *clink*. "Not the part about growing up," he says. "The part about jumping in with both feet. Worst-case scenario? You get wet. Best-case scenario?" He pauses here to insert a snicker. "Best-case scenario, *she* gets wet."

I snatch the beer cap off the floor and lob it up at him.

It hits him squarely on the forehead.

At this time of year, Copper Drive is actually canopied by a medley of copper-colored leaves. They cling to the branches overhead, flitting in the breeze, and then eventually release their grips and tumble to the earth below. A few tap against my truck's windshield; most mingle with those that have already fallen and line the road, forming a crispy crust atop the grass. The sky is a crazy shade of blue—bright and clear—and it peeks through the autumn umbrella overhead as I head out to the old farmhouse.

Today is the day.

At five o'clock on the dot, the Brewhaha's doors will open for the very first time, and with any luck, members of the public will step through them.

The event is being talked about in town. The *Lake Caywood Times* ran an article last week about the refurbished establishment, and this morning's headline boasted "All About the Beer and the Laughter." Charley welcomed a reporter and a photographer to the house yesterday, and today both her words and her photograph are above the fold. My name was mentioned once or twice, too, and my phone's been ringing because of it, but potential customers will have to exhibit patience because my schedule is booked solid for the next several days.

Gravel crunches beneath my tires as I make a right into five-nineteen and navigate the long drive up to the house. Oscar and his crew are out picking apples, dressed in denim and flannel and heavy work boots; ladders and bins filled with shiny red fruit dot the orchard. I put up a hand in greeting as I roll past.

Petey's bike is propped against the barn and Addy's newly purchased old clunker is parked out front. I pull in beside it, shut off the ignition, and hop out of the truck. Then I turn to face the farmhouse, taking a moment to consider the transformation that's occurred over the past nine months. The siding is no longer dingy, the shutters no longer skewed, and I sanded the porch a few weeks ago, staining it a ruddy, red hue that couldn't be more perfect. High-gloss white paint gleams on the porch rails and a simple crimson-and-gold placard has been mounted beside the front door, advertising the establishment's name: The Brewhaha. "It's come a long way," I whisper to myself, both proud and amazed, and with my hands in my pockets, I start across the yard.

The porch spans the front of the farmhouse, wraps around the side, and then disappears around another corner, stretching partially across the back. Charley has taken it upon herself to embellish not only the handrails and posts with twinkling lights, but each and every baluster has also been encased. In addition to this, I've been told that a jack-o-lantern will adorn each step of both the front porch stairs and the side. What Charley has neglected to mention is that a professional pumpkin carver will be in charge of this task, so I'm rather surprised to find a complete stranger straddling a gourd in the front yard and scooping heaps of gooey, orange innards onto a sheet of newsprint.

"Hi," I say to the kid as I approach. He looks to be in his late teens, with dark hair that falls across his forehead and slightly sunken cheeks, and it's obvious that he knows how to wield a carving knife. A lineup of jack-o-lanterns watches from a few yards away, beneath the cherry tree, each wearing a different devilish expression. I look at them, then back at him, and ask, "Who're you?"

"Courtland MacArthur," the kid answers, "but you can call me Mac. Everyone does. You're Juli, right? I'd shake your hand, but." He cuts himself off and waggles his goo-covered fingers, employing the gesture as the second half of his sentence. "Addy and Charley are roasting pumpkin seeds inside. Will you let them know there's another batch coming?"

"Sure."

"Thanks."

Talk about a surprisingly direct introduction. I can feel myself smiling as I walk away.

Compared to the chilled outdoor air, the kitchen is toasty. It smells like the inside of a pumpkin after it's been scorched by an unscented candle. I feel my cheeks turning rosy about ten seconds after stepping inside. Last week Charley had me hang a coat rack on the wall behind the door (it's cool because it's made from old beer tap handles—I don't know where she found it) and I slouch out of my jacket, looping it over a hook. Rhett is there to greet me almost immediately, sniffing my ankles and then shoving his wet snout against the palm of my hand. "Hey, fella," I say, wiping the dampness from his nose on the top of his head. "What's going on in here?

Are you helping in the kitchen?" I walk over to the bar and lean against the copper-plated counter, watching Charley rinse pumpkin seeds at the sink and Addy toss a fresh batch of them with olive oil and herbs. "I thought the ingredients consisted of olive oil and salt," I muse, and Addy glances over at me, a slightly distracted grin lingering on his face. "We already made regular pumpkin seeds," he explains. "These are going to be spicy: minced chili peppers, curry, cinnamon, cayenne, and of course… salt."

"My taste buds cower just *thinking* about that combination of flavors."

Addy laughs. "They're not *that* spicy," he assures me, "but they do have some heat to 'em."

Charley shuts off the faucet and lifts the colander from the sink, fat droplets of water streaming off the newly cleaned pumpkin seeds. "It occurred to me this morning," she volunteers, apparently changing the subject, "that Rhett shouldn't really be down here while the bar is open. I think that goes against a restaurant code or something… unless I give him the label of 'service dog,' which I could do."

"Really? You can do that?"

"Well, I mean, he's *pleasant.* He makes people *smile.* That's a service, isn't it?"

"I guess so," I say, but it seems like a stretch. "He could just hang out upstairs and make the occasional guest appearance, though. And I could bring Scarlett over to keep him company sometimes. Like tonight."

"That'd be great! You don't mind?"

"Not at all. What do you need me to do *now*, though? Anything?"

"I'm sure there are fifty million things that still need to be finished," Charley says, picking up a dishtowel and wiping her hands on it, "but right now I can't think of what they are. My brain is so jumbled with half-thoughts and horrible hypothetical situations that I can't think straight. Will you just walk around and make sure that everything *appears* to be put together? That way I can continue to help Addy with the cooking."

"Sure," I agree. "Where's the rest of the kitchen staff?"

Charley hasn't hired many people, but she's recruited a few. Petey Goode has agreed to work one night a week, at least for the first few months, and Molly Dixon, a twenty-something starving artist who always smells a little like turpentine, will tend bar the majority of the time. Charley will help out, too, of course, and I may even have an opportunity to step in every now and then.

Addy was given a large say when it came to choosing extra hands for the kitchen and I have to admit that I'm sort of surprised by his selections. Boomer Matthews is only five years older than he is, so the two of them have a good bit in common, but Cordelia Fritz is in her *sixties*. I aim to retire once I hit sixty, but Cordelia claims that retirement isn't all it's cracked up to be. "At least for me it isn't," she's said on numerous occasions. "I like to cook, and I've got no one to cook for except my husband, and *he's* already gone up two pant sizes since I quit my day job." Therefore, what she needs is a place that enables her to feed the masses.

The Brewhaha fits the bill.

"Plus, she does crazy stuff with goat cheese," Addy's informed me. "Crazy *good* stuff."

I look forward to trying some of these crazy-good goat cheese concoctions, but it doesn't sound like today will be the day for tastings. "Molly's not coming 'til later this afternoon. Boomer and Cordelia will be here soon," Charley announces. "They'll be prepping for the quesadillas. Addy, you've got the chowder under control, right?"

"Yep," he says with a nod. Addy is nowhere near as flustered as Charley, which I attribute to the fact that he's already spent some time in the restaurant industry. Bussing tables, waiting tables, helping out in the kitchen when necessary… he has an idea of what to expect. I figure he's more of a help to Charley than I am, so I disappear to do as she's asked: walk the premises to make sure everything is in order.

I straighten a picture in the living room, water the plants in the claw-foot tub, and relocate a few of Rhett's chew toys to the upstairs office. Overall, though, the first floor of the farmhouse is pretty well put together. Satisfied, I head outside to consider the yard.

Oscar mowed for probably the last time of the season just yesterday, so the grass is neat and trim and there aren't too many leaves littering the lawn. The end of the driveway has been expanded to create a sort of gravel parking area. It's situated to the left of the barn, close enough to catch whiffs of the hops growing around back in the summer months, with a flagstone walk that leads from it to the porch steps.

On the porch steps is where I stand now, observing Rhett as he prances over to where Mac is still kneeling and inserts his snout into the teenager's ear. "Hey!" Mac laughs, managing as best he can to push the dog away without smearing his wiry fur with pumpkin innards. "Stop it, Rhett! That tickles. Come on…"

I clap my hands and Rhett turns to face me, his eyes bright and his tail erect. He barks once, a puppy-like yip, and gives Mac a final kiss before trotting over to a low-standing bush and lifting his leg. I slide my hands into my pockets and saunter toward Mac. "How many more are you planning to carve? I can help if you want."

"This is the last one," the boy tells me, "but if you want to carry the finished jack-o-lanterns to the porch and get 'em set up for tonight, that'd be great."

"I can do that. Are there candles somewhere?"

"Should be. I think they're in a brown paper bag. Check the side porch."

I lift the largest pumpkin first. He wears a wicked smirk and has slanted eyes; his brows are arched and jagged. This is the type of jack-o-lantern that the Headless Horseman would choose to ride with, grasping it with his left hand and lifting it high above his shoulders as he gallops through the woods of Sleepy Hollow on Halloween night.

I position the ghoulish gourd to the right of the front door and then disappear around the corner of the house in search of candles, allowing a moment to stand at the railing and take in the view below. It's a sea of autumn: green-to-brown leaves lifting in the wind; gnarled boughs fighting gravity, their limbs laden with crimson and gold fruit; glossy apples dotting the orchard floor, still hoping for a chance to be rescued. This is where Charley grew up—where she spent her childhood into early adulthood—and I can see now why she felt so passionately about bringing the color scheme indoors. "Five-nineteen Copper Drive," I say aloud to myself. "What a place."

The paper bag is where Mac said it would be—on the side porch, near the door—and as I stoop to pick it up, Charley slides open a kitchen window and says, "Cordelia's here. She brought goodies from Piping Hot."

"Cinnamon rolls?"

"And apple turnovers, and caramel coffeecake muffins, and—"

"Pecan sticky buns!" Cordelia calls from inside. "My favorite!"

I tuck the bag of candles under my arm and give Charley a lopsided smile. My stomach issues an audible grumble in anticipation. "Give me two minutes," I say. "I'll let Mac and Petey know, too."

"Oh, Mac knows," Charley assures me. "He's already laid claim to a turnover and a muffin. The only reason they haven't been devoured yet, I think, is because his hands are covered in pumpkin slime. He's washing them now."

"So what you're telling me," I start.

"Is that you should hurry," she finishes.

I laugh and deposit the candles to the front of the house before heading out to the barn. Inside, I can hear Petey muttering to himself about hops or malt or something. I clear my throat, not wanting to startle him, and he looks up, flashing a smile embraced by parentheses. "I'm attempting a sugared cherry-infused IPA," he says in greeting. "For the Christmas season."

"Sounds decadent."

"It should be. I'm realizing that the alcohol content is going to be through the roof, though," he muses. "We'll have to serve it in snifters instead of regular pint glasses. Know what I mean?"

I nod, pointing out, "But that'll make it seem extra festive."

"True." Petey fiddles with some sort of gadget on one of the brew kettles and I rub my hands together, trying to keep them warm. It's cold outside and even colder in the barn. There is heat for the winter months, but I'm guessing it hasn't been turned on yet. "Cordelia brought stuff from Piping Hot," I tell him. "Wanna take a break?"

"Yeah, I can do that." He adjusts a temperature gauge, gently touches a tube that's running from one container to another, and finally pulls his attention away from the complicated mess of equipment. "Let's go."

We lope back across the yard, up the porch steps, and stomp our feet on the welcome mat before stepping into the house. In addition to scorched pumpkin seeds, the kitchen now smells like coffee. There's a fresh pot of hazelnut gurgling away on the counter, a trickle of dark brew slowly filling the container. Someone (my guess is Addy) has already retrieved a container of half-and-half from the refrigerator; a package of sugar cubes has been set off to the side, ready for use.

The oak table that Charley's grandmother once used to roll out piecrusts and core apples has been relocated behind the bar. It will serve as an island on most days—a place to garnish dishes before delivering them to customers, or chop vegetables for an autumn chowder—but it will sometimes still be employed as a gathering spot for friends. Like how it's being used right now. Cordelia stands behind a white bakery box, pointing out the different sugar-crusted delicacies hidden inside. She grins, laughing at a joke or a comment or an amusing facial expression of some sort, and behind her wire-rimmed glasses, her eyes twinkle. Addy and Charley stand side by side, each clad in a red apron dusted with flour, looking a lot like brother and sister with their short dark hair and comfortable smiles. He's taller than she is by more than a few inches, and her eyes are emerald while his are the color of ash, but there's a similarity in their postures. Shoulders casually slumped, backbones contradictorily straight and confident... almost as if they know more about life than the average person.

Whereas Charley and Addy seem wise beyond their years, Boomer exudes boyishness. Having only recently graduated from college, he still has that frat-boy appearance about him. Short hair, big biceps, polo shirts from Abercrombie and Fitch. "A typical Chad" my college roommate, Curt, would have called him, but Boomer is more than that. I've known him for approximately two weeks and I've already heard him quote Shakespeare twice. He's also ridiculously skilled at mental math; the guy can quadruple recipes almost without thinking. I still struggle to remember how many teaspoons are in a tablespoon, and how many cups are in a pint.

I *can* sand the floors that we're standing on, though, so there's that.

Mac's among the throng of people, too. He leans against the counter, not officially joining the others at the table, but close enough to Cordelia and Addy that one might be generous enough to concede that he's standing *between* them. He wears a thin mustache of confectioner's sugar and holds an apple turnover in his right hand, a paper napkin in his left. He laughs when the others laugh, and listens when they speak, but doesn't readily contribute much to the conversation, which is unlike Petey Goode, who slips behind the bar and squeezes in beside Charley. "Big day today," he states, reaching for a sticky bun. "You nervous? I can't wait to see this place alive with customers. Are you going to make an opening-day toast? Maybe raise a pumpkin ale to the occasion?"

"You'd better believe I'm nervous," Charley states. "Now I'm even *more* nervous. I hadn't even thought about making a toast… Thanks, Petey. Thanks a lot." She sighs and Petey rests a hand on her shoulder, offering comfort with its weight. "Everything is going to work out perfectly," he assures her. "I feel very confident about that."

"Oh, you do, do you?"

He nods. "I also feel confident in stating that if Juli doesn't soon snag a pastry, then he will be pastry-less for the remainder of the day. Which do you prefer, man: a muffin or a cinnamon roll?"

I opt for the latter and Charley plucks it from the box, carrying it over to me. She lays a napkin on the bar and sets the cinnamon-spiraled bun on top of it. Then she rests her elbows on the copper plating and cups her chin in her hands. "There's an entire flock of butterflies in my stomach right now," she very seriously states. "I feel as though I might puke."

Rhett and I are still on the other side of the bar. He stands with his front paws resting on the seat of a tall stool, his nose working overtime in order to capture every sweet scent floating in the air; I'm right beside him, but slump down in order to be eye level with Charley. "I'm pretty sure that 'flock of butterflies' is the wrong terminology."

"Oh yeah?" she queries. "What would you call it then? A swarm?"

"Or a kaleidoscope."

She rolls her eyes.

"I'm serious," I counter. "I'm almost positive that a group of butterflies is referred to as a kaleidoscope. Like, I'm ninety-nine percent positive about that fact. You can look it up if you don't believe me."

Charley fixes me with her clear green eyes, searching my face for a hint of a smile. Finding none, she eventually tilts her head to the side and asks, "Why do you know that?"

I shrug. "When I was in sixth grade, my teacher invited a butterfly man to speak at our school. He brought Monarchs and Swallowtails and Painted Ladies and caterpillars." I pause, don my most knowing look, and share, "A group of caterpillars is called an army."

I think she might laugh, but what she does instead is drag a finger through the icing of my cinnamon roll, smear it on my nose, and say, "You're a constant surprise, Juli Singer. A constant surprise."

At three o'clock, I head home to get cleaned up and invite Scarlett to opening night. At the mention of Rhett's name, she yips once and wags her feathery plume of a tail, dancing eagerly around my feet. It's cute until her needle-teeth snatch at the hems of my jeans. "Hey now," I warn. "That's enough. I know you're excited, but I'm not ready to go yet. Give me half an hour."

It takes closer to forty-five minutes because I spend way too long in the shower. In addition to lugging kegs with Petey and jack-o-lanterns with Mac, a portion of my day was also spent crawling around under the porch in an effort to hide the extension cords used for Charley's twinkling white lights. I've got threads of spider webs clinging to my face and hair and no matter how many times I attempt to brush them away, I still feel sticky. Plus, I'm nervous about tonight, and when I get really nervous about something, I tend to slow down. Like, get tired. Standing beneath that steady stream of water, letting the soap mingle with the day's grime before circling down the drain, I must yawn no fewer than thirty times. I think it's a defense mechanism or something: if I'm too tired to do something, then I obviously can't do it—no matter how important that something is. I mean, I can remember feeling absolutely *exhausted* before giving a twenty-minute presentation in college. That can't be normal.

It's my normal, though.

I have no intention of bailing on Charley so that I can take a nap instead. I throw on my nicest pair of jeans, a button-down shirt, and my favorite pair of Converse sneakers, grab my wallet and keys, and lock the front door on my way out. By four o'clock, Scarlett and I are cruising down Copper Drive with a bouquet of grocery-store flowers occupying the passenger's seat and a bottle of unopened bubbly standing upright in one of the truck's cup holders. "This is for now," I say to Charley, handing her the autumnal assortment of mums and dahlias and copper-colored roses, "because this is really happening. You did it! And this," I add, flashing the champagne's label before hiding it in the back of the refrigerator, "is for later."

"You're too much," she whispers, and her voice is watery. It takes me a moment to realize that she's on the verge of crying. So I walk over to her, wrap my arms around her shoulders and hold her close, resting my chin on the top of her head. "*You're* too much," I insist. "You're amazing."

Her voice is muffled when she answers, "I couldn't have done it without you."

"Yeah, well... with the exception of stripping the walls of ancient wallpaper, I had a lot of fun doing this renovation. I should probably actually thank you for giving me the opportunity."

"No you shouldn't," Charley says, pulling away so that she can look up at me. "Don't thank me. Please don't thank me, Juli. I didn't... You don't need to..." It's a struggle to find the words and her voice trails off, leaving me to ponder the weight of what *hasn't* been said. But then she plants her hands flat against my chest and stands on her tiptoes and presses her lips gently against mine. "Thank you," she says. "Just... thank you." Followed by, "You smell really good, by the way. Like men's deodorant."

There's a part of me that all of the sudden wants to sniff my armpit, but I refrain from doing so, and Charley continues, "You look good, too; I'm digging the rolled-up shirtsleeves and the absentee baseball cap. Maybe remember this look for future events."

"I'm making a mental note right now," I assure her, blushing despite myself. She giggles and walks away, and although I don't say it (maybe I should), Charley is looking pretty damn beautiful herself. She's got on this crimson sweater dress that's fitted-but-not-tight, with a slouchy neckline and three-quarter-length sleeves. Baseball-jersey-length sleeves. It hits an inch or two above her knees, which are bare, but then she's wearing these tall boots with fun teal-and-green-striped socks that stick out the top. Very cute. I watch her skirt around the bar and dart into the living room, checking for the thousandth time today to make sure that everything is in its rightful place, and as she's making her rounds, Addy hustles down the stairs and into the kitchen. His hair is damp, leading me to believe that he's recently showered, and his face is flushed. "I put the dogs in a spare bedroom," he informs me. "Do you think that's alright? I made sure they had water. Cordelia is 'freshening up' and Boomer will be here in five minutes. I sent him to pick up some more Brie; I'm worried we might run out of supplies. I have no idea where Molly is… checking a keg or something? And what about Charley?"

"Addy," I say. "Calm down. It's going to be fine."

He looks at me, eyes wide, and states very seriously, "I'm freaking out right now."

"Take a breath."

"I don't have time to breathe," he insists. "Go-time is twenty minutes from now."

"Addy," I say, walking over to place a hand on his shoulder. "You need to take a breath. Come on." I steer him out the side door and onto the porch, where we stand side by side, shivering. The night is crisp and clear. Stars blink above the orchard; the devilish grins of jack-o-lanterns flicker in the darkness. Addy's hot breath forms clouds of condensation that float upward and away, dissipating into nothingness. He runs a hand through his hair, across his face; he walks to the railing and leans heavily against it. "I am so nervous," he confides. "So incredibly nervous. I can't remember ever being this *nervous* before! What if I mess up? And overcook the quesadillas? Or what if we run out of Brie? Or chowder?"

"You will not run out of Brie," I assure him. "You will, in fact, probably have a ridiculous amount of Brie left over. And if you run out of chowder, customers will order quesadillas instead. It's possible that you *will* mess up, but if you burn a quesadilla, you'll toss it in the trash and make a new one. And Addy?"

He turns to face me, panic still loitering in his eyes. "Yeah?"

"If you mess up, no one's going to hold it against you. Charley and I? We've got your back."

It's this statement that finally allows him to take a real breath. To completely fill his lungs with fresh air, hold it there for a few seconds, and then release some of the worry and fear that's weighing him down. The change is visible: his slumped shoulders straighten, the crease in his forehead disappears, his face relaxes. And to think that all he needed was for someone to say, "I'm looking out for you. You're not alone." I give him a half-smile and he reciprocates the gesture and then Petey is suddenly rounding the corner, a cello strapped to his back, a microphone case clutched in one hand, and his wife at his side. "Hello, friends!" he says in greeting, and a grin lights his face. "Are we excited or what?"

"I'm excited!" Jenny exclaims. She climbs the porch steps and gives first Addy, then me, a tight squeeze. "I'm *really* excited to try this pumpkin ale that Petey keeps talking about. I swear he's mentioned it at least a dozen times today!"

"Because it's delicious," Petey insists. "After experiencing it tonight, ten bucks says you'll be mentioning it at least a dozen times tomorrow."

"Is that a bet?" Jenny confirms.

"It can be," her husband shrugs.

"Then you're on!"

They shake—Addy and I serving as witnesses—and then I hold the side door for everyone as we enter the kitchen. Boomer has returned and is stocking the refrigerator with more Brie than I have ever seen in one place while Cordelia busily peels apples at the sink. Charley, unsure of how to handle her nerves, flits about from one task to the next, checking to make sure the outdoor lights are on, and the jack-o-lanterns are lit, and the pictures on the walls are straight. When she notices Petey and Jenny, she claps her hands together and heaves a quiet sigh of relief. "I'm so glad you two are here! Where do you want to set up? In the living room?"

"That sounds perfect," I hear Jenny say as she follows Charley out of the kitchen. "We still have amps in the car that need to be br—"

"I'm on it!" I call after them, and duck back into the chilly night without bothering to grab my jacket. Goosebumps immediately sprout on my arms and I book it across the lawn, my sneakered feet soundless until I reach the parking lot, where although the gritty crunch of gravel is quiet, it is still audible. Even more audible is the hum of an approaching engine. I glance over to see headlights slowly navigating the drive, bouncing and blinking as they maneuver small hills. "This is it," I whisper to myself, and reach into the car to retrieve one of the amplifiers. Emerging, I give a polite nod to the newly arrived customers, but am slightly surprised when the driver lowers his window and asks, "Need some help with those?"

The voice is familiar; I'd recognize it anywhere. So I set the amp on the ground and walk over to the couple in the silver hatchback. "Hey guys," I say to my parents. "Where'd this car come from?"

"It's new," my father informs me, as if I couldn't determine that on my own. He shuts off the engine, unfastens his seatbelt, and opens the driver's side door, planting one foot on the ground and beaming up at me. "Just bought it today. What do you think?"

What I think is that the decision to purchase a new set of wheels is long overdue—if cars are anything like cats, then Dad's Buick was definitely on its ninth life—but what I am is surprised. I'd just assumed that the Electra would remain in the family until it died. Now I see that that assumption was less than accurate. As soon as I lean down to examine the leather seats, brightly lit dashboard, and six-disk CD changer, that classic new-car aroma meets my nostrils. My eyes must turn a little bit glassy because my ma, sitting in the passenger's seat, gives me a warm smile and says, "Honey, are you in shock? I bet you never thought you'd see the day that Dad would show up with a new car, did you?"

"Never," I have to agree. And then to my father I pose, "Are you sick or something?"

"Sick?" he repeats, confused.

"Like, deathly ill? Just given a month to live?"

He laughs as he climbs from the vehicle. "If I were sick," he assures me, clapping a hand firmly on my shoulder, "then you'd be admiring a cherry-red sports car right now. Not a Subaru. I can promise you that."

I shrug out of his grip and return to the abandoned amplifier. Another set of headlights has just turned into the farmhouse's drive and Charley will want to have all of the Goodes' equipment set up before it gets too busy. "If you don't mind grabbing that other amp," I say to my father, "that'd be great. Petey and Jenny are inside setting up. They're tonight's entertainment."

"And Charley?" my ma wonders, hurrying after me.

I know what she's asking, but I decide to be a smart ass about it. "Charley's not performing tonight," I say over my shoulder. "She's not much for singing and she doesn't play an instrument, but she will be serving beer."

The rolling of eyes may be a silent action, but I swear I can hear my ma execute a hardcore eye roll. I can also hear her ask of my father, playfully, "How did we manage to raise such a brat?" to which he responds, "I think that's one area where he takes after you." I don't turn around, but I know Ma slaps Dad lightly with her purse, and Dad reaches out to grab hold of her hand, and then they walk like that, with their fingers intertwined, all the way to the porch. When I finally stop outside the door and turn around, I see that I am right. My parents are very much in love. Way more in love than most people who have been married for going on forty years. "Come on," I say, propping the front door open with my foot and motioning them inside. "I'll introduce you to Charley."

I've had girlfriends before. Not many, but a few, and while obviously none of them proved to be *the one*, a couple of them managed to stick around long enough to meet my parents. The introductions always went smoothly enough (handshakes followed by "We've heard so much about you from Juli!" followed by awkward stories about me as a child followed by "Thank you so much for dinner; everything was delicious!" followed by pleasant-enough goodbyes that rarely turned into second hellos) but the introduction of Charley to my parents is different—*completely* different—because Charley handles everything perfectly.

She's flustered and flushed as she enters the kitchen, having heard the door and wanting to greet her first guests, but as she glances from Ma to

Dad, and then back to Ma, she must recognize a few similar features because she looks then to me and asks brightly, "These are your parents?"

I nod, preparing to offer up the necessary names, but before I have a chance to speak the words, Charley has already crossed the kitchen and is embracing first my mother, then my father, in a hug. "Your son," she says, standing before them and beaming, "is probably the best thing that could have happened to me at this point in my life. You must be so incredibly proud of him! I don't know how I would have pulled off any of this without his help." She opens her arms in acknowledgment of the kitchen, spinning around to marvel at all of it, and when she turns back around to face my parents, she tilts her head and widens her eyes and asks excitedly, "Would you like the grand tour?"

We take them around the house together, pointing out the newly sanded floors and discussing the narrowness of the before-renovation doorways and sharing the story behind the hop-garden acrylic. Ma laughs out loud when she sees the claw-foot tub-turned-planter ("Juli may have mentioned this once or twice") and Dad can't get over the craftsmanship that went into the cuckoo clock hanging in the living room ("A wedding gift from one of Gramps's old friends," Charley explains. "Oliver Clay, I think was his name. They had a falling out of some sort, but Gramps kept the clock. It stopped ticking a long time ago.").

As the night progresses, curious townspeople slowly trickle into the Brewhaha. Asher brings Annie, Hank escorts Eileen, and Lucy Campbell brings the gift of a ceramic jack-o-lantern. "Just because," she explains pleasantly to Charley. "Just to say congratulations!" The customers sip pints of Petey's pumpkin ale and tap their feet to the folksy tunes provided by the Goodes and some of them are even bold enough to dosey-doe a few times around the living room. Addy does not run out of Brie, but a dent is definitely made in his stockpile of cheese: the quesadillas are a huge success.

And Charley herself is over the top.

She greets each customer as if he or she is an old friend, lost and gone for a decade, but now back for the long haul; she opts for hugs instead of handshakes every time. I hang back, right on the cusp of corners and shadows, content to simply observe her self-assured interactions and casual conversations. When Doc Delaney stops by to sample the Fuzzless Hopper, she jokingly tries to coerce him into sharing his recipe for sweet potato fries, and though Doc chuckles and averts his gaze, his mouth definitely forms a secret three-syllable word: paprika.

The owners of Simply Clay and the Tavern aren't the only entrepreneurs to wander into the Brewhaha on opening night. Joe Abbott, of Bottomless Joe's fame, sidles into the farmhouse around nine o'clock and takes a seat at the bar. Charley—her emerald eyes twinkling—perches on the stool to his left and blends sarcasm with pleasantries when she wonders if he might like a shot of espresso with his chocolaty stout. "Sort of like an Irish Car Bomb?" I overhear him ask.

"More like a Lake Caywood Caffeine Bomb," Charley answers, and Molly laughs from behind the line of taps. "Or a Lake Caywood Caffeine *Buzz*," she volunteers.

Joe shrugs. "It sounds better than Red Bull and vodka," he admits. "I'll try anything once."

So Addy brews extra strong coffee and Boomer carries two shot glasses over to the bar and Charley and Joe plop them into their beers on the count of three. "Cheers!" they exchange in unison, quickly clinking pint glasses before chugging their frothy beverages. They both sport mustaches of foam when the competition concludes. Joe wins by a sip or two, much to Charley's chagrin, but the duo nevertheless commemorates the event with a selfie. "Making memories," she whispers to me on her way from the kitchen to the study, dancing her fingers across my chest. "That's what tonight's all about, right?"

Shortly after midnight, Rhett and Scarlett join the party. Although still very much alive, the crowd has definitely dwindled, so Charley deems it safe for the pooches to make an appearance. They run downstairs with their tails wagging, eager to greet each visitor and accept any scraps of food that might be up for grabs. I keep an eye on the front door and Petey keeps tabs on the side entrance, neither one of us wanting to put a damper on the night by losing a dog.

For the most part, Scarlett sticks close to my side. She's a shy girl, often wary of strangers, and tends to be intimidated by large crowds. Rhett, on the other hand, is about as sociable as they come. He disappears for long stretches, happy to say hello to new faces and have his ears scratched by unfamiliar hands, but does make it a point to check in every now and again. At one point, he turns up with a billiard ball in his mouth. It's striped with royal blue and bears the number ten, and when I show it to Charley, she widens her eyes and asks excitedly, "Where did he find it? Did another room show up?" It's almost as if she's *expecting* a specific room to make itself known.

We search both the first floor and the second, but if some sort of game room *had* made an appearance, it's since vanished. "That doesn't mean it won't show up again later," I assure Charley, acutely aware of the disappointment she's experiencing. "This old farmhouse is weird. You know that. When it's time for you to find the room, you will."

"You're right," she agrees, her tone flat. "I know you're right. I was just really hoping—"

"For a game of pool?" I predict.

She grins, but the gesture is obviously forced.

"Hey," I say, resting my hands on Charley's shoulders and leaning in to plant a quick kiss on her forehead. "We just need to be patient, okay? Tonight is only opening night. We've got all the time in the world to find a room with a pool table, and when we finally do, I can *guarantee* that you will kick my butt. That's not a sport at which I excel."

She raises her eyes to meet mine, wondering, "Is pool really considered to be a sport? I think of it as more of a game."

I shrug and take the blue billiard ball from her, relocating it to a shelf in the study. "I don't know," I tell her, gripping her hand in mine and leading her back to the kitchen, "but whatever it is—sport or game—I'm really bad at it."

The beer she drinks with Joe is the only one Charley has all night. It isn't until after Molly's last call for alcohol officially clears the Brewhaha that the bottle of chilled champagne is retrieved from the refrigerator. "Noni used to have fancy, long-stemmed flutes," Charley says, placing the bottle on the bar. "Anyone know if they were saved? And if they were, where they might be?"

Addy doesn't answer, but he does walk over to a cabinet near the sink and swing the door open. I watch him reach a hand inside, rummaging the whole way in the back, eventually unearthing the flutes in question. "I noticed them the other day," he says, pulling them out one at a time, "and thought they might come in handy at some point."

"You were right," Molly praises. "Good call." She hands a bar towel to Charley, who peels away the bottle's foil before wrapping the towel around the bulging cork. There's a muted pop followed by the trickling of golden liquid into eight glasses. Even Addy is served a sip, despite being underage, but before he's allowed to indulge, Charley clears her throat and asks all of us—Addy, Molly, Boomer, Cordelia, Petey, Jenny, and I—to raise our glasses to Gramps. "Because he was all about good beer and good times," she says, and I can't help but laugh as she narrows her eyes, considering the beverage that she's holding. "Good beer, good times, and the occasional glass of champagne," she corrects. "To Gramps!"

And we all cheerfully chorus, "To Gramps!"

We stand on the porch, side by side, my arm wrapped around Charley's waist and her arms crossed over her chest, holding in body heat. The taillights of Addy's car bump down the long drive, shrinking from vibrant orbs to faded specks, and then eventually disappearing completely as a left-hand turn is made onto Copper. Charley leans her head against my chest, resting it just below my collarbone. "I can't believe we did it," she sighs. "And even more than that… I can't believe we'll be doing it all over again tomorrow."

"This is why so many restaurants are closed on Mondays, I guess."

"This is why the Brewhaha is closed on Mondays," Charley giggles. "I literally feel like I could sleep for days."

I reach over and brush the bangs from her forehead, caress her cheekbone with my thumb. "Then maybe I should let you get to bed, huh? I'll round up Scarlett and head home for the night, but I can come back in the morning if you need me. Or…" My voice falters as my thoughts travel back in time, remembering words spoken by Asher. About taking my own advice.

About jumping in with both feet.

"Or?" Charley prompts, and I swallow once, find my voice, suggest, "Or I could just stay."

She's quiet at first, impossible to read. I worry that I've somehow offended her, am about to issue an apology... but then she nuzzles closer and buries her face in my chest, warm. I can feel the change in the shape of her cheek as she slowly begins to smile. "Or," she finally whispers, "you could just stay."

I take a breath, hold it in my lungs, wonder if I've heard correctly. Those are five words that she's never spoken before, and now she's spoken them so softly that I can't help but wonder if the sentence was a figment of my imagination. But it's not, because Charley turns her head, stares up at me with heavy-lidded eyes, and grins. "I think that you should."

"Then I will."

Her shyness is adorable as she fumbles to hold my hand in hers, leads me inside, upstairs, down the hall to her bedroom. I've been in here before, but not at night. Charley walks to a nightstand and switches on a light, illuminating a spread of patchwork. Squares of blue and green—some light, some dark like the midnight sky—join together to form a solid cover. I reach down and run the tips of my fingers over a piece of corduroy fabric. "Did your grandmother make this?" I ask, and Charley scoffs, amused. "Noni? No way. She wasn't much of a seamstress. She could bake a mean apple pie, but sewing wasn't really her thing. I'm pretty sure this was purchased from one of those soulless department store chains, where you can buy anything from underwear to a new spaghetti strainer."

"Oh," I say, feeling foolish, but Charley seems not to notice the color rising in my cheeks. She flops onto her back, crossing her arms behind her head, and closes her eyes. "Three, five, and seven," she mutters. "I've seen all the odd numbers except for one. Will you show me now?"

It takes me a second to understand what she's talking about. "You mean my tattoos?"

"The footnotes, yeah."

"You want to know about the first one?"

She nods, her eyes still closed. "I want to see it."

"Alright," I agree, sauntering to her side of the bed and perching there beside her. "You'll have to open your eyes. It's right here, behind my left ear. As a kid, I got into a living-room wrestling match with one of my friends and conked my head on the side of a coffee table. Two stitches—not a big deal—but it left a mark."

"Not a mark that you can see," Charley points out, reaching with a hand to brush my hair aside. Her fingers tickle as they gently touch the faintly elevated scar on the back of my head. "But I guess you can feel it, can't you?"

"Yep." I allow myself to fall back on the bed, landing beside Charley with a quiet thud and turning my head to face her. She has a soft profile: subtly sloped nose, slightly parted lips, perfectly arched brows that always make her appear a little bit excited. "You're beautiful, you know?"

"You're not so bad yourself." And with those same fingers that were just in my hair, trailing down my neck, lingering on my shoulder… those same fingers traipse across my chest, slip between the placket of my shirt, fumble to unfasten a pearly button. "Do you need some help?" I ask, flashing a lopsided smile in her direction, and when Charley mirrors the expression, she pairs it with the words, "Right now, I just need you."

Her voice is a whisper and her breath, when she leans in for a kiss, is sweet champagne. The gesture leaves me feeling a little bit tipsy. She kicks off her boots and peels off her dress, lifting it over her head. The result is a crackling of static. Wisps of her short hair stand on end, catching the lamplight and glowing mahogany. She straddles me—wearing nothing but striped knee socks, panties, and a bra—and even though now is not the most opportune of times, I can't help but wonder, "Are there holes in the heels of those socks?" Because to know that there are would make me love her more.

Charley pauses, her face inches from mine, and answers almost patronizingly, "You know that there are, Juli Singer. And please… don't ever let anyone tell you that you're not romantic, because your ability to say just the right thing at *just* the right moment is, as illustrated tonight, uncanny."

She unbuttons my shirt then, and the buckle on my belt, and I run my hands through her hair while she disappears to make it erect, performing magic with hands and tongue and those perfect lips. The jolt of excitement is almost immediate; that heat in my groin wonderfully intense. It courses up my spine, down my legs. I moan, and Charley returns, suddenly above me, her emerald-slit eyes half-open, half-closed, the insides of her thighs tight against the outsides of mine. I reach behind her, scramble to undo the clasp of her bra, toss the garment aside and cup her small breasts in my hands. Her skin is so soft. And then I am in her, just like that—the rhythm more adagio than allegro: peaceful and good.

I've had plenty of firsts with plenty of girls and on some level, every single one of those interactions could be described as awkward. But nothing about making love to Charley is awkward; nothing about it is wrong. The experience is, in a word, *comfortable.* I feel closer to her now than I ever have before, and while the feeling is positively terrifying… it's at the same time staggeringly *right.*

Afterwards, we lie side by side on the bed, under the patchwork comforter: me in nothing but a button down with the shirtsleeves rolled up, Charley in nothing but her knee socks with the holes in the heels. She rests her head on my shoulder, inhaling the mingled aroma of sex and man-scented deodorant, her breaths growing shallower and shallower as she slowly drifts to sleep. But I stay up for a while longer… to hold her, and marvel at the contours of her face, and simply *be aware* of this beautiful creature known as Charley Lane.

It isn't until the sun is creeping up over the orchard that I finally allow my lids to fall closed.

18.
Charley

"I kept my arm around you all night," Juli had greeted me the morning after, one of those crooked grins lingering there on his lips. He'd sounded proud of the accomplishment. "My arm didn't even cramp up."

I'd snuggled in closer, not really answering, and rested my face on his bare chest. There'd been a lot of thoughts coursing through my head at that moment—if I'm being honest, there still are—and talk about what had happened between us the night before hadn't really been something I'd wished to delve into. So I'd kept my lips pressed together, muting the whispers in my mind.

Juli hadn't forced conversation. He'd just lain there, breathing even and rhythmic breaths, until too much sun lit the room. And then he'd wondered, "What time will Addy and everyone show up today?"

"He could already be here," I'd answered, because the *click-clack* of Rhett's nails could be heard clattering down the stairs, traveling toward the front door in order to greet a possible newcomer. "Everyone on staff has a key."

"Then we should get up." He'd gently slid his arm out from beneath me, sat up, and thrown his legs over the side of the bed. His shirt was still on, hanging open in the front, but that had been his only article of clothing. That's how I'd managed to notice the small *2* positioned toward the bottom of his right butt cheek, situated in the middle of an almost-heart-shaped scar. "What happened?" I'd asked, commenting on the tattoo, but of course Juli's back had been to me so he hadn't noticed.

"What happened," he'd answered, "is we had sex last night and I managed to lose my boxers in the process. Are they on your side of the bed?"

"No!" I'd laughed. "I mean what happened to your backside? I want the story behind the little two that's inked there."

Juli'd glanced at me over his shoulder, throwing a painfully embarrassed expression in my direction. And then with a grumble he'd recounted the story of that drunken summer night spent with an ex-girlfriend on the shores of Lake Caywood. "It was a Saturday in July, between my junior and senior years, and we'd had enough beer to think it was a good idea to go skinny-dipping. Normal geese go to bed with the sun," he'd informed me, "but the goose I encountered came straight from Hell. A devil goose. I must've gotten too close to her nest or something because she came out of nowhere and did her best to take a chunk out of me. The girl I was with was still in the lake when it happened, safely treading water, and she thought the whole thing was hilarious." He'd grimaced at that point; the shudder had hunched his shoulders and caused him to involuntarily duck his head. And then he'd concluded, "I did not think it was hilarious. Still don't. I sprinted a quarter mile buck naked down the shoreline trying to get away from that evil, feathered thing… And," he'd added, smacking his own butt, "I have the scar to prove it."

"So when did you start recording them?"

"The scars?"

"Yeah. When did you start getting the tattoos?"

"Senior year of college, but I came up with the idea in high school, when one of my English teachers, Mr. Kent, taught us about footnotes. I just didn't have a whole lot of scars to go with it at that point in time."

"But you do now?"

I'd watched him retrieve his jeans from the floor and pull them on, never-minding about the forgotten underwear; I'd waited while he'd pulled on his socks and charcoal-colored Converse sneakers. And then he'd returned to the bed, his shirt still unbuttoned, and said after delivering a quick kiss to my forehead, "I have seven."

Now, lying alone in my bed on this frigid November night, I force the memory out of my head, pull the covers snug beneath my chin, and try to drift back into the Land of Nod. But it is no use. The bar will be open for another hour and downstairs someone is playing the piano, which means the room with the expansive windows has revealed itself for the second time this month. The Brewhaha had been hopping earlier this evening when I'd called it a night, the pounding in my head making it too difficult to tend bar or talk to customers. "You can handle it," I'd said to Addy. "Just lock up tight when you leave."

He'd given me a sympathetic look, almost as if he too was capable of experiencing the pain in my head, and promised, "I will. You can trust me."

"I know I can."

I hadn't bothered with pajamas, choosing to climb under the covers still wearing that day's clothes. Now, though, with the throbbing behind my eyes somewhat subsiding (despite the belting of "Piano Man" from below), I decide to change. Rhett lifts his head when he hears the covers being thrown back; the metal tags on his collar jingle and his chocolate eyes peer up at me from the floor. "It's okay, pup," I assure him. "Go back to sleep." But of course he can't because he is awake now, anticipating a one o'clock-in-the-morning adventure. There's the familiar sound of him clambering to his feet, the hollow *tap-tap-tap* of his toenails against the hardwood as he prances over to me, the cold dampness of his nose pressed against my palm. I take a moment to pat him on the head, massage his silky ears, tell him he's a good boy—and then he sits, waiting patiently while I swap jeans for sweatpants, a wool sweater for a soft thermal. My bed beckons to me, but not to my canine companion. Rhett walks to the closed door and scratches at the wood, asking to be released from the confines of my bedroom. What he wants is to socialize with the company downstairs, and even though I know Addy would toss him scraps of uneaten quiche and Molly would watch him like a hawk, making sure he didn't slip out with a borderline-tipsy customer, I want him here with me. If Rhett desires a brief change of scenery, though, I can at least provide him with that.

We quietly slip across the hall to the office. Rather than flip on the overhead light, I shuffle to the desk and tug the chain of the glass-shaded lamp that resides there. Snap-flicker-bright. It springs to life, casting a dull greenish glow on the walls and a puddle of light on the desk. I take a seat in the recently purchased ergonomic swivel chair and pick up a gel pen, clicking the end so that the inky tip vanishes and reappears, vanishes and reappears, vanishes and reappears, vanishes and reappears…

Juli has been working on the upstairs of the farmhouse one room at a time and this is the first space on the second floor to be completed. Sage walls, white trim, a braided rug on the floor. It's a peaceful little room that sometimes opens into a tower. I've taken to paying the bills here, and sorting through the day's mail.

Yesterday's mail brought something unexpected.

Addy had been experimenting with cranberry-jalapeno salsa, and Cordelia was chopping cilantro for chicken-tortilla soup, and Molly was conversing with some handsome fellow who couldn't say enough about Petey's pumpkin ale, so Rhett and I had ventured outside for a walk. I'd bundled up in my black woolen coat and red cashmere scarf (the only cashmere I own, a gift), because the air in November is crisper than that of October's. Its flavor is blue-grey and it carries the aroma of woodstoves and its temperature is capable of invoking shivers so powerful that they'll knock a person's knees together.

We'd taken the southern route, meandering among the bare trees that only months before were laden with peaches and pears and plums. Rhett had run ahead, his tail standing tall and always at attention, his nose rarely more than an inch off the ground. Every now and again he'd catch sight of a squirrel, out gathering nuts for the winter. The desire to chase it too intense to resist, Rhett would bound ahead, ears bouncing, until the furry creature disappeared into the treetops, out of reach, but not quite out of mind. "Come on, pup!" I'd call each time, commanding his attention away from the overhead branches. "Come over here!"

The mailbox had been our destination, just as it always was, and when we reached it, I'd stuck my hand into the large metal box and extracted a pile of bills and sales fliers and catalogs. But this time there'd also been a scarlet envelope marred by no return address and very recognizable handwriting: capital R's.

I hadn't opened it right away.

I'd merely tucked it between an oversized department-store coupon and the electric bill and walked back to the house, feigning to all the world that everything was still very much wonderful. But later that evening, before Juli came over for a Brewhaha dinner and the happy hour crowd filled the seats at the bar, I disappeared upstairs and sat in this exact seat and slid Gramps's silver letter opener beneath the flap of the envelope. There'd been a card inside.

There still is because I'd hidden that card in its red envelope in the back of a desk drawer, under a box of unused Christmas greetings and behind an extra tape dispenser that's currently void of tape. But I unearth it now. Someone continues to pound the piano downstairs and a chorus of joyful laughter and off-key singing carries up the staircase. With this soundtrack playing in the background, I place that card in the pool of light on the desk and stare at the cover: a lone cardinal whistling a tune from its perch on a snow-covered branch.

Saw this and thought of you, he's written on the inside. *I guess you'Re doing okay...? I'm not suRe whetheR you Received my last letteR oR not, but I think about you often, ChaRley. EveRy day. I know I messed up – I'm not asking you to foRgive me – but could you just, when the time comes, somehow let me know?*

He signed it with the L-word.

Love.

Love, ChaRlie.

The sight of it—of his signature and his words and the familiar capital R's—causes my stomach to clench and my throat to close in on itself. The realization that he believes he's done something that requires forgiveness... he doesn't *need* to be forgiven. The only thing that Charlie Flynn ever did wrong was love me too much; *I* should be the one asking for forgiveness. Not him.

To put it into words… to write it down in a way that makes sense… I'm just not sure that it can be done, but it's probably worth a try. I find a legal pad and flip to a fresh sheet of yellow, lined paper; click the end of the pen so the tip once again reappears; jot today's date on the first line. "That's most likely the only part of this letter that'll come easily," I mutter aloud, staring at the three sets of numbers divided by long hyphens. And then I start to write.

∞

At nine o'clock on Thanksgiving morning, when Juli still hasn't emerged from the bedroom after I've showered and dressed and brewed a strong pot of coffee *and* fed both Rhett and Scarlett heaping-because-it's-a-holiday scoops of kibble, I return to the second floor of the farmhouse and reenter my bedroom. "Are you planning on getting out of bed today at some point?" I wonder, more flirtatious than sarcastic. "Or is this unusual behavior a ploy to get me back under the covers?"

Juli opens his eyes and stares at the ceiling, not really looking in my direction. There's a lopsided little smile on his face, but it doesn't seem genuine, and I understand why when he asks, "Do you remember when you told me not to lug all those kegs from the barn to the house by myself yesterday?"

"I do."

"Well, I'm now realizing that I should've listened to that advice."

"Because you hurt your back?"

"Destroyed," Juli groans. "I'm fairly confident that I've *destroyed* my back."

I lean against the door jamb and rest my head against the wooden frame, considering the situation. I know very little about injured backs. It's not something I've ever experienced firsthand. "Destroyed, huh? Are you able to sit up?"

"No."

"Have you tried?"

Juli makes a noncommittal "eh" which causes me to question his desire to leave the bed.

"What if I help you?"

"I don't know," he groans. "I think that I'm definitely going to need your help if my goal is to *stand* up. I've pulled muscles in my back before, and messed up my neck before, but nothing like this. This is, like, *excruciating.* But I want Thanksgiving dinner. I want turkey and mashed potatoes."

"Then give me your hands," I say, walking across the room to join him. "I'll be gentle."

He doesn't cry out as I help to pull him into a sitting position, but he does wince quite a bit; his eyes are watering by the time he eventually manages to plant his feet on the floor. I'm thinking that maybe I ought to call his parents and tell them that we won't be over for the much-anticipated midday feast, but Juli vetoes that suggestion and forces himself to his feet. The poor guy can barely stand up straight. "Maybe a shower will help," I propose. "Because of the heat."

Juli agrees to give it a try and we shuffle down the hall to the bathroom, taking it one agonizing step at a time. He manages to step out of his boxers just fine, but I have to help him lift the t-shirt he's wearing over his head. "I'd offer to shower with you…" I begin, but trail off without finishing the sentence because it's obvious that this task has already been checked off my list. I'm fully dressed and minor makeup has been applied. Juli shakes his head absentmindedly and gingerly steps over the avocado-hued lip of the tub, disappearing behind the curtain. "That's okay," he assures me. "I'm not feeling especially frisky right now. It's like I went to bed a thirty-seven-year-old and woke up forty years later, Rip Van Winkle style. My beard should be to my knees."

The idea of Juli Singer with a beard makes me laugh. I'm not sure that four decades would be long enough for him to grow facial hair; he's always so clean-shaven, and part of that is due to the fact that his whiskers don't seem to be capable of amounting to more than mere scruff. "Don't beat yourself up, old man. I'm happy to help."

"But Charley," he says, "I can't even bend over to wash my *feet* right now. You are going to, like, have to help me get dressed." The sorrow in his voice makes my heart ache; despite not being able to see it, I know that his face is burning right now.

"It's really okay," I assure him. "I don't mind at all. I'm going to make the bed and then I'll be back to check on you. Just shout if you need something."

I leave the bathroom door open and disappear down the hall to the bedroom, quickly smoothing the sheets and straightening the blanket and tucking everything snugly under the mattress. Over the sound of running water, I can make out a few butchered lyrics from The Clash's "Train in Vain," letting me know that Juli isn't exactly wallowing in the depths of despair… but then again, it would take a *lot* to keep that boy from singing. I pull up the comforter, fluff the pillows, and toss them on the bed before racing back to my patient.

"In the second stanza," I say as I step into the room, announcing my presence to Juli, "I'm pretty sure the line isn't 'I'll remember who sings the most.'"

"It isn't?"

"No. But if *I* had written that song about *us*, then I would have used that line."

"Because I sing the most," Juli states, charmingly matter-of-fact about it, and I have to agree, "Yes. Because you *definitely* sing the most."

The water shuts off and Juli pushes the shower curtain aside, reaching for a towel. He does that thing that boys do: blots the excess water from his hair, wipes his face, drags the terry fabric across his chest, around his back, and then ties it casually at his waist. "My back feels approximately five percent better," he volunteers, carefully stepping out of the tub and onto the bathmat. His feet leave wet footprints there. "Will you slather me up with Bengay? I think that might help."

I apply the cream like sunscreen, massaging it into his skin until the white streaks have been completely absorbed. My fingers and palms tingle from the effort and the humid air smells strongly of mint.

Back in the bedroom, I help Juli lower himself onto the bed and do my best to comfortably prop him up with a mound of pillows. "Jeans or sweatpants?" I query, expecting him to choose the latter, but he surprises me by answering, "Jeans. I don't want my ma to suspect anything's wrong."

I carry the denim and a few other articles of clothing over to the bed, toss them down beside him, and say, "I'm pretty sure she's gonna be able to tell, Mr. Van Winkle, but if jeans are what you want, then that's what you'll get." I guide his feet through the boxers and the pants, sliding them up over his knees and allowing Juli to take it from there. It's while I'm assisting with his socks, though, that I finally make it a point to really study the bottom of his right foot. There, printed in a very tiny sans serif font, are seven numbers followed by seven brief descriptions, and at the end of each description is a date listed in parentheses. It occurs to me that now is my chance to discover footnotes four and six. "Stepped on a nail," I read aloud, and then glance up to meet Juli's gaze. "So I'm guessing number four is on your *other* foot?"

He nods. "It is."

"And number six…" I scan his foot, silently skim the succinct account of the incident, and look up, wide eyed, to confirm, "You fell through a deck?"

"I was in the process of building it," Juli explains. "Just the frame was in place. I lost my footing and slipped right through a gap, but somehow managed to catch myself on the way down. I landed with a board under each armpit, and the bruises I sported as a result were beyond impressive, but I also acquired a splinter below my left arm in the process. A big splinter. It got infected and left a scar." He carefully lifts his arm and points to a very small *6* that's been inked among the wiry hair sprouting there. "And those are all of my tattoos."

"Do you think you'll end up with more?"

"I hope not," he confides. "Getting those tattoos on the bottom of my foot hurt like a son of a bitch, so unless something really big and worth remembering happens, I'm content with seven. It's a decent number."

"Some even consider it lucky," I say, directing the sock over his foot and partway up his calf.

"But not you?"

I shrug and rock back on my heels, debating whether or not I have an actual opinion about the number seven. Deciding that I do not, I conclude, "I just like eights better, that's all."

Juli's eyes travel to the ring on my finger. "Because sometimes an eight is more than just an eight. Sometimes it lasts for an infinity." He pauses, flashing an off-kilter grin in my direction before asking, "Do you know what the zero said to the eight?"

I give him a questioning look, but neglect to provide a verbal prompt. Juli is snickering when he answers, "Nice belt!"

Mrs. Singer—or Marcela, as she tells me to call her—most definitely notices that her son is more than a bit out of commission. It takes her approximately three-point-five seconds to do so, too. "What happened?" she demands, sternly, upon swinging open the front door and finding Juli struggling to navigate the single porch step. Scarlett, nimble as ever, charges right past all of us and into the house; Rhett follows closely on her heels, though he does pause to lick the back of Marcela's hand in greeting.

The easy athleticism of the dogs only results in making Juli appear even more injured than he already does. And yet, he insists, "I'm fine, Ma." It's a blatant lie, and an unconvincing one at that. "I just pulled something in my back is all. Not a big deal."

"You sure are shuffling around like it's a big deal," Marcela retorts. She walks to her son and wraps an arm around his waist; I'm holding the same position on his other side. By using the two of us as crutches, he makes it onto the porch and through the front door, wincing with each step. "Maybe we could set up the heating pad," he suggests once he's gotten his breath back. "Would that be alright?"

"Of course. Did you take anything?"

"Pills, you mean?"

She nods.

"Just some ibuprofen."

"How many?"

He speaks the word sheepishly, hanging his head when he says it: "Five?"

"Julian!" his mother exclaims. "*Five?*"

He shrugs. "It really hurts."

Marcela shakes her head, obviously concerned, and calls up to her husband on the second floor: "Ed! Bring the heating pad along with you when you come down. Juli hurt his back. He's hobbling around like an eighty-year-old."

I do what I can to stifle my laughter because the expression on Juli's face is one of misery. "Come on," I say, linking my arm through his. "Let's get you situated at the table. Mashed potatoes and turkey, coming right up! Maybe you'll even be able to surpass your five-pound Jamboree goal today."

He gives me an appreciative grin and provides directions to the dining room, pointing out interesting home details along the way. For example, there's a framed piece of artwork in the hallway that Juli created when he was only six years old: white and black crayon on aqua construction paper. The image is that of a white tiger standing in a river. If I'm being honest, it's not very good, but Marcela apparently has a real fondness for it. "I went through a phase where I was a little bit obsessed with white tigers," he tells me. "I had a white tiger stuffed animal—Rocky—that I slept with at night, and I dressed up as a white tiger for Halloween that year, and I used to check out nothing but white tiger books from the library. Weird, right?"

"Not so much. I mean, I had pretty much the same experience, but not with white tigers," I share. "My fascination was with sloths."

"Sloths?"

"Yep. I had a giant poster of one above my bed. They're pretty gnarly-looking creatures."

"Yeah, they are," Juli agrees, because how could he not? They've got those crazy-long fingernails and smooshed-up faces and shaggy, moss-infested fur. But there's really only so much a person can say about sloths, and by the time we finally trundle our way into the dining room, Ed Singer is right behind us. "You must've lifted something you shouldn't have," he observes, plugging in the heating pad and situating it behind his son's back.

"Kegs," Juli admits. "The night before Thanksgiving is just an impromptu class reunion waiting to happen. *Many* impromptu class reunions, actually. We didn't want to run out of beer."

"And we didn't," I add, "thanks to Juli."

Ed moves to the other side of the table and stands behind the chair that he'll probably end up occupying a few minutes from now, drumming his thumbs against the slatted back. "So it sounds like business is good," he observes. "You've had a decent turnout most nights?"

"We have," I answer. "Last night was probably the busiest so far, if you don't count the grand opening."

"Either last night or Halloween," Juli pipes up. "Halloween was pretty nuts."

"Oh, that's right… You told me that, but I forgot." On the evening of October thirty-first, I'd been hit hard by a migraine and ended up going to bed around eight o'clock. My doctor would have instructed me to take two pills and call it a night; I swallowed three because the pain was that bad. Downstairs, the majority of Lake Caywood's twenty-something population had turned out for homebrewed beer and festive food. Addy's pumpkin-Brie quesadillas, having received a standing ovation, returned for a second performance and Cordelia made personal pizzas topped with apple, goat cheese, and toasted pecans. Customers wore ill-fitting fangs that glowed in the dark, painted their faces to sport triangle noses and long whiskers, and adorned their heads with devil horns that shimmered with red glitter. Petey Goode brought his cello and Jenny brought her voice and the two led everyone in a "Monster Mash" sing-along.

I'd missed all of it, of course, but had been provided with a full account the next morning when Juli showed up in my bedroom with lattés from Bottomless Joe's and Piping Hot almond scones. He'd kicked off his Converse sneakers, flopped down on top of the patchwork quilt, and filled me in on all the important details.

Ed nods his head once, considering all that we've shared and the recent success of the business, and then he asks, "Legally, you've taken all of the necessary steps, right? Not just about a liquor license and restaurant codes—I know that stuff's under control—but about ownership? In the event that something would happen?"

"I, um—" I begin, because the question catches me more than a little off guard, and Juli must sense my discomfort because he reaches over and squeezes my knee, explaining, "Dad's an attorney; he's always asking this kind of stuff. Don't let it freak you out."

"Singer and Freund," Ed says, offering proof by naming his law office.

"I went to Starner, Sterner, and Baust," I volunteer. "Elliot Baust was my grandfather's lawyer, so he was already handling the estate, and I just stuck with him because it seemed like the easiest thing to do. I think we've got everything in order... He seems to know what he's doing."

"Oh, Elliot's a great guy," Ed assures me. "He'll take good care of you. I had to ask, though; it's the attorney in me."

I force a smile, still slightly shaken by the unexpected question, but neither Juli nor his father seems to notice. I listen to them fantasize about sweet potatoes and mashed potatoes and stuffing, and feign interest as they debate which pie is better: pumpkin or pecan. But I'm not really listening because there's a small part of me that wonders if Ed Singer *knows*. He couldn't, of course, because that would completely negate any sort of existing attorney-client privilege—and besides, Elliot Baust works for a different firm altogether—but the unasked question eats away at me, gnawing at my mind and occupying space that could be better spent on other, happier thoughts. I force myself to compartmentalize and voice my belief that pecan pie is the way to go.

"See?" Juli beams. "This is why I like her."

"That's the only reason?" I counter. "Because I like the same kind of pie as you?"

"Well, I mean... you've got some other nice qualities too," he concedes.

Marcela appears then. Her hands, hidden inside thick oven mitts, hold a steaming container of green bean casserole. "If you two wouldn't mind helping with the food," she says, glancing from her husband to me, "then I think we'll be able to eat in just a minute. And you," she adds, fixing Juli with a Mom Look, "stay put."

"I'll load up my plate awhile," he calls after her as she walks away, and over her shoulder Marcela responds, "No you will not."

It doesn't take very long to carry everything to the table and mere moments later we find ourselves seated around a smorgasbord of delicious food: quartered sweet potatoes roasted with thyme and garlic and red pepper flakes; mashed red potatoes with the skins still on; savory stuffing flecked with rosemary, parsley, and sage; fantastically moist turkey; creamy gravy; tangy-sweet cranberry salad loaded with apples and pineapple and nuts… My eyes are bigger than my stomach and I end up sneaking bits of stuffing to Rhett and Scarlett, who wait patiently beneath the table with their heads in my lap.

Juli's eyes are not bigger than his stomach. He, in fact, manages to consume seconds, thirds, *and* fourths. "This is my favorite meal of the year," he says with a shrug, dousing nearly everything on his plate with a brimming ladleful of gravy. "I've gotta take advantage of it." I must widen my eyes to about the size of his expanding stomach because he laughs and admits, "I *am* wishing that I'd opted for the sweatpants." He tugs at his waistband and I can't help but notice that his normally flat stomach is very much convex.

"You'll probably almost double the Jamboree weight gain," I predict. "Eight pounds. That's my guess."

"At least," Ed chuckles. "When this guy says that Thanksgiving is his favorite meal of the year, he means it. My money's on ten."

"There's money involved?" Marcela verifies.

"Might as well be," her husband responds. "Charley, are you willing to make it a ten-dollar bet?"

I have to laugh. Never before have I experienced a holiday quite as intentionally gluttonous as this one. Beside me, Juli stabs at a green bean with his fork and drags it through a puddle of gravy. "Don't take the bet," he warns me. "It'll be like you're throwing your money away. I'm aiming high… not stopping at ten…"

"If you'd worn sweatpants, I might be inclined to take your advice, but I'm trusting my own gut. Eight pounds. You'll explode if you eat more than that."

"Suit yourself," he says around a mouthful of food.

To Ed, I say, "Count me in."

"Unbelievable," Marcela groans. She puts down her fork and knife, resting them on her plate, and pushes her chair away from the table. I expect her to announce that she won't condone such a competition, but she surprises me when she says, "Did the two of you just meet this child *yesterday*? At least one of his legs is hollow. If he doesn't put on eleven pounds today, then I'll consider myself a failure as a cook. I'm going to get my purse."

She disappears for a moment. When she returns, she has with her a ten-dollar bill that she tosses down in the center of the table, right beside the turkey; Ed and I do the same. "We weigh him after dessert," Marcela announces. "Is everyone in agreement?"

We are.

So after Juli finishes his fourth helping of Thanksgiving dinner and polishes off two slices of pecan pie, Ed retrieves the scale from upstairs and I help the still-incapacitated but endearingly round-bellied Juli step onto it. He announces his starting weight before placing both feet on the sensitive deck. The four of us stand there, waiting for the digital numbers to register a final decision, and when they do, we all perform quick math in our heads. "Eight and a half pounds?" Ed confirms, glancing around the group. He pulls his cell phone from his pocket and checks his subtraction with a calculator. "Eight and a half pounds," he repeats. "That makes Charley the winner."

"See?" I whisper, nudging Juli with my elbow. "I trusted my gut."

"My gut is too full to trust," he woefully responds, staring down at his outcurved stomach. "If I'd taken your fashion advice and opted for an elastic waistband, I'm pretty sure Ma would've won the bet." He looks up at her and says very seriously, "Please don't consider yourself a failure in the kitchen. This meal was amazing."

"It was," I have to agree. "If I didn't already have a full kitchen staff, I'd hire you."

Marcela laughs. "That's very sweet of you, Charley," she says, her smile warm, and then she continues, "I'm thrilled you could join us today; it was my pleasure to cook for you. And… if I could just ask one favor in return—"

"Of course!"

"—it would be that you take this kid of mine home and make sure he spends the rest of the day on the couch with a heating pad."

"I can do that," I assure her. "No problem."

We stick around long enough to help with the dishes. Marcela provides Juli with several containers of leftovers and Ed carries them out to the Jeep, hiding them beneath a seat and thus out of the pups' reach. I help Juli ease into the front seat, load Rhett and Scarlett into the back, and honk twice as we pull away from the house. "Your parents are awesome," I say, the recent experience having filled me completely: full stomach, full wallet, full heart.

To my right, Juli nods sleepily. "They are pretty great, aren't they?"

I'm happy he has them in his life.

19.

Addy

"What'd you do for Thanksgiving?" Charley asks. She's standing at the bar, nursing a cup of hazelnut coffee and watching Addy chop vegetables for soup: carrots and celery, onions and potatoes. Her hair's getting shaggy and Addy likes the way it falls across her forehead, almost-but-not-quite brushing the tips of her eyelashes.

"Just hung out at the apartment and watched one made-for-TV Christmas movie after another. What about you?"

"Went to the Singers' house," she answers quickly, apparently not interested in exploring the experience further. Charley seems more focused on the fact that Addy *didn't* go anywhere. "Did you cook or anything? Was Mac around?"

"I made a turkey melt and oven fries. Mac went home to see his parents, so I just cooked for myself."

"Addy!" Charley exclaims, and Rhett, napping on the other side of the kitchen, raises his head at the sound of her voice. He surveys the situation, glancing back and forth between his owner and Addy, and then finding everything okay, he eagerly returns to dreams of rawhide and peanut butter-flavored bones. "Why didn't you tell me?" Charley continues. "We could've spent the day together."

The teenager shrugs and slides a pile of chopped carrots from the cutting board into a tall copper soup pot. Then he starts in on a head of cabbage. "I don't know," he answers as he slices the pale green leaves into rubbery ribbons. "I didn't mind being alone. It was kind of nice having the apartment to myself."

Charley can appreciate this, of course. As much as she loves an eventful night at the Brewhaha, an occasional lull in business doesn't have to be such a bad thing. Sometimes it's kind of nice to have a row of empty seats at the bar.

Today is like that.

The air smells like frozen peas and the sky is the color of chimney smoke. It feels like it could snow, but the meteorologists aren't brazen enough to commit to even a flurry of precipitation. "The storm system might veer to the north," they reported on the noontime broadcast. "Cold air might be all we get." The public hears the word "snow" and nothing more, though, so lunch breaks are spent in line at Main Street Market as people rush to stock up on milk and eggs and toilet paper.

The Brewhaha has seen a few customers today. Addy served them Manchego-mushroom paninis and cups of vegetable soup and happily obliged when they asked for extra slices of bread to wipe clean the insides of their bowls. While they ate, Charley talked to them about beer and offered each a sample of Petey's latest concoction: salted caramel stout. "This'd be alright with a scoop of vanilla ice cream," one had said, laughing. "Make a beer float with it! I bet it'd be damn good."

But the lunch crowd had eventually fizzled out and now only a few college students, armed with thick textbooks and the last of the pumpkin ale, remain. Charley checks on them periodically, meandering back to the study to make sure that no refills are required. They slump in the plush chairs, notes open on their laps, highlighters at the ready. She thinks what they're poring over is math, but if that's the case, the math is complex. There are angles and charts and little italicized letters involved; the pages of their texts contain more than just numbers. "I think," she confides to Addy upon returning to the kitchen after one of these visits, "that beer would only make studying for finals more difficult. When I was in college, cappuccino was my elixir of choice."

"You should've seen Bottomless Joe's this morning," Addy tells her. "I stopped in for a coffee before coming here. The LCU kids have pretty much taken over."

"The library must be a madhouse," Charley observes. "So much to learn, so little time." It's difficult to determine whether her tone is pensive or nostalgic, but Addy imagines her thoughts have probably wandered back to Ferris State and the years spent there, broadening her education. He doesn't interrupt—doesn't ask her to verbalize what she's thinking—but eventually Charley hints at what is running through her head. "You know," she quietly muses, "I haven't spent a Christmas in this house since my first year at college. After that, Gramps always came to me. Isn't that crazy?"

Addy doesn't answer because it is and it isn't, and saying both is the same as saying nothing at all. So he checks the vegetables on the stove and waits for Charley to continue and she does by saying, "We should have Christmas here. You, me, Juli… maybe the Goodes and Juli's parents?"

"How about Mac? He's spending Christmas Eve with his parents, but the next day they have to leave for Chicago or something, so Mac is driving back to Lake Caywood on Christmas morning."

"Okay. And Mac. What do you think?"

"I would like that."

"Yeah?"

"Yeah." He doesn't share any information about past holidays. He doesn't say that June Birch preferred to spend her Christmas bonus on a mani-pedi rather than a Douglas fir, or that the last time he woke to find gifts in his stocking was when Charley had put them there, or that there's a box of homemade ornaments—crafted in elementary art classes—that still takes up space in his bedroom closet on Blackstone Drive. He doesn't volunteer details of the time that he asked his mother to buy the ingredients for a special meal, having wanted to prepare ham and scalloped potatoes and roasted Brussels sprouts for Christmas dinner, and she came home with individually frozen turkey dinners instead. "Because this is just easier," she'd insisted. He doesn't mention the dangly earrings made of blue glass that he'd worked so hard to earn money toward, raking leaves for Mrs. Grady and selling homemade cookies to his teachers, and which he eventually purchased from the school's annual Santa's Workshop. He doesn't talk about the fact that he'd been giddy to give them to his mother, wrapping them in tin foil because it was the shiniest paper he could find. He doesn't say anything about not being able to sleep on Christmas Eve—so excited was he to present June Birch with the beautiful jewelry. Or how he anticipated the giant smile that would light her face. And he certainly doesn't open up about her reaction: down-turned mouth, narrowed eyes, wrinkled nose. "Are they glass?" she'd asked. "They look cheap. Where'd you get them?"

He doesn't say any of this.

But even though Addy has his back to Charley, making it impossible to read the expression on his face, it's easy for her to read his posture. She understands that a barrage of joyless memories have caused his shoulders to slump and his head to droop. She realizes that Christmas memories for Addy aren't gingerbread-scented; she imagines that Santa Claus occasionally forgot to stop at his house. But Charley also knows that when she mentions having Christmas at the farmhouse, Addy stands up a little bit straighter. He stirs the soup a little bit faster. And so when Addy *does* provide that simple, one syllable of confirmation—"Yeah"—she knows that this year's December twenty-fifth will mean something different than the others.

"Then we'll do it," she decides. "We'll have a feast. Turkey, ham, shrimp… whatever you want. Maybe we can even make snowflake sand tarts like Noni used to, with sugary icing drizzled on top and then dusted with raw sugar. You can stay at the house the night before if you want, and you and Juli and I can open our stockings together on Christmas morning."

It sounds to Addy like the best holiday ever, but he doesn't need to put this into words because the smile that lights his face says it all. What he does share is, "I'll start thinking about the menu," and that's enough.

Since her job of tending bar isn't especially taxing today, Charley refills her coffee, splashes it with cream, and carries the steaming mug to the other side of the bar. She slides onto one of the empty stools and rests her elbows on the copper counter, cupping her chin in her hands. Tendrils of vapor waft upward, warming her face. "What's the deal with you and culinary school? Are you in?" It's an inquiry that Charley's thought to make several times, but one that she's neglected to voice. Enrolling in a program for second semester *was* a stipulation of being hired. Not only does she expect Addy to uphold his end of the bargain, she expects him to do it without being nagged. Winter break isn't that far off though, and now, having asked the question, Charley waits with bated breath, fearful that his response will be an unsatisfying one.

But Addy surprises her.

He hadn't wanted to disappoint Charley, so after conducting some research of his own, he'd made an appointment with Mrs. Pennington and shown up in her office with notes. "Look at you!" the guidance counselor had marveled, obviously impressed by the recent graduate's sudden interest in higher education. "I'm thrilled that you've chosen to pursue something in the culinary field, Addy. This is a really wise decision that you're making." She'd pulled out a legal pad, assisted in creating a list of pros and cons, and helped to make sense of the financial-aid fine print that jumbled together in Addy's brain. It had taken hours, but Mrs. Pennington had been incredibly patient, and that patience had ended up paying off. "I got accepted to the West Orensdale Technical Institute," Addy announces. "I start in January."

Charley widens her eyes; they're greener than ever and bright with pride. "That's fantastic!"

"The letter came this morning. You're the first person I've told," he admits, the color in his cheeks darkening. He fights to hide a grin as he retrieves the folded mail from his back pocket. With a slightly shaking hand, he passes it to Charley, who reads it aloud and involuntarily inserts an exclamation mark at the end of each sentence: "Dear Addison Birch! Congratulations on your admission to the West Orensdale Technical Institute! It is with great pleasure that I write to invite you to join the first-year class in the School of Culinary Arts! You should take great pride in receiving this invitation…"

She reads the whole thing, and Addy blushes the entire time, and once the farewell is concluded—"Sincerely, Marta Olewiler!"—Charley races over to him and executes a ferocious bear hug. "I am so proud of you!" she squeals. "So, so, *so* proud of you! And I'm going to want to sample *everything* that you make. Understand?"

"I understand," Addy laughs. "You do that anyway, though."

"I know," Charley agrees. "I do. But I want to *keep* doing that."

"You will. I promise."

With the soup simmering away on the stove and no one to cook for at the moment, Addy pours himself a cup of coffee and joins Charley at the bar, standing across from her as she silently rereads the acceptance letter, over and over again. She looks happy, despite the fact that the sparks of crimson that leap from her person seem somewhat duller than usual. Not nearly as vivid. They spring from her skin, from her hair, from her fingernails... swarming around her like an army of fiery gnats. Addy notices the change in intensity, but he does not comment on it. He says instead, "My friend Gabe needs a job."

"How old is he?"

"Seventeen. He's looking for a way to earn gas money."

Addy had visited the Wynne household on Monday evening after wrestling practice because Gabe needed help with his math homework. "I hate stupid numbers and I hate stupid calculus," he'd grumbled, "and I wish stupid Mr. Coleman would teach in a way that makes sense. I don't understand *any* of this!"

So Addy had sat beside him at the family's kitchen table, declining the cookies and milk offered by Mrs. Wynne since her son, needing to cut weight for the following night's wrestling match, couldn't partake in the goodies. Grumpy from lack of food, Gabe had tried his best to comprehend limits, P's paired with *x*'s, and denominators of Q(*x*). Addy had done his best to channel Mrs. Pennington and exhibit great patience.

At one point Mr. Wynne had wandered into the kitchen and contemplated whether he might have a bowl of ice cream for dessert. He'd stood there in front of the refrigerator with the freezer door hanging wide open, billowing clouds of cold air spilling onto the floor as he'd silently debated between Moose Tracks and mint chocolate chip. The latter had eventually won out, but before a decision was made, Mr. Wynne had temporarily abandoned his sugar fix and wandered to the table, peering over the boys' shoulders to squint down at the textbook lying open before them. "Looks like hieroglyphics," he'd joked, and Gabe had angrily muttered, "You're telling me. This stuff is so stupid. Calculus is, like, the dumbest class ever."

It wouldn't have taken a rocket scientist to sense Gabe's frustration, but it's hard to know the right thing to say to someone whose stomach grumbles each time "Sandwich Theorem" is mentioned. Mr. Wynne had sympathized with his son, though, and that had been shown when he'd reached out with one hand and gently tousled Gabe's unkempt hair. "You just need to pass the class," he'd reminded the boy. "No one's asking you to pass it with an A."

The words had calmed Gabe a little, but that gesture—that tousling of the hair—had had more of an effect. And as Addy'd observed it, it occurred to him that it was an experience he'd never had with a fatherly figure. For as many men as June Birch had introduced into his life, not one of them had ever proven to be much of a role model. Not one of them had ever thought to tousle his hair.

"So how many hours a week is he looking for?" Charley wonders, drawing Addy back into the present. "A day or two?"

"More like a weekend or two each month," he answers. "Could he bus tables or something?"

"Or something," Charley says. "I'm sure we can figure something out."

"Really?" Addy hadn't been expecting such an easygoing response; with a reliable staff already in place, it didn't seem like additional help was really needed at this point in time, but if Charley felt she could afford to bring someone in for a weekend or two each month, then he wasn't going to argue it. The news would certainly please Gabe. "Should I tell him to drop by for an interview or something?"

"Let's just have him come in on a Saturday and we'll put him to work. See how he does."

Addy shrugs, obviously surprised, but simply answers, "Okay. I'll let him know."

"He might even be able to help Juli with renovation stuff," Charley suggests. "There's a lot going on upstairs, and when it comes time to revamp the bathroom… I don't know. The more people on deck, the better, right? I mean, that's the only shower we've got."

Addy lifts his coffee mug to his face, inhales deeply and fills his lungs with the nutty aroma. He's used that upstairs bathroom more than once or twice. On opening night, for sure, because he'd spent the day cooking and was sweating bullets before the doors even opened—but as a little kid, too. There'd been a few times when his mother had needed to be away all night, whether it was for a job or a man, and rather than stay at the Birch house, Charley had gathered a toothbrush and a pair of pajamas and carted Addy off to the farmhouse. He'd taken many a bubble bath in that avocado-hued tub, splashing in lavender-scented suds and racing plastic boats: blue tugboat, red speedboat, yellow sailboat. As unlikely as it may have been, the tugboat always won.

After the bath, Charley would wrap him in a plush yellow towel and hand him his pajamas and wait while he brushed his teeth. They'd read a few picture books together—*In The Night Kitchen* or *Strega Nona* or *Make Way for Ducklings* usually—and then Charley would tuck him in with the promise of something decadent for breakfast: pecan pancakes with maple syrup, waffles topped with fresh fruit, apricot-almond coffee cake… Noni was always in the kitchen, and she was always creating, and her creations were always divine.

Even though Addy's childhood memories of the farmhouse aren't nearly as plentiful as Charley's, he does hold a few of them in his brain. That's maybe why he thinks to ask the next question. "Do you mind not having the house to yourself most of the time? Do you ever wish you didn't *live* here?"

"Someday," Charley confides, "I think the only off-limits room of the farmhouse will be the upstairs office. Everything else—my bedroom and the guest bedrooms and the bathroom—will all be open to the public. There'll be a few tables up there, and maybe even an upstairs bar, and the beds will be replaced with couches and comfortable chairs. But that's way down the road."

"And where will you live?" Addy wonders. "With Juli?"

Charley lowers her head and fiddles with the ring on her finger, spinning the copper band so that the typewriter key with the eight on it spins around and around. "I don't know," she says. "Maybe."

Her words and her posture indicate that there is more to be said, but Addy doesn't pry. He simply sips his hazelnut coffee. Watches the crimson sparks as they dance on her skin. Wonders if the fragmented worries in her head are the cause of the flickers' diminishing luster. But he doesn't ask. If Charley wants to share the thoughts running through her head, then she will, but Addy will not force her to do so.

She must want to share, though, because a moment later, after silently corralling the scattered information in her brain, Charley closes her emerald eyes and says very quietly, "I stopped Juli from saying 'I love you.' He was so close to saying it, but I cut him off, and I don't know *why* I cut him off… but I did."

It had happened on Thanksgiving night, after Charley had helped him to the couch and placed a heating pad behind his back and brought him yet *another* piece of pecan pie. It was then that Juli had looked up at her and warned, "I'm going to say something incredibly cheesy… but I'm thankful for you, Charley Lane. I'm doing this a little bit out of order, I think, of what a real gentleman would do, and I should have said this earlier, I know, because I've known it for a while, but I—"

"I'm thankful for you, too," Charley had cut in, "because without your help, none of this could have happened. You're great, Juli. I'm thankful for you everyday." And that had been that. The mood was lost and Juli, sensing that those three words were simply too much for her to hear, hadn't pushed the issue. He'd simply lain there on the couch, his head in Charley's lap, enjoying the way her fingers felt as they ran through his hair.

Now, remembering it, Charley opens her eyes and fixes Addy with an intensely emerald gaze. "I'm horrible," she says. "Horrible. Most girls swoon when a guy voices those three words, but not me. I wish I could just be… I don't know. Normal?"

Addy sets his coffee mug on the bar and sticks his hands in his pockets. He's never been in love—never acted on any of the crushes he's had over the years—so his wisdom regarding matters of the heart isn't really wisdom at all. What Addy knows is that "I love you" doesn't always mean what it's supposed to. Like when June Birch says it. Those three words, although meant to leave a person feeling full and warm, always hollow him right out. In his experience, actions are louder. English muffin pizzas and walks through the orchard and bedtime stories are all a thousand times louder than a shouted "I love you." And so even though Charley is peering up at him, waiting for *something*, Addy struggles to find the right words. He settles for "Normal is overrated," which makes Charley laugh a sardonic laugh, and then she blinks a long blink to erase the entire conversation. "I just need to stop thinking about it," she decides. She stands, glances across the kitchen to her snoozing wire-haired friend, and asks, "Hey, Rhett. Do you want to go for a walk?"

He does.

If he'd still been dreaming of twisted rawhide bones, then the dream must have been shallow because as soon as the question is presented, Rhett is on his feet. He prances across the kitchen, holding his head high and wagging his tail rapidly. Addy laughs as the dog dances enthusiastically around his owner, bouncing and circling and getting himself so worked up that he eventually stops to execute a sudden and unexpected sneeze. "Goodness!" Charley exclaims. "Excuse you!" To Addy she adds, "We'll be back in a bit. Hold down the fort, will you?"

"Consider it done." He carries the abandoned coffee cups to the sink, pours the remaining cold liquid down the drain, and fills the basin with hot soapy water, preparing to wash them. When the front door opens only a few moments after clattering shut, he assumes that Charley's forgotten something and is back to retrieve it, but when he turns, soapsuds clinging to his forearms and water dripping from his hands, he's surprised to find Miss Flora walking over to the bar. "I'm not much of a beer drinker, Mr. Birch," she admits, "but I'm willing to give one a try. What do you recommend?"

At nineteen years of age, Addy should legally know next to nothing about the flavors of stouts and lagers and ales. Charley isn't a complete stickler for the law, though. She *did* give him an earful when he got caught shoplifting, and she'd *never* challenge the speed limit by more than six or seven miles per hour, but underage drinking—if practiced responsibly—is okay in her eyes. "Just speak with a British accent when you drink beer," she'd instructed him on more than one occasion, "because all this'd be legal if we were in England." Considering his status of chef and stand-in bartender, Charley has deemed it important for Addy to, at the very least, have an *idea* of what's on tap, and while he's by no means an expert, he knows enough to suggest a Sweet Potato Pint. "It's like Thanksgiving in a glass," he explains to Miss Flora. "And I can serve you a half-pint if you prefer."

"I would like that very much," Miss Flora consents. While Addy fills a snifter with the tea-colored liquid, she meanders around the kitchen, wool coat draped over an arm, examining the architecture and the artwork. The most interesting piece is the painting of a ten-year-old Charley on her yellow bicycle, a basket of peaches and flowers mounted to the front. This is where the old woman lingers longest, studying each aspect of the image, squinting to glean information from even the minutest details. She stands there for several minutes, not commenting on the acrylic, and doesn't turn away from it until Addy slides her beer across the bar and clears his throat. "I'm glad you stopped by," he says. "It's a good day to visit. We've been pretty slow, I guess on account of the—"

"Snow," Miss Flora finishes for him. She fingers her silver locket as she says it, rubbing a wrinkled thumb over the snowflake that's etched there. Tiny explosions of yellow-green light jump from her skin like little bursts of electricity. "I suppose you're probably correct in this assumption. So tell me, how have you been? What's new in the world of Addison Birch?"

He leads with the acceptance letter from West Orensdale Technical Institute, which earns him a round of applause from Miss Flora, and follows it up with a brief description of life at the Brewhaha. "Charley used to take care of me," he confides, "back when I was just a little kid. I'm not sure if I ever mentioned that to you before or not."

Miss Flora shakes her head and takes a very small sip of her beer. "No, I don't think you did."

"She taught me to cook, and how to read, and how to tie my shoes. If it hadn't been for her, I wouldn't know much of anything, and having her back..." He trails off, trying to find the words to describe the feeling in his heart. It's a challenge. "Having her back," he finally decides, "is the best thing that could have happened to me."

Behind thick bifocals, kind eyes twinkle. "Is she here?" Miss Flora wonders, glancing around. She doesn't say that she's hoping the answer is yes—doesn't say that she'd like to meet the woman who saved this boy's life—but Addy likes to imagine that this is what she's thinking, and so his tone is regretful when he answers, "She isn't right now, but she ought to be back pretty soon."

Miss Flora waves her hand, dismissing the unspoken proposal to wait. "No, no," she mutters, so softly it's almost impossible to catch the words. "It's probably better this way." She swallows a bit more of her beer, sets the not-quite-empty snifter on the counter, and eases herself off the tall barstool. "I should be on my way, Mr. Birch, but before I go… I'd like to share something with you."

Addy raises his eyebrows and the old woman turns her back to him, pointing to the acrylic on the opposite wall. "That painting right there?" she asks very simply, and in a way that implies no answer is expected. "It's one of mine."

"It is?"

"Indeed. You may tell your friend Charley, if you wish. She might be interested to know." She gives Addy a final smile and says, "It's nice to see that you're happy, Mr. Birch" before turning to exit the bar. The front door opens, blowing in a cold gust of wind, and then softly clicks shut behind her.

By the time Charley and Rhett return from their walk, the afternoon sky is nearly as dark as calligraphy ink. "Feels like snow," Charley says. Her nose and cheeks are rosy; she claps her mittened hands together. "Come outside for a minute."

And Addy, whistling a strange little tune as he wipes the countertops, tosses aside his rag and temporarily abandons his duties. The notes that he creates float upward, bounce against the ceiling, break into cacophonic pieces that ricochet off the walls. He follows her out the side door to stand on the porch. Their breath forms translucent clouds. Addy shivers, crosses his arms, looks to Charley for guidance. "The sky," she says, pointing with a finger hidden inside a red mitten. "It's too early for stars."

There are stars, though.

So many stars.

They twinkle and blink and shimmer in the ultramarine evening, having woken earlier than usual under the false pretense of snow. Snow makes the world sleepy, but no flakes have fallen, and so the stars have been suckered into working an extra-long shift. "On a night like tonight," Charley whispers, "a wish on a shooting star would have to come true." And so they wait, watching the sky, as their teeth chatter and the tears in their eyes threaten to freeze. And then, without warning, Addy notices a streak of pale blue light. "There."

Both Charley and Addy squeeze shut their eyes.

Both Addy and Charley wish hard their desires: one for a quick tousle of the hair, the other for a painless goodbye. And then, their aspirations still fresh in their minds, they wordlessly return to the warmth of the old farmhouse.

20.

Juli

Shaggy garland and twinkling lights spiral up and around each lamppost lining Main Street; every single local business seems to have at least one wreath with a giant red bow hanging somewhere on its storefront. Every window display that I pass boasts something to do with Christmas: stockings crammed full of art supplies, trees trimmed with mittens and scarves and hats with earflaps, snowmen wielding chainsaws and wearing tool belts. Even the post office has orchestrated a makeshift snowstorm in its front window, oversized crystals mingling with letters addressed to the North Pole, each flake and envelope suspended by fishing line. Lake Caywood has yet to experience a snowfall of its own, but the lack of a white winter blanket hasn't done much to lessen the town's Christmas cheer. There are so many oversized candy canes planted in the lawns of my neighborhood that I had to swing by Main Street Market and purchase a box of the striped sticks; my hankering for peppermint has lately been unreal.

Now, with one of these half-eaten candy canes clenched in my teeth, I dash up the steps to the Tavern and duck inside. Compared to the blustery conditions outside, it feels almost as though I've just stepped into an oven. The air is heavy with the aroma of baked goods, reminding me instantly of the decadent peanut butter cookies that Doc Delaney only prepares during the week leading up to Christmas. The fresh-from-the-oven treats are a small token of appreciation to every customer, no matter the order: appetizer or full entrée, martini or pie à la mode. Everyone gets a cookie.

And knowing this, I opt for a beer that complements the anticipated dessert. "I'll take a double-chocolate stout," I say to Petey.

"That's the same thing Asher ordered," he informs me, and then motions to the jukebox in the back when I glance around for my friend. It's become somewhat of a tradition to meet Asher for a beer or two after his last day of school before Christmas break. I'm not really sure why… since he gets to sleep in the next day while I, nine times out of ten, have to work. But we've done it for years, and we're doing it again this year, and chances are, it'll happen next year as well.

Content with his musical selections, Asher carries his beer from the back of the bar to the front and joins me near the lineup of taps. As he does, Bob Seger's "Sock It To Me, Santa" seizes control of the Tavern's airwaves and a wide grin breaks out on Asher's face.

"Really?" I ask him, crunching down on my candy cane. It explodes into miniature particles of sweetness, sticking in the crevices of my back molars. "Of all the Christmas songs available, this is the one you chose?"

"There are plenty more where that came from," he assures me. "I just dumped ten dollars worth of quarters into that thing. Bing Crosby, Elvis Presley, John and Yoko… The Kinks… They're all invited, because I invited all of 'em. Don't worry."

"But I *am* worried," I say. "If someone finds out that you're the reason for this atrocious playlist, then we're gonna have to find another bar."

"So we'll head out to the Brewhaha," Asher shrugs. "No biggie." He hoists himself onto a stool and wraps his hands around his beer. "I probably ate, like, two dozen Christmas cookies and half a pound of fudge at school today. Do you like those pretzel-thingies with the white chocolate melted on top? I'm not real crazy about 'em."

"No, me neither," I agree. "Why?"

"One of my students filled a *tin* with them and gave it to me as a gift. Why can't they just give me a new pack of pens? Or a pad of fun-shaped Post-Its? Or a tin full of chocolate chip cookies?"

"Because they're kids," I remind him, "with parents who like to whip up a few batches of those weird pretzel-thingies because they're easy to sort and then package in plastic baggies tied shut with curling ribbon. That's why."

Asher takes a sip of his beer, laughing. "You're so right, man. *So* right. And most times the little plastic baggie has my name written on it in red Sharpie."

"Or sometimes green, maybe?"

"Or sometimes green. And every now and then dollar-store reindeer stickers are stuck to the bag."

"But it's the thought that counts," I remind him. "They're just kids."

"I know, I know… It just kills me to hear the stuff that you get, though." He turns to look at me, shaking his disheveled hair away from his face. "Like, how many jobs have you gone on this week that've earned you an extra tip or a gift? Be honest."

It's a question that I need to put some thought into. This week has been busy. Just because I was out of commission with an injured back for a few days didn't mean the phone stopped ringing. I installed a garbage disposal at the Finley's house and re-caulked one of their bathtubs (it gave me a chance to reconnect with Myra); I stopped by my former phys ed teacher's house and fixed a bedroom door that kept sticking; I made it a point to replace the furnace filters for Mrs. Wilkinson, my parents' neighbor, who just recently had surgery on her hip, and then went ahead and strung Christmas lights for my ma since I was right there; I tiled a backsplash for the Goodes; I painted a living room for Mr. Jeffries, a guy who lives in my neighborhood, because he works weird hours and never seems to be home long enough to do it himself; and I repaired Mrs. Fletcher's garage door (it kept getting stuck on the way down). Not to mention the time I put in at the farmhouse. "Four or five monetary tips, a pint of Mrs. Finley's homemade butter pecan ice cream, and a few sexual favors… courtesy of Charley Lane."

"See?" Asher sighs. "I'd take bedtime antics with Charley over pretzel-thingies any day."

"Hey now!" I warn. "That's my girl you're talking about!" But it almost feels weird to refer to Charley as "my girl." She is, I suppose, but I've never been bold enough to use the word "girlfriend" when describing her, nor have I witnessed her referring to me as her "boyfriend." A month ago, I would have dismissed the confusion by telling myself that titles don't matter, but after Thanksgiving night—after coming a fraction of an inch from saying "I love you" and basically being shut down in the process—I'm no longer sure what we are. For the most part, things have remained the same: I work at the farmhouse, I eat at the farmhouse, sometimes I sleep at the farmhouse… but there's something different between us. Not necessarily bad-different, but different-different, and as much as I've wondered about the right way to handle it, I'm still not sure that pretending nothing happened is the best way to go. So I've kept my mouth shut and played it off like everything is hunky-dory. It's not, though. Not quite.

Asher chuckles and Petey, pouring an amber ale for someone at the other end of the bar, pauses for a moment to check in on us. "You guys still good, or do you need a refill?" His eyes dart back and forth between our more-empty-than-full glasses, already predicting what our answer will be.

"We'll take a second round when you get a chance," I request. "There's no rush."

Although it's only a little after four o'clock, business at the Tavern is hopping. Asher isn't the only teacher participating in a holiday happy hour by a long shot; it's evident, too, that one doesn't need to work in the world of education to imbibe on the eve before Christmas Eve. I recognize a couple of coffeehouse attendants, a group of bankers with their ties loosened, and even the woman who grooms Scarlett once or twice a year. Emily. She toasts me from afar, raising some sort of milky martini into the air, its garnish a cinnamon stick. "To dogs and eggnog!" she shouts.

"To dogs and eggnog!" I chorus.

Petey sets a duo of stout-filled pints and a plate of warm peanut butter cookies down in front of us just as Elvis comes over the speakers, crooning about how blue his Christmas will be. "A gift from Doc," Petey reports, "but I expect you know that already."

"Tell Doc we love him!" Asher says.

We each take a cookie. I break mine where the tines of the fork left its imprints, dividing the confection into even halves; Asher does not. He lifts his cookie, directs it to his mouth, and takes a large bite. The expression on his face as he chews is one of pure bliss. "This is *so good*!" he eventually mumbles through a mouthful of sugary crumbs. "I wish I had some milk."

"Drink your beer," I instruct, which he does, taking a big swallow and then wiping his lips with the back of his hand. "You won't believe what I'm doing for Christmas," he volunteers. "Try to guess."

"Spending it with your mom and her boyfriend?"

Asher shakes his head. "Nope."

"Spending it with your dad and your stepmom?"

"Nope."

"Spending it with Charley and Addy and me at the farmhouse?"

"No, but that sounds like fun. If I'd known that was an option, I might've chosen to join you. Thanks for the last-minute invite," he says with all the sarcasm he can muster, but then he grins and informs me, "What I'm actually doing is driving to Pittsburgh with Annie, where we will be celebrating Christmas with *her* family. Are you shocked?"

"Shocked" may be too strong of a word, but I am surprised. Spending the holidays with a significant other's family is something that Asher has done only once before. The experience was less than stellar, which is why he normally makes it a point to dump the girl he's dating right before Thanksgiving. Annie must have survived Turkey Day with his mishmash of a family, though; it's obvious she's still in the picture. The fact that he's traveling to *her* hometown, to meet *her* parents…? Well, this is a huge event. "I'm proud of you, buddy!" I say, clapping a hand against his shoulder and giving it a squeeze. "This is a pretty big step for you. What made you decide to take it?"

"That lecture you gave me," Asher answers, not bothering to beat around the bush at all. "I thought about it a lot—about why I was so reluctant to jump in with both feet—and then I realized that I was scared."

"To commit?"

"Nah," Asher muses, tilting his beer so that the remaining stout creeps up the walls of the glass. "I don't think it was so much about being scared to commit as it was about being scared to admit to myself what I feel for Annie. I really care about her, man. I know that makes me sound like a big, dopey marshmallow, but…"

"It doesn't," I assure him. "You're not a dopey marshmallow."

"Yeah, well… even if I am, it's probably not such a bad thing. And so I wanted to say thanks."

"For the lecture?"

"For the lecture, yeah, and for calling it like it is."

I brush off the accolades by taking a quick swig of my beer. "Not a big deal," I say to Asher, and casually change the topic of conversation to something a bit lighter: the possibility of dinner. So while he rambles on about whether we should opt for burgers or wings, I ponder whether it might be possible that Charley's afraid of her own emotions. In the midst of a dream world is the last place I want to be living; I prefer to see the big picture rather than wear blinders. So if the reason Charley halted my words on Thanksgiving night is because she's looking for a humane way to dismiss me from her life—for a kind way to say goodbye because she's too afraid to get attached—then I *do* want to know that.

But I also can't deny that there's a part of me residing in that dream world. There's a part of me that's hoping Charley will work past her fears and identify what she's feeling because I, more than anything, know that I want to be with her. Forever. And if that's not going to happen… well, then maybe I've done a disservice to Asher by telling him to jump in with both feet.

Maybe jumping in with both feet is the fool's approach to love.

21.
Charley

The Brewhaha closes early on Christmas Eve. I stand by the front door, arms crossed against the night's chilly breath, saying goodnight to each customer as they file out to their cars. "Merry Christmas!" I say again and again. "Have a safe holiday!" And once the last person has gone, I close and lock tight the door, turning to face Addy and Juli. "Pajamas first, dinner second, *A Muppet Family Christmas* third. Deal?"

"Deal," the boys chime in unison.

"Great. Meet back down here in ten minutes!"

We leave the kitchen together and dash single file up the stairs. At the top, Addy slips into one of the guest rooms while Juli and I continue down the hall. I throw myself onto the bed and he flings himself down beside me, planting a soft kiss on my forehead. "You smell like cinnamon," he says.

"Because Addy and I baked so many of those sugared pecans." I sit up, place a hand on his cheek, and stare down at his face, studying everything about it: the laugh lines by his eyes, the creases along either side of his mouth, the straight bridge of his nose, the silver hoop that hugs his bottom lip… Three words—three syllables—come to mind, but I swallow them and say instead, "I bought matching Christmas jammies for you and Addy, since neither one of you owned any."

"You did?" he laughs, almost disbelievingly.

"Addy already has his. I gave them to him this morning."

"But you said that we weren't opening gifts 'til tomorrow," Juli reminds me. "You lied."

"I didn't lie. I'm just not counting the pajamas as gifts. They're extras."

Juli narrows his eyes and peers up at me, debating whether it's worth it to argue. He must decide that it is because he continues, "You made a twenty-five-dollar spending limit, though. Remember?"

"Of course I remember. But the pajamas don't count toward the spending limit because they're *extras*," I explain. "They're day-*before* gifts, not day-*of* gifts."

"That's faulty logic," he harrumphs, to which I respond, "But at least you recognize it as logic. So, do you want to see them or not?"

"Fine."

I imagine that his response is meant to come across sounding more lackluster than it does, but I'm well aware of the fact that Juli Singer finds even my quirkiest quirks to be endearing. Case in point, he pairs the "Fine" with a lopsided smile and an amused shake of his head.

I hop off the bed and scamper to the closet, which is where Juli's new bedtime apparel is currently being stored. Admittedly, I did for a split-second consider purchasing ridiculous sleepwear—like footed pajamas with long nightcaps, or gowns similar to those worn by Wee Willie Winkie and Ebenezer Scrooge—but then I decided to just go with flannel PJs from a little shop in town called Eclectic. They're red with white fluff in all the right places: hems, cuffs, and the lapel down the front. The bottoms have drawstrings; the tops have buttons and collars. "Here," I announce, tossing the garments to Juli. "What do you think?"

He catches the fabric and unfolds it, thoroughly examining both pieces while determining the best way to respond. "I think," he finally muses, "that this looks like nothing I've ever worn before. You saw it and thought of me, huh?"

"I saw it and thought, 'How cute would Juli and Addy look wearing these?' So I bought two."

Juli pulls the thermal he's been wearing over his head, sinews rippling in his abs as he does, and drops it on the bed beside him. Then he stands, unbuttons his jeans, and allows them to fall around his ankles. "If Addy and I have to dress up like Santa," he asks as he pulls on the flannel pajama bottoms, "then does that mean you'll be decked out to resemble Mrs. Claus?"

"I'll be wearing my standard Christmas Eve attire," I assure him.

"Which is…?"

"My Rhett Pupler nightshirt."

There's a definite knit of his brows and a crinkling of his forehead, but Juli doesn't request further information. I assume he knows the answer will be provided in due time, so he just keeps quiet as I walk over to my dresser and rummage in its bottom drawer.

The Rhett Pupler nightshirt was a gift from Charlie, six Christmases ago, and came into existence because I'd once commented on the fact that every good dog deserves to have his face printed on a pair of pajamas. I remember saying it. The weather had been chilly—an evening in October or November, probably—and we'd made spaghetti for dinner. All of the pasta was eaten; all of the sauce was not. Charlie had fancied up Rhett's dinner by pouring the remaining sauce over the beef-flavored nuggets and Rhett had eaten with gusto, chomping the kibble with great satisfaction and turning his wiry beard red. When he'd finished, full and content, my pup had walked over to where I'd been sitting at the table and done his best to initiate a kiss. With my face out of reach, he'd settled for my wrist, and then placed his head affectionately on my lap. His face, with extra attention paid to the beard, was immediately and permanently printed on the white nightshirt I'd been wearing at the time. Rather than get upset, I'd rationalized that "every good dog deserves to have his face printed on a pair of pajamas," and so that Christmas Charlie had really made it happen: a new white nightshirt, made of super-soft cotton, with a life-sized photograph of Rhett's face on the front. His torso has been altered to appear as though he's wearing a highbrow suit and old-fashioned tie, and the quote "You should be kissed and often, and by [a dog] who knows how" is printed in a speech bubble to the right of his mouth. The line is credited as being spoken by Rhett Pupler.

I hold up the masterpiece so that Juli can view it and even though he tries to hide a smile, one shines through nevertheless. "Where…?" is all he can manage, and so I share very simply, "Charlie gave it to me. He did the artwork himself, and then had it screen printed by a friend of his. He was always messing around with things like this. Probably still is."

"But you haven't spoken to him to know?"

I shake my head and quickly undress, aware that the designated ten-minute timeframe has come and gone; Addy is probably waiting for us downstairs. Besides, I don't feel like talking about the cardinal card with that one request, or sharing the story of why I left Charlie. It's Christmas Eve, and there's chili simmering on the stove (Noni's recipe: extra heat, two pints of stout, a tablespoon of baking cocoa), and *A Muppet Family Christmas* is airing at eight. I'm looking to make new memories tonight, not relive the old ones.

"I'm hungry," I announce, changing the topic. "Are you ready to eat?"

"More than ready," Juli answers. He grabs my hand and leads the way down the hall, down the stairs, and into the kitchen where Addy has already set three places at the bar. The cornbread has been sliced, relocated to a basket, and covered with a linen towel to hold in the heat; two heaping dishes—one with sour cream, the other with grated cheddar—sit on either side. Addy hears our footsteps and turns to greet us, a wide grin on his face. It's evident that this Christmas, already, has exceeded those experienced in his past. I just want to make sure that it continues to get even better from here.

"It smells incredible!" I gush. "And you look adorable! Stand by Juli so I can get a picture!" I whip out my phone and motion them closer together, not satisfied until their arms are around one another's shoulders and their heads are tilted together and Rhett is seated at their feet, looking up at Juli instead of at the camera. Scarlett, as much as we coax her, is less than interested in having her image captured. "So it'll just be the boys," I laugh. "Say 'cheer!'"

"Cheer!" they humor me, even going so far as to show their teeth.

With the photo op complete, Addy wields a soup ladle and officially declares it to be dinnertime. We fill our bowls and carry them to the bar and I pour a beer for each of us. Addy's is significantly smaller than the ones that Juli and I enjoy, but I have no qualms about teaching him to drink responsibly… even if the law might deem it illegal, or some obsequious snoot might declare it unconscionable. It's a holiday, and he's not driving anywhere, and half a beer isn't going to get him drunk. Not to mention the fact that once upon a time, Gramps did the same thing for me.

The first few minutes of the meal are relatively quiet, due to the fact that our mouths are full, but Juli eventually stops for a breather. He rests his elbows on the counter and turns to his left so he can look at both Addy and me. "Explain the significance of the Muppets," he says. "If you guys were adamant about watching *How the Grinch Stole Christmas* or *It's A Wonderful Life,* then I might get it. But the Muppets?"

"It was Addy's choice," I disclose. "You'll have to ask him."

To which Addy responds, "Wait. You don't remember?"

I look sideways at him, a spoonful of chili halfway to my mouth, melted strings of cheddar still clinging to the bowl. "Remember what? Something about the Muppets?"

"Yeah! The Muppets and the turkey and the Vicks VapoRub?"

He seems so confident about the details that I feel sort of guilty admitting, "I have no idea what you're talking about."

"Wow," Addy muses. "It's one of my most vivid memories. But, okay... I was seven, and Christmas was three days away, and I came down with the worst cold *ever.* My mom was working extra hours at the restaurant, or so she claimed, and you spent the night at my house. You fed me chicken noodle soup, and smeared Vicks VapoRub all over my chest so I could breathe, and moved the television from my mom's room to my room so that we could watch *A Muppet Family Christmas* in bed. And then after that, all the time and for no apparent reason, we were always quoting—"

And now I remember, chiming in, "Ooowee, bork! That's the gobbla-gobbla humonga!"

"See!" Addy exclaims. "You *do* remember!"

"But I'd completely forgotten until now. That's funny, though... We *did* say that all the time." And together, in unison, we both exclaim for the second time, "Ooowee, bork! That's the gobbla-gobbla humonga!"

"Ooowee, bork," Juli groans. "This is going to be a long night..."

It's been years since I've cared about waking up early on Christmas morning, but I definitely wake early on *this* Christmas morning. Not just because I'm excited, either. A little before seven o'clock, I hear a very loud and rattly engine making its way up the drive to the farmhouse. At first I assume it must be Oscar, out to inspect the orchards on one of Gramps's old tractors, but the vehicle doesn't veer off toward the barn: it chugga-chugs closer to the house and idles there for a moment before being silenced by the mystery driver. Juli, lying in bed beside me, remains oblivious to the visitor. His eyes are closed, his lips slightly parted, his silky hair mussed from sleep. Rhett and Scarlett, however, are watching me from their stance at the door, waiting to participate in an adventure. "Okay," I whisper, pulling sweatpants on under my nightshirt and hiding my feet inside a pair of fuzzy moccasins. "Let's go."

The dogs clickety-clack their way downstairs and I follow, tiptoeing past Addy's closed bedroom door and skipping over the squeaky step that falls third from the top. The kitchen is chilly and if I weren't in such a hurry to discover who's parked outside the farmhouse, I'd stop to crank up the heat. The pups are already at the front door, though, whining to go out, and as I wedge myself between them, my hand turning the cold copper knob so that the door swings open, I learn that the car parked out front is a Ford Model T. A wreath with a floppy red bow is tied to the front and my uncle is seated behind the wheel. When he sees me, he opens the door and climbs down. Both Rhett and Scarlett bound off the porch and over to greet him, sniffing at his boots and his pants and the tires of the old car. I trail behind, shivering and pulling at my sleeves so they cover my hands. I wish I'd thought to grab a coat. The temperature is in the twenties; frosty blades of grass crunch beneath my feet, the sound a sort of muted crackle.

"Uncle Kirby? What are you doing here?"

He gives me a wry smile. "Wasn't expecting you to be up. I intended to just leave everything by the front door. Had to get an early start, you know. It's s'posed to snow later."

The air's been damp and heavy for weeks, and even though the weather report continues to include that disclaimer—"we might see a flurry later today"—I've yet to notice even one flake. This year is shaping up to be a snowless winter. I dismiss his last comment and focus on the words that came before it. Kirby has yet to visit the Brewhaha for a tour, so it seems odd that he'd make it a point to drop by before even the birds are fully awake, and on Christmas morning no less. "What do you mean 'leave everything by the front door'? What're you dropping off?"

"The bowls," he says, as if this much ought to already be known, but noticing the blank expression on my face, he quickly realizes that some elaboration is required. So he adds, "For the punch? They've been taking up space in my kitchen cabinets for years, and I figured you'd want 'em for the party, so here they are." He lifts a large cardboard box out of the car and cradles it in his arms. "I can carry it inside for you if you want. It's not heavy."

"Only if you want to," I say, still confused.

Kirby starts toward the porch, so I jog ahead of him and open the door, whistling for the dogs to follow. Scarlett darts in ahead of my uncle while Rhett takes a moment to mark a patch of dead grass. A hasty sniff confirms that the territory is now his and then, satisfied, he sprints across the yard to rejoin the excitement. By the time I enter the kitchen, Kirby has deposited the box on one of the small dining tables and is standing with his hands in his coat pockets, studying the renovations. "It's different," he mutters. "Real different. But just 'cause I say that don't mean it ain't at the same time nice."

The praise surprises me and I thank him for it, making it clear that the words mean a lot. He smiles thinly, apparently having nothing more to say, and I walk over to peek in the box on the table. Inside is a collection of punch bowls, nestled within one another, their clear plastic ladles tucked in beside them. "I'm sorry," I hear myself saying, "but why do I need so many punch bowls? I'm really sort of puzzled right now…"

"Ain't you hosting the party?" Kirby asks, and now it's his turn to sound a bit baffled. "I thought you would, seeing as you got the place up and running again. Jasper stopped having it once your mother passed, but I overheard some folks in town chitchatting about it last week, so I thought to myself, 'Better run those punch bowls out to Charley.' He used to serve up that cherry-wheat beer punch in 'em, if I remember correctly, but maybe you're planning something different this year."

And it's *then* that I realize what he's talking about: the massive New Year's Eve party that Gramps, in his heyday, was known to throw. It's rumored that half the town would turn out for it, both young and old, and everybody brought *something* to share. Doc Delaney and his Tavern staff provided heaps of crab-stuffed mushrooms and garlic-parmesan chicken wings and sweet potato fries glistening with sea salt. Still perfectly crisp on the outside and delightfully soft on the inside, the recipe hasn't changed at all.

Ruby Gallagher, before she became the town's recluse and later died one night in her sleep, used to bring lavender thumbprint cookies, made from her own lavender preserves. Gramps once described them to me as tasting like April… rain and sun and fresh.

There'd be shrimp and smoked salmon and chicken on skewers; there'd be colorful vegetables and baked Brie and a cheese platter piled high with sharp cheddar, aged Gouda, Asiago, and Pecorino. Dorothy Kirkland, married to Lake Caywood's local shoe salesman, always showed up with the richest chocolate cupcakes heaped with the most decadent peanut butter frosting, and Noni served homemade Romano gnocchi with marinara dipping sauce. People ate them with tasseled toothpicks.

Of course, my knowledge of the festivities isn't firsthand; all of the information I've gleaned has been through anecdotes shared when I was a child, so if they weren't embellished to begin with, then my memory has most likely altered them to be more fairy tale than fact. Still, if what Kirby has said is true—if there's honestly talk among townsfolk of a big New Year's to-do at the farmhouse—then maybe the stories are more accurate than I'd imagined. "What are people saying?" I ask him now. "Who's talking about it?"

Kirby raises his shoulders in a disinterested sort of way. "Oh, just that there'll be music and food like there used to be. Desserts 'n' such. I heard it mentioned at the grocery store last week, and then again at the garage, and Dale asked about it yesterday when I met him for lunch. Told him I didn't know nothin' about it."

"Because until this morning, I didn't know anything about it either," I inform him, worried that he's offended or upset about not receiving a personal invitation. "I'm glad you let me know."

"Well, I'm glad I did too," Kirby says, almost laughing. "Imagine all those people showing up here a week from now, expecting a party and finding the place dark and empty… That'd make for some talk around town, wouldn't it?"

"It would," I have to agree. And then, realizing that there's really no other choice, I say, "So I guess I'm hosting a blow-out event on New Year's Eve, Uncle Kirby. You're more than welcome to attend. There'll be food and music and beer and laughter, just like Gramps would've wanted."

This time Kirby does laugh—a *real* laugh—and a smile lights his round face. He rubs a hand over his mostly bald head, smoothing the few hairs that still grow there, and chuckles, "We'll see. I'm an old man, Charley, and midnight is way past my bedtime."

"Well, just know that you're invited," I say, because it seems important for him to understand this.

He doesn't say anything, but instead reaches into an inside flap of his jacket, extracting a red envelope. Rhett, hopeful that it might be a gift for him, prances over to give it a sniff, but Kirby passes the envelope right over his head, handing it to me. "It's just a card," he informs me, "nothing special. But I wanted to say Merry Christmas." This last sentence is mumbled as he starts toward the door, studying his feet as he walks, and so it takes him a little by surprise when I reach out and touch his shoulder, stopping him in his tracks. I hadn't thought to purchase a gift or even a card for my uncle, but he's right: it is Christmas. I wrap my arms around him, feeling the chill that still clings to his coat, and give him a tight squeeze. And Kirby, not entirely sure how to react, places his hands on my back and does the same. "Merry Christmas," I say to him, pulling away. "And thank you."

I walk him as far as the porch, watching as he plods across the lawn to Gramps's old Model T and slides behind the wheel. It takes a couple tries before the engine turns over, but it eventually does. Kirby backs the car out of its spot, and as he guides it down the long stretch of gravel to reconnect with Copper Drive, he issues a short honk and a single wave.

There's no eggnog for Christmas day. We indulged in some on Christmas Eve, but then someone (me) forgot to return the carton to the refrigerator before heading up to bed. "Not a big deal," Juli assures me. "We'll have hot chocolate instead. That's something even *I* know how to throw together."

So Juli warms milk on the stove and Addy slides a pan of sticky buns into the oven and I plug in the white lights that twinkle and blink and shine on the tree. The ornaments are those that Noni used to use: glass snowflakes, red apples, and golden pears. There are a few out-of-place additions, too, like the light bulb that I painted to resemble a penguin when I was in junior high, or the uncooked pasta snowflakes that Addy and I glued together one winter and then coated with silver spray paint, or the pinecone owl from elementary school. Mostly, though, the tree captures the essence of a wintertime orchard, which is precisely what I'd been going for.

While the sticky buns bake, slowly perfuming the air with cinnamon, we carry our mugs of piping hot cocoa, each sporting a dollop of whipped cream, into the living room. Juli and I occupy one of the couches; Addy situates himself on the plush rug adorning the floor. We've limited ourselves to a twenty-five dollar budget, and everything purchased *must* fit inside a stocking. I bought one gift for Juli (a knit hat with earflaps because he always wears a baseball cap, regardless as to how low the temperature plummets) and one gift for Addy (a turning knife, which is apparently a very useful knife for chefs to own according to West Orensdale Technical Institute's School of Culinary Arts' website; truthfully, it exceeded the price limit… but not by much). The boys each did the same.

Addy distributes the stockings. They share a color scheme of crimson and white, but differ in their patterning: chevron stripes for me, polka dots for him, argyle for Juli, bones for Rhett, and paw prints for Scarlett. The boys, to humor me, keep their Santa pajamas on for a bit longer and go so far as to stuff pillows under their shirts, bellowing "Ho! Ho! Ho!" at every opportunity. It's a little obnoxious, but no more so than "Ooowee, bork!" must have been the night before. We sip hot chocolate and open our gifts and laugh a lot. Juli gives me three pairs of new knee socks that *don't* have holes in the heels and Addy sends me on a scavenger hunt that takes me upstairs and downstairs, outside and inside, upstairs again… and finally concludes in the freezer, where he's packaged adorable gingerbread man ice cream sandwiches. "Everything's homemade," he assures me. "The cookies, the gingerbread ice cream… everything." And boy, are they ever delicious! We each have one for dessert after a breakfast of gooey sticky buns.

Petey and Jenny Goode, Marcela and Ed Singer, and Addy's roommate Mac show up around noon. There's an enormous spread that includes everything from ham and shrimp, to asparagus and roasted Brussels sprouts, to scalloped potatoes and ricotta-mushroom lasagna just like Noni used to make. Marcela's brought dessert—chocolate, cherry, and almond bread pudding—and we all indulge in a scoop topped with vanilla ice cream, even though none of us is still hungry.

The afternoon is spent playing board games like *Trivial Pursuit* and *Monopoly,* and talking about the New Year's Eve party that I only just recently learned I'd be hosting. "If you need entertainment," Petey pipes up, "we're available. I'm happy to play the ol' cello while my wife sings along." He grins an affable grin and moves his top hat piece to land on Marvin Gardens. "That's mine," Jenny informs him. "You owe me money." But to me, she says, "I wouldn't mind doing that at all. We'll bring something too, an appetizer or a dessert, because any time someone talks about those crazy New Year's parties your Gramps used to throw, they also talk about the food that the townspeople brought. Will you charge admission, or will it just be a wildly fun gathering?"

"I don't think I *can* charge admission," I confide. "I mean, this 'wildly fun gathering,' as you put it, is legendary… and Gramps never had an entrance fee, so I don't think I can either. It'll just be a party."

"A really big one," Juli muses.

"And one that the whole town might turn out for," his father points out.

Addy lets out a low whistle, probably already thinking of the food he'll have to prepare, and Mac, being a realist, asks the logical question: "How will they all fit?"

A year ago, I would have wondered the same thing, but I've since climbed the spiral staircase that leads to a studio tower; I've stood in a room that overlooks the orchard and I've listened to customers pound the ivory keys of a piano that doesn't always exist. And what I know is I *don't know* everything this old farmhouse has to offer.

I probably never will.

Juli catches my eye, sharing in the secret of the mysterious rooms that come and go as they please. We exchange furtive smiles, our eyes twinkling, feeling powerful because of a knowledge that is solely ours.

To Mac I simply say, "I guess we'll figure it out."

22.

Addy

Several months ago when Addy packed all of his belongings into a knapsack and five cardboard boxes and moved them into the apartment above Whirligigs and Whatnots, he understood that his new living conditions weren't going to be luxurious by any means. He did, however, expect a few basic commodities: a place to sleep, a place to prepare food, and a place to shower.

Up until this morning, these needs had been met, but now he stands in a clogged bathtub, soapy water sloshing around his ankles. He tries not to think about the fact that *some* of the water he's standing in is leftover from the shower his roommate took last night… or that his landlord is currently away, visiting family in Canada, and won't be back until the new year has already been rung in. He tries not to think about how deep the dirty fluid might be by the time a plumber is finally called. And then, unable to not think about any of it, he exits the tub, wraps a towel around his waist, picks up his phone, and calls the only handyman he knows.

"Addy," Juli answers on the second ring. "What's up? Everything okay?"

Seeing as both men spent Christmas night at the farmhouse and only parted ways three hours ago, the concern in his voice is understandable. "What could have possibly happened between now and then?" is the thought running through Juli's head, and Addy lets him know right off the bat: "My tub is clogged. It's got, like, seven inches of water in it. Can you fix it?"

From the other end of the phone, Juli laughs. "I probably can, yeah. I'm installing window blinds for the Sullivans right now, but I'll swing by when I'm done. It shouldn't take too long. Maybe an hour or so?"

"That's fine," Addy assures him. "There's no rush."

He spends the next sixty minutes flopped on his bed, reading through the course selection guide that West Orensdale Technical Institute recently sent in the mail. Introduction to Professional Cooking doesn't sound especially exciting, and neither does Food Safety and Sanitation, but some of the higher-level classes—like International Cuisine and Desserts of the World—have the potential to be not only interesting, but also fun. Pastries, too, might be worth knowing about; Addy's experience with puff pastry and phyllo dough is pretty much nonexistent, but he's willing to learn. There are several Greek dishes that he wouldn't mind attempting, if given the right education. His thoughts are on spanakopita when a knock sounds at the back door.

Mac, painting in the kitchen, beats him to it, but Addy shows up a moment later to find Juli lingering just inside the apartment, toolbox at his side, eyeing the artwork that lines the counter and clutters the table. "So this is where you guys live," he observes, an expression of bemused bafflement on his face. "Wow. I wasn't expecting a kitchen studio, I guess. But, hey... whatever works."

"Best light in the house," Mac says, shading an abstract building that vaguely resembles Bottomless Joe's. "It's where I create."

Addy likes his roommate just fine, but sometimes Mac's artistic aloofness, disorganization, and inability to focus on more than one thing at a time grates on his nerves. If left up to Mac, the tub would have to overflow in order to get noticed.

"Come on, Juli," Addy says, fighting the urge to roll his eyes. "I'll show you where the bathroom is." He leads the way down the hall and into the narrow space that just manages to fit a tub, sink, and toilet.

"Ew, yeah..." Juli mutters, eyeing the standing water. "That's a problem." He sets his toolbox on the floor and rummages through it, searching for some sort of tool that will disassemble the drain. "How long's it been like this?"

Addy leans against the sink with his hands in his pockets. "Mac said since last night."

"Last night? Yikes. Okay. I'll *try* to clear this clog with a coat hanger but, I mean, if the water hasn't really moved at all since yesterday, I'm thinking we're gonna need a snake." He pushes up the sleeves of his thermal and reaches down into the milky liquid. He's singing the chorus of No Doubt's "Bathwater" before his wrists even get wet, and without thinking about it, Addy goes right ahead and whistles the bridge between the lyrics. The musical accompaniment makes Juli smile, but he doesn't stop until he runs out of song, and even then, Addy is the first one to speak. "Do women really do that?" he wants to know.

"Do what?"

"Take baths in their boyfriends' dirty bathwater? Use someone else's toothbrush?"

"I've never had a girlfriend who's used my toothbrush," Juli answers honestly, "and the few times I've bathed with a girl, I've bathed *with* the girl—she didn't just climb into the tub once I was finished using it, if you know what I mean."

"Yeah, I know what you mean," Addy answers shyly. His cheeks are warm; he can feel the rosy splotches taking shape. His intention isn't to guide the conversation any further, but Juli must have an uncanny ability to read between the lines because he asks, "Are you thinking about taking a bath with a girl?"

Addy's face burns, but Juli, with his back to the teenager, remains ignorant of this fact. "If you are," he continues, "I wouldn't do it here. Does Mac sometimes paint in the tub? There are orange and red splatters all over the ceramic."

"He does," Addy says, thankful for a change in topic. "Not often, but occasionally."

"He probably shouldn't if he wants to get his security deposit back."

Addy considers the teal streaks on the kitchen ceiling, the trail of green spatters down the hallway, the yellow stain on the living room carpet. "I think it's too late for that," he determines.

"You know what I think?" Juli asks, rocking back on his heels. "I think it's too late for Drano and coat hangers. This clog isn't going anywhere without a snake, and since I don't own one, a trip to Honey-Do is in order. Wanna tag along?"

Addy shrugs. The hardware store is one of those places he's walked by a million times and never set foot in. Since Cordelia and Boomer are in charge of the kitchen today, and since he didn't make plans to be anywhere else, there's really no reason why he shouldn't accompany Juli.

They slip into their coats, hustle outside and down the back steps, and cover the distance on foot. The sidewalks are totally clear: not a single flake of snow has fallen yet this year. Juli wears the new hat that Charley gave him, but even with the earflaps it's still cold. The men duck their heads against the biting wind and jam their hands into their pockets. Their breath fogs in front of them. Addy would be content to not talk because the chill of the air is actually painful against his teeth, but Juli prefers to pass the time with conversation. "So who's the girl?" he wonders. "The one you're hoping to bathe with?"

"I'm not hoping to bathe with a girl," Addy sighs. "At least, not any time soon. I just… I don't know. I'm not real comfortable with girls. I never know what to say around them, or how to act. And, like, how can you tell if a girl likes you or not?"

"You can't. Not all the time, anyway. Girls don't really make a whole lot of sense."

"But Charley makes sense, right? You understand Charley."

"I understand Charley about seventy-five percent of the time," Juli admits. "Sometimes less than that. But, you know… the sooner you understand that you'll *never* understand women, the better off you'll be. That doesn't mean you shouldn't pursue one, though."

"Really?"

"Yeah. Just tell me who you're being all cryptic about. Who's the girl?"

Addy allows his thoughts to wander back in time, to a few hours ago, before he'd become aware of the cold puddle taking up occupancy in his tub. Just this morning he'd associated the word "relaxing" with showers, and although this has since changed, when his phone chimed this morning to indicate that a text message had been received, Addy had been in the midst of considering a relaxing shower.

He assumed that it was from Charley, checking to make sure he got home okay… or from Gabe, using him as a sounding board to voice his opinions on the subject of math. A part of Addy had even worried that it was June Birch, expressing her anger about spending Christmas alone, despite the fact that the holidays have never seemed to much matter to her in the past.

The text had been from Eleanor Ames, though, long-lost classmate and graduation partner who'd traveled south for college in the fall and hadn't, to Addy's knowledge, been back since. Or if she had been, she wasn't in touch… which is fine, really, since they were more constant than close: always a part of one another's lives, but never outside of a school setting. In the scheme of things, Addy knows little about Eleanor Ames. Her middle name is a mystery, he has no idea whether she lives with one parent or two, and he can't recall whether or not she ever mentioned having siblings. What he does know is that she looks especially pretty in blue, prefers strawberry Twizzlers to other candies, and has the glossiest ponytail of anyone in school. If it were possible to take the colors represented in the skin of a Gala apple—that buttery yellow base with those deep red streaks—and mix them together like paints on a palette, then it's likely the end result would be the exact color of Eleanor Ames's remarkably shiny hair.

Addy Birch hasn't on very many occasions let himself develop feelings for girls. That feat hasn't been especially difficult, either, since he's always been more focused on surviving than falling in love. But he supposes that if he's being honest with himself, then the truth of the matter is what he feels for Eleanor Ames is a little different than what he felt for Maria Rodriguez in elementary school, and for Chloe Fitzpatrick in eighth grade. And so now, keeping pace with Juli as he books it down the sidewalk on this frigid afternoon, he hears himself admitting, "Her name's Eleanor. Eleanor Ames. We graduated together."

"And?"

"And I don't see her much anymore, because she's away at school, but she texted me this morning to find out if I'd be at the New Year's Eve party."

"Wow, word travels fast!" Juli exclaims.

"Yeah. I was surprised that she contacted me about it."

"But you wrote back, didn't you? To tell her that *of course* you'll be there?"

"Not yet," Addy says, which causes Juli to shake his head in frustration. "Addy, Addy, Addy…" he mutters. "You need to respond. Tell her you'll be there, and that it's gonna be a great time, and that you're looking forward to seeing her."

"That's it?"

"That's it. Don't make it more complicated than it needs to be," Juli says, guiding him through the door of Honey-Do Hardware. The copper cowbell clangs, announcing their arrival, and both boys stand on the front mat, blowing warmth back into their fingertips.

"Why in the hell are y'all out walking the streets on a day as cold as this one?" Hank demands. He's standing behind the register, sorting through a stack of receipts with one hand while petting the black cat sprawled on the counter with the other.

"We need a drain snake, Hank," Juli offers up as explanation. "Addy's got a tub with a bad clog."

"Plumbing section," Hank says. "Want me to grab one for you?"

"Nah, I've got it." Juli knows the layout of the hardware store like the back of his hand and could probably find the necessary aisle with his eyes shut. Addy follows right behind him, taking in the bins of flanges and drains and pipes and wondering why some men are good at fixing things while others are better at baking. Addy's never had to use a drill; he'd in fact never owned any tools until yesterday, when he'd discovered a hammer, some screwdrivers, and a couple of wrenches in his Christmas stocking. It amazes him to think that Juli can look at just about any object in this hardware shop and have an idea of how it works, and that he can study nearly any broken thing and have an idea of how to make it function again. Is it a genetic gift, or is it learned? Rather than keep his questions quiet, he voices them, and Juli answers truthfully: "I have no idea. I used to watch my dad tinker in the garage, and then *I* started tinkering in the garage, and I took a bunch of shop classes in high school… so I guess it's a combination of things. But if you're worried about knowing how to fix things, don't be. I can show you the basics, and you can call me for the big stuff, and all I ask in return is for you to hook me up with an occasional pie. Pecan is good… or cherry. I'm a big fan of apple, too."

"Are you being serious right now?"

Juli grins one of his lopsided smiles, friendly little flickers of blue bouncing off his skin, and heads back to the register. He calls over his shoulder, "I can install a ceiling fan and I can build a second-story deck easily enough, but I'm a disaster in the kitchen. Trust me." He sets the snake on the counter and pulls his wallet from a back pocket, dismissing Addy's attempts to contribute. Then he looks at Hank and asks very seriously, "Why don't you just adopt that cat? It's obvious you've grown attached."

The store attendant chuckles and uses a calloused hand to scratch the creature's furry chin. Robert purrs contentedly, lifting his head and squinting his eyes. "Eileen and I, we don't need anymore critters. Two's probably enough. We do what we can to support the shelter, though, by giving a few fellows in cages a temporary romping ground. And sometimes we do get attached." He pauses and tenderly rubs the black cat's nose with his square-nailed finger. "Like Robert here… he's a good boy, and he's come a long way. Remember how sad he was when we first got him? It took weeks just to get him to purr."

Addy extends a hand, allowing Robert an opportunity to sniff him, and when the cat doesn't back away, he gently massages his left ear. The fur there is soft and fine. Growing up, Addy wasn't allowed to have pets, but after spending a substantial amount of time with Rhett and Scarlett, he's begun to think he might someday like a dog. Or a cat, perhaps; Robert seems pleasant enough, and he imagines a cat would be a nice thing to have curled at the foot of his bed at night.

"Hey," Hank says, changing gears completely. "You're not by any chance headed out Lucy Campbell's way, are you? She ordered some cabinetry hardware that just came in this morning. It's already paid for—just needs to be dropped off."

Juli starts to shake his head and say "No," but Addy interrupts by asking, "Is she the potter?"

Hank nods and Juli queries, "Why? Are you in the market for a salad bowl or something?"

"No, but Mac ordered a… um… I don't know. He ordered something from her that needs to be picked up. I'm not really sure what it is, but it's been paid for already, and he mentioned recently that if I went out that way, I should feel free to get it for him."

Juli gives Addy a funny look, but doesn't say anything other than, "So you want to drive out there and do a quick swap?"

"I mean, if you don't mind," Addy says. "If you do, Mac can get it some other time. I just thought—"

"No, no," Juli cuts in. "It's fine with me. We'll run it out to her, Hank. Not a problem."

Addy carries the drain snake; Juli totes a paper bag with cabinetry hardware clanking against one another inside. They hurry down the sidewalk, covering the distance with long strides, neither one of them speaking because all of their energy is focused on walking against the icy wind. The truck is closer than the apartment, and Simply Clay closes early today, so they make the only logical choice and pile into the cold vehicle as quickly as they can. Juli fumbles with his key, inserts it into the ignition, and coaxes the engine to life. It isn't until his seatbelt is fastened that he turns to Addy and asks pointblank, "Mac bought a bong, didn't he? That's what we're picking up."

It's like the Eleanor Ames conversation all over again, only this time Juli isn't oblivious to the fact that Addy's face is turning scarlet. "How did you…?" But his voice trails off as Juli begins to laugh. "Don't think that Mac's the first person to buy a bong from Lucy Campbell," he says, and leaves it at that.

"This is what I call service," Lucy greets them when the men enter her shop armed with goodies from Honey-Do Hardware. "I told Hank to just call when the shipment came in. I would've stopped by and picked everything up."

"It's not a big deal," Juli assures her. "This is actually a two-birds-with-one-stone kind of thing. Addy has to procure something for his roommate while he's here. We're under the impression that it's already been paid for…?"

"When you say it like that—'procure something'—I have to assume you're talking about a water pipe. Am I right?"

Addy nods and confirms, "For Courtland MacArthur."

"Yep, I've got it," Lucy says. "It's behind the register." She walks over to the front counter and slips behind it, her chin-length hair curtaining her face as she bends down to retrieve the hidden merchandise. Addy takes in his surroundings while he waits. Floor-to-ceiling bookcases line many of the walls, their shelves stocked with pitchers and bowls and platters fired in all different glazes. Large pots stand at attention on either side of the entrance, decorative plates run parallel to the doorframe, and the wall behind the register is adorned with beautiful, handcrafted mugs: ombré tones of brown and gold, blue and green, purple and red. Some mugs are round and squat, others are tall and thin, but each is distinctly different from the next. They hang from hooks, enticing customers to splurge on last-minute sales. Addy's debating upon whether he should perhaps purchase one for himself when Lucy resurfaces with a surprisingly tall, tissue-wrapped package. "This is it," she says, setting it on the counter. "I hope he likes it."

Addy's eyes must widen considerably because the others in the room begin to laugh. Juli's is more of a breathy snicker, but the sound of Lucy's is almost musical. "He requested an eighteen-incher," she explains, "so that's what he's getting." She lifts her shoulders in a what-can-I-say sort of shrug before turning her attention to Juli. "It's weirdly convenient that you stopped in today because you're on my list of people to call."

"Oh yeah?"

"Yeah. Can you tell me what the deal is with this New Year's Eve party that everyone's talking about? Is it true it'll be Jasper Lane-esque? That the whole town's invited?"

Juli exchanges a quick look with Addy; both men seem more than a little surprised by the question. "How is it that Charley just found out about all this yesterday, but the entirety of Lake Caywood has known for weeks?" Juli voices, obviously baffled, but he does follow his question with an answer to Lucy's: "Yes, there's going to be a big-ass party at the farmhouse on New Year's Eve. And you should definitely bring some sort of food item to share because poor Addy here can't be expected to feed everyone."

Addy's slight grin is almost bashful; it's both different and nice to have someone—an adult—speaking on his behalf. Whether Juli is cognizant of its significance or not, the gesture is reminiscent of something Mr. Wynne might do for his son Gabe.

Neither Juli nor Lucy seems aware of the words' importance, though. They merely continue their conversation, Lucy reassuring, "Oh, I'll bring something. Maybe guacamole. I'm more interested in the music, though. Do you have anything lined up?"

"Petey and Jenny said they'd play," Juli shares. "Why?"

"Because the guys were talking about it last night. Bert and Russo and Finn came over for Christmas dinner and Bas brought it up, asking if anyone knew anything about it. Doc had mentioned it to him, saying that back in the day there was always, and I quote, 'banjo strumming and whatnot,' so they were just wondering about it."

"About…?" Juli knits his brows, not totally sure of what's being asked, but Addy's pretty sure Lucy's about to say what he's hoping she'll say. He isn't Flannel Lobster's number-one fan by a long shot, but he knows Charley is; she used to play their albums all the time and had every lyric memorized by heart. Addy still to this day whistles "Kick It One More Time" when rolling out piecrusts, because that was the song playing in the background when Charley taught him to make quiche for the first time. He holds his breath, looks to Lucy, and anticipates her words.

Her answer is nonchalant; spending time with the boys of Flannel Lobster has become second nature to her. They jam in her living room, sneak food from her refrigerator, and have become, in a word, family. "The guys are available if you want 'em," she says. "They'll play."

The excitement Addy feels is different than that which he experienced when the acceptance letter from West Orensdale Technical Institute arrived in the mail, or when Charley suggested having a *real* Christmas—his first *real* Christmas—at the farmhouse. This excitement is different because it's not for him, it's for Charley, and the thrill that accompanies that is a thrill all its own. When Addy looks over at Juli, it's evident he's feeling the same thing.

"I'm going to go ahead and say that we want 'em," Juli decides, and Addy vigorously nods his agreement.

"Then they're yours," she announces. "I'll call Bas and let him know."

Addy and Juli beam. "And we'll tell Charley."

They place bets on the drive to the farmhouse, fifty cents each. Juli thinks Charley will squeal as soon as she hears the news; Addy suspects she will plop down on a chair in a near faint. In the end, neither ends up being exactly right.

Charley's reaction is a slow enthusiasm. Her first words are "Wait, what?" and the men are forced to repeat the information, saying for a second time, "Flannel Lobster wants to play at the New Year's Eve party. Right here in the farmhouse."

Charley does sit down after that, and Addy begins to think that he's won the bet, but then a big smile breaks out on her face and she hops right back up. "They want to play *here*?" she confirms, her voice definitely an octave or two higher than usual. "In the *farmhouse*?"

"Yes," Juli assures her. "Lucy suggested it to *us,* not the other way around."

"Let me just get this straight," Charley clarifies, talking with her hands to further punctuate her dialogue. "Flannel Lobster, my favorite band—the band that I've traveled far and wide to see, sometimes even camping out at rainy festivals and standing in six-inch-deep mud puddles to watch them perform—Flannel Lobster wants to perform *here,* at the *Brewhaha,* and I don't even have to *pay them*? Are you *kidding*? I hope, I hope, I *hope* you said yes!"

"We said yes," they assure her, in unison, and then wince as she embraces them in the tightest group hug either has ever endured. She squeezes them close, nearly knocking their heads together and constricting their ribcages to the point that they're gasping for air, but neither Juli nor Addy really minds.

So no one wins the bet.

Money doesn't change hands.

But both Addy and Juli walk away feeling like winners.

23.
Juli

On the day of the party, the Brewhaha remains closed until six. Addy, Cordelia, and Boomer spend the morning assembling prosciutto-wrapped dates, washing vegetables for an enormous veggie platter, and baking various types of quiche: mushroom 'n' asparagus, bacon 'n' broccoli, green pepper 'n' onion, sundried tomato 'n' mozzarella… The list goes on, and the kitchen smells amazing. My mouth is watering as I stand on the bar, helping Charley to hang twinkling lights and sparkly streamers and glimmering beads. The color scheme is silver and gold, and lots of it; I'm belting out Burl Ives and calling Charley by the name of Yukon Cornelius before we've got even half the decorations hung. Cordelia loves it, though. She chuckles and sings along and says, "Juli Singer, you *do* make me laugh." I'm pretty sure that if she weren't in her sixties, she'd have a little bit of a thing for me.

Charley hands me a final string of lights and waits while I hang it. Then she lifts a large cardboard box filled with more decorations and rests it against her hip. "Next, we move to the living room," she informs me. "Bring the ladder, okay?"

"Aye, aye, Cornelius." I hop down from the bar, retrieve the ladder from where it's standing in the middle of the room, and prepare to lift it just as Petey wanders in from outside. His nose is red and his hands are raw. Today is blustery, for sure; the wind whips bare tree limbs together, creating a hollow clattering sound, and crackling brown leaves somersault through the air with each gust. "Do you need some gloves, buddy? You can borrow mine."

"Nah, I'm good. We're just about done." He cups his hands and blows warm air into them. "Molly and Mac are lugging the last keg to the basement. I think we're set for tonight. I'll probably head home soon if that's okay. I promised Jenny I'd do some stuff around the house before the party tonight. Do you guys need anything else before I go?"

"I think we're alright. Hey, sorry about—" I begin, trying to apologize for my lack of help transporting this evening's beverages, but Petey cuts me off by saying, "Don't be. Charley was right to forbid it. The last thing we want is for you to be out of commission for the biggest party Lake Caywood's seen in decades. You need to be upright and mobile, not flat on your back with a heating pad. Tell Charley I'm heading out, but that I'll be back by five."

"Will do." I give him a quick wave and hoist the ladder onto its side. I cart it carefully into the living room, not scuffing a single wall or ramming a single doorjamb in the process, and prop it beside the fireplace. "Petey left, but he'll be back by five," I inform Charley before I forget. "And the kegs are in the basement."

"Awesome," she says, not really listening. Her hair, grown shaggy over the past several months, has a folded bandana wrapped around it and tied on the top of her head. I'm not sure of its purpose, but it's cute; the short little knot reminds me of mouse ears. I think this while at the same time wondering what *she's* thinking. Her emerald eyes dart around the room, across the ceiling, glancing every now and then into the study. Finally she says, "It's gonna be a madhouse tonight. *So* many people. If there are more rooms that show up… will you come and find me? No matter what?"

"Of course," I assure her. "Absolutely."

"Even if Flannel Lobster is in the middle of playing 'Kick It One More Time'?"

"Even then. I promise."

She sighs, apparently relieved by this vow, and walks over to rest a hand on my chest. "Hey," she whispers. Her fingers are warm; I can feel her heat through my thermal. "Thanks for helping with all of this."

"You're welcome." I kiss the top of her head, the bandana-mouse ears tickling my nose. She smells like cinnamon and nutmeg and other things nice, and I remember that she and Addy baked star-shaped spice cookies first thing this morning. She turns her face toward me, melting me with those unbelievably green eyes, and asks in a secretive tone, "So… what're you going to wear tonight?"

Party attire isn't something I've put much thought into, but as soon as she asks it, I know what she wants me to say. I might be a guy, but I'm a guy who pays attention to the important stuff every once in a while. "Jeans and a button-down?" I respond, phrasing it as a question on the off chance that I'm wrong.

"With the sleeves rolled up," Charley adds.

"With the sleeves rolled up," I repeat.

"Good." She pulls away and returns to her box of decorations, unearthing yet another string of lights and another half dozen streamers. "Let's get these hung so we can move into the study. Then we'll be done. Unless… Do you think…?" She brings her lips together, forming an adorably apologetic smile. "Maybe we should put a few lights in the bathroom, too. What do you think?"

"Whatever you want, Cornelius. You're the boss."

Seeing as Charley had little to do with the actual planning of this particular event, no one's quite sure as to when the guests will start to arrive. Petey and Jenny roll in around five, and we start watching for headlights at six, but it's not until seven o'clock that the first car veers off of Copper Drive and navigates its way up the bumpy gravel lane. At seven-oh-one, a second vehicle's right on its tail.

"Show time," Charley says, stepping away from the door. She looks a little bit panicked as she scans the kitchen and the bar and the five smallish round tables that have been reserved for food. "Are you *sure* we have enough beer?" she asks. "And what about that punch Gramps used to serve? Cherry-wheat beer or whatever it was… Did we figure that out? Does it taste okay?"

"It's surprisingly good," Addy informs her. "I didn't think it would be, but it is."

"And we've got plenty of beer," Petey says for probably the tenth time tonight. "Trust me."

I walk over to stand beside her and place a hand on her back, moving it in soothing circles. "Just breathe," I remind her. "It's going to be fine. And then later, after it's all over—"

"Next year, you mean," she interrupts, and forces a smile to let me know that she hasn't lost her sense of humor.

"Yeah, next year," I agree. "Next year, sometime, I'll give you a massage, okay? Sound good?"

"Sounds great. I'd like to schedule it for January first, maybe around three A.M."

"You book your schedule that far in advance?" I ask, feigning surprise. "Wow!"

Charley laughs. A real laugh. I can feel some of the tension melt from her shoulders. She leans her head against my chest and asks very quietly, "So… are you available at three, or do you have other plans?"

"No, I'm free," I assure her. "I'll pencil you in."

I could probably keep going with this flirtatious banter for another thirty minutes or so, but we get interrupted by a sudden influx of people. Guest number one is my buddy Ernie, who's brought a bottle of bubbly and a platter of bacon-wrapped scallops. "I splurged," he tells me. "This is kind of a big deal." Guests two, three, and four are Louise Robinson, a Flannel Lobster mom; Gertrude Coinstepper, an odd woman who decorates her house with birds and who sometimes hires me to help her hang art; and Gertrude Coinstepper's hunchbacked friend Wallace, who walks with a cane and smells strongly of Skin Bracer aftershave. Five, six, and seven are Addy's friend Gabe; Gabe's girlfriend Lydia; and Sam Finley, the greatest swimmer *yet* to come through Lake Caywood High School. Back when I was a student, Sebastian Porter was the one to beat… and he's guest number eight, which is when I lose count.

"Juli Singer," he says, sliding his hand right into mine and giving it a firm squeeze. "It's been a long time. How've you been? Everything going okay?"

"Everything's good," I tell him. "Things are really good right now."

"Glad to hear it." He gives me an almost-smile, because that's Bas's way, and fixes me with a long look. Now, I know I'm a guy and I'm not supposed to notice things like this, but Bas Porter has *really* blue eyes. *Strikingly* blue. They're, like, a shade of blue that's so unnaturally icy and pale that when he stares at you, it's a little bit disconcerting. Sort of like he's looking *through* you... I always forget that, and when I see him for the first time after a long stretch of *not* seeing him, it takes me by surprise. Tonight is no exception. "So," he continues, scanning the room with his frozen-blue eyes, "you renovated this place?"

"Yeah. It belongs to Charley. She's..." I skim the crowd, searching, until I find her standing just a few yards away. She's talking to the lead baker of Piping Hot and sampling some sort of sugary confection that he's brought along. I catch her eye and motion her over, nodding discreetly toward Sebastian. She blinks once, twice, bites her bottom lip and quickly excuses herself from the conversation. I watch her cover the distance between us, noticing the way that her hips sway slightly as she walks... noticing how her simple evergreen tee makes her cheeks appear extra flushed and her eyes appear extra bright. When she gets close enough, I rest my hand on the small of her back and say as casually as I can muster, "Charley, this is Bas."

"Oh my gosh," she gushes, blending the syllables to form one word. "It is so nice to meet you. I can't thank you enough for offering your support tonight. When Juli told me... I couldn't... I just... I can't even talk right now. That's how excited I am. I can't even talk." She clasps her hands together, giddier than I've ever seen her, and asks, "Am I allowed to make one request?"

Sebastian shrugs. "Sure." I see him glance quickly over Charley's shoulder and make a funny little movement with his head, almost like he's beckoning to someone, but I don't turn around to see who's there. My attention is fixed on Charley, who wonders, "I know you probably get this all the time, but... could you play 'Kick It'? Would you mind?"

"*Really*? 'Kick It One More Time'? I mean, *really*? Can you guys think of a single fucking show where we *haven't* played that song?" The tone is one hundred percent joking and the voice is one hundred percent Bert

Robinson's. He comes up behind Charley and extends his hand, offering "Did you guys know that my mom's here? She got here before we did!" instead of an introduction. And then he rattles on a bit longer, saying, "You're Charley, right? This place is fucking awesome. Thank you so much for letting us play here. If you want 'Kick It,' consider it done. Just tell us where to set up. The living room, maybe? Or that room with the piano?"

Charley turns to me right away. I meet her gaze and hold it. And even though neither one of us speaks a single word aloud, so much is said in that moment. "How about the room with the piano?" she eventually says in answer to Bert's query. "If that works for you guys."

"Yeah, that definitely works for us. I'll tell Finn and Russo."

Bas, probably feeling like he ought to help his bandmates load all their amps and guitars and drums into the house, claps a hand on my shoulder and prepares to slip away. "Juli," he says, "I'll track you down a bit later. There's a lot that we need to catch up on, but I've gotta help those guys with setup. And Charley." He tilts his head to one side, causing a few loose curls to fall across his eyes. "Thank you. The band and I really appreciate you giving us this opportunity." His tone is totally sincere; I can see Charley swooning a bit.

"Anytime," she responds. "You guys are welcome to play here anytime at all."

"Careful," Bas warns as he walks away. "We might take you up on that!"

Charley leans into me, watching him saunter across the kitchen and disappear into the living room. She doesn't say anything for a long time. Around us, people mingle and talk and laugh and joke. I wrap an arm around her, pulling her close, and whisper very quietly into her ear, "You're not thinking of leaving me for him, are you? I know he's a rock star and all, but…"

She snuggles closer and comments, "He *does* have beautiful eyes."

"And nice hair," I have to admit.

"I know, right? It's like a shaggy mop of curls… And does he walk with a limp?"

"Only when it's really cold," I tell her, because I remember well that horrible accident Sebastian was in so many years ago—nearly two decades ago now—long before Flannel Lobster signed with a label and waded into the mainstream. "Is that a turn-on? When a guy has a limp?"

"It can be," Charley informs me, "when the guy's a musician."

"I had no idea. Should I walk with a limp?"

"Are you a musician?"

"I played trumpet in high school…"

Charley slips out from under my arm and takes a step back. "You did?"

I nod. "I was in the marching band."

"Really?"

"Yep."

"Huh," she muses. "I had no idea. You probably *should* walk with a limp. Actually, you should limp right over there to the bar and get us each a beer. I'm up for whatever: stout, lager, IPA… Surprise me. But I'm gonna need *something* if I'm expected to mingle with all these people." She scans the room, obviously overwhelmed by the turnout; her eyes are the size of those two quarters I *didn't* win in that bet with Addy.

"Let's strategize," I suggest. "I'll get the beers, we can drink the first three sips together, and then we'll split up so that twice the mingling can be accomplished in half the time. Operation: Mingle Hell. How's that for a name? If we haven't reconnected by the time Flannel Lobster plays the opening chords of 'Kick It One More Time,' then when that song comes on—no matter what's happening at that exact moment—drop everything and meet me by the piano."

"Really?"

"Really."

"You're the best, you know that?"

"Better than a musician with a limp?"

She grins, but doesn't respond. She doesn't have to.

"Wait right here," I instruct. "I'll be back in a flash."

Molly Dixon's tending bar, providing free drinks to anyone over the age of twenty-one, and Petey's planning to help out once he and Jenny pump up the crowd with an opening set. He's tuning his cello now; his wife's testing the mic. "Check, check, check," she says over and over again. Petey drags his bow across the strings, issuing a deep, smooth chord. They'll open with something fast like they usually do, follow it up with a few ditties that get people dancing and clapping and singing along, finish the set with "Me and Bobby McGee," and then Flannel Lobster will be up.

Molly looks swamped, though. I'm half-tempted to offer my services as a tapster, but then I notice Boomer's also pouring pints and ladling beer punch. "Hey," he says when he sees me leaning on the bar. "What d'you need? We just tapped a keg of dark-chocolate stout that's supposedly pretty delicious."

"I'll try it," I say. "Give me two."

"Make it three," a deep voice says from behind, and I turn to find Doc Delaney standing just to my left. He smiles in that way he always does—like he's amused to see you, but a little bit aloof at the same time—and peers down at me with watery blue eyes. Almost the same shade as Sebastian's, his are more sparkly than icy. I give him a nod and Doc gives me a firm clap on the shoulder. "How're you doing, Juli?"

"I'm good. You? I saw that you brought the sweet potato fries."

"I never leave home without 'em," he says, trying his best to keep a straight face. "So talk to me. Tell me what's new. You and Jasper Lane's granddaughter, eh? How'd that happen? Where'd the two of you meet?"

"At the hardware store, actually, when she hired me to fix up the farmhouse."

"Huh," Doc muses. "Interesting. And do you think she's the one?"

I have to laugh. The thing about Doc Delaney is this: If asked a question that he's not keen to answer, he'll simply create a response that makes little to no sense. For example, I once asked him why, as a lifelong resident of Lake Caywood, he'd never tried waterskiing. His reply? "Because I don't want to scare the fishes." But when Doc has a question of his own, he has no qualms about asking it pointblank.

Thankfully Boomer returns with our drinks and I'm able to dodge this last question. Is Charley the one? I don't know. My gut and my heart say she is, but my brain won't let me forget Thanksgiving night. So I pass a beer back to Doc, fake a distraction, and quietly slip away.

Charley is waiting just where I left her, munching on a piece of celery that's piled high with some sort of orange concoction. "What is that?" I ask. "Buffalo chicken dip?"

"Mmm-hmm."

"It looks good."

"It is."

"Who brought it?"

Charley lifts her shoulders to indicate she has no idea and takes the beer from my hand. "Petey's new stout?" she confirms. "He was telling me about this. Did you try it yet? What do you think?"

"The deal was we drink the first three sips together," I remind her.

"Oh. I forgot. Are you ready?"

"I am."

We raise our glasses to our lips and sample the thick, creamy brew. It's a little bit bitter, but not unappetizingly so, and I take a second sip without thinking. "You've only got one more," Charley monitors, "and then you're on mingling duty."

"It's really good," I say, pressing the rim of the glass against my lower lip for the third time. I swallow a final mouthful of the chocolaty brew, give Charley a light peck on the cheek, and wave goodbye as I attempt to maneuver my way out of the kitchen. I spy Asher and Annie standing by one of the many tables heaped with food. They consider the smorgasbord, filling a sturdy paper plate with shrimp and garlic-stuffed olives and artichoke dip that's gooey with cheese. Addy, too, can be spotted. He's munching one of the spice cookies baked earlier this morning and talking to a girl with strawberry-blonde hair. Eleanor, I assume. She's cute, and seems happy to be with him, and definitely stands a little closer than necessary. I catch her glancing at his lips periodically.

My trek to the study isn't exactly treacherous, but I do get jostled around quite a bit. By the time I finally reach my destination, I've already stopped to chitchat with two former teachers, three clients, one friend from high school, and the Honey-Do owners. "I've got some news," Hank starts in when he sees me, already raising his glass for a toast. "I've made myself a New Year's resolution."

"What is it?" I look to Eileen for a clue. "Should I guess?"

"No," she answers, rolling her eyes. "You shouldn't. And you won't be surprised."

Hank beams. Without further prompting, he announces, "I'm keeping Robert! We're adopting him."

It's great news, and Eileen's correct—I'm not the least bit surprised—but I pretend the resolution is a bit of a shock and I ask Hank a bunch of unnecessary questions. Like "What made you change your mind?" and "When did you decide?" He answers all of them, just as proud as any new father, and then I continue on my way, moving as speedily as possible through the congested hallway, eager to find a room that isn't quite as cramped as the kitchen.

Unfortunately, the study is nearly as jam-packed as the room I just came from. People lean against the walls, lounge in the mismatched chairs, and laugh jovially with one another while having the most obscure conversations; I overhear one girl tell her boyfriend that a single elephant tooth can weigh more than nine pounds. I've no idea how that managed to come up in conversation, but I make a mental note to check its accuracy tomorrow. If it's true, it might be worth filing that trivia away with my knowledge of butterfly kaleidoscopes and caterpillar armies.

The only person of interest in this room is Mac, and since I can see him just about whenever I want, I give him a curt nod of acknowledgment and keep walking, pushing my way through clusters of people and squeezing around occupied furniture. While navigating, I keep a close eye on my beer, not wanting to lose any to the floor, so this is maybe how I inadvertently end up entering into a space that doesn't contain a chaise lounge, a couple of couches, or a piano. It's darker here; I blink a few times, giving my eyes a chance to adjust. Strings of lights don't outline the windows; there aren't any streamers draped from the ceiling. The only source of illumination comes from low-hanging pendant lights with lampshades made of copper. There are six of them, aligned in two rows of three, positioned directly above a green-felted pool table.

It's centered on a large oriental rug situated in the middle of the room. The walls here are paneled, the artwork hanging on them old-timey photographs of now-old men who were once young. Some are sepia-tone; others are black and white. I find myself drawn more so to them than to the few partygoers milling about the room. Many of the faces mounted on the wall seem familiar. I stare long and hard at one in particular: a twenty-something fellow wearing a trilby hat and holding a cue stick. He has light eyes and a smug grin and it takes me a long time to recognize him as the Tavern's very own Doc Delaney. I whistle low, not quite sure if what I'm seeing is real, and move to the picture hanging to its right. It's of a couple and a hound that's much larger and scruffier than any I've ever seen. The man is juggling billiards balls, his face set in a look of determination. The dog and the woman watch from afar; one appears wide-eyed, anticipating a game of fetch, while the second wears an expression of awe. Her eyes twinkle, her mouth is open to form a very round O. She looks to be fairly young—no more than thirty, for sure—but her hair, perfectly sculpted to frame her face, is pure white.

The thought that should have occurred to me immediately suddenly occurs to me now: I have to tell Charley. And as soon as I think it, a mix of panic and uncertainty settles in the pit of my stomach. What if when I leave, this room vanishes? What if at the end of the night, Charley has only my word that it happened?

I spin around, pulling my eyes away from the old photographs and focusing them on the room instead. There's only a handful of people. Five, to be exact: three girls and two guys. They stand around the pool table, holding cues and beers and plates of appetizers. I scan their faces, recognize a high school friend of Petey's, take a few steps in his direction. The group is talking about break dancing, or step dancing, or something along those lines. "Hey, Geoffrey," I interrupt. "How's it going?"

"Juli," he greets me, momentarily abandoning the previous conversation. "Hey there. Things are good." He raises his glass and clinks it against mine, toasting the new year several hours early. From the way his lager sloshes around in his glass, I can tell he's already sort of tipsy. "How're you doing?"

"I'm okay, I just… Would you mind doing me a favor?"

"Nah, man," he says, eager to help. "What d'you need? Another beer or something?"

"Or something. I need to find Charley Lane. Have you met her? Do you know who she is?"

"Sure, I know Charley!" Geoffrey exclaims, making it sound like the two have been friends since kindergarten and used to ride the school bus together. "She's missing, huh? I'm gonna be needin' a refill pretty soon, so I can scope the place out for you. See if I can track her down."

It's not exactly the response I'd been hoping for—I'd wanted him to exit the billiards room posthaste (that's a Mr. Kent word), scouring the first floor of the farmhouse until he found Charley, wrapped his hand around her wrist, and guided her back to this very spot—but I guess the only choice I have is to accept what he's offering.

Unless I risk the possibility of the game room's disappearance...

But then one of the women standing among the group props her cue stick against the table and steps forward, gently resting her fingers on my bicep as she offers, "I'll do it, I don't mind, but is everything alright?" She's tall—surprisingly tall, in fact—and her hair is an explosion of very tightly spiraled curls. She looks kind of familiar, but I don't think it's because we've ever actually met before. "It is and it isn't," I say in answer to her question. "It will be... I just really need Charley, and I can't leave to get her, which I know sounds super weird—"

"I'll find her," she promises, cutting me off. "I'll bring her to you."

I watch her turn and stride to the door, slipping out of the room and into the throng of people occupying the study. There's no telling how long it will take her to locate Charley. There's also no reason for me to linger on the fringe of a conversation that I don't care about, and so as the group resumes its previous discussion, I quietly slip away and return to the gallery of old photographs.

There are twenty-four of them in all. They span three walls, eight images displayed on each, recording a history of this room in this house, so very many years ago. Some of the people captured on film are unknowns. Maybe they spent their youth in Lake Caywood and moved away as adults, or maybe they've just changed so much over the years that it's hard to associate faces now with faces then. I pause in front of a picture of a dark-haired woman perched on the edge of the pool table. She wears a flour-dusted apron and a dark bandana, similar to the one Charley was sporting just this morning. She has an amused grin on her face, well aware of the youthful gentleman standing off to her side. He's leaning across the table, one eye squinted shut, using his index finger to steady the cue stick. Vibrantly colored balls, depicted here in varying shades of grey, are scattered across the felt. Though the man's aiming for the cue ball, his gaze is on that black orb printed with an eight… and the woman to his left is watching. "Noni and Gramps, I'll bet," I mutter softly, the observation not much louder than a thought. "How cool is that?"

It's a question that I phrase to no one other than myself, and although I'm not expecting an answer, one is whispered in my ear: "Pretty damn cool."

I turn and there is Charley, looking flushed and frazzled and beautiful. "Axa said you needed me. I guess you found another room." Her eyes twinkle, green and bright, and then she very nearly squeals, "You found another room!"

"I did."

She twirls, taking it all in: the wood-paneled walls, the framed history of folks who have come and gone over the years, the copper-shaded pendant lights that hang low, illuminating an array of scattered stripes and solids… Her gaze lands on that pool table and tarries there, as if something has just occurred to her. A thought? A question? I wait, wondering, anticipating a clue of some sort… and then she says, "Corner pocket."

Charley appears not to care that there's a game currently in progress. Her movement across the room is slow but purposeful, almost as if she's on a mission of some sort. I observe her as she nimbly clears the cue stick that Geoffrey is wielding and comes to stand quietly at the end of the table, right there near one of the corners. She earns a few sideways looks from the players and their friends, but this doesn't faze her at all. Without a word or an explanation, Charley peers down into the corner pocket and slowly reaches inside.

24.

Charley

A pool table has four corner pockets. The odds of me finding what I'm looking for on the first try are exactly twenty-five percent. On top of that, I'm not entirely sure what I *am* looking for.

Or feeling for, rather.

I'd expected the felt lining to spill over the edge of the table and into the compartment, thus softening the thud of the balls as they tumbled over and clattered through those hollow tunnels that lead to a gathering ground. The interior is just wood, though… smooth and polished. I run my fingers over the bottom, along the sides, feeling for some sort of secret compartment, but there is none. No tiny hook on which to hang a smallish key; no tricky drawer in which to conceal one. I remove my hand slowly, ignoring the puzzled expressions on the faces around me, and glance to the other end of the table, considering another option. But as I remove my hand from the pocket, I notice a tear in the felt, right where the rail ends and the abyss begins. I wonder if it might not be possible to slide a very small object beneath that soft green fabric, and deciding it might, I move my fingertips over the felt and make a discovery: a very subtle bump.

Once found, it takes only a minute to slip the key from its hiding spot.

I place it in my palm and hold it there, studying the tarnished silver with its smooth edges and tiny hole cut in the bow. And then I tuck it snugly into my pants pocket. "What did you find?" Juli asks, coming over to join me, but I silence him with a kiss and a promise to explain everything later. Right now, we need to get back to the party; I can hear Jenny singing Bobby McGee's name for the last time tonight and I know that what follows will be something I don't want to miss. I slip my hand into Juli's, interlocking my fingers with his, and pull him with me as I try my best to interpret the farmhouse's current floor plan.

The piano room, its expansive windows frosted with condensation, is alive with energy and cheer. Lights twinkle overhead, casting muted reflections in the foggy glass. People socialize. They joke. They reminisce about the past and plan for the future; they compliment the Brewhaha and comment on the food. I see that Doc Delaney clutches a beer with one hand and a cupcake with the other, chuckling pleasantly with a few staff members from the Tavern. Nearby, *our* newest staff member, Gabe Wynne, speaks animatedly with a group of friends. He talks with his hands, flailing them about, recounting a drama that pertains somehow to a mug or a mutt… I can't quite make out what he's saying, but the story's conclusion results in an eruption of laughter. Jenny Goode witnesses this commotion and rolls her eyes, which only causes the teens to laugh harder.

An entire book club has come out for the event: one dozen women, all in their sixties, with a fondness for literature and wine. "It's a good thing you stopped by tonight," I'd informed them. "Normally we only serve beer." It had been right in the midst of Juli's aptly named Operation: Mingle Hell that I'd happened upon them, and their colorful personalities had definitely been the bright spot of my mission. "We've read everything from Alice Hoffman to Zora Neale Hurston," they'd told me. "Everything from *Lolita* to *Fifty Shades of Grey*!" A banker and a financial advisor, a realtor and a retired teacher… I'd wondered aloud what they all had in common and the children's librarian had responded, "Books and booze, honey! Books and booze!" I spy her now, standing with her friends in the middle of the room, holding a glass of white wine. She's watching as Petey packs up his cello and Bert Robinson unpacks his guitar.

"Let's move closer," I say to Juli, and he nods in agreement.

We weave our way through the crowd, squeezing between college students who've come home for the holidays and around couples with their lips locked together, and landing near the piano, which is where Lucy Campbell is leaning. "Hey!" she greets me, excited, her brows shooting skyward. "Great party!"

"Thanks!"

It's too loud to talk—to have a real conversation—so I simply smile and lean against Juli as he wraps his arm around my waist, pulling me in close. He smells like fabric softener and deodorant. I inhale, filling my lungs with his scent, and rest my head against his solid chest.

The Flannel Lobster boys perch on stools: Sebastian, Bert, and Finn Gregory in the front with guitars; Kenny Russo, on drums, seated behind them. He holds a set of wooden sticks with one hand, waiting while his bandmates "check, check, check" into the microphone over and over again. When it's his turn, he pounds the tom-toms, kicks the bass, and crashes the cymbals, listening for discrepancies that my ears aren't skilled enough to hear. And then, satisfied, he issues a simple thumbs-up.

The sound check takes fifteen minutes.

Only deep-sea divers are capable of holding their breath for that long, I know, but I think I come close. Eighteen times, I've seen this band. I've traveled to Indiana, Illinois, and Ohio to watch them play; I've road-tripped to Tennessee, West Virginia, and New York for festivals. Once, Flannel Lobster even played at Ferris State, but never before have I seen them perform in Pennsylvania. Never before did I dare to dream that they'd be tuning their guitars in the very house I grew up in… But here they are, and the experience is beyond surreal.

They kick off the show with "Up Tempo, Down," a track off their sophomore album, which aims to do just what the title suggests. The song starts out fast, slows for the chorus, accelerates in the middle, slows for the chorus, and concludes at full-speed. The audience stomps its feet, claps its hands, cheers for more… and obviously gets its wish. Flannel Lobster keeps the music flowing. Every song is a crowd-pleaser and the set list is a happy blend of old and new: for every original, there's a cover; for every cover, there's something from a time when albums were released as LPs and not MP3s. The banter among the band members is fun; there's a lot of sarcasm and teasing that goes on. At one point, Bert dedicates an arrangement to his mother—claiming the song always reminds him of her—and then a minute later the boys start dee-de-dee-dee-deein' the introduction to Simon and Garfunkel's "Mrs. Robinson."

The Beatles earn a plug, too. I'm pleasantly surprised when the boys playfully ease into "I've Just Seen A Face," quickly and quietly tickling the strings of their guitars until the drum jumps in, kicking a lively and lighthearted beat. I half expect Sebastian to make eye contact with Lucy while he sings this one, and he does once or twice, but it's the chemistry between he and Bert that has me laughing. The facial expressions that those two exchange with one another are humorous, to say the least. "If you think they're funny now," Juli shares, speaking directly into my ear in order to be heard, "you should see 'em once they've had a few. Backyard cookouts at Lucy's studio? They get silly, for sure. You'll have to come sometime."

"I'd like that," I shout up to him. "I hope it happens."

He grins crookedly and pats my hip. "I'll make it happen."

I don't have the heart to tell him that might not be possible. I push the inevitable from my mind and focus on the stuff that I can control: this party, at this moment in time, with Juli's arm around me and my favorite band jamming in a room that shouldn't even exist… If it were an option, I think I might choose to stay like this forever, but midnight is near and Flannel Lobster's set list is drawing to a close. "We have one more for you," Sebastian shares with the crowd, "and I'm gonna bet that you already know what it is."

Bert looks right at me and rolls his eyes, doing his best to hide a smile. "This song," he grumbles. "This fucking song…"

I laugh as Kenny Russo lifts his drumsticks, steadily tapping the tom-toms to set up a fast and steady beat; Sebastian taps his foot on the stool's rung, listening for his cue to chime in with guitar and vocal. "This one's for Charley," he says very simply. Then he closes his pale eyes on the world, losing himself in the music. Dark curls bounce as he bobs his head, keeping the rhythm. I watch him for a moment, and then I follow suit, lowering my own lids, losing myself in the lyrics… enabling a flood of memories.

"*There's the past and there's the future / And the here-and-now between…*"

Somewhere, right now, there is a fat album of photographs that were taken at festivals where Flannel Lobster once performed. It lives in a box in an attic in a small town in Michigan, right along with all of the other albums that document my life spent with Charlie Flynn. They will exist into the future, and they will tell my story long after I am gone. Somewhere in an album in that box in the attic is a picture of me struggling to eat a triple-decker ice cream cone without losing a scoop to the sidewalk. Pistachio, vanilla, and strawberry. The melted cream runs down my arm and drips off my elbow, a flood of green and white and pink.

"*I want you here for all of it; / I want you here with me…*"

Somewhere there's an image of me when my hair was long—*so* long—standing in the middle of a tall-grassed meadow, picking wildflowers and humming an easy song to myself, taken by Charlie as he lolled on the picnic blanket a few yards away. Somewhere there's a picture of us both making snow angels, and kissing beneath a covered bridge, and cannonballing off the end of a dock, into Lake Huron. Somewhere in a box in an attic in a small town in Michigan is my past…

"*So even when we disagree / When opinions just won't jibe…*"

But my past is here, too.

My past is here in this farmhouse, around the heavy oak table in the kitchen, coring apples and rolling piecrusts with Noni. It's out there in the barn, helping with the harvest of the hops and sipping golden lagers with Gramps before my age had even reached double digits. It's down there in the orchard, perched in the plum tree surrounded by peach trees, dreaming of a life on the other side of Lake Caywood.

Now, years later, I've no desire to escape this tiny town.

Now, I like to think maybe my future is here, as well.

"*Know that I'll be back again / To kick it one more time.*"

The song ends abruptly, that last note final and short, and as the crowd puts its hands together, creating a cacophony of noise, I turn to face Juli. The line of his jaw is so strong and angular, with the faintest hint of a five o'clock shadow, and as I gaze up at him, he feels me watching. "Hey," he whisper-shouts into my ear, his breath warm against my skin. "We're less than two minutes away from a brand new year."

I've no desire to step into tomorrow; I'd just as soon relive this past year than step into a new one. But I smile and nod and lie, "I'm ready."

The countdown starts at thirty seconds 'til midnight, but participation doesn't peak until about twenty seconds into it. At that point, voices join together, ringing clearly and loudly: "Ten!"

"Nine!"

"Eight!"

Juli spins me around to face him, placing a hand on each of my hips.

"Five!"

"Four!"

"Three!"

His eyes twinkle… so boyish and kind.

"One!"

The band, as a single unit, strums the opening notes to "Auld Lang Syne" as the crowd erupts in an animated declaration of "Happy New Year!" Someone pops champagne. And Juli…? Well, Juli leans in and delivers a kiss that would put that one all those months ago in the hop field to shame. The magnitude of it sends electric coursing through my body, singeing my fingers and toes and the tip of my nose. That kiss takes my breath away. It lasts and lasts. As far as I'm concerned, it could last forever, because even though my lips ache and my lungs feel as though they might burst, the pain isn't enough to make me want to pull away.

It's in that moment that I realize how much I truly love him.

Just as the stories have always claimed, the festivities last into the wee hours of morning. Flannel Lobster takes the stage for round two, this time inviting the Goodes to play along if they recognize the tune, and on a whim Jenny and Bert throw together an impressive version of "Tangled Up In Blue" while Sebastian puffs away on the harmonica. At one point, even Doc Delaney gets involved in the night's musicality. Without any sort of warning—but much to everyone's delight—he claims a seat at the piano and pounds out a booming adaptation of "Great Balls of Fire."

Molly and Boomer switch out the kegs yet again; Rhett and Scarlett escape from the second floor and venture down for a visit, panting and wagging their tails; and dear, grandmotherly Cordelia packages all of the leftover appetizers and desserts into tiny to-go bags, distributing them to guests as they slip into the chilly night-morning.

By two, the crowd has dwindled considerably; by three, only staff members of the Brewhaha remain. I give each one a hug, thank them for their help, and instruct everyone to spend the rest of today (because it is technically already tomorrow) lounging and catching up on sleep. Addy looks exhausted, but content, and when Juli asks him how "things went with the girl," his only reaction is a sleepy smile. "Are you awake enough to drive?" I ask him. "You're welcome to stay."

"No," he assures me. "I very much doubt that I'll be able to sleep tonight."

Juli snickers. "That good, huh?"

I wrap Addy in one last hug and tell him to be safe on the roads, but opt not to walk him out to his car. Juli accompanies him instead, taking the dogs along for a final rendezvous before bed. I hang back, though. The farmhouse seems ultra quiet now that all of the guests have gone home to their beds. I walk through the rooms, picking up fallen streamers and crumpled cocktail napkins and toothpicks abandoned on coffee tables. As I wander through the rooms, unplugging strings of lights and stacking sticky pint glasses one inside the other, the task of cleaning up isn't really my main priority. What I'm curious about is the rooms. Have they gone already, or is the floor plan still a maze of unrecognizable spaces? Having overheard a few comments this evening, I suspect an additional bathroom or two made an appearance, but now, as I meander through the living room and into the study, from the study to the back bedroom, what I find is the layout is just as it should be. The pool table has vanished; the piano is gone.

In the kitchen, a door opens and then clatters shut. Dog nails *click-clack* across the hardwood, halting periodically to investigate an odor or snag a morsel left on someone's discarded plate. Juli calls my name, wondering where I am, and I meet him at the foot of the stairs. "That boy is more love-struck than tired," he says with a grin. I let him pull me in for a hug and hold me close for a long minute, his chin resting on the top of my head.

"It's about three o'clock, you know, and I *do* have you penciled in for a massage. Still interested?"

My shoulders feel tight and there's a dull ache forming behind my eyes, but what I can't help thinking about more than the pain is the silver key in my pocket. It's been there all night, emanating a comfortable coolness against my thigh, reminding me of the locked box that resides beneath my bed and the note from Gramps that's folded beneath it, mentioning a corner pocket. "Actually," I hear myself saying, "I might take a rain check. I have something else in mind."

As any man would, Juli assumes I mean sex, and this assumption is only further confirmed as I lead him upstairs to the bedroom. Scarlett remains on the first floor, her nose to the ground, busily scavenging for forgotten food, but Rhett tags along with us. He sticks close to my side, his head drooping, a very tired pup awake long past his bedtime. As soon as we enter the room, Rhett lumbers right to his usual spot: an old blanket folded into a rectangle, situated on the floor beside the bed. He steps onto it, paws at the worn fabric, and turns in a complete circle before throwing himself down, resting his chin on his feet with an exhausted sigh. His eyes close almost immediately.

Juli walks over to the bed and collapses onto the mattress, leaving room for me to land beside him, but I kneel down instead, reaching for the box that hides among shadows and dust bunnies. "Corner pocket," I explain. "That's where the key was, just like Gramps said it would be."

"What key?" Juli lifts his head and furrows his dark eyebrows, not understanding.

"The key to this box. Kirby dropped it off months ago, but I haven't been able to open it because it's locked. Tonight, though… Well. 'The key is in the game room. Corner pocket.' That's what the note says. And I found it."

Now Juli sits up, intrigued. "What do you think's in it?"

"No idea." I pull the key from my jeans pocket and sit down on the bed, resting the rusted box on my lap. It's heavy—heavier than I remember, anyway—and cold. The key slides right into the lock and turns easily to the right. There's the slightest *pfft!* of a latch being released and the lid raises a fraction of a centimeter, confirming that whatever may be concealed inside is now readily accessible.

I lift the lid. It swings open on tarnished hinges, revealing a clutter of handwritten notes, dog-eared photographs, and sealed envelopes that never made it into the mail… and one very simplistic silver band studded with a single diamond. On top of all of this is an envelope with my name on it—*Charley*, written in Gramps's shaky hand—and inside the envelope is a story every bit as complicated as the one Colleen McCullough weaves in my most favorite novel… only this story isn't a work of fiction.

My dear Charley, the letter begins.

So with Juli beside me and Rhett curled at my feet, I learn the truth about my past.

Gramps never spoke much about World War II. He told me tales about his childhood, like how he and his friends used to meet late at night, soundlessly escaping through curtained windows while their parents lay slumbering in their beds, only to hide in the shadows of Baker's Alley and watch drunks stumble home at two in the morning. He'd talk about Miss Redfern, his favorite teacher, who used to drink honey-sweetened tea and taught him how to write in cursive with a piece of white chalk and a little slate that was kept in his desk. Occasionally he spoke of receiving notice that he was being drafted—about the rock that settled into the pit of his stomach and the tears that his mother shed—and every now and again he'd even mention an old war buddy by the name of Oliver Clay. "Gave me that clock on the wall," Gramps would say, motioning to the round face and the iron hands. "Made it himself. A wedding gift. Used to tick, even, if you can believe it." And often he recounted his experiences from that cross-country trip taken upon his return to American soil. But never until now did I know that the reason he always gave for the sojourn—the need for a change of scenery—had more to do with a woman than it did with the war.

As it turns out, when Gramps gained acquaintance with Oliver Clay all those years ago in the army, they became more than just friends: they were one another's lifelines. Specific details aren't provided, but Gramps states very clearly in his letter to me that he "wouldn't have survived those long months had it not been for Oliver." They were very different men, Gramps and Oliver Clay. One grew up in a small Pennsylvania town, shooting guns and riding tractors; the other hailed from New York City. "About the only thing we had in common was apples," Gramps used to claim. "I picked 'em, and he lived in a real big one." In reality, though, apples weren't their only commonality.

On the eve before he left for war, Oliver Clay asked his longtime girlfriend to marry him. She said yes, of course, because she'd known him for half her life and found him to meet all of the necessary requirements that one looks for in a husband: handsome, kind, and intelligent. According to Gramps, Oliver spoke of her quite often… commenting on her sweet smile, twinkling eyes, and tendency to secure with long-handled paintbrushes the bun she wore in her hair. Her name was Flora Higgins and she loved reading as much as she loved art. When the war ended she and Oliver traveled south, landing in Lake Caywood, where they fell in love with the land and rented a little home in the country, covertly living as a married couple before vows had actually been exchanged. The land wasn't the only thing Flora fell in love with, though…

My grandfather—or Jasper, as she knew him—caused her heart to palpitate in a way that it never had for Oliver. Whereas her fiancé provided her with a sense of comfort, Jasper afforded something else entirely: passion.

Flora wasn't faithful; she did things she shouldn't have done.

So did my grandfather.

It was a short-lived affair, lasting no more than a handful of months. His hope was for the wedding plans to falter and fade. Flora didn't have to go through with the arrangement, he reasoned; no one had yet said "I do." But no matter how much he wished it—no matter how *hard*—in most instances, a wish is just a wish. Unless a person plants it on the right shooting star, the odds of it happening are slim to none. So even though he'd splurged on a diamond and thought out the words he'd speak while down on one knee, that time never came because Flora married Oliver.

That's why Gramps traveled west.

Isabella Crocetti, whom I came to know as Noni, was merely a distraction.

A distraction who became my grandfather's wife. He loved her, sure… but not like he had loved Flora. Not in the way he *continued* to love Flora.

He returned to Lake Caywood a married man; Oliver Clay sent a clock to congratulate him, along with word that the wife he'd been married to for six months was nearly eight-months pregnant. "I think you probably already know that the baby's not mine," he told Gramps in a letter, "and I don't intend to raise it as such." So when Fiona—my mother—was born, Noni accepted her with open arms and raised her with all the love in the world. And then when Fiona was killed at too young an age, Noni did the very same thing all over again, but this time for me.

It should come as no surprise that the friendship between my grandfather and his brother-in-arms didn't last. Oliver and his wife moved out of their country home and returned to the city, where they settled into a life among skyscrapers and walked to work in the morning beside suit-clad strangers carrying briefcases and folded up copies of the *Times*. Oliver made a living selling clocks; Flora worked for the New York Public Library, but kept a hobby of capturing cityscapes in acrylic. These were sold for mere pocket change at a tiny shop down the street. Her husband knew nothing about Flora's earnings from the art, so he didn't miss the miniscule payments when she sent them to Copper Drive rather than deposit them in the bank. It was her way of supporting Fiona, I suppose. And then me, because the checks kept coming long after my mother had passed away.

Gramps never cashed any of them; they're still in the box, Flora's small signature on the back of each one. He wrote to thank her for them, though, and included a bit of their daughter in every envelope: a flower she'd picked in the orchard, a crayon sketch that she'd drawn in school, a perfect spelling test with all ten words neatly printed in the script of a child. I know all of this because Gramps never mailed any of the letters he wrote. They are all right here, held together with a piece of twine, not a single stamp marred by the inked seal of the United States Postal Service.

In the letters, at the end of each one, he'd expressed the exact same wish: that things had worked out differently. But the past is the past and there's no undoing it once it's been done. Perhaps this is why none of his words ever made it to Flora. The taste of regret is a sour one; there's really no reason to share it.

At some point, though, he *had* posted a letter. Two letters, in fact. One, to inform Flora of her daughter's untimely death, and then again, long after my mother died and well past my tenth birthday, he'd sent that photograph of me on my yellow bicycle. And Flora had painted it, perfectly detailing its basket loaded with sun-kissed peaches and purple flowers, the glint of the rainbow tassels as they held tight to the ends of my handlebars, skipping and dancing down the dirt drive. She'd painted it and then sent it to him, and Gramps had stored it in a studio tower that only occasionally revealed itself to the world. But why? Why had he sent the photograph to begin with? Because he'd wanted Flora Higgins Clay to have an idea of *me*?

Because she came back, Gramps explains in his letter. There'd been two visits to the farmhouse. The first occurred when Fiona was four. She'd been a chubby little girl with dark ringlets, blue-green eyes, and a laugh that bubbled right out of her like a fountain. Flora had shown up unexpectedly, in town for no reason other than a desire to see her daughter, and so Gramps had walked with them to the hop field. They'd sat on a blanket spread out across the grass, sunlight filtering through the tall vines and dancing on their golden skin. The musky aroma of hops surrounded them as they spoke of past and present and future while at the same time speaking of nothing at all. Noni knew not of the visit. She'd had no desire to marry a man with more than one love or to raise a daughter with more than one mother; she'd said as much when she first agreed to raise Fiona as her own.

So Gramps never spoke of that single afternoon encounter that lasted no more than two hours. And neither did Flora. They went their separate ways, communicating through never-cashed checks and never-mailed letters, until one day, more than thirty years later, Flora *did* come back. She'd found my grandfather in the barn, fiddling with his brewing equipment. Noni and I weren't home at the time; we'd gone into town to run errands and weren't expected back for at least another hour, which is most likely why my grandfather felt safe enough to invite Flora into his home. She'd been distraught, so Gramps had sat her down at the solid oak table, poured her a small glass of wheat beer, and listened to her talk.

Eleven years earlier, in the winter, Flora Higgins Clay explained, she and her husband had traveled to England for a long, rainy month. While they were gone, a nice neighbor lady looked after their home and collected their mail, stacking it neatly on a heavy bureau beside the front door where it was read upon the couple's return. Had the kindly woman realized that a few envelopes slipped behind the cumbersome furniture, wedging themselves between it and the wall, she surely would have made note of it, but alas, this small fact went unnoticed. Therefore, it was more than a decade after the fact that Flora learned of her daughter's death and her granddaughter's existence.

Grief-stricken, she'd come back to Lake Caywood because she'd wanted to talk about Fiona with someone who'd known her and loved her… but she'd also wanted to learn about *me.* So Gramps dug out an old album and she flipped through it, thoroughly studying every picture on every page. There I was in cowboy boots, dancing around the Christmas tree, wearing a makeshift kerchief fashioned from discarded wrapping paper. And there I was again at age nine, standing on a stool at the kitchen sink, helping Noni to peel potatoes for soup.

The most recent was of me on my bike. Flora had stared at it for a long time, smiling a sad and faraway smile, but it wasn't then that Gramps gave the photograph to her. Not until years later, when Flora wrote and asked for a copy, did he slip the image from its frame on the mahogany desk and put it in the mail. It ended up being one of the only letters he ever actually posted to her, and with it he'd included a note: *This has to be it. I've made a commitment, and it is to Isabella and Charley, but you will forever be in my heart.*

Flora initiated contact only one more time after that: when she sent the artwork and note to express both her appreciation and respect. She never challenged my grandfather's request. Not after Noni passed away, not after her husband Oliver died of a stroke. Not even after she moved back to Lake Caywood and took a part-time job at the college library. Never once did she dial Gramps's number or show up on his doorstep… but he eventually realized she was back in town. It was he who suggested they meet for a cup of coffee. And so it came to be that three mornings out of every week—Monday, Wednesday, and Friday—Gramps would wander into the Tavern for breakfast. He always ordered the same thing: a spinach-and-cheese omelet, white toast spread with blackberry jam, and a steaming mug of joe, black. And not always, but sometimes, Miss Flora Higgins would join him.

That old quote—"'Tis better to have loved and lost than never to have loved at all"—it's true, Gramps writes in his letter to me. *But if you have the opportunity to get that love back, to find it again, then take it, Charley. Even if it only means sharing an occasional cup of coffee… something is almost always better than nothing.*

I blink a long blink, trying to process the earth-shattering information that's been offered to me on a few measly sheets of stationery. It's close to four in the morning, and that dull ache that settled in behind my eyes a couple hours ago isn't so dull anymore, but with the amount of newly acquired knowledge that's buzzing around my head, I know there's no chance of sleep. I close my eyes, rest my head on Juli's shoulder, the weight of the box and this newly discovered history so heavy in my lap. "So my *real* grandmother—"

"*Noni* is your real grandmother," Juli cuts in, correcting me. "Flora Higgins is your mother's birthmother. Those are two completely different things."

"That's true," I agree. "You're right. But Flora Higgins… I don't know. She was important to Gramps. *Really* important. Just look at all these letters he wrote, all the stories he'd wanted to share. You know that painting of his that I hung in the living room? Of the dark-haired woman sitting at the easel? I bet that's her."

"It might be," he assents. "That would make sense."

"He must've… he must've really loved her."

Juli rests his hand on the back of my head, smoothing my hair. "But he loved Noni, too. I saw that picture hanging in the game room… him acting all cocky, her giving him a coy grin. It's obvious how they felt about each other."

"How *she* felt about *him*," I correct, because suddenly it's all becoming clear. I remember them in the kitchen, talking about their separate days, sitting side by side but never touching. Now and then Noni would reach out and pat his face or his knee, ruffle his hair, rest a reassuring hand on his shoulder… but Gramps didn't reciprocate the act. Or, if he did, it somehow didn't convey the same sentiment. Sort of like how he always gave her an expensive piece of jewelry for her birthday: a diamond necklace, a sapphire ring, a brooch embedded with rubies. To make up for the guilt, most likely. Noni always oohed and aahed, of course, but her reaction was never more sincere than it was that time Kirby gave her a plush rug to place before the kitchen sink, so her feet wouldn't hurt while she did what she loved to do most.

"Gramps might've loved her," I reason, "but not like my uncle Kirby did. That's why he was so weird about the burial, I guess. He wanted Gramps laid to rest beside Noni, probably because he felt it was the last right thing—and the very least thing—Gramps could do for his wife."

Juli wraps an arm around my shoulders, giving me a squeeze, and slants his cheek so it's resting on the top of my head. A few sandpaper whiskers rub against my forehead. "Talk about turning a person's life upside-down," he whispers. "How does he end it?"

Gramps's cramped chicken-scratch scrawl etched in blue ballpoint pen has filled the fronts of five sheets of paper. There's still one left to go, though. Mentally, I am completely exhausted, but I turn to the final piece of stationery and read the concluding paragraph: *I've made some mistakes in my life, Charley, and I've kept an awful lot of secrets. Looking back, I'm not so sure it was the right thing to do. A better man wouldn't have kept all of this from you for so many years. What I should have done is told you the truth from the start, and I'm sorry I didn't until now.*

There's no way Gramps could have predicted the effect his words would have on me—no way he could have imagined the significance they'd impart—because Gramps himself knew nothing of the secret that's been weighing me down for the last several years. His apology hits me at full force, though, and leaves me struggling for air. Because in reality, it's more than just an apology. It's a warning.

"Hey," Juli soothes, cupping my face in his calloused hands and using his thumbs to wipe away my tears. "It's gonna be okay, Charley. Hey… come 'ere."

He draws me closer, lets me soak his shirt while I sob on his shoulder, but I eventually pull away because I can't do this to him. Everything will *not* be okay. With Gramps's words ringing in my ears, I look right at Juli and speak the truth that I should have spoken months ago. Before he electrocuted me with a kiss and gave me knee socks without holes in the heels for Christmas. Before he held me while I cried about Addy's arrest. Long before he bought me a scone and a popover at the town's annual berry festival. Looking back, I should have told him that first day in the hardware shop, when I shook his hand with the *5* tattooed on the palm and asked if he had the skills to refinish hardwood floors. What I should have said is, "Hi. I'm Charley Lane and I have a brain tumor. It's inoperable. My doctor tells me I only have one or two good years left to live, but I'm hoping for more. Juli, is it? So nice to meet you."

I didn't say that, though. I allowed him to think I was normal because normal was what I had wanted at the time… I'd had no idea that a handyman with a lip ring and a lopsided smile had the power to send me somersaulting head over heels.

Gramps would tell me to be honest, though; that had been reinforced just tonight.

And so I tell Juli now, a year later, holding both of his hands in mine and watching his face as the tears stream down his cheeks, over day-old stubble, dripping onto his jeans to leave dark splotches of blue. I tell him the entire truth, starting with the diagnosis that came two years after my college graduation and detailing the surgery and radiation and hair loss that accompanied it; I tell him about that blissful year of remission that followed, when the doctors felt confident enough to employ the term "cancer-free" when describing my status. And then I tell him about the headaches that started out mild enough, but eventually grew to be blindingly painful, and about how sometimes my memory faltered, enabling candles to remain lit overnight and full cartons of milk to spoil on the kitchen counter. Charlie went with me to that appointment; he was sitting right beside me when the doctor shared the grim news: "The tumor's back."

They gave me between three and five years.

Between three and five years is where I am right now. I guess there's still the possibility of another New Year's Eve celebration, but I've started to view my future in months rather than years. "I will eventually die," I say now to Juli, "and there's nothing that can be done to prevent it."

He doesn't pull away like I feared he might, but he doesn't offer anything in the way of words. I fill the space with apologies and hindsights until finally he asks, so earnest and frank, "Why didn't you tell me?"

"Because when Charlie looked at me, he looked at me like I was dying, and I didn't want to spend the rest of my life being looked at like that. I didn't want my last years to be nothing but downcast eyes and constant reminders and unspoken wonderings about when it will happen. I wanted normal… or as close to normal as I could manage." I look at him, meeting his gaze and holding it because I want him to really hear what I'm about to say. "I didn't think I was going to fall in love—I didn't think it was even possible to fall in love with someone else, after loving Charlie as much as I did for all those years—but then I met you, and… and, Juli, if Charlie loved me even half as much as I love you, then I can't bear to think of what I've already done to him. *You* are the love of my life, but I really hope I'm not yours… because when I think of how much I'm going to end up hurting you…? I am so sorry, Juli. I am so, *so* sorry."

I choke on the words, barely able to get them out.

Juli holds me tighter than he ever has before, maybe thinking that if he doesn't let go—doesn't loosen his grip—then right here is where I'll have to stay forever. That fate won't stand a chance. He kisses my neck, my ear, my forehead; he buries his face in my hair and soaks the mussed locks with his tears. When he does speak, his voice is barely a whisper and muffled from crying. "You know that I love you too," he says. "More than anything. And whatever you need…"

"There is one thing."

"Anything."

I look to my pup on the floor, sprawled there on his blanket, so calm and serene in his slumbering state. Fragments of broken tissue-paper leaves cling to his shaggy beard; tufts of caramel-colored fur curl out from between the worn black pads of his feet. Utterly exhausted from a long day of joyful activity, his only movement is the tiny widening of nostrils as he intakes steady, peaceful breaths.

"When the time comes, will you take care of Rhett?"

"Yes," Juli assures me, swallowing hard. "When the time comes, I will."

25.

Addy

The first thought that popped into Addy Birch's head when he woke up this morning and looked out the window was "It's a mac 'n' cheese kind of day."

It's cold and the air smells like woodstoves. Although there still isn't any snow on the ground, the sky is grey and a thin film of frost coats the grass, making it crunch beneath his feet as he crosses the yard to the farmhouse. He carries a canvas bag in each hand. One contains several boxes of uncooked macaroni; the other is weighted down by milk, butter, and multiple types of cheese. He clambers up the porch steps and tries the door, expecting to find it locked, but the knob turns easily.

Charley must already be awake.

The warmth of the kitchen slaps his face, turning his cheeks a rosy shade of red. Addy walks across the room and sets the groceries on the bar, shrugs out of his coat and tosses it over the back of a stool. The recipe that he has in mind isn't difficult, per se, but it does require quite a bit of prep time. Plus, he has a mind to pair the meal with a side of stewed tomatoes and a warm mushroom salad tossed with bacon-vinaigrette dressing. Needless to say, an early start is his goal.

Addy slips one of the Brewhaha's crimson aprons over his head, wrapping the long straps around his waist and tying them in the front. He salts a big pot of water and sets it on the stove, lights the gas burner beneath it, unearths the cheese grater, and rolls up his sleeves. Blocks of cheddar and Colby and Monterey Jack line the counter. Addy whistles while he works, the notes bouncing against the ceiling and finding their way upstairs as he forms one mountain of shredded cheese after another. Sharp and mild, white and orange. He deposits the sticky mounds to a large aluminum bowl, where the flavors and colors mingle with one another.

On the stove, elbow pasta softens and cooks in a slow, rolling boiling. Addy tests a piece (al dente!) and is in the process of pouring the noodles into a colander when he hears Rhett's fast footsteps on the stairs. Charley, dressed in loose corduroys and a long-sleeved t-shirt, appears a moment later. "Hey," she greets him. "You're here early. I wasn't expecting you 'til closer to nine." She walks to the bar and picks up his coat, relocating it to the beer-handle rack behind the door before taking a seat on one of the tall stools. "Have you eaten yet?"

"Just a granola bar," Addy informs her. "What about you?"

"Same. Do you want some coffee or something?"

"Sure," he answers, noticing the dimness of her ruby-red sparks; they fizzle to nothingness mere seconds after leaving her skin. She seems extra tired today. Drained. The two days off between New Year's and now must not have been quite enough recuperation time. "I can make it. Give me just a minute."

"Okay. Thanks."

With the macaroni draining in the sink, Addy scoops hazelnut coffee into a filter and fills the maker with water. It gurgles to life right away, sputtering and coughing and filling the kitchen with its buttery, nutty aroma. "So?" he asks, sensing unspoken words hanging between them. "Everything okay?"

"Not really," Charley confides, "but I'm not quite ready to talk about it yet. How about you talk to me first instead? Tell me about that girl you were spending time with at the party. Juli says you're in lust."

"I might be," Addy admits, feeling his cheeks warm. "I don't know."

Charley giggles half-heartedly, prompting, "Well, what's her name? How'd you meet her?"

"Her name's Eleanor. We went to high school together. She, uh… she asked me to kiss her."

"And did you?"

"Yeah." He turns away, pretending to check the status of the coffee, but really he's just too embarrassed to look at Charley as he says, "I think I did alright. I… That was the first time I ever kissed a girl."

"I'm sure you did fine," Charley assures him, "but I know what you mean. I spent years preparing for my first kiss. I used to practice on one of those hand-held mirrors. I even drew a mouth on it. For some reason, I was so worried my aim would be off and I'd miss the guy's lips… You didn't miss Eleanor's lips, did you?"

"Nope."

"Then, yeah. I'm sure you did just fine."

"We met for lunch yesterday," Addy says, filling two mugs with coffee and retrieving a pint of cream from the refrigerator. "I had a sandwich and she had a salad and then we split a piece of cheesecake for dessert."

"What kind of cheesecake was it?" Charley wonders.

"Just regular, but there were cherries on top."

"Sounds good." She sighs, remembering something from her past, and then asks, "Have you ever had Guinness cheesecake? When I lived in Michigan there was this little hole-in-the-wall restaurant that was known for three things: dirty martinis, loaded baked potatoes, and Guinness cheesecake. And the cheesecake? It was *amazing*." She's quiet for a minute, probably lost in a memory of cream cheese and stout and dark chocolate, but then she looks back to Addy. "Did you make plans to see her again?"

"No. Her dad drove her back down to school yesterday afternoon. She goes to Appalachian State in North Carolina, so she won't be home again for a while."

"But I bet you'll see her over spring break. And, I mean, *something* is almost always better than *nothing*." The way that she says this, Addy almost wonders if she's quoting someone. He doesn't ask, though. He doesn't have to; Charley shares without urging, "Words of wisdom spoken by my gramps." She lightens her coffee with cream, watching the liquid cloud of white transform black to toffee, and then holds the mug in both hands, not lifting it off the bar. Not taking even one sip. "I have something to tell you, Addy. It's not good."

Addy divides the cooled pasta into two casseroles and opens a carton of eggs. He doesn't ask what this not-good something is because he already knows it isn't anything he wants to hear; he already knows the words she's about to speak aren't just "not good." They are in fact much worse than that. So he waits.

And he cracks six eggs against the side of a large mixing bowl, yolks bleeding yellow.

And he measures out two cups of whole milk.

And through tears, he whisks together the ingredients until they are creamy pale.

And then, because Charley can't say it, he does: "You're dying."

Charley looks up, her emerald eyes brimming with saltwater. "How did you…?"

"Your sparks," Addy says, plain and simple. "They've been fading for months. I just knew."

He doesn't stop working. Charley watches him add heaps of cheese to the pans of cooked macaroni and tells him she's met with a lawyer. "When I'm gone," she informs him, "the Brewhaha will be yours. I'm leaving all of it to you: the land, the barn… the farmhouse." Addy nods, letting her know that he's listening even as he pours the milk-and-egg mixture over the pasta. So Charley keeps talking, explaining that she's written two letters that will need to be mailed. "Once I'm gone," she clarifies. "Will you do that for me?"

Addy shakes salt and pepper over the pans. "Yes."

"They're in the upstairs office, in the middle desk drawer. One is in a big manila envelope; the other is just a small white one. I already put postage on both of them. And Addy?"

He pulls a box of foil from the drawer by the sink, unrolls it, and tears off two long silvery sheets. Charley waits while he lays them on top of the casseroles, folds down the edges, slides both pans onto a bottom shelf of the refrigerator. He'll take them out in a few hours, popping them into the oven so they're done right as the lunch crowd begins to roll in, but now, with nothing left to do but clean up, Addy turns and meets Charley's gaze for the first time since his fears were confirmed.

"Addy," Charley repeats. "I want you to know that I'm sorry. All those years ago when I left…? I didn't want to. And I don't want to leave you now. If there was something I could do to change it, I—"

"I know," Addy interrupts. "I know you would." He hangs his head, fiddling with the strings of his apron, not really sure of the right thing to say. So he says the first thing that comes to mind, which is, "I'm really going to miss you."

"I'm going to miss you, too," Charley cries, quiet tears rolling down her cheeks. "So much."

"You're the best mother I ever could have asked for, you know? The very best. If it hadn't been for you I don't know what would have hap—"

But now it's Charley's turn to cut him off, and she does it with a hug. Addy's still fumbling to finish his sentence as she walks around the bar and pulls him in close, standing on her tiptoes to rest her chin on his shoulder. And for the second time in a less than three days, Charley holds a grown man as he weeps for the loss that he hasn't yet fully experienced.

26.
Juli

Rain splatters against the windows of my living room, tap-tap-tapping like too-long fake fingernails, fat droplets racing down the glass. The sky is that same silver-grey as a chainsaw bar and the ground is soggier than a kitchen sponge after it's been dunked in dirty dishwater. I pull the fleece blanket up under my chin and snuggle deeper into the couch. Since Scarlett's occupying a cushion of her own, I've only got two-thirds of the space to claim as mine; needless to say, I'm pretty scrunched up. I will give her this, though: that little Irish setter sure does know how to keep a person's feet warm.

We're watching Sunday football with our eyes closed, silently cheering for the Ravens because audible support requires too much energy. Scarlett is actually snoring. I haven't quite reached that point yet, but I'm close…

It's been a long day. It's technically only four o'clock, but already it's been a long day.

Normally, I'd reserve the first day of the week / last day of the weekend strictly for snoozing or boozing (just one or two beers) or anything else that strikes my fancy, but this morning was busy. The basement flooded. Not like a deluge or anything, but there was definitely some standing water. Fortunately, I don't keep a whole lot of stuff down there—just some boxes of Ninja Turtles action figures that Ma sent home with me, a pile of scrap lumber, and an old recliner that should've been tossed years ago—but it *is* where I do my laundry. I *do* have a washer and dryer that aren't meant to sit in an inch of water.

My initial reaction was to petition Asher for his help, but he must've spent the night at Annie's because when I pounded on his door at seven o'clock this morning, no one bothered to answer. So I pulled on a pair of rubber boots and moved everything by myself, dragging the machinery to a patch of cement that wasn't quite as level as the rest of the basement floor. Who knew I had an island in my basement? Michelangelo, Master Splinter, Genghis Frog, and the rest of the gang are now hanging out on top of the washer, newly secured in a non-soggy cardboard box. Some of the lumber *might* be salvageable, but that chair's going out with the trash. Finally.

I spent the majority of my day down there with a Shop-Vac, a squeegee, and every old towel I could find in the house. I'm tired and my back hurts. It's not the kind of sidesplitting pain that occurs after lugging keg after keg from the barn to the house, but it is a dull ache that I'd prefer not to be experiencing. A massage right about now would be nice, but so would a large pizza with mushrooms and extra cheese. I didn't eat breakfast and there was no time for lunch. About thirty minutes ago, my stomach issued a low, threatening rumble… but even placing a call for delivery seems like an awful lot of work: my phone's all the way back in my bedroom.

Sometimes, though, good things come to those who wait.

The headlights that turn into my driveway cast a long beam of light through the windows and onto the wall, reflecting off a framed picture of a pineapple that Asher once sketched for me while drunk. It's not very good, but the story behind it is. At least, what I *remember* of the story is good, which admittedly isn't much. It definitely had something to do with SpongeBob.

The headlights shut off and so does the car's engine. A door slams. I hold my breath, wondering if it's possible that Luigi's Pizzeria telepathically received my order and is now delivering a pizza to my doorstep. The odds of this wish coming true are slim to none… but then the doorbell rings.

Suddenly wide-awake, Scarlett leaps off the couch and barks incessantly, alerting me to the fact that we may have an intruder on our hands. "It's fine," I tell her, tossing the blanket aside and forcing myself to stand up. "Settle down."

It's not a pizza deliveryman.

It's Asher. He's wearing a soggy hoodie and looking a little bit like a drowned rat. "Hey," he says when I open the door. "Can I come in?"

"Sure." I step out of the way and walk back to the couch.

Asher follows my lead, the soles of his wet sneakers squeaking against the floor. I return to the sofa and he perches on a chair, leaning forward to rest his elbows on his knees. He spends a minute observing the Ravens game, but quickly loses interest and directs his attention to me instead, preparing to initiate a dialogue. I'm surprised when the question he voices is, "Why are you here?"

"I live here," is my response. "This is my house."

"Right," Asher sighs. "But why are you here *now*? And why have you been here every night this week? Did something happen? Are things not good between you and Charley? Because, dude… I can't remember the last time you were home five nights in a row. I'm worried."

"You're worried?"

"I am!" Asher insists. "Charley is, like, the perfect match for you. You can*not* let her get away. So whatever differences you're having, figure them out. Be honest with her. Tell her you're scared, if you're scared. Or upset, if she did something to piss you off or whatever…"

I roll my eyes. "Okay. Thanks for the pep talk, buddy."

"Hey, I'm just telling it like it is," Asher informs me. "You'd do the same for me. Hell, you *did* the same for me. That lecture you gave me? Yeah. It made all the difference. So this is me paying it forward. *Call* her. *Fix* whatever's broken between the two of you. But don't let her slip away. You'll regret it, man. I know you, and you'll regret it. You're a nice guy, Juli, not a douche. But you sure are acting like one hell of a douche right now."

I'm not sure what to say, which is okay since Asher doesn't seem to expect any sort of response. He stands up, walks to the door, and lets himself out without so much as another word. "Definitely not a pizza deliveryman," I mutter to Scarlett, but even as I say it, I realize the comment is more a defense mechanism than anything else. The truth is, Asher isn't too far off base. I maybe *am* a little bit scared of everything that's going on with Charley, but even more than that—and I feel bad admitting it—but even more than that, I'm angry. I'm actually *incredibly* angry.

Without any sort of warning, Charley Lane allowed me to fall in love with her.

And because there was no warning, I fell. Hard.

The anger wells up, forming a fire-red wave of intense rage, and I turn to the pillow beside me, punching it with every ounce of strength I can muster. My fist lands squarely on the cushion's only button, wide and flat, positioned right there in the center so as to decoratively secure a flap of the linen-like fabric. A sharp pain stabs my knuckle, drawing blood. "Shit," I swear, because the little knick sort of hurts.

"Shit-fuck-*damn!*" I elaborate, because I don't want Charley to die.

Scarlett, her chocolate eyes awash with worry, hops onto the couch and curls herself onto my lap, reaching up with her snout to nuzzle my neck and give my chin an affectionate lick. I wrap my arms around her and bury my face in her fur, inhaling her doggy scent. She doesn't care that I'm making her fur damp, and she'll be happy to lick the salt from my cheeks once I've shed all the tears that are in me. She's the perfect girl, albeit a dog, and she lets me hug her for as long as I feel the need.

In the end, I realize what Asher's told me is true: honest *is* the best way to be. Even Charley's grandfather would agree; he basically issued the same advice in that life-altering letter he left. So once I've cried myself out and wiped my face clean—and once Scarlett's offered her services as well—I trudge back to my bedroom, find my phone, and dial the only number that matters.

"Hi," I say when Charley answers on the second ring. "It's me."

"Hi."

"Hi. I'm coming over. Have you eaten yet?"

"Dinner?"

"Yeah."

"It's not even five o'clock yet."

I glance at the clock on my nightstand. She's right. "Oh. I'm really hungry."

"Okay, well… I've been craving Chinese."

"Veggie lo mein?"

"With a spring roll."

It's not what I want, but in the scheme of life, that doesn't matter. "Okay. Give me half an hour," I say, and grab my coat on the way out the door, hunching my shoulders against the pouring rain.

∞

One never knows what a Sunday at the Brewhaha will entail. Sometimes the joint is hopping, other times it's relatively slow. Today, the latter version applies. I park among the automobiles of staff members; only two cars in the lot are not recognizable.

Scarlett hops out first, splattering mud as she lands. "Come on," I call to her, clutching the Chinese food against my chest and dodging raindrops on my way to the farmhouse. The turf is so soggy it suctions my feet. Each step requires a bit of extra effort, and each time the ground releases one of my canvas shoes from its grip, it does so with a sickening *squish-slop*. By the time we leap onto the porch, I'm the walking definition of the word "drenched" and Scarlett's looking a lot like a sopping-wet mop. She executes a full-body shake while I stand beside her and drip, a puddle of water forming around my Converse sneakers. We leave as much dampness as possible on the Welcome mat before venturing into the establishment.

The kitchen smells salty. It's Boomer and Addy's responsibility to man the stove this afternoon, but as I walk around the bar, it's not dinner they appear to be working on. It's a dessert. The counter is littered with discarded containers of heavy cream, sour cream, cream cheese, and beer: dark-chocolate stout, bottled by Petey. The Brewhaha's label—Old Orchard Brews—appears on each one, that tree of life with its deep-running roots, crimson ink printed on gold paper. I have to arch my brows and give pause, stopping to wonder aloud, "What're you guys doing?"

"We could ask the same thing of you," Boomer observes. "Why would you bring Chinese food to a restaurant? We would've fed you—we've got ham 'n' bean soup simmering on the stove right now."

"Charley was craving lo mein," I say with a shrug, but the simple response earns a quick glance from Addy. Although we haven't talked about it, he knows that I know, and I know that he knows, but we are the only two aware of the truth-bomb Charley dropped last week. Everyone else remains completely oblivious to the devastation it's left in its wake. "So all that cream cheese and stuff," I continue. "It can't be for ham 'n' bean soup."

"Nope," Boomer says, but then Addy cuts in.

"Stout cheesecake," he informs me. "That's what we're making. Charley and I were talking about it earlier in the week, so I just thought…" He looks away, plucking empty containers from the counter and tossing them into the trash. It's evident that he's not really sure of how to conclude the sentence.

"It's a good thought, Addy. She'll love it."

"I just hope it turns out okay."

"Even if it doesn't, she'll still love it," I assure him. "Is she upstairs?"

He nods, and Boomer elaborates, "In the office paying some bills."

I head to the second floor, urging Scarlett to tag along by promising her a fortune cookie of her own, but it takes some coaxing. The salty scent of ham is hard to walk away from; she keeps looking over her shoulder, her nose in the air, sniffing relentlessly. I do manage to guide her up the steps, though, and once she notices Rhett curled just inside the office door, she forgets about ham and starts thinking about gnawing on her best canine-friend's face.

Charley is at the desk, but it's not bills that she's paying. Rather, she's filling a small leather journal with words. "Hey," I whisper, coming up behind her and kissing the top of her head. Her hair smells like sleep and soap. "What're you up to? Writing a book?"

"I might as well be," she sighs. "It's for Addy. I'm trying to record all of my memories of him as a kid, just so he has it, you know? So he can look back and remember. I don't want him to *ever* forget how much I love him… I don't want him to ever forget, because, you know… I'm going to be gone, but his mother won't be, and that's… that's just not *fair*. It's not fair and I, I just— I *worry* about him. That's all. I just really worry about him."

"I know you do." I set the food on the desk and stand beside her, running my hands through her sleep-scented hair as she leans her head against my stomach. "He knows how much you love him, Charley. He won't ever forget that."

"I hope you're right."

"I *am* right."

"Your stomach's growling."

"Because I'm starving."

"Then let's eat."

We sit facing each other on the floor and use chopsticks to pluck our food right from white cardboard cartons. I try Charley's veggie lo mein, she tries my shrimp and broccoli, and the dogs attempt to try some of each, but ultimately fail. Although admirable, their persistent efforts are equally obnoxious; I'm about one snout-in-the-face away from taking them out of the equation all together. The hallway isn't such a bad place, I reason, and am about to act on this thought when Rhett suddenly diverts his attention and refocuses it on the funny little door with its wrought iron latch. He paws at it once, his nails scratching softly against the wood. I turn to Charley. "You can open it for him," she says with a shrug. "That's fine."

So I do, and the dogs wander inside to explore the undersized closet.

Now that it's no longer necessary for us to devise a strategy for each bite, we find ourselves with little to say. There's no longer a need to fill the space with "Scarlett, no!" and "Rhett… *stop*" so I find myself filling Charley in on my flooded basement instead. "So what you're telling me is that you hurt your back again?" she confirms.

I stare into my carton of Chinese food, attempting to spear a piece of soy sauce-soaked broccoli. "It's not bad, just a little sore. I'll be fine."

"Do you really mean that?"

"Mean what?"

"That you'll be fine."

I give up on the broccoli because I can't focus on it *and* what Charley is asking. But I don't have a chance to answer before she continues, "I don't just mean about your back, Juli. I mean about… *everything*. Will you really be fine?"

It's impossible to fully describe the emotion that wells up in me at that moment. I'm hot and cold all at the same time; my hands shake and my head pounds. Almost violently, I toss aside the carton of shrimp and broccoli. Soy sauce speckles the wall and my chopsticks fall to the floor and when I speak, my voice is scary-calm. It portrays a calm I definitely do not feel. "No," I say, adamant about this fact. "I will *not* be fine. I am not *fine*, Charley. I am… I am a *wreck*. I love you more than I have ever loved anything or any*one* before, but I am so *mad* at you because you *didn't* tell me—you conveniently waited for me to fall madly in love with you before you bothered to mention *anything* about a brain tumor—and so right now I am furious with you, but I'm also feeling guilty *because* I'm furious with you… because I shouldn't be furious with you because I *love* you… and so there are just so many things that I'm feeling, all at the exact same time, and I have no idea what to do. I have absolutely no idea what to do with these feelings. The only thing I *do* know is that I am definitely *not* fine."

I say all of this, and I say it without screaming or crying. I just shake. I sit there and shake and Charley sits there and watches me because how is she supposed to comfort a person who's basically just said he loves her and hates her, all at the same time and all in the same breath?

I tug at the sleeves of my shirt and interlock my fingers. I raise my hands to my mouth, fiddle with my lip ring, bite down on my left index finger, just hard enough to leave an imprint of my teeth. I have no idea what I'm doing. No idea what I'm feeling. No idea how I'll handle the future. And then Charley says, very softly, "It's okay that you're angry."

"It *has* to be okay that I'm angry," I point out, "because I don't know how to turn the anger off. I wish I did. Maybe then I could stop feeling so guilty, too. I feel *guilty* about feeling *angry*… and… I think I'd honestly rather just feel sad."

I close my eyes, take a deep breath, open them again and focus on Charley. She's nibbling her bottom lip and looking right *into* me with those astonishingly green eyes of hers. They're brimming with tears. One's actually spilled over and is slowly navigating her cheek, taking with it the faintest trace of mascara. "I'm sorry," I tell her. "I am really, really sorry."

"For feeling angry?"

"For feeling *everything*. For not knowing how to handle any of this."

"But you are handling it," she says, hugging her knees to her chest. "You're handling it the only way you know how. And your way… At least your way is honest. It's real. Charlie used to… he used to always claim that 'showing up was half the battle.' Like just being there was enough. But it wasn't. It *isn't*. Being there isn't worth much if you're not being honest." She pauses, meets my gaze, offers a weak smile. "I guess I'm one to talk, right?"

I don't answer.

"Anyway," she continues, "I'm glad you're not hiding what you're feeling. Glad you're not tiptoeing around the issue, pretending everything is okay when it's not. Charlie never did that. He pampered me and told jokes and insisted that everything would be fine."

"Even though it won't be," I whisper.

Charley reaches out to me, her fingers long and thin, and I reach out to take her hand in mine. "It won't be fine at first," she says, "but eventually it will be. Life will go on, and you will meet someone even better than me, and I will be so incredibly happy for you."

"I will never find someone better than you," I tell her. "Never."

"But I want you to."

I pull her hand closer and press it to my lips, kissing each individual finger. Kissing that infinity ring that she's never without. There are tears streaming down my cheeks and the room smells like soy sauce and my stomach feels queasy and hollow and I say the most truthful thing that I can: "I don't want to lose you."

"You won't," she says, crawling into my lap so I can hold her. So I can feel her warmth and her knobby elbow digging into my ribcage; so I can smell the soapy lotion on her skin and the Chinese food on her breath when she promises, "You won't ever lose me, Juli Singer. I will always be with you. Always."

We sit like that for a long time.

Me holding her, her holding me, the only sound that of the shaky breaths we inhale.

And then when her elbow pressed against my ribs gets to be too painful, and my hand wrapped around hers gets to be too clammy, we slowly disengage ourselves from one another. It doesn't occur to me until Charley starts tossing crumpled spring roll wrappers into the trash that the clean-up is entirely too quiet. "Where are the dogs?"

She stops what she's doing and looks up, tilting her head to the ceiling, almost as if listening for something. The way she cranes her neck—the thinness of it, and the perfect slope of her skull—makes me think she has the most beautiful neck of anyone I know, which is maybe an odd thing to think, but given the circumstances… it makes perfect sense that I'm admiring Charley Lane's neck; soon enough, I will no longer have that option.

"I think…" Charley starts, trailing off before resuming her thought. "I think they might be in the tower." She turns to face me, widening her eyes just a bit, and confirms, "You haven't seen it yet, have you? Do you want to go up?"

I nod and follow Charley through the undersized doorframe. She feels her way to the first step, leading the way since she's done this before, and I crawl along behind. At one point she reaches back with her left hand to grip mine, pulling me along.

Not quite halfway up the spiral staircase, I'm able to stand at my full height. The low ceiling disappears and the steps widen, opening into an octagonal room comprised mostly of windows. Steady rain *rat-a-tats* against the glass. Right now the sky is ink-stain black, but I imagine that when the sun is shining, the view this room affords is something to behold. I mean, a vantage point like this one pretty much allows for the entire orchard to be observed.

In the studio itself are a worktable and two fresh canvases propped up on two easels. Each easel is accompanied by a stool, and each stool has resting on it a blank palette. "I don't remember there being two of everything last time I was up here," Charley mutters, and I can't help but wonder whether *she's* wondering if this is a result of the room's magic, or a result of the tumor in her brain. I keep this thought to myself, though, because it doesn't matter if the memory is faulty. This setup of two easels and two stools and two canvases and two empty palettes means something, so I say the only thing that makes sense: "Let's paint."

We find brushes and tubes of acrylic on one of the table's built-in shelves. Charley squeezes glistening globs of color onto our palettes, dotting them with cadmium yellow, cerulean blue, and titanium white; burnt umber, phthalo blue, and naphthol crimson. The dogs, utterly exhausted after conducting a thorough investigation of the room, lie in a heap between the easels. Scarlett nuzzles Rhett with her nose and Rhett pins her face to the floor with a furry paw, licking her eye and her ear in a great show of affection. "What should we paint?" I ask, and Charley, sliding onto the opposite stool, answers, "Paint your favorite memory of me, and I'll do the same for you."

"I don't know how to do that. I don't know how to paint your quirks."

She grins, but doesn't glance over. "It's okay if it needs to be abstract."

The truth is, almost anything I'd come up with would look abstract; I'm not the world's greatest artist by a long shot. Charley starts painting right away, but it takes me a while to sift through all of the memories—there are a lot of good ones—before I finally decide that my very favorite would have to be that day at the Jamboree, when Charley agreed to label our outing as a first date. "But, if that's the case," she'd adamantly stated, "then I'm not buying your scone."

And she hadn't, true to her word.

My canvas ends up being a swirl of yellow and blue (representative of the lemon-blueberry scones we ate that day) with a few splashes of red (because Charley likes the color red) and green (because her eyes take my breath away every time I look into them).

The final product is atrocious. I apologize when I show it to her and tell her I won't be offended if she burns it. "That is, hands down, the most hideous painting I've ever seen," she laughs. "And I love it."

Her canvas turns out a lot better than mine. It too is abstract, but in an entirely different way. The image details us as blurred silhouettes, kissing between two flecked columns of green. "Columns of hops," Charley explains, grinning. I'm depicted as blue, she is red, and the sparks that fly above us, like fireworks, are various shades of purple.

I glance from the canvas to her, surprised. "I didn't know you could paint."

"I'm no Van Gogh," she claims, "but I can wield a paintbrush better than I can a screwdriver."

"Boy… not me."

"Oh, really?"

I give her a look, and she tries to stifle a smile, but it's no use. She lifts my painting from the easel and holds it out in front of her, studying the swirls and the splotches and the poor execution. "It really is awful," she admits, "but I meant it when I said that I loved it. Let's take them downstairs. We've still got fortune cookies waiting for us."

Somehow the dogs manage to determine that fortune cookies are edible, so their interest is instantly piqued. They hop up, shake themselves awake, and snort gruffly in one another's faces. Rhett licks Scarlett, Scarlett bites Rhett, and then they are off… racing downstairs in the hopes of receiving a snack.

We carry our respective canvases and prop them on a windowsill to dry. Side by side, mine looks worse than ever, but the contrast makes Charley laugh so hard that she's practically crying. "Wow," she gasps, struggling for air. "Just, wow!"

I roll my eyes and toss a fortune cookie at her. Rhett lunges forward, trying to catch it in his mouth, but his owner is too quick. She pats him gently on the head and promises him a bite. I look at Scarlett, who's watching me with eyes about the size of Saturn, and assure her that she, too, will receive at least a few crumbs. "Okay," Charley announces. "We have to break 'em at the same time, eat half, and then read our fortunes. Deal?"

"Deal."

The plastic wrappers crinkle as we tear into them.

Charley counts out, "One, two, three!"

I'm not a big fan of fortune cookies—I think they taste a little bit like sweetened sawdust—but I follow the rules and chomp down on half of my cookie. Then I unfold the little slip of paper tucked inside and read the prophecy that's printed there in blue ink: "You will always be surrounded by those who love you."

"See?" Charley says, making light of what feels like the heaviest fortune ever. "Told you."

I avert my gaze, not sure I can look at her without crying again. She pushes onward, though, and reads off her own forecast for the future: "A nice cake is waiting for you."

"Downstairs."

"I think the more common closure is 'in bed,' isn't it?"

"It is, but I doubt there's a cake waiting for you in bed. I know for a fact that there's one in the refrigerator downstairs, though. A dark-chocolate-stout cheesecake. Addy was working on it earlier."

"He was?"

"Yep."

Her green eyes dance. "Do you think that it's ready?"

"Doubtful. Don't cheesecakes have to chill for, like, four or five hours? I can't imagine it's been in the refrigerator for all that long. Addy had just put it in the *oven* when I got here this afternoon."

"Oh." She bunches her lips together in a sort of contemplative pucker. "Do you think we should check anyway? I mean, the fortune says that a nice cake is waiting for me… We should probably just walk downstairs and ask, right?"

She looks so cute standing there with her eyebrows arched, waiting for me to concur. I don't answer right away. Instead, I take a moment to study her. To memorize Charley Lane. To capture mental snapshots of her mussed hair and the way it falls across her forehead… of the dimple-creases that form when she smiles, and how the one to the right of her mouth is more prominent than the one to the left. I notice hints of the freckles that spatter her cheeks in the summer, growing more visible with each day of sunshine, but lie dormant during the winter months. I want never to forget those long, dark lashes; I need always to remember how they perfectly framed Charley's too-green eyes.

I let my gaze travel downward, over that perfect neck, along the curve of her shoulders. She's wearing a simple white t-shirt—not tight —and it flows gently over her small breasts, down to her waist, where it billows and floats when she moves.

"Hey," she says, aware of the fact that my eyes have traveled south. "Earth to Juli…?"

"Sorry. I was just…"

"Thinking about surrounding yourself with the people you love? In bed?" she guesses. "I can make that happen for you, but not until later. Right now, there's a nice cake waiting for me. Downstairs. So come on."

Not unexpectedly, the cheesecake is still several hours away from being deemed "sliceable." Addy informs us that it needs at least another sixty minutes in the refrigerator. Preferably more.

"*I* don't care if it falls apart on the plate, though," Charley assures him. "*I* don't mind if the middle's still gooey."

Frustrated, Addy shakes his head and grumbles, "But *I* do. Just one more hour… Please?"

Charley agrees to wait if I'll agree to dance with her. I offer up fair warning that my footwork is about as pathetic as my artwork, but she dismisses my words with a wave of her hand. "We've never danced together before," she points out. "I just want to have the *experience* of it. Don't you?"

"He does," Addy pipes up. "He wants at least an hour's worth of the experience."

I narrow my eyes and shoot him a look, but it's in jest. The Brewhaha is virtually empty. Even Boomer is gone, having left early when the dinner crowd turned out to be nearly nonexistent, and outside, the rain still falls in sheets.

Charley disappears for a moment, wandering off to fiddle with the sound system. There are speakers in each room, but the actual stereo and her collection of outdated albums are stored on the shelves in the study. She must have a song in mind because a tune that sounds like it was released in the eighties hits the airwaves almost right away. It takes me only a second to recognize it as something by The Clash, and when Charley returns to the kitchen, she is wearing a mischievous grin.

I don one as well. "'Train In Vain,' huh?"

"Your shower song," she says with a wink.

I let her grab my hands and pull me to the center of the kitchen; I let her sway her hips and coax me into swaying mine. We swing our arms and tap our feet and spin in circles—I even dip her at one point—and all the while, I serenade her with my own version of the song (because I *am* the one "who sings the most").

Addy leans on the bar and watches us, executing a piercing two-finger whistle at the conclusion of our dance number. He's clapping and looking pretty happy until Charley motions for him to join her on the floor, announcing, "Okay! You're up!"

"No way. I don't dance," he insists.

Charley scoffs. "What do you mean you don't dance? We used to dance all the time!"

"Yeah, when I was *five*." Addy's cheeks are definitely more flushed than they were a minute ago. "And besides, I'm on the clock. What if someone walks in and asks for a beer? I need to be ready."

"You need to get your butt on the dance floor is what you need to do," I tell him, laughing. "Go on, get out there! I can man the taps for five minutes."

Addy slumps his shoulders and issues an incredibly exaggerated sigh, but he does untie his apron and slip it over his head, tossing the wad of red fabric down on the bar and trudging over to join Charley. She puts her hands on his shoulders and pushes them back, forcing him to stand up straight. "Hey, Juli? Can you run into the study and skip ahead to track four?"

"Sure thing!"

I dash down the hall and tap the button printed with double arrows, pointing to the right. Maracas blast instantly from the speakers; the beat they keep is both steady and sandy. By the time I get back to the kitchen, Charley and Addy are following one another around the room, walking like Egyptians with their chins jutting first forward and then back again. Rhett darts in front of them, skirts around them, attempting to be a part of the musical celebration. "This was Addy's favorite song when he was little!" Charley informs me.

And Addy agrees, grinning. "When I was six, I dressed up as King Tut for Halloween!"

He whistles the melody while Charley and I sing the chorus, and with the rain beating its own steady rhythm on the roof, we pass the next hour dancing in the kitchen. Rick Astley, Kenny Loggins, Wham!, Katrina and the Waves… they all show up. The CD that Charley's chosen has not one single slow song on it, so when Addy finally deems it an appropriate time to slice the cheesecake, all three of us are literally dripping with sweat. I fill three pint glasses with water while he slides the spring-form pan from the refrigerator and Charley gets us each a fork and a plate.

"Do you think real chefs slice cheesecakes with dental floss?" Addy wonders. "Or is that just a rumor?"

"You'll find out soon enough," Charley muses. "Don't classes start next week?"

"Classes? Yes. Bakery classes? No. First I need to learn the basics: tools and safety and cleanliness." He unhinges the side of the pan and picks up a carving knife, holding it so it hovers just above the beautifully golden-brown top-crust. He's managed to bake the thing to perfection: there's no Grand Canyon splitting the cake in two. "Addy," I praise him. "You've outdone yourself, buddy."

"Well… taste it first," he says, blushing. "This is the first dark-chocolate-stout cheesecake I've made. It might be awful."

"Or it might be deserving of the Nobel Prize," Charley says, accepting her extra-large wedge of a piece. She's practically drooling; her bright eyes dance like candle flames.

"Yeah," I agree, "because the Nobel Prize is awarded to folks from the culinary world all the time. Didn't Emeril Lagasse win it last year? Or was that two years ago?"

"Bam!" Addy exclaims, laughing, and Charley gives us each an exasperated look. "Just hurry up and finish slicing the cake," she grumbles. "You guys are so—"

"Hilarious?" I predict.

"Charming?" Addy suggests.

"I was going to go with 'annoying,'" she informs us, "but 'obnoxious' works just as well."

"Ouch!" I exclaim.

"And after I baked her this nice cake…" Addy laments.

Charley rolls her eyes and offers, "This nice cake that's *waiting for me.* Hello? Can we please eat." It's more a demand than a question, so we gather around the bar, pick up our forks, and guide them right through the very dense and *very* rich dessert. It's still a little bit gooey in the middle, but no one's complaining, and although there's no counting to three this time, we all somehow manage to chomp down on our individual bites at exactly the same time.

Not much is said after that.

Most of our energy is devoted to the issuance of satisfied sighs and close-to-climactic groans. "This is *so good,*" each of us moans at least once. And then we indulge in seconds. While we eat, we talk about hole-in-the-wall restaurants and dirty martinis and olives. "The first time Addy tried an olive," Charley shares, "he scrunched up his face and spit it right back out, shooting it onto the table. He said it tasted like—and I quote—'salty yuck.'"

"But I like 'em okay now," he says. "It was a required taste."

I raise my eyebrows at him. "A 'required taste,' huh?"

"Yeah. If you want Charley Lane in your life, then you'd better want olives in your life too."

Charley laughs. "I wasn't that persistent, was I?"

"Fancy cheese, crusty bread, and olives," Addy reminds her. "Any time I asked for a snack, that's what you fixed. Fancy cheese, crusty bread, and olives. So, yeah... you were pretty persistent."

"Sorry."

He shrugs. "Don't be. I wouldn't change it for the world."

The comment makes Charley grin, but her smile is definitely watered down.

Eventually, every good night has to come to a close, so the cheesecake gets covered and returned to its shelf in the refrigerator; our water glasses are stacked with our plates in the sink. "I'll take care of them tomorrow," Addy says. "Not a big deal."

Charley offers to escort him to his old clunker, but he dismisses the suggestion with a wave of his hand. "It's pouring," he points out. "Stay in here where it's dry." So we equip him with an umbrella and accompany him to the door, and then we watch as he bolts quickly across the soggy yard. Once his car is disappearing down the lane to meet up with Copper Drive, I turn to Charley. She looks tired, but happy. "Hey," I whisper.

"Hey," she whispers back.

I rest my hand against her cheek, stroke her skin with my thumb. "I'll stay if you want."

"I'd like that."

The dogs linger on the first floor while we walk to the bedroom together: hand in hand, side by side. Charley makes a few references to our fortune cookies from earlier, and I crack a few jokes about what might happen "in bed," but what ends up occurring isn't anything anybody'd be interested in knowing about. I hold her while she tells me about helping her grandfather harvest hops, and describes how sickeningly sweet the kitchen smelled when Noni canned strawberry preserves. I hold her, pulling her as close as humanly possible, as she recounts a tale of getting lost in the orchard at a young age. "I was so scared," she murmurs. "So, so scared." I wrap my arms around her, tight, and hold her while she talks about leaving Lake Caywood and moving to Michigan and starting a new life in a new place.

I'm content to just hold her.

Content to experience the solidness of her in my arms, her head on my shoulder.

I'm content to simply experience the solidness of *us*.

27.

Charley

My plan had originally been to package all of the never-sent love letters into a box, cart them to the post office, and stick them in the mail. I'd looked up an address for Miss Flora Higgins and used a black Sharpie to neatly print the information on the parcel's brown-paper wrapping; I'd carried the box to my Jeep and placed it on the passenger's seat and checked my wallet to be sure it contained cash for postage. And then I'd driven into town with every intention of visiting a United States postal worker… but somehow I'd ended up parked in front of a tiny red brick home with navy shutters and a pistachio-colored door.

Technically, I have met Flora Higgins once before: at the Lake Caywood Jamboree. Though I hadn't known who she was, she must have known who I was, and the fact that she said nothing at all is somewhat infuriating. But then, what could she have said? "I loved your grandfather once, long ago, and we had a child together"? Or how about, "The woman you remember as your grandmother was nothing of the sort"? It would have been impossible to employ the right words because I'm pretty certain the right words don't exist. I'm sure on that warm, early-summer Saturday of the berry festival, Flora Higgins struggled in the same way I'm struggling now. Because what *does* one say in a situation like this?

I sit in my Jeep, outside the little house, for a good ten minutes before I build up enough courage to shut off the ignition and reach for the door handle. It takes another five before I'm ready to actually open the door and plant my feet on the street, but eventually this happens. My legs carry me up the cement walk and onto the porch and my sweaty hands clutch the brown-paper package and even though I'm aware all of this is happening, I can't fully comprehend *how* this is happening. It's like I'm on autopilot.

My brain must command my hand to reach for the doorbell because that's what it does. I can hear the musical chime echo through the house; I imagine Flora Higgins, reading a book in her living room, tilting her head and marking the page with a lace crocheted bookmark. Or perhaps she's making tea in the kitchen, the kettle on her stove starting its slow, high-pitched whistle at the same moment the doorbell alerts her to a visitor.

Or maybe she's not home at all, I realize.

But then there are soft footsteps and the turning of a lock and the door swings open to reveal a petite woman with snow-white hair and soft-looking skin. She's wearing corduroy pants and a heavy sweater and bifocals that make her eyes appear overly large. What she is not wearing is a smile, but there is a kindness in her face nevertheless. "Charley Lane," she greets me. "This is a surprise."

"I'm sorry to bother you," I begin, "but I have something that belongs to you."

She raises her eyebrows but doesn't speak. Instead, she allows her gaze to travel to the box in my hands. "It's full of letters," I explain. "Letters that Gramps wrote to you, but never mailed. He left them to me, so I've read through all of them, but I thought… I thought you might like to have them."

Flora brings her hands together in a silent clap and holds them there in front of her face, her eyes glistening with tears. She is speechless for a long moment, and because I don't know the right thing to say, I do the only thing that makes sense: I extend the box to her.

She lowers her hands slowly; they are shaking as they move to accept the gift. I watch the way she caresses the sturdy paper with her fingertips and rubs her thumbs over the folds at the ends. I observe how she halfheartedly picks at a piece of packing tape, eager to explore the package's contents, but fearful of the sadness that will accompany the investigation. Maybe this is why she invites me to stay, because she needs a buffer between the present and the past.

Or it might be that she wants to share her side of the story.

Regardless, she leads me to a brightly lit kitchen and tells me to have a seat at the mahogany table while she heats milk for hot chocolate. She's quiet while she works. I watch silently as she whisks together bittersweet cocoa powder and glistening sugar and just a splash of almond extract, and wait patiently as she pours the creamy concoction into large mugs printed with snowflakes. With a cup of cocoa in each hand, she walks carefully to the table and takes a seat catty-corner to where I'm sitting. "So," she sighs, knitting her wrinkled fingers and placing them in her lap, "I assume you already know most of what there is to know."

I say nothing because, since I don't know *all* of what there is to know, it's impossible for me to determine if *most* of what there is to know has already been shared. Whether Flora realizes this or not, I've no idea, but she does take a sip of cocoa and clear her throat and begin to talk. "I didn't expect to fall in love with Jasper," she says very quietly, "but I did. It was Oliver who introduced us, and had he known of the spark that would ignite, I'm sure he would have thought twice about making that introduction." She pauses, remembering the past; a single tear slides down her pale cheek and tangles tenuously along the line of her jaw. "Oliver was furious when he learned of my pregnancy. He refused to entertain the idea of raising your mother as our own. He, in fact, wished to hand her off to an orphanage."

This was not part of my grandfather's version of the story. I warm my hands against my mug of cocoa and raise my eyebrows. "In his letter, Gramps made it sound like Oliver wanted him and Noni to take the baby. Gramps said your husband sent a clock as a wedding gift, and word that he had no interest in raising Fiona as his own."

"That's partly true," Miss Flora informs me. "Oliver did send a clock."

"A cuckoo clock," I add. "It stopped working years and years ago, but it still hangs in the living room, occupying wall space and not keeping time."

Flora seems surprised by this announcement. She widens her eyes and her jaw becomes slack. "Good heavens," she mutters, her tone one of disbelief. "Do you mean to tell me Jasper kept that clock?"

I nod. "Why wouldn't he?"

"Well, because of the note that Oliver sent *with* it. That's why. He built that clock so that it would eventually stop keeping time; Oliver told your grandfather in his letter that time is supposed to heal all wounds, but he didn't believe there was enough time in the world to heal the wound Jasper had inflicted on him."

"Oh."

Miss Flora smiles a sad, knowing smile. "Yes," she agrees. "Theirs was a friendship that was never repaired. But *my* relationship with your grandfather…" Her voice trails away, remembering the man who we both loved in our own ways.

I give her time to speak, but when she remains quiet, I volunteer, "Gramps said the two of you still met for coffee sometimes."

"We did," she confirms. "Usually at the Tavern, but once at the farmhouse. He'd wanted to show me the library."

"The study, you mean?"

Flora shakes her head and forms a thin line with her lips. "No," she muses, "I don't think so. Jasper referred to it as the library." And then she goes on to describe a circular room, its walls lined with books, a plush leather couch in the middle of the cluttered space. Its hardwood floors had been stained a shade of golden honey and gleamed as if just polished. Apparently, nearly as many hardbacks had been piled around the sofa and along the baseboards as had lined the shelves, with their titles ranging from *Alice's Adventures in Wonderland* to *Middlemarch* to *Wuthering Heights*. As Miss Flora uses words to paint a picture of the room, I slowly realize that this is a place I *have* visited before, though not for a very long time.

I couldn't have been more than six or seven when it happened, but there had been a winter night when Gramps and I had sat in the living room, him smoking his pipe and me sucking on sour-sweet lemon drops, discussing whether a pig might really fall in love with a frog. We'd most likely been watching *A Muppet Family Christmas* or something along those lines, but that particular bit of the memory isn't clear. It's the debate I remember. Gramps had insisted that love *could* span species, because Edward Lear had written about just such a thing in his poem "The Owl and the Pussy-Cat."

"I don't know it," I'd stated, and Gramps had begun to recite it, but then he faltered in the second stanza and puffed his pipe, racking his brain for the right rhymes. Not finding them, he'd hoisted himself to his feet, hitched up his pants, and motioned for me to follow him out of the room.

Where he'd led me was all through the house, mixing me up so much with the quick turns and sudden backtracking that I probably would have been hard-pressed to find my way back to our starting point. We'd ended up in a room very much like the one described by Miss Flora: herringbone-patterned floors; walls lined with leather-bound books, their spines various shades of browns and burgundies; an overstuffed sofa in the center of the room. Gramps had known just where to go; I'd watched him climb the rolling ladder with its brass hardware, watched him reach for a thin book on a top shelf. "Ah," he'd sighed when his fingers made contact. "Here it is." He'd slipped it from its hiding place, eased himself down the ladder, and joined me on the couch, wrapping an arm around my shoulders and pulling me close. With the picture book lying open in his lap, he'd tugged lightly at one of my pigtails and mused, "Let's see then, shall we? 'The Owl and the Pussy-cat went to sea / In a beautiful pea-green boat, / They took some honey…'"

Gramps had read the entire story aloud, changing his voice for each character. The Owl, exceedingly wise, had sounded a bit snooty, whereas the Pussy-cat had spoken with a rather high-pitched, singsongy tone. The voice of the Piggy-wig had been gruff and to-the-point: he was, indeed, willing to sell for one shilling the ring at the end of his nose.

Until now, this memory had been lost.

Until now, I'd had no recollection of experiencing a nonsensical Lear poem in a library that didn't truly exist… but suddenly, everything comes flooding back: the fluttery whispers of the pages as they turned, Gramps's scent of strong tobacco, the taste of sugary lemon clinging to my tongue… My grandfather had had a handle on the rooms. He'd understood them.

Known where to find them.

Had an inside knowledge of how to make them appear.

Maybe, with more time, I would come to understand them as well: understand why they exist, and how they exist, and who gets to experience them, and when. Maybe, with more time, I would learn to summon them when needed. But since more time isn't something I have, I will have to content myself with what I know: the rooms *do* exist.

I glance up. Miss Flora is watching me, waiting for an answer or a reaction, and it occurs to me that she's spoken while I've been time-traveling to the past. "I'm sorry," I apologize, "but what did you say? My thoughts were wandering."

The old woman forces a pensive smile and repeats, "Life. It's a funny thing. People come and they go, because that's what's supposed to happen… but some people are so much harder to say goodbye to than others."

"Like my grandfather?"

Flora Higgins nods. Behind thick bifocals, I can tell that her magnified eyes are wet. "Like your grandfather," she agrees, speaking barely above a whisper. "Jasper Lane was the love of my life, so isn't it silly that we lived *separate* lives?"

I'm not sure how to respond, so I remain silent and wait for the woman sitting beside me to continue. She takes a sip of her lukewarm cocoa and runs a fingertip across the snowflake printed there on the front of the mug, maybe thinking about my mother and her love of snow. Maybe thinking about my grandfather. Eventually, her thoughts align and she verbalizes them, quietly declaring, "At least we had that last year, nursing cups of coffee at the Tavern and sometimes sharing a spinach-and-cheese omelet. Jasper liked cheddar, but I preferred Swiss." She pauses, smiles, adds, "He always ordered it with Swiss when I was there."

"That sounds like something Gramps would do."

"Jasper was a good man," Flora says. "A *great* man. And we spent a great year together."

"Just one?" I hadn't realized the couple's reunion had taken so long, and that they'd only had twelve months to spend with one another, but the wistful expression on Miss Flora's face tells me this is the case. "Just one," she informs me, "but isn't a single year spent together better than none at all?"

"It is," I agree, not entirely sure that I mean the words I've spoken. For me, this past year has contained even more than what I'd hoped. But for

Juli… is a single year spent together better than none at all? Or would it be better for him had he never met me?

I finish my cocoa and push back my chair, suddenly ready to go.

"Thank you for the hot chocolate," I say to Miss Flora as she walks me through her home, back to the door. "It was delicious. And it was really nice to—" I cut myself off, not sure of how to finish the sentence. "To get to know you" seems wrong, since this woman who loved my grandfather is still more mystery than anything else. And "to meet you" is too generic for the situation.

Fortunately, Miss Flora seems not to expect a conclusion. She reaches out, pats my left cheek gently with her cool hand, and says simply, "You cannot possibly imagine what this visit has meant to me."

She stands with the front door open, watching me navigate her front walk. I can feel her eyes on my back. Even after I've climbed behind the wheel of my Jeep and started the engine, her gaze lingers, and she is still watching as I pull away from the curb.

I imagine she continues to watch long after my taillights have vanished.

January becomes February.

It seems the sky is always grey and the grass is always frosted by ice crystals that aren't quite snow. My headaches become more frequent and more intense. Most days, I feel fine, but the majority of others are spent in bed. "It will happen soon," I confide to Juli. "I can tell."

Even my doctor says that my good days are numbered. He gives me a timeline: what to expect, and when. He mentions the word "hospice."

The margin of error for a shooting star is about ninety-nine-point-nine percent—I know that—but I made a wish for a painless goodbye and I'm *still* wishing for a painless goodbye. I don't want to lose my memory, my speech, or the ability to control my own body; I don't want the people who love me to be forced to watch as I slowly deteriorate. I want to leave this earth as *me,* not as a shell of the person I used to be, so I keep wishing, and

I keep telling myself that ninety-nine-point-nine percent isn't one hundred percent, and I keep reminding myself that there's always a chance.

Juli spends as much time as he can at the farmhouse. He'd spend all of his time with me if I'd let him, but whereas my life will soon end, his will continue, and the last thing he needs is a long stretch of days that are void of distractions. "You can't just stop going to work," I tell him very firmly. "You can't neglect your customers." So he grudgingly goes off each morning to install a ceiling fan or grout a backsplash or caulk a window while I stay behind in bed, curled beneath the covers, thinking of all the things I like best about him: the sound of his breathing at night, the pointed tip of his nose, the way he tugs on his lip ring when lost in a forest of thoughts…

When I'm not feeling my greatest, Addy doctors me by serving steaming dishes of the things Noni used to make. One day it's slippery potpie, the next it might be noodle soup with juicy chunks of chicken. On the days that my head doesn't pound, though, we cook together. Grilled cheese and minestrone, lasagna layered with spinach and ricotta and sauce that tastes of summer, buttery shortbread cookies that glisten with sugar… Yesterday we made English muffin pizzas, just like old times, with mozzarella and diced tomatoes and fresh sprigs of basil. Addy talked to me about culinary school while I listened and chewed, posing a question every now and again, but mostly content to simply be with him. He seems to like his classes—seems happy with the program—and knowing this fills me with a sense of relief.

That's where he'll be today: learning about food safety and preparation in West Orensdale. Juli, too, is off doing something. He received a call from his father early this morning, wondering if it might be possible to swing by his law office sometime before nine. "I've got a water heater that's not producing hot water," he'd complained, "and before I call in some plumber who charges an arm and a leg, I'd like your opinion."

Juli was willing, but unenthusiastic.

Scarlett was eager beyond belief.

"I guess I'll take her with me," he'd said when the glossy-furred setter went so far as to retrieve her leash from one of the hooks by the front door. "She seems pretty keen on tagging along. Maybe she heard Dad's voice and put two and two together…?" Juli had looked so adorably perplexed as he'd stood there, watching his pup dance circles around his feet, that I'd had no choice but to laugh.

"Be back in a bit," he'd said, planting a quick kiss on my cheek. "Love you."

That had been fifteen minutes ago. I'd accompanied him to the door, a mug of hazelnut coffee warming my hands, and watched as he'd walked across the yard to his truck. Scarlett hopped up first, Juli climbed in after her, and then they were on their way. I'd watched them go from my stance on the porch, waving goodbye as they bumped down the gravel drive. Wisps of caffeinated steam, white and vaporous, swirled upward to merge with the smoke-colored sky; beneath the gnarl-limbed cherry tree, Rhett snuffed for the odors of chipmunks and squirrels. The atmosphere felt heavy and frostbitten. "Like snow," I'd whispered to no one at all.

Now, a quarter hour after filling my lungs with great gulps of air that smelled of glaciers and peppermint, I don my black woolen coat and red cashmere scarf and slip my hands into a pair of thick gloves. "Come on, Rhett," I say, leaving my lukewarm coffee on the bar. "Let's go for a walk."

We lock the door behind us. It's Monday, so Molly Dixon won't be coming in to tend bar; Cordelia and Boomer won't be warming the kitchen with soup on the stove or mushroom-goat cheese empanadas in the oven. Nobody will be stopping in for a beer with lunch or a great-start-to-the-workweek happy hour because the Brewhaha is closed until tomorrow.

Rhett bounds ahead, marking tufts of dead grass and fallen tree branches with his scent, and alerting orchard rodents to the fact that this property is now his. I wonder how he doesn't run out of urine, how his bladder never *quite* manages to empty completely, but this doesn't seem to be an issue for him. He could probably mark every blade of grass if he chose to…

We loop first around the pond, tucked tight beneath a solid layer of ice. As a kid, I learned to skate here, and spent many a winter afternoon forming sloppy figure eights while imagining myself as the next great

Olympian. Gramps stood among the cattails and cheered, acting as audience and judge, using fingers instead of cards to issue scores.

From there we amble past peaches, pears, and plums. The trees are bare now, but they weren't always. I can remember passing many summer days up in the branches of that plum tree, reading books and eating fruit and dreaming of a grown-up future very different than the one I'm currently living. As a kid, I never saw myself growing old… but then, which kid ever does? It's possible I knew without knowing what was to come.

But it's also possible I was just being a kid.

Up toward the barn is where we head next. Rhett leads the way, having come to memorize this route over the past year: down by the pond, through the orchard, up to the hop field. We go there to visit Gramps every now and then. Sometimes I talk to him. Once in a while I talk to him about Juli and Addy, but mostly I confide my own fears. *Will it hurt?* I wonder. *Will I know what to do when it finally happens?* He doesn't answer, of course, but there's something about being among the viny rows of Cascade and Chinook that comforts me.

Rhett comes to stand by my side for a moment, giving my hand an affectionate nudge before darting down to explore that narrow stretch of land nestled between the dried-to-brown Nugget and Willamette hops. I watch him go, amused by his jaunty gait and the way he holds his tail so erect, and as I laugh, a snowflake floats down and lands on the tip of my nose.

"Finally," I breathe, my breath visible in the chilly morning air. "Snow."

It's a flurry and then it's a storm. What begins with one becomes one million. I turn my face to the sky, blinking against a platoon of fast-approaching flakes as they parachute to the ground and quickly blanket the grass beneath a cover of white. I catch one on my tongue and hold it there, thinking of snowmen with carrot noses and hot cocoa piled high with whipped cream and Gramps pulling me on a sled through the orchard. And when it happens, it doesn't hurt at all. When it happens, I don't realize it's happened until I'm looking down on myself, lying there beside a row of Cascade hops still months away from bloom, snow wrapping soft arms around my still body to hold me in her warm embrace. I'm above the earth, but not in it… I'm alone, but not really. Those who once loved me surround me, and those who still love me continue to exist below.

I see Rhett turn to check my status, watch as he lopes back to sniff my ear, nuzzle me with his damp nose, gently lick my cheek with his pale pink tongue. With a front foot, he paws once at my shoulder, and when still nothing changes, he flops down beside me with a sad sigh and rests his head on my chest, watching the sky with his soulful brown eyes.

I can't feel the weight of him, but I sure can feel the weight of losing him.

28.
The Boys

It's Oscar who stumbles upon her body, and only because Rhett, hearing his truck idling outside the barn, alerts him to the fact. The wiry dog doesn't ever leave Charley's side, but he issues a plaintive, drawn out howl that lasts just long enough to pique the orchard hand's curiosity.

Oscar finds her tucked beneath a blanket of snow, the expression on her face both peaceful and serene. He calls first for an ambulance, then for Juli.

Ed accompanies his son to the farmhouse. It is he who talks to the medics and answers their questions when his son can't form the words. The lights of the ambulance dance in the morning's grey glow, its siren muted. Juli stands, watching, slumped and broken, one arm crossed over his chest and the other reaching down to hold Rhett's collar. The dog whines, wanting to go with Charley, but that's a wish that can't be granted.

Marcela, alerted by another lawyer from her husband's practice, arrives at the farmhouse not long after the rest of her family. She throws her car into park and leaves the keys dangling in the ignition, racing at top speed to reach her son.

Juli doesn't notice his mother until she's right in front of him, but when he sees her, he breaks down. Barely holding it together before, he now collapses into her, sobs racking his body. It takes all of her strength not to crumble right there beside him, because to witness her son experiencing this much pain is almost too much to bear.

Eventually, the ambulance pulls away with Charley in it. Marcela wraps an arm around her son's waist and guides him toward the house; Ed takes hold of Rhett's collar and pulls him gently along. Not much is said because there's nothing really to say. There are things in life that aren't fair and this is one of them. So Marcela holds her son while he cries and Ed makes tea because it seems like the right thing to do and Rhett wanders the house, searching each room again and again in the hopes of finding the girl he loves even more than mud-marinated rawhide. But she is gone.

Kirby stops by around noon. He and Ed share a hush-toned conversation in the study while Marcela scrambles eggs in the kitchen. "I'm not hungry," Juli insists, pushing aside the plate and resting his head on the bar. Charley's coffee cup from this morning still resides there and he observes it with red-rimmed eyes, remembering her love for hazelnut and the hearty splash of cream that she'd always use to lighten it.

Marcela takes a seat beside him and places a hand on his back, rubbing small circles there between his shoulder blades. "Addy doesn't know yet, does he?" she confirms. "Will you be the one to tell him?"

"I'll have to be," Juli whispers, still focused on the mug of cold coffee.

The men return to the kitchen soon after, exchanging firm handshakes and somber goodbyes before Kirby slips back into the snowy afternoon. Ed explains to his family that Charley's uncle will take care of the funeral arrangements and Kirby will be in touch with details just as soon as he knows something.

Juli listens, but doesn't say anything until his mother asks if there's something he needs—something they can do for him. "Call customers to let them know what's happened? Explain that you won't be available this afternoon?"

"No," he answers, shaking his head. "That's okay."

"What about Scarlett?" Ed wonders. "She's still at the office. Should we keep her tonight?"

Juli, his head still resting on the bar, blinks. A tear slides sideways across his cheek. "Can you drop her at my house?"

"Or we can bring her back here," Marcela offers.

"No," he whispers, finally turning to meet his mother's concerned gaze. She looks so worried right now. So sad. "I think I just want to be alone right now. With Rhett. But thank you. Thank you for everything you guys have done."

"Oh, honey..."

He lets her pet his face and smooth his hair; he allows his dad to wrap him in one of those giant father-son bear hugs that are reserved for moments of intense pride and intense grief. He watches them go, listens for the click of the door behind them, and then he promptly falls apart. It's an anguish he's never before experienced and it aches a thousand times more than any nail-gun injury or second-degree burn. He cries until he has no more tears left to shed; he cries until his throat is raw and he thinks his lungs will burst. And when he can't cry anymore—because it hurts too much and because an exhaustion like no other suddenly plagues his body—he drags himself upstairs and crawls into Charley's bed and curls there beneath the covers with knees tucked against his chest, until he falls asleep.

It's a slumber that is deep, but brief, and when Juli wakes up, Rhett is sprawled there beside him, breathing doggy breath into his face and whimpering softly. The force of what's happened suddenly hits him head on; the morning comes rushing back. It is three o'clock, and even though Juli is tired of crying, he thinks it might be possible for him to cry another gallon or two of tears.

But a person can tire of feeling sad.

Sometimes a person can decide that even though he *is* sad, it's okay to pretend he's not. If only for just a little while. Sometimes a person can decide that maybe for one hour of one day… it's okay to choose not to be completely *consumed* by sadness.

It's a decision that might backfire, yes, but Juli decides to give it a try. He reaches over to smooth the wiry terrier's fur, running his hand across Rhett's face and rubbing that soft spot behind his ear. "Hey buddy," he says. "How about we go for a drive?"

So they roll out of bed and plod through the house and pass all of the things that still scream of Charley: a chair that she bought, a rug that she chose, a big oak table where she once rolled piecrusts with her grandmother. They exit through the front door, climb down the porch steps, and walk across the snow-covered yard, leaving footprints in their wake. Juli opens the door of his truck and motions for Rhett to hop up; Rhett only half obliges. He willingly plants his front feet on the seat, then turns to stare at his backend, glancing from it to Juli, waiting for a bit of assistance.

Forcing a lopsided smile, Juli gives him a boost. "You're spoiled, you know it?"

They bounce down the bumpy drive and turn left onto Copper, following it into town. Juli avoids Main Street, choosing to stick to the back roads instead, even venturing down Howard to sit at the traffic light that rarely glows anything but red. But this is where he first saw Charley, that day in the rain, when she fought with her uncle on the sidewalk after bursting through the funeral home's doors. Kirby could be in there right now, Juli realizes, making plans for later this week. This knowledge, when it occurs to him, nearly results in a new onset of tears, but Juli swallows the pain and the reality and stares straight ahead at that never-changing traffic light… and turns right instead of left.

Beside him, Rhett stares out the window. He studies the snow and he looks at the storefronts and he watches for anyone who might resemble his owner. But of course Charley isn't out shoveling sidewalks or walking through town, shopping in family-owned stores… because Charley is gone. And Juli, sensing the confused pup's pain, reaches over and runs a hand over Rhett's coarse fur, offering what little comfort he can.

They turn off of Copper and onto a little street called Chester and it's not until Juli reaches his destination that he realizes where he's going. It's a place he's not visited for a long time, but once he pulls up to one of the meters out front, he understands why he's here. "This won't take long," he says to Rhett, and leaves the truck running as he hustles inside.

The Illustrated Man, named after one of Ray Bradbury's most memorable characters, is the only tattoo parlor that can be found in Lake Caywood. It's where Juli came for footnotes one through seven, and it's where he's returned today. He meets the gaze of the heavily inked artist standing behind the counter and announces, "I'm back for number eight."

She has him take a seat and asks him what he wants and then she permanently sketches a tiny eight, tipped onto its side, right there above his heart. "So it can go on forever," Charley would say, "just like an infinity sign."

"And on your foot?" the tattoo artist asks. "Same as the others? A description with the date?"

"Today's date," Juli informs her. "And for the description… just write 'Charley.'"

So that is what she does.

∞

Addy learned of the news from Juli, who'd been waiting outside his apartment on Monday evening as he'd returned home from class. "An aneurism," Juli had said, his eyes brimming with tears. "That's what one of the paramedics thought might've happened, anyway. Very quick, very painless."

People with brain tumors don't die of aneurisms. They die of brain tumors. The odds of such a thing happening are less than two percent, but Addy remembers that cold winter night on the porch, standing by Charley's side, watching the sky for shooting stars. Maybe that's what Charley had wished for.

And maybe sometimes wishes do come true.

Addy hadn't cried right away. He'd stood there in silence, stoically acknowledging the report, but not quite ready to accept its meaning. The tears had come later, after he, Juli, and Rhett had wandered numbly through the snowy town, slowly adjusting to a world without Charley in it. Later, he, the man, and the dog had parted ways on the sidewalk in front of Whirligigs and Whatnots, voicing hollow goodbyes before heading home. It wasn't until Addy had locked his bedroom door and hidden himself beneath a heavy down comforter that he'd allowed the tears to flow.

It was only last night he'd cried himself to sleep, but it seems like so much longer ago than that. Possibly because he's running on only a few hours rest; his slumber had been short-lived, and having woken early, the place he'd thought to visit is the old farmhouse. Charley had left him with a task to complete, after all—she'd trusted him—and so it seems important to fulfill her request as soon as possible.

The house is disturbingly silent when he enters it, and cold. He leaves his coat on and stands for a moment in the quiet kitchen, considering the copper-plated bar and the low-hanging lights and the shadow they cast as their glow lands upon the cold mug of coffee still sitting there from yesterday. Addy understands it had been Charley's; he notices the splash of cream and the thick skin that's formed across the top as a result. He knows pouring the cup's contents down the drain is in no way representative of dismissing the memory of Charley… but he leaves it there anyway, not yet ready to dispose of anything that once was hers.

Addy's footsteps echo as he crosses the room, slips into the hallway, climbs the stairs to the second floor. She'd said the letters were in the office, in the middle desk drawer: one in a bulky manila envelope, the other secure within a small white one. And that's exactly where he finds them, held together with a paperclip, accompanied by a short note. *The sooner these find their way into the mailbox,* Charley's written, *the better. The larger envelope is for my uncle. It contains a picture of Noni, a bundle of paperwork, and a letter deeding Gramps's cemetery plot to Kirby. She was the love of his life, you know; I like to think someday they will be together.*

The other letter is for Charlie—an explanation—because he deserves to understand.

And if you look, Addy, there's also a leather journal tucked back in this drawer. That's for you.

She's concluded the letter by drawing a small heart and signing her name beneath it. A final goodbye. Addy stares at her signature for a long time, studying the curve of the C and the slightly sloppy tail of the y and remembering things like the sound of her laugh and how much she loved olives. And then he blinks away the tears and takes a shaky breath and carries the letters to the mailbox.

Two inches of snow, crusted with a thin film of ice, coat the ground. Addy's feet crunch against it, leaving oblong indents as he cuts across the yard and walks down the unplowed lane, meandering along the tire tracks left by his car. He's not in any hurry, so his pace isn't especially fast, and he certainly doesn't quicken it when he notices the grey car with only one headlight turn off Copper and coast toward him. The vehicle itself isn't familiar, but as it grows closer, he recognizes the driver as none other than

June Birch. She eases to a stop beside him and rolls down her window. "Baby," she croons, "I just heard abou—"

"What do you want?" Addy interrupts, his voice every bit as icy as the current temperature.

His mother winces, wounded by the harshness of his words, but continues in the kindest tone she can muster. It sounds fake coming from her; she's never cared much about anyone other than herself. "What do I *want?*" she repeats, donning a mask of sympathy. "Can't a mother check up on her son? I just heard the news, and I love you, baby, and poor, poor Charley…"

"Don't say her name," Addy demands. "Don't ever say her name."

"But I—"

"No." He holds the letters tight in his fist, his knuckles turning white, slightly crumpling the paper and the words scrawled there in Charley's artistic hand. "You don't have the right to say her name," he tells his mother, low and angry. "You aren't worthy enough to use her name in a sentence."

"Addison!"

"No," he reiterates, slowly fitting the pieces together and realizing the truth for the first time. Finally figuring out the past. "No. You don't get to say her name because… because you're the reason she left, aren't you? You sent her away."

"Addison Birch!"

"You did. All those years ago. You sent her away. You sent her away because you felt threatened by her. By Charley, a *kid*, because I loved her more than—"

"I am your *mother!*"

"No," Addy tells her, his voice hard and dangerous. "You're not. Not really." And then, in a whisper laced with quiet fury, he says simply, "I'd like you to go now. This is goodbye."

June Birch sits there for a long minute, exhaust coughing out the muffler of the grey car and polluting the atmosphere. She's holding a cigarette with her right hand and the ash continues to grow longer and longer, threatening to fall off like the spent end of a Fourth of July sparkler. Addy stares at it instead of his mother, focusing on the orange-to-grey and wondering when it will crumble. Mere seconds before it does, and without speaking another word to her son, June throws the vehicle into reverse and slowly backs down the lane. She doesn't look at Addy and Addy doesn't look at her and it isn't until she's vanished completely that he resumes his walk to the end of the drive, whistling a half-hearted tune and kicking at the snow.

His hands are still shaking as he slips the letters into the mailbox and raises the metal flag.

The service is held on Friday morning. Folks from all over town turn out to show their support, offering hugs and condolences, and at eleven o'clock, when Leonard Turley clears his throat to offer opening remarks, only standing room remains. He offers the few memories he has of Charley, having met her briefly only a little over a year ago when she returned to Lake Caywood to say goodbye to her grandfather. She hadn't wanted a big ceremony then or now. She hadn't wished for a drawn out farewell, he informs the congregation; Charley made that very clear when she sat down with her lawyer to sort out all the nitty-gritty details that tend to accompany death. "All she requested," Leonard says, "was that the lyrics to her favorite song be read. And so… I'm here to read them."

It had always been the chorus she'd loved the most. That much, Charlie Flynn remembers. He stands there against the back wall, a stranger among strangers, wearing his only suit and the crimson tie Charley had once used to wrap around one of the Christmas presents she'd purchased for him. "Instead of ribbon," he remembers her giggling. "Pretty clever, right?"

And Charlie'd had to concur: "Pretty clever."

"There's the past and there's the future / And the here-and-now between," Leonard reads. "I want you close for all of it; / I want you here with me. / So even when we disagree, / When opinions just won't jibe, / Know that I'll be back again / To kick it one more time."

The funeral director goes on to connect the meaning of the song's lyrics to the meaning of Charley Lane's life, but Charlie isn't really listening because he's thinking about a rainy concert so many years ago. Rain hadn't been in the forecast, but it had poured every day of that three-day festival. Charley traded half a dozen special brownies for a red umbrella and the couple had spent the weekend caked in mud, huddled beneath it. The following week, they both came down with bronchitis; Robitussin and hot toddies thickened with honey is how they'd survived. Charlie remembers all of this while he only half pays attention to the funeral director relating to the mourners how Charley Lane felt about reincarnation. He doesn't need a refresher course on the content; he recalls quite clearly how she felt about cardinals and second chances and forever.

The service is over before noon. According to Leonard, the burial itself will be private—Charley, like her beloved grandfather, has requested to have her ashes scattered on the land that she loved—but a local restaurant owner opens his doors to the public, inviting them to join him for spicy corn chowder and three-cheese paninis and crunchy sweet potato fries. It's not the Tavern that Charlie wishes to see, though; it's not Doc Delaney whom he's driven all this way to meet. And so he skips the refreshments and reminiscences altogether, choosing instead to follow Copper Drive outside of downtown… allowing the tree-lined street with its canopy of skeleton-fingered branches to lead him to an old farmhouse on the outskirts of Lake Caywood. He's seen pictures, but he's never visited; he's heard stories, but never witnessed the soft quiet that envelopes the orchard.

It's a large white house that welcomes him, its copper roof an oxidized green and its raised panel shutters a brilliant shade of red. "Charley no doubt had a say in those," he mutters, smiling despite the day's heavy sadness.

He parks beside the only vehicle there: a truck with a sign on its door. "Singer Services," it reads. "Service with a Song." It seems unlikely that anyone would be here, what with the luncheon occurring in town, but Charlie grabs his portfolio from the backseat and lopes across the yard anyway, sliding his keys into his pants pocket so that they jingle faintly with each step. Traces of snow still linger, but the ground is more green than white. Despite this, Charlie stomps his feet against the bottom porch stair before covering the last few steps to the door. The sign that's posted there clearly says "Closed," but he issues a quick knock nevertheless.

No one answers, but a dog barks, and Charlie recognizes the bark as belonging to Rhett. "Pupper?" he asks, wishing the door had a window so he might see inside. "Rhett, my boy!" He knocks again, louder this time, not stopping until his knuckles begin to ache, and inside, the terrier mix and another dog join together to issue a melodic howl.

"Rhett and Scarlett!" someone scolds them, his voice somewhat muted. "Enough already..."

And then the door swings open to reveal a tallish man with dark hair that falls across his forehead, a silver hoop glistening there on his bottom lip. He's wearing black pants, Converse sneakers, and a white button-down shirt with the sleeves rolled partway up. A loose tie hangs around his neck. He studies Charlie with red-rimmed eyes and says pointedly, "We're closed."

"I know. I'm sorry. I..." Charlie stops and swallows, because he realizes this must be Juli. Charley mentioned him in the letter. She wrote about his sarcastic sense of humor and lopsided smile and his ability to speak the truth no matter how painful... and even though she never once said that she loved him, Charlie could tell that she did. So he knows. He knows what Juli is feeling right now—the words are written right there on the wrecked man's face—which is why he says the only thing that he can think to say: "I'm Charlie Flynn. I loved her, too."

Rhett sniffs the newcomer's leather shoes and leather portfolio and then gently licks his hand, an indication of recognition. "I brought along some photographs," Charlie says, "of Charley. I thought you might like to see them."

Juli studies this man with the trim beard and mussed blonde hair, remembering him from that single picture Charley shared of her past; he eyes the oversized briefcase clutched in the fellow's hand. And then, without saying so much as a word, he holds the door open wide and motions for him to enter. Rhett wags his tail, seemingly pleased by this small collision of worlds, and follows both men inside.

They walk to the bar.

Addy is already there, nursing an IPA, tracing his finger over the tree of life's roots printed on his pint glass. He looks up when Juli returns, raising his eyebrows to pose a question without words. "Charlie Flynn," comes the answer, and Addy nods, familiar with the name.

Juli retrieves a third glass, fills it with beer, and slides it over to Charlie. "She once donated a single loafer to the rescue mission," he volunteers without prompting, "because she said it was possible that a one-legged man might need it someday. But, I mean… what are the odds that a guy with one foot—a *left* foot—would wander into the mission looking for a size-ten loafer? Slim to none, I'll bet… I think about that story a lot, though."

Charlie forces a sad smile and sighs a heavy sigh. "Because that was Charley. Her thoughts were different than the thoughts that the rest of the world tends to think. More poetic, I guess. More full of possibility." He bends down to unzip the portfolio leaning against his barstool, giving Rhett a quick pat on the head before unearthing a slim leather-bound album. Setting it on the bar, he flips open the front cover and pushes it over for Juli and Addy to view. "That picture was taken soon after I met her," he shares, "at this little bar in town that served the very best dirty martinis. Charley only drank one the whole night, I think, but she asked the bartender to replenish her olives at least six or seven times."

"A required taste," Juli half-laughs, nudging Addy with his elbow, and the younger boy almost smiles. They bow their heads and consider the happy girl in the photo, obviously posing for both the camera and the boy behind it. Dark waves of hair spill over her shoulders, framing her face as her lips form a round O as she marvels at the three olive-skewered toothpicks wading there in her drink. Juli reaches out and touches her cheek, wishing it were really her cheek and not just a black-and-white image tucked inside a plastic sleeve. "Do you have any of her with short hair?" he wonders, his voice cracking a bit. A lone tear escapes; it leaves a saltwater trail across his skin. "With short hair is how I remember her."

Charlie skips ahead, fast-forwarding through images of Charley picking wildflowers, Charley making snow angels, Charley leaping off the end of a dock and landing in the chilly water of Lake Huron. He flips past one of her with buzzed hair, a C-shaped scar still visible on her scalp, taken soon after the operation that had removed a then-operable tumor from her brain; he skims over another of Charley wearing a navy bandana and holding the fluffy remnants of a giant dandelion, her cheeks puffed as if ready to make a wish. And when Charlie finally stops turning the glossy pages in the leather-bound album, what he lands on is an image of Charley sitting across from Rhett, their noses practically touching, participating in a staring contest the canine hadn't fully understood. He'd only wanted to be close to his favorite person; he'd only wanted to plaster her face with puppy-dog kisses and leave her skin feeling sticky from dried saliva.

"Rhett won," Charlie announces, studying that picture. "Every *single* time Charley challenged him to a staring contest, Rhett won." He reaches down to pat the wiry terrier on the head and adds, "Keep that one if you want, of Charley and Rhett."

Juli turns to face him, knitting his brows. "Are you sure?"

"Absolutely. She'd want you to have it."

Addy watches as Juli removes the photograph from the album. He watches as he holds up the picture and studies it through eyes brimming with tears. And then Addy, quiet until now, says, "Charley's the reason I whistle."

Juli turns to face him.

Charlie turns to face him.

Addy continues, "She was teaching me how to make onion soup, right before she went off to college, and my eyes were watering like crazy. From the onions," he clarifies. "I had to slice four onions. And Charley said to me, real matter-of-fact, 'Just whistle. If you whistle while you slice 'em, then you won't cry.'" He pauses, stares down into the bubbly brew that he grips with both hands, and concludes, "That's the best advice she could've given me; it's helped me to get through all the tough times."

Three men in a row, all clutching lukewarm beers and remembering a woman so full of life, swallow their tears. Three men in a row, all at the same time, lift their pint glasses into the air. And three men in a row, their hearts heavy with grief and their voices hoarse from crying, toast "To Charley."

Juli touches his chest, and adds in a whisper so soft that the others can't hear, "Forever."

∞

The afternoon passes.

The boys share many beers and many tears; they view many pictures and share many stories. Sometimes they even laugh. But as the sun begins to set and the cold February night sneaks in, Charlie zips his portfolio and prepares to go. He squats down in front of Rhett, rubbing the pup's velvety ears and reminding him that he's a good dog before planting a firm kiss in the middle of his wiry head. Standing, he pulls his keys from his pants pocket and walks to the front door.

Juli, Addy, and Rhett follow him out.

They stand on the porch steps, staggered in height, watching him go. Charlie strolls across the yard. The ground lies frozen beneath his feet; his breath forms frothy white clouds of chimney smoke that float up, up, *up*. Above his head, a brilliantly red cardinal soars, swoops, lands on one of the cherry tree's bare and gnarled limbs. It perches on the smooth bark and tilts its head to the side, acknowledging the boys, staggered in height, who line the porch steps: Rhett, Addy, Juli.

Juli, Addy, Rhett.

All three boys turn to face the bird, and just as they take in its crimson feathers and carrot-orange beak, the cardinal sings a funny little melody. It's not so much a chirp as it is a song, and as the beautiful bird whistles, Addy cups his ear and listens. "I know that tune," he whispers, because it sounds so very similar to the chorus of a song Charley Lane used to love.

Juli smiles, tears streaming down his cheeks, and reaches out to tousle Addy's hair. "How 'bout that?" he murmurs. "She's back to kick it one more time..."

"There are times in our lives where you can't run on the gun;
There are times in this world where you just gotta let go.
No need standing in your sorrows, 'cause there's no way out of here.
You got to take one step at a time, turn around and do it again."

-Erick Macek, "On the Other Side of the Road"

JUST WHISTLE

Playlist

"I've Just Seen A Face" - Dawn & Hawkes

"Stubborn Love" - The Lumineers

"You Got Growin' Up To Do" - Joshua Radin

"Where Apples Grow" - Preston Hull

"Empire" - Trampled by Turtles

"Ways of Man" - Old Crow Medicine Show

"Home" - Edward Sharpe and the Magnetic Zeroes

"Laundry Room" - The Avett Brothers

"Jump Rope" - Blue Öctober

"Let Her Go" - Passenger

"I'll Be Fine" - Erick Macek

"Gone, Gone, Gone" - Phillip Phillips

"Carry On" - fun.

"Train In Vain" - The Clash

"I Will Wait" - Mumford & Sons

"Hey Brother" - Avicii

"On the Other Side of the Road" - Erick Macek

"I've Just Seen A Face" - The Beatles

∞

Acknowledgments

Everyone deserves a buddy as solid as Nicole Starner. She literally provided feedback for every last page of my manuscript. We passed many an evening at Starbucks, sipping mugs of caramel apple cider and hazelnut latté as we analyzed things such as characters, plot, and theme. Without her suggestions and corrections, *Just Whistle* wouldn't be what it is. Nicoleo is a top-notch editor and a top-notch friend; I'm incredibly lucky to have her.

Rob Baust, defender of the English language, was kind enough to not only offer a male perspective regarding all things Juli Singer, but he also adjusted my grammar whenever necessary *and* provided such generous praise that I felt myself blush. His words meant a lot. So did his willingness to offer feedback.

In addition to allowing me to use the opening lyrics of his song "On the Other Side of the Road," Erick Macek said something that's really stuck with me: "Every single person you interact with matters. I appreciate being part of your journey." I'd like to thank him for his support. I'd also like to encourage readers to be a part of *his* journey and look him up on Spotify.

Last but not least, I need to acknowledge a few additional early readers who have become an integral part of *my* journey: my mother, Nancy Newman, because her recurring dream about a house with too many rooms is what inspired the magic in *Just Whistle*; my brother, Curtis "The Pip" Meeson, because even though he's gone, his eye for design continues to impact my novels' covers; my father, Craig Meeson, for always saying wonderful things about the books that I write; my pretend aunt, Dorothy Puhl, for her warm words; Miss Jane Nutter, for her sky-high praise; Amy Gorman, for her advice regarding verbiage; Heather Baugher, because she's read every version of every manuscript I've ever written and offered spectacular encouragement and advice for all of them; Bonnie Ott, who has told me that whenever I share one of my manuscripts with her, she feels as though I'm entrusting her with my child; and Rich Sterner, because he doesn't know how to give anything *other* than compliments.

Hannah Rae's books,
listed in the order in which they occur:

The Way Back

Like A Flip Turn

Just Whistle

Made in the USA
Middletown, DE
19 November 2022

15272841R00205